Gypsy in Her Soul . . .

"Ah," Shandor sighed. "How wise you have grown in the ways of the Rom. A Gypsy needs the evening campfire the way the flowers need the rain." He turned a smiling face toward her, showing strong white teeth below the dark mustache.

Graciela looked into the dark eyes, so impenetrable until now, and found them not mysterious at all. They were warm and understanding and appreciative, filled with an immense sweetness and strength. And inside her, for all her excitement, there was an unusual calm. Her own answering smile was ardent and accepting.

As she moved into the circle of light around the roaring fire, he stepped closer, the firelight playing crazily over his brown body with its powerful muscles. She'd never seen a man naked before, and the sight of him standing there unashamed before her was the most thrilling thing she'd ever seen.

With a look of intense pleasure on his face, Shandor opened his arms. "Come," he whispered softly. "Come to me, Graciela."

A great surge of warmth flowed into her and she felt the real strength of him as he skillfully brought her along to one delicious new feeling after another, mastering the Gypsy in her soul.

Then, as the excitement mounted, she no longer knew, or cared, who it was that was experiencing this . . . nothing mattered but the experience itself, and it was savage and tender and holy above all things. . . .

ACKNOWLEDGMENTS

With respect and appreciation to George Warren, who was a great help on this story from the very beginning, and to Arthur Andrews, Joe Curcio, Andrew Ettinger, Stanley Corwin, and with very special thanks to my editor, Gaye Tardy, for her patience, professionalism, and spirited enthusiasm throughout the endeavor.

FRISCO LADY

Jeraldine Saunders

PINNACLE BOOKS • LOS ANGELES

FRISCO LADY

Copyright © 1979 by Jeraldine Saunders

An original Pinnacle Books edition, published for the first time anywhere.

First printing, July 1979

ISBN: 0-523-40408-5

Cover illustration by John Solie

Printed in the United States of America

PINNACLE BOOKS, INC.
2029 Century Park East
Los Angeles, California 90067

The road leading to a goal does not separate you from the destination; it is essentially a part of it.

—Gypsy saying

BOOK ONE

Chapter 1

Exhausted and out of breath, legs aching and feet bleeding, Graciela McGee turned in at a magnolia-shaded driveway on Carondelet and paused to rest for a moment in the dark comforting space of a wrought-iron *porte cochère*. Her breath coming in deep gasps, she listened intently for signs of pursuit on the gaslit street behind her.

For the moment, it seemed, she could afford to stop and catch her breath. Leaning back against a masonry wall, she let the deep heaving breaths bring life back to her spent muscles and slowly—achingly slowly—still her racing heart.

She listened; she didn't dare stop to think about anything. If she once gave in to the temptation to think about the terrible things that had happened today, she'd never be able to bear up, to fight for her life and freedom, to keep her headlong flight from the only world she'd ever known—a world that, in the space of twenty-four hours, had become a living nightmare, peopled with horrors she had never imagined in her wildest and most frightening dreams.

No! Don't think of that now! Think only of survival! she told herself angrily. Anger was a good emotion right now; anger made you keep fighting, keep running. It made you crafty and cunning and wise. It would keep you alive. Anything else . . . but anything else wasn't worth thinking about. No, no; the best thing was to stay angry and wary. And alive and free . . .

Free? What a bitter joke. Yesterday she'd been free, perhaps. Yesterday and all the yesterdays she remembered. At least she thought she'd been free. No matter

3

that it had all been a terrible sham, a fraud, a thought-less, careless oversight of her father's that. . . . No. No matter. The illusion had been just fine while it worked. While her father was alive and out of debt, and while there'd been no one around to contest the status of his house and his chattels and his issue. But now?

Now she was no longer a person, no longer a human being with feelings to consider. Now she was no longer a free white virgin female of marriageable age (for all her convent upbringing). Now she was no longer a black-Irish beauty with Spanish blood. Now she was no longer anything that fit into any category anyone would care about.

Except as property. Except as an unfree quadroon chattel. Except as a slave to be bought or sold—or passed over as legal tender, to pay off her father's creditors after his death. There alone she was worth something. Graciela shook her head in bitterness now as she remembered, the salty tears scalding her eyes. Worth something? She certainly was. The legal settlement that had awarded her to Louis Thiebaud in partial payment for a gambling debt left unresolved at Tom McGee's death had canceled a good fifteen hundred dollars of that debt in exchange for proprietary rights over her body and soul. She, alone of the girls she'd known in her short life, knew, once and for all, exactly what she was worth. Perhaps someone would tattoo it on her shoulder after they caught her. . . .

No! No! Stop thinking that way! You're not going to let them catch you! she told herself. But it was with a sinking heart, as she thought of the odds against her escaping from New Orleans and from the man who owned her now as of this twenty-seventh day of June, 1844. She was *property*. Property didn't get up and run away with impunity. If your dog ran away you hired men to catch it. If it wouldn't return, if it had turned "bad"—if it showed signs of disobeying again—you had perfect license to shoot it. You could shoot anything you owned. Shoot it—or do anything else you wanted to with it. Things like . . .

Behind her, behind the masonry wall that screened off the garden of the big house in whose coachport she had found temporary shelter, a door slammed. Close after

4

the slam of the door came the low rumble of a growl, deep and hostile, the growl of a large dog.

Now the growl became a snarl. Then the fierce, vicious bark of the unseen animal behind her nearly scared her out of her wits. Graciela cringed in terror against the iron uprights of the *porte cochère*; then, her wits coming back to her, she remembered that there was—at least she hoped there was—a stout brick wall separating her and the dog. He couldn't get through to her.

Outside, in the street, she heard the sound of horses' hoofs again: steel-shod hoofs that clattered on the cobbles of Carondelet Street. And metal-tired wheels, guided by a careless hand, that slammed hard against a cypress *banquette* before the vehicle—a light buggy, perhaps similar to the one that had been following her— careened crazily back into the middle of the street, to the muffled curses of its driver.

Please, dear God, let him pass, she thought. *Please let him go right on by.*

Behind her the dog's barking grew louder, more insistent. In the street the buggy slowed as the hoofbeats dwindled to a slow *clop-clop.*

On silent bare feet she moved closer to the front of the *porte cochère,* keeping back from the area dimly lit by the gaslight from the street. She peered out into the pool of light as the buggy slowly hove into view. It must be around eight-thirty or nine by now, she was thinking. It could, after all, be anyone, just anyone, coming home from dinner at a friend's, or from a card game on one of the moored riverboats down at Tchoupitoulas Levee. It could be . . . but her heart sank as she saw the heavy shoulders under the broadcloth coat and the grizzled hair poking out from under the tall beaver stovepipe hat the man wore. No, it was Thiebaud himself. Louis Thiebaud—her owner, her lord and master.

Not while I'm alive! she said fiercely to herself. She'd die first. Better yet, she'd kill him herself. She reached into a pocket of the convent-school dress she'd escaped in, feeling the comforting coldness of the sharp dressmaker's shears she'd stowed there. At the very worst, she decided, she'd sell her life dearly, and whatever happened he'd find her no easy prize. She'd show him you didn't trifle with a girl of Irish and Spanish blood. . . .

Her lips twisted into a bitter smile. Spanish? Well, that was what her father had told her all her life: that her mother had been a Spanish beauty from the Caribees whom he'd met and married back when he was still in the sugar trade. Graciela was sure it had seemed like a kind lie to him at the time, and after all, he'd raised her, after her mother had died in childbirth, in as warm and loving a manner as any father could provide. But it *had* all been a lie. She'd seen the papers to prove it that afternoon. Her father had bought her mother, not married her. And while he'd lived with her as a husband and even introduced her as his wife, he'd never got around to manumitting her. That made their daughter a slave, too—a slave who shared her mother's dusky half-Negro blood. It was a lot to learn about yourself in eight hours' time—the eight hours that had passed since the nuns at the convent had, with tears in their eyes, been forced to refuse her admission for the first time in the five years she'd been there. That was a place where the students were kept from knowledge of the sinful outer world—a good background for the making of a rebel, she thought to herself.

Behind her the dog's barking grew louder. Outside in the street the buggy stopped dead, and Louis Thiebaud turned his square face on its bull neck toward her. No! He was coming this way! What could she do? The *porte cochère* was closed on three sides. If he trapped her inside . . .

In a wild panic she dashed from the door, out into the street, past Thiebaud's stocky figure, and, keeping to the smooth cobbles of the street rather than the rough wooden planks of the raised *banquette,* ran like the wind down the street to the corner.

"*Eh! Arrêtez!*" Thiebaud bellowed after her. "Come back, you little nigger bitch!" Behind her she heard him once again place the burden of his heavy body on the squeaking springs of the buggy and bellow an impatient "Hyaaahhhh!" to his horse. Her heart pounding, she turned the corner and ran as fast as her legs could carry her down the half-lit street, heading—where else could she go?—for the Swamp.

6

A day earlier she'd have been frightened half to death at the thought of going into New Orleans's infamous Fiddler's Green, one of the toughest Sailortowns in the world. Of going there at all, in broad daylight, much less of going there at night, friendless, alone, barefoot, her hair and clothing in disarray. There she'd have no protection, no friends, not one person to aid her. But how could that be worse than going back to the nice part of town, only to be the slave of a swine like Thiebaud?

She turned another corner, hearing the horse's hoofs behind her. Faster . . . faster . . .

Now she was in a street of taverns and grog shops, where the sailors staggered down off the broken *banquettes* to dance in the middle of the street under the lights. There was singing and the sounds of loud roistering. As she hesitated, slowing her pace, she saw one drunken salt tossed out of a doorway to land on his face in the gutter, awash with water these days when the River, swollen from the abnormal spring rains upstream, lay so high above them on the levee that steamboat passengers could look down into the upper-story windows of houses all along the waterfront.

She stopped, looking right and left, and heard behind her the sound of Thiebaud's horse pulling into the narrow street. Of course there was nowhere to go but straight ahead. She eluded the grasp of a drunken tar and dashed forward again. One man grabbed her arm. As he spun her around she caught a frightened glimpse of Thiebaud, farther back, his whip held high, cursing the dancers in the street as he struggled to maneuver the buggy down the narrow avenue between the twin rows of houses.

"Let go of me!" she yelled, and swung her thin arm at the man. The scissors-blade flashed in the dim light.

"Saucy bitch!" the sailor said. He released her arm and stepped back, reeling drunk and half-smiling. She turned and pushed past another pair of sailors who were trying to dance on the uneven cobbles.

"Out of my way, you scum!" The voice was closer than she'd thought; she looked back over her shoulder and saw Thiebaud gaining on her. As she looked he swung the whip and laid open a sailor's cheek. The horse pushed forward.

7

Where could she go? To one side a door loomed: a door that led into a long hall. Perhaps the hall led to a back door. She bit her lip; then, taking a deep breath, she plunged through the open door.

There was a light at the end of the hall. She made for that. Hope still glowed inside her, a fierce ember; but at the sounds that came from the closed doors to one side and the other, the glow guttered. What could she do? At the end of the hall only a closed door could be seen— that and the inert body of a drunken man lying on the floor. Gathering up her courage, she pushed the door open and shut it. Her back to the lit room, she listened for sounds of pursuit as her heart pounded.

"Well, look here, won't you?"

Graciela whirled. On a battered love seat sat a tall man, his shirtsleeved arms around a woman. She wore only a shift, its hem riding higher on her pretty legs than anything Graciela had ever seen, its open neck showing an ample bosom. She didn't seem to be disconcerted by the invasion; it had been her voice that Graciela had heard.

The man spoke. "Well, now. You're an odd sight, my dear. Aren't you a bit out of your element?"

She looked at him. The voice was deep, humorous, almost mocking. The face was long, sharp-boned, aristocratic, with a wide sensual mouth; the eyes were green and the hair red. His eyes swept her up and down, from the torn collar of her convent-school dress to her muddy bare feet. "I . . . there's a man after me. . . ."

"And no surprise," the man said, giving the woman on his knees a quick friendly hug. "Scrub you down and you'd be pretty enough, I'll wager. I might even be tempted to go after you myself, if I were not otherwise, and so pleasantly, occupied," he added gallantly. The *galanterie* earned him a luscious kiss on the neck. "What are you doing in the Swamp, though?"

The door burst open then, and Louis Thiebaud stood in the archway, whip still in hand, his broad form almost filling the doorspace. "What's she doing? Running away, that's what! Running. . . ." He paused, his eyes going to the tall man, who hadn't moved. "Here. I know you, don't I? Oliver . . . Tolliver. . . ."

"Beau Tolliver," the tall man said. "And you're . . .

8

oh, yes, don't tell me. Thiebaud. Louis Thiebaud. We met over the gaming tables above the Bourse Michelet, I think last Wednesday. Now," he said, his voice calm and with that mocking edge still on it, "what brings you here to interrupt me at my sport?"

"Sport. Hah." Thiebaud's voice was carelessly contemptuous. "This nigger wench ran away. I'm just here to claim what's my own."

Tolliver's green eyes went to Graciela, then back to the hulking Frenchman. "Nigger wench? Since when does a nigger wench wear a convent uniform? Last I was in New Orleans"—he pronounced the word casually, *Nyorlins,* the way a Kaintock might, a Kaintock who didn't give a damn for Creole manners—"the ladies who run that sort of place weren't in the habit of admitting blacks, even if they were as pretty as this young lady here."

"Lady?" Thiebaud laughed coarsely. "Come here, bitch!" He reached for Graciela's hand. She shrank back against the far wall, one hand in her pocket clutching the shears.

"Hold," Tolliver said in a commanding voice. He eased the girl in the shift off his lap, not at all unpleasantly, and stood up. He was better than a head taller than the square-built Frenchman. "I ask you to hold. You've invaded my privacy now."

"Privacy?" Thiebaud said harshly. "You speak of privacy on public premises? In a whorehouse?"

"I speak of privacy," Tolliver said. His smile was courteous—and cold as ice. "And I speak of premises whose public use I haven't yet determined. Whorehouse it may have been. Yesterday noon it became mine on the turn of a card at *vingt-et-un.* I may decide to make a cotton warehouse of it, for all you know. And when I do will the Runaway Slave Law give you license to invade my premises and carry someone away, with no more bond than your word?" That icy smile still on his craggy face, he stepped softly into the line of sight between Graciela and the open door.

Chapter 2

"Word?" Thiebaud said, his manner going from bluster to something rather more deadly. "You presume to doubt my word?"

"Systematic doubt," Tolliver said, "is the philosopher's stance the world over, Monsieur Thiebaud. There is a certain point past which I must take you on faith, and you me. I'm being asked, for instance, to take on faith your statement that the girl is yours and that her status is what you say it is. I may in fact do so in the end, but I'm a hard man to hurry. All things in good time." He held up one hand, not so much in warning as in gentle admonition. "On the other hand, you must take on faith, and right now, *my* statement that the premises are mine. I occupy them, after all, and I can produce witnesses to back me. And the property laws of this city would be damned lenient on me if I were to have you shot for trespass." His hand reached out and touched a bell cord. "I can summon a man who would kill you for me."

"You will answer for this!"

"Perhaps, in due time. I can, after all, hold the girl until you get a court order for her."

"Damn you, I have a packet to catch for New York!"

"All the worse for you. I—"

"You—you'll hear from my lawyer!"

"Lawyer? I thought you were going to say your seconds. That, now, would require proof that you were a gentleman."

"I? Fight with a common gambler?"

"Please. Gambler, yes. A common one, no. It is an

10

uncommon gambler indeed who wins half a city block, whatever its pedigree, on the turn of a card."

"What is it that you want from me?"

"Only time to hear the girl out. Here we've been arguing back and forth, and she hasn't said a word. I think she has a side to be told."

"You keep out of this!"

"Moderate your tongue under my roof," Tolliver said. His hand was still on the bell rope as he turned to Graciela. "Tell me what happened, my dear," he said gently. His green eyes did not mock now as they swept from her to the other girl, nodding to her to dress behind a screen and go.

Graciela, her back still pressed to the wall, started telling him of the terrible events that had occurred since her father's death. "I know . . . I know Father always meant to get around to it, but : . . well, I suppose it didn't seem important until. . . ."

"Yes," Tolliver said. "Most unfortunate. And who did you say your father was, my dear?"

"I didn't, sir. My father was Tom McGee. Don't you believe me?"

"McGee . . . wait, now. Black Irish like yourself, then? A man about so high? Turned a bit stout?"

"Yes, sir. He was . . . he was a gambler. A gambler on cards, on cotton futures. . . ."

"I knew him. Poor devil, he was losing his stone face these last days. You could bluff him. I watched him drop a fortune on the *Belle of the West* last February up the River. And your mother? Spanish, you say?"

"Yes sir. That's where I got my name. My father was—he didn't get along with *his* father. He was turned out of the house young. His family—they were from Natchez-on-top-of-the-Hill—they didn't recognize him, or his . . . his wife. I mean my mother."

"Wife, hell! His nigger whore!"

"Hold your tongue, Thiebaud. I'll not ask you again." His tone changed abruptly from command to kindness. "And your father went on the beach at Natchez-under-the-Hill, I take it? And found he liked it better than life among the Mississippi gentry, eh? Well, I can understand that. That's how some of my best friends got their

11

start. Some of them are bankers now." His smile was appreciative, but it wasn't gentle. Only his voice was gentle now. "Well, you've had a rough day and a half of it, I'd say. I don't know. . . ."

"Tolliver! Stop this nonsense and return my property to me, or I'll—"

"You'll what? Fight me? We aren't armed. When does your packet leave?"

"Tomorrow at nine."

"And I've an appointment aboard the *Paragon*, for *piquet*, at eight. When does that leave us time for formal fighting? For the duelling code, with all its sober little punctilios? I could put you on my calendar and shoot you at seven, but damn it, I have an appointment with a lady at midnight and I'm damned if I'll disappoint her by not staying for breakfast just for the likes of you."

"Please, sir, don't give me back to him!"

"Easy now, my dear. Tell you, Thiebaud. Possession is nine-tenths of the law, and the other tenth you'll have to deal with after you get back from New York, won't you? Complicates things, doesn't it? Well, I do know a solution. Will you cut the cards for her? Fair and square? Your deck or mine? I'll call across the street, to a place I don't own, for a clean deck."

"Gamble? You are asking me to gamble?"

"Certainly. Haven't you any sporting blood at all?" His grin was mockingly Irish, Graciela thought. And there had to be Irish blood in him, with that hair and those eyes and that pale Byronic skin. "Here." He threw a fat leather wallet on the big bed beside him. "Before dinner there were four thousand dollars or so in there. The wallet's contents against the girl. Fair enough?" He didn't wait for an answer. "Annie!" he called to the girl behind the screen. She came out, not suitably clothed for anywhere but the Swamp but with enough bosom tucked into her dress to avoid arrest. "Annie, go across to the Admiral's Cabin and get me a good deck of cards if they've got one."

"Good deck?" The girl grinned. "They wouldn't know what a good deck of cards was if you told 'em. There's an honest game at the East Indiaman. I'll ask there."

"Be back as fast as you can!" He watched her scamper through the door, brushing past Thiebaud who

12

shrank from the contact. "Oh, don't worry, Thiebaud. She won't give you the pox. She's probably as well born as you are—if on the wrong side of the blanket." He winked at Graciela, the grin still on his face. "No offense intended, Miss. There are damn few of us whose provenance would stand up under scrutiny, here in New Orleans."

"You go too far, Tolliver!"

Tolliver turned back to the Frenchman. "I was just going to explain to the lady the curious trick of history which I'm sure the nuns at school were not at liberty to teach her."

"And that was?"

"The one, my dear sir, by which the whole of polite New Orleans is descended from the *filles à la cassette* of 1728, each of whom seems to have had at least a hundred children, and not from the correction girls—the dregs of the French jails, who were sent here to keep the rivermen and landowners happy, and who seem, every *Jeanne et Jeanneton*, to have been barren. It has always seemed to me a curious coincidence that the pedigrees of the French of New Orleans have never been examined more thoroughly."

"You insolent swine!"

". . . especially in view of their manners."

"You speak to me of manners? You. . . ."

"You can't think of a word? Try *aventurier*. Or perhaps *parvenu*. You cannot insult me except by intimating that I resemble you in any way." His grin turned to Graciela, his eyes gentle again, his whole posture a dismissal of the hulking Frenchman. "Ah, but I fear our lesson in history will have to wait, my dear. I hear Annie's footsteps in the hall." Sure enough, the girl with the low-cut dress entered just then, handing Beau Tolliver a deck of cards, its ribbon seal intact. "Here, Thiebaud. Examine the seal if you will. Examine the cards if you like. Take your time."

Thiebaud, however, dismissed the cards with one contemptuous glance, his arms crossed over his broad chest. "It is your game, Tolliver. Shuffle the cards. I will cut them."

"Very well," Tolliver said mildly. He picked up the cards, broke the seals, and, taking them to a bedside

13

table, shuffled them expertly, his long-fingered hands a blur. "Here," he said. "Take your cut." Thiebaud stepped forward and cut the cards four ways, in what amounted almost to a second deal. Graciela, her heart pounding, leaned forward. "All right, Thiebaud. Four thousand in cash against Miss McGee. If my wallet's short you'll have my note for the rest, payable by dawn. I'll redeem it myself. Your draw. *Après vous, monsieur*." His grin was cool, controlled.

"*Mais non. Après vous.*"

"All right." Beau Tolliver's Irish panache was put to the supreme test as he reached for the deck, his eyes mockingly on Thiebaud's own. His grin did not waver for so much as a moment as he let his hand fall, carefree, on the top card and peeled it up as if he were dealing a hand of draw poker, the deadly new Kaintock game Graciela's father had brought downriver from St. Louis a year before.

He laid the card down. It was low—painfully low. The seven of hearts.

Seven of hearts! Graciela's heart almost stopped. Not only was the card on which her life and fortune depended a low one, and easy to beat, but it bore an unmistakable symbolic message, according to the system her father had used in reading the cards for her: *Beware of treachery.*

Thiebaud smiled—a mean, callous, brutal sort of smile, in which the sweet smell of victory was evident. His broad, coarse hand reached again for the top card and turned it over. Graciela leaned forward; she held her breath and her heart seemed to stop as she strained for a sight of the second card.

It was the two of spades. Thiebaud's smile sat frozen on his square face. All the life went out of his eyes.

When Thiebaud had gone—fuming, silent, taking his loss badly—Tolliver pulled the bell cord. A face appeared at the door: scarred, unshaven, the face of a fallen angel. "Bludger," Tolliver said, "This is Miss McGee. This, on the other hand"—he held up something shiny—"is a Spanish piece of eight. I'm sure you don't need instruction on how to spend it, or on how much it will buy."

"No, sir," the man said. "How do I earn it?"

14

"Miss McGee is to be conveyed to my rooms. I'd send Josh, but he's off on an errand and won't be back until late. No matter; you'll do. You're to call a hack, and accompany her to my place. She'll be taking the boat north with me in the morning. And mind you, nothing is to interfere with her getting there. Nothing. If she's lost I don't want you to come back alive. You get my meaning?"

"Yes, sir. I'll go get a hackie." The face disappeared.

Beau Tolliver called to the girl Annie. "Annie, my love. Miss McGee will need shoes, and perhaps a change or two of clothes. Go upstairs and see what you can scare up. One of the girls ought to be her size. Make haste, now, and I'll consider putting you in charge of this place while I'm gone, you and Bludger."

"Oh, Beau!" The girl stepped into his indulgent arms, kissing him hard. Then she slipped out of her room, too elated to look at Graciela.

Tolliver turned to her at last. "Miss McGee," he said. "You've had a terrible time of it today, I think. Well, I hope the way's clear to ending that. I'm taking you north—"

"Please," she said, "I. . . ."

"No, hear me out. You can't stay here. These slave-holding swine have ruined you for the black states. Even if you're manumitted here formally, you'll have no so-cial status at all, mainly because they feel your blood has been impugned—and, remember, there'll be nobody left here to defend you and stick up for you now that both your parents are gone. Your pa was disowned, and God knows where your mother came from. I gather you don't."

"I never had a chance to ask her. She died when I was born."

"I gathered as much." His long-fingered hands took hers; the touch was like lightning striking. His green eyes on hers were exciting, in a way she'd never felt excitement before. "Well, I can't help you in the South. What I'm going to do is put you on the boat with me north to St. Louis. My black man Josh will come with us; the moment we reach free-soil country I'll make a stop and lay over a couple of days while formal manu-mission papers are filed on both of you."

15

"Mr. Tolliver. . . ."

"Please." His carefree grin had a serious note about it, and his green eyes were earnest indeed. "There are goddamned few topics in the world that I feel strongly about, one way or the other, but this swinish slavery business is one of them. No man, no matter how bad, should ever be owned by another man. Now I'm neither rich nor powerful. I gave up all chance of that for the freedom from convention that the gambling life gives me. But I make it a point, every time I come South, to take a couple of nonfree people back North with me. It never costs me anything, because I get my living and my temporary slaves at the turn of a card. I'm no hero. I'm just a man who has good sense on every point but this, and most of the time I have the wherewithal to indulge myself in this one madness."

"I don't know how to thank you. You're too kind."

"Now, no damned Southern hyperbole! Not for me. I have a hard enough time talking horse sense to the men down here without having to tackle the English—or the French—languages as the ladies use them. Look: I'm from the wrong side of the blanket myself. I'm a rich man's bastard. You think you've had it hard. My father never tried to acknowledge me. He never had any intention of doing so. My mother took until my third birthday to die of having me, and she suffered the agonies of the damned from a crushed spine all the way. She was small and delicate, a redheaded Irish type like myself, only she had little bones that broke easily. She should never have been left with a child in her belly, much less with no money for doctors and hospitals."

"Oh, my God," Graciela said, her eyes on his. She was on the verge of tears.

"I went to the workhouse when I was six. I ran away seven times before I finally got it right. I was twelve by then. For six years I was owned. The workhouse could sell my labor and pocket the money any time. Lord knows they tried often enough. Trouble was, I wouldn't work. Sell me, and I go dead on you. Well, never mind all that. The main thing is, that's not going to happen to you. Not while I'm alive. Thus. . . ." His hand waved the whole problem away airily. "At any rate, you'll be safe at my place until morning. Joshua will be along

16

soon, and he'll take over guarding you when Bludger leaves. Josh is strong and true; he'll look out for you until I can. And I'll be along shortly after dawn. We leave at ten on the *J.M. White*." He squeezed her hands, then released them. "Bludger!" he bellowed. "Where the hell have you got yourself to?"

Chapter 3

To Graciela's surprise the conveyance Bludger found for her was not an open buckboard or surrey but a big six-passenger rockaway, all shiny black paint and red trim on the outside, with bright brass sidelights and lovely leather fittings inside. The driver was a tall, regal-looking black in elegant livery, the dress of an earlier and more aristocratic age.

Bludger handed her up and then stepped up to sit opposite her. He'd found a battered hat somewhere, and a broadcloth coat with many patches. She fancied she could spot the tell-tale bulge in his coat where he carried a sidearm. After a couple of moments he shifted in his seat and confirmed her suspicions; the distinctive-looking heel of a big Colt's Texas Paterson percussion-cap revolver much like her father's poked its way out from under his coat.

Her father's. . . . There wouldn't be much left now of the small store of possessions she'd thought he was leaving her. Her own wardrobe, her books, her small box of jewelry—they'd all be sitting in disarray on the floor of some grubby warehouse owned, like as not, by Thiebaud. There was nothing left for her. And why should there be? After all, she was property herself. How could property own property? And here she was in a dress and shoes borrowed from a tart from the Swamp.

No! She forced the hot tears from her eyes. That was mean and snobbish of her. After all, the girl—Annie—had been kind to her. Who else had, in the last two days? Only Beau Tolliver, for sure.

No, it would be mean and ungracious of her to look

18

down on a girl from the streets after the girl had gone out of her way—and, like Beau Tolliver, defied one of the city's most sacred laws—to help her. She was past that sort of caste snobbery now. You could never look the same way upon the social status quo in the South after you had had the kind of education she'd just had, with all her so-called friends turning their backs on her. Even the manner of her father's old lawyer had changed to make her a non-person all of a sudden just because her father had inadvertently flouted some law. And to cap it all, being handed over like a horse or a cow to a man like Thiebaud, a man who would, no more than half an hour later, try to. . . .

She shuddered. Better not think about that. She'd try to think of the future, because she had a future again! In no more than a matter of hours she'd be leaving this terrible, vicious place, where people treated you like dirt, heading upriver to safety and a new life on the *J.M. White*, the fastest, most elegant steamer in the whole river trade. With the strong, gallant arm of Beau Tolliver to protect her.

Tolliver! A little shiver of a totally unfamiliar kind of pleasure ran through her at the thought of him. How handsome and fearless he was! How strong and upright and kind and manly—everything she'd always wanted to find in her father. But Tolliver was a gambler, too. She wondered if all gamblers fell prey to the same disease her father had had: the one that turned them into foul-tempered, drunken beasts when they were in the middle of a losing streak. Thinking of Beau Tolliver, she found it hard to imagine him in that sort of condition, whatever the circumstances. High-tempered, perhaps, for he was half Irish—and didn't she have a bit of a temper about her herself? But drunken—Beau Tolliver didn't seem the type. He had the air of a gentleman, and a gentleman held his liquor. Well, perhaps her father had been like that, once. He'd always said that he was never the same man after her mother died, and she'd often found him up late, sitting and staring into the fire, perhaps thinking of her. He'd said he saw her mother in Graciela, with her raven-black hair and dark flashing eyes and dusky skin. . . .

Yes, she thought bitterly. Dusky is the word. She'd

better get used to the fact that the very qualities her father had found attractive in her mother, and in her, were now to be considered reprehensible. Well, down here in slaveholding country, anyhow. It might be different up North. Beau Tolliver had intimated that, particularly once she had the formal papers of manumission in hand. Whether people would look down on her was another thing. With freedom papers in her pocket, though, she'd at least be able to defend herself should anyone challenge her.

Well, Pa had never said life was easy. At least now she had a chance. And she was free of Thiebaud forever.

Under her she could feel the springs of the wagon registering the touch of each cobblestone. They were in the *Vieux Carré*, the old part of town. She looked out the window but failed to make out any landmarks she knew in the dim gaslight.

"Be there in a minute or two, Miss," the man Bludger said. "Don't worry."

"Thank you," she said, settling back. "It's just that . . . I'm not used to having to run for my life all the time. I jump at every shadow."

"Right you are," Bludger said. "But after ten years or more you get used to it, and it don't bother you no more. You're doin' best to get a change of air, though. Life ain't easy in New Orleans, but I can think of at least one other seaport where I'd be looking forward to the same kind o' life you'd be livin' if you stayed here." From his accent she'd say that seaport would most likely be an English one.

"Mr. Tolliver told Annie that you and she would be taking over management of the—the place we were in."

"The False Love? Yair. That'll be a cushy one. Won't be as rich a post as some. Beau won't tolerate crimpin', and that's one o' the biggest ways o' makin' money down here in Fiddler's Green."

"Crimping? I'm afraid I don't know the word."

"Sellin' crews to merchantmen, Miss. 'Pressin' sailors for service on the windjammers. Whether they likes it or not. Well, I'm well quit o' that line o' work, I reckon A man can make a bad name for himself that way."

"Mr. Tolliver doesn't approve of any kind of slavery, then?"

20

"No, Miss. Only thing he hates worse than slaveowners is traders. Yesterday, when he won the False Love and half the block, it was from a man 'at dealt in blacks down to the Market. Beau could have gone easy on 'im after a point, you know, but instead he went to bearin' down. He's a tough customer when he's riled. He. . . ."

Instantly alert, Bludger sat up as the coach slowed and then stopped. His hand went to his lapel and his fingers closed around the big butt of his gun.

"What's the matter?" she said, leaning across to the window and trying to peer out. As she said this a weight seemed to fall first on one side of the carriage, then the other. Bludger leaned forward, gun in hand. As he did someone yanked open the side door of the coach and swung a heavy cosh at Bludger's head. He was halfway turned around when the club hit him; the gun fell from his hand and he toppled forward onto the floor of the big rockaway. At the same time a rough hand reached in from the other side and grabbed Graciela by the hair, dragging her headlong through the opposite door. She fell heavily on her knees; then hands were on her, hauling her out headfirst.

There were five of them, she could see now as strong hands set her on her feet. One man stood on the cobbles, his gun trained on the black coachman. Two others held her while a fourth man, mounted on a white horse, looked down on her, a savage smile of triumph visible on his square face in the dim light. Thiebaud! As she looked, her face falling with her hopes, the fifth man came around from behind the carriage and stood looking up at his leader.

"All right, boys," Thiebaud said. "You've done well. Get her to my place—that's the warehouse down in Exchange Alley—and there'll be a fat purse in it for you. I'll be along in a moment. There's something I want to do first." His face turned to her, a look of hatred on it. "Your Mr. Tolliver isn't likely to make that morning departure on the *J.M. White*, girl. I think he'll find he has another, more *pressing* appointment." He accentuated the word heavily, his words trailing off in a laugh of bitter triumph.

Thiebaud was no more than a couple of minutes behind the men who took her inside the big warehouse. By

21

the time he arrived, however, the lanterns were lit. There was enough illumination to show her the tight, controlled smile on Thiebaud's cruel face as he stepped forward, closing the big doors behind him.

"Do you want chains on her?" one of the men said. "She's already got away once:"

"All in good time," Thiebaud said. "Strip her."

"No!" she cried out. "Please. . . ." But as strong hands grasped her arms on both sides, a third man behind her reached for the neck of her borrowed dress. As she struggled his hands ripped the gown down. The dress fell at her feet. "No! Please! Stop him!"

"Not bad," Thiebaud said. "Now the shift."

"Right you are." The rough hands pulled hard, and her shift fell to the floor around her ankles.

And there she was, stark naked and defenseless, before the eyes of five men. She, who had never been naked in front of anyone since she was a babe in arms, was sobbing uncontrollably. She could almost feel their hot, lustful gaze on her breasts and pure body. She writhed, moaning, "No . . . please don't . . . I've never. . . ."

As she fought with all her might, she could hear Thiebaud's merciless, hard, soulless laughter, which seemed like the sound of a snarling animal. A cataclysmic torrent of foul words sprang from his evil cistern of a mouth. Although the waiting men were drooling like a pack of wolves, out of desperation she cried to them, "Help, help me!"

"Don't worry, you'll get help from us. We'll show you what it's like to be with a *real* stud as soon as it's our turn."

"She'll soon be yours, boys," Thiebaud said, as he began to maul her.

Throughout this contemptible and repugnant situation she was surprised to find foremost on her mind the struggle for survival—her physical danger was first in her thoughts. It seemed as though the fear of her life being at stake gave her the strength she needed to keep her from going completely mad.

"Well, boys," Thiebaud said. "I think the little nigger bitch is trying to tell us she's a virgin. Can you believe that?" A general murmur told him no. "Right! They're like animals, no matter how they're raised. Let 'em loose for a moment and it's back to the bushes in a flash. If there's a one of them that's a virgin it's because she's too goddamned ugly to attract anyone. Well, we'll see. There's a cot over in the corner." He reached inside his jacket and pulled out a fat clinking purse; he tossed this to the men. "Here. Hand her over and enjoy yourselves. If she fights, I may throw her to the lot of you when I'm done with her." Boastfully he said, "But I'll wager she'll be tame enough. If," he added with a faint leer, "I haven't tamed her myself by then. Hand her over, now."

Alone in the near dark with him she fought like a tigress. It was no use, however. That square form of Thiebaud's was not fat but solid muscle and felt to her as though it weighed a ton. His hands pinned hers; his heavy body straddled her at first, holding down her kicking legs; his repulsive thick lips descended on her naked nipples, kissing, biting, sucking, tonguing.

She struggled with all her might, her head tossing. There was no aid to be reached by her loudest screams, and the fight for her virtue was, of course, in vain. Only when he temporarily released one of her hands to fumble with his own clothing did she strike out, frantically, hitting him hard in the face with her free hand, using her fingernails to scratch him deeply. The respite was brief, though, and his large hand took both her wrists, holding them tight, as first his knee, then his coarse-skinned, brutal hand forced her naked thighs apart. Now she felt pain as something began to penetrate her, slowly at first, then quicker and deeper. "N-nooo," she moaned. "Please don't, please, you're hurting me."

Shivers of fear shot through her body in a burst of loathing and repulsion. She couldn't define her feelings of hatred mixed with a new, self-preservation instinct that she had never needed before. The next time she cried out it was at the height of sharp pain so intense she almost fainted. She would have just lain there, inert, feeling him withdraw and then leave her, but then his hard hand swept across her face, snapping her head to one side in an effort to revive her.

"Damned little bitch," he said. As he stood, tucking his clothes about him in the dim light, she could see the thin lines of blood running down his face where she'd scratched him. He wiped his mouth with the back of one broad, powerful hand. "I told you not to fight. Now you'll learn the consequences of disobedience, all right. *Boys! She's all yours!*"

Straightening his ruffled neckcloth and pulling the twin points of his collar up around his neck, he smiled a mean and bitter smile. His voice lower, he added, "She's yours—until morning, anyhow. Then we'll see how much she brings in the market when we stick her bare-assed on the stand. I think I'll make money on the present deal."

He turned and walked away. She cringed against the rough wall of the warehouse, behind the cot, hearing the several sets of footsteps coming closer.

Chapter 4

The big door slammed behind Thiebaud. Graciela kept the cot in front of her, peering into the darkness for the eager faces. Now two of them stepped into a pool of light from the spirit lantern that hung on a nail driven into an oak upright. The face of the nearer one bore a long, disfiguring scar that ran from the corner of one eye across one cheek to the point of his chin. As the full light fell on him she could see the puckered flesh around the empty eye socket.

She blinked and looked back into the darkness. A weapon, somewhere, anything! But nothing came to hand. From the darkness strong fingers closed around her wrist. She cried out in panic, "No! No, please! Please don't—"

"Easy, my dear," came the tight voice of Beau Tolliver at her side. Then his voice boomed out in the unmistakable tone of command. "You there! Another step forward and I'll put out that other eye!" His big boot lashed out and shoved the cot toward Thiebaud's man. The metal edge caught the one-eyed man in the shins; he bellowed in pain.

Three others stepped into the light now. She could see a knife in the hand of one of them. "You clear out, whoever you be," said a man with hair as fiery as Tolliver's own. His Irish accent was thick and harsh, with not a trace of the gentle sing-song her father's voice had sometimes fallen into.

Tolliver's voice beside her in the darkness was calm and reassuring, but there was a curious huskiness in it that had not been there before. He gave the impression, although she still couldn't see his face, of great self-control. "Graciela—that is your name, my dear?—get behind me. Between me and the wall. Here, put this on." He handed her his own coat; she slipped it on gratefully. "Now edge over to your right. There's a back door. My man Josh is outside holding the horses. Don't make any commotion. Quietly now." His big hand squeezed her own.

"You, Nobby, get on his left." The harsh voice of the one-eyed man cut through the stillness. She could hear their rough bootsoles sliding across the floor. "Eddie? Stay here with me. All right, boys."

In the pause she heard Tolliver's loud sigh. "Do as you choose, then. I've got an Allen revolver with more than enough balls for killing every man that comes at me." Graciela, edging along the wall away from him, once again marked the huskiness in his voice. "*You!*" he barked now in that peremptory tone. Back a step or I'll. . . ." He didn't finish the sentence. Graciela saw the flash and heard the sharp report at the same moment. The one-eyed man stopped in his tracks, looked down at the small hole in his chest, and collapsed like a puppet whose strings have been cut. There was a cry and a curse from the men beside him, and their forward motion stopped.

"All right, damn your eyes!" Tolliver's voice was powerful and authoritative even through the husky note. "Clear out and take him with you before I—"

Then she saw the heavy form in the darkness beside him. One of them had crept around beside him. "Mr. Tolliver!" she cried. "To your right! He—"

A heavy blow fell on Tolliver, driving him to his knees. She saw a knot of them rush forward into the light again. She backed against the wall, feeling for that door he'd said she would find.

Then another shot rang out, and a second brigand pitched headlong onto the floor of the big warehouse. Out in the middle of the big room she could see the tall, slim man, looking dapper and powerful in clothing as good as Tolliver's own. Blackpowder smoke still curled upward from the just-fired pistol in one hand. The other held a second sidearm, and it was pointed with cool efficiency at the man with the harsh voice. "Mr. Tolliver!" the black

26

man said in a voice with only the smallest trace of accent. "Are you all right, sir?"

"By Christ," the rough voice of the man in his sights said, interrupting him. "By Jesus Christ, a nigger with a gun. And he's shot a white man. Tolliver, you'll hang for this. But this black bastard won't live long enough to hang."

Tolliver stepped into the light now for the first time, wiping the blood from a fearsome-looking knife with his kerchief. "It's all right, Josh. The one in the corner won't be bothering anyone again." In the light Graciela could now see the great red spot on Tolliver's waistcoat. He was hurt! "Keep them covered," he said in a voice that showed strain. "Now—you. Both of you. Clear out. And if I ever see either of you again, so help me God, I'll kill you on sight." His face was as cold as his voice. "Now—*out*! And tell Thiebaud he's a dead man. You hear that? Be it soon or late, I'll have his heart in this hand. Tell him not to sleep soundly." His mouth twisted in contempt. "Out, damn you!"

Graciela's hand went to her chest. She watched the look of hatred in their eyes as they sidled past Josh's waiting pistol and headed for the door Thiebaud had taken only moments earlier. Only with the door safely shut behind them, however, did they obey instinct and hurl parting curses at Tolliver and his man.

"Now," Tolliver said. "Josh! The horses! Good work, man! And Miss—Miss McGee. Can you ride? There are two good Virginia geldings out by the door. If you can make it up behind me onto one of them. . . ."

Graciela, with his big coat buttoned loosely about her, moved forward into the circle of light. "Mr. Tolliver! You're hurt!"

"Yes, I am, my dear," he said. His eyes on her were full of anger. "Thiebaud tried to have me waylaid and sold to a crimp. I took a bit of a knife cut across the ribs. Otherwise I'd have been here faster, and you. . . ." His sigh was full of fatigue. "Are you all right? Did Thiebaud and his men . . . ?" But his eye caught hers and he nodded gravely. "Ah, God." His big fist clenched and unclenched. "Thiebaud's a dead man. It may take me some time to find him, but. . . ." He threw his shoulders back, wincing at the pain in his chest. "Here," he said. "We've got to get out of here. Not only am I harboring runaway slaves, but one of them has committed the murder of a white man." His gaze fell on the bodies at his feet. "Well, I've killed one of them myself, haven't I? Not that the likes of these will qualify easily as human beings. Ah, but I'll hang for them anyhow if we don't make haste." His arm went around her, herding her gently toward the back door.

The first sign Tolliver had of the gravity of his wound was the unexpected difficulty he encountered getting into the saddle. After two unsuccessful tries he allowed Josh to help him up. "Damn me, Josh," he said through lips held tight against pain. "Look at me. I vault into the saddle nine times out of ten like a jockey-boy. I must be getting old." His voice held a note of cavalier contempt for his own mortality.

"You're hurt, sir," Josh said in his even voice. "Don't you think Miss McGee would be better off riding with me?"

Tolliver's voice regained its earlier note of anger. "North of Cairo, Josh, I'd say why not? But you know the kind of reaction we'll get if we run into the night watch here. A black man riding at the gallop with a white woman behind him on the same horse—and her riding astraddle at that?" His short laugh wasn't humorous at all. "I'm sorry, Graciela. There wasn't time for finding a sidesaddle for you. If you can get up here behind me it'll just be a matter of hanging onto me." He smiled down at her reassuringly, and even in the dim light of the gas lamp far down the street she could see in his expression how badly he'd been hurt.

Then she was feeling Josh's strong hands lifting her up, effortlessly—goodness, how strong and fine the two of them were!—and putting her bare foot into the stirrup so that she could swing the other leg up and around. When she settled in the saddle behind Tolliver there was a sharp pain between her legs, a reminder of her assault. Now there was a compensating feeling there as well, something she could not name, as she settled herself close up against Tolliver's hard rump and felt the soft leather of the saddle against her bare behind under Tolliver's big coat. God! She'd almost forgotten. She was naked underneath that borrowed greatcoat! Naked! And pressed tight against this man's body! She couldn't understand how Thiebaud's body had repulsed her so and here she was wanting to be even closer to this man.

Beside her she could feel rather than see Josh's long, lithe body slip effortlessly astride the second horse. "All right, sir," he said. "Mr. Tolliver? You're sure you're fit to ride?"

"I'm sure of nothing, Josh," Tolliver said. His voice was hard and determined. "Graciela, hang on, now. Arms around my belly. It'd be a blessing if you didn't let them slip up too high. That's fine. Josh?" And without further word he spurred the horse to a walk, a trot, to a full gallop.

They rode at full pitch for an hour, Tolliver and the powerful horse beneath them showing no signs of fatigue. Tolliver and Graciela held the lead, with Josh keeping an eye out behind them. Twice Graciela craned her neck around to look at him. He looked like a centaur, tall and erect in the saddle, his head held high and proud on his long neck. Man and horse were one. Well, she thought, turning again to burrow her head into the comforting expanse of Tolliver's broad back, this was something else again. She'd never seen a black man like Josh. You'd almost think he was white. You'd almost think. . . .

She hugged Tolliver all the harder. Heavens, she thought. Here I am thinking like these Creoles I was raised with. The ones who turned me out as a black girl, as a slave, a person without rights. Well, why shouldn't Josh carry himself with pride? Who was she, a slave herself, to give herself airs about being better than he was?

Suddenly Tolliver's broad shoulders and strong back seemed a veritable Rock of Ages for her, a bulwark as strong as the Church had been—had seemed, for indeed what had they done for her? They'd thrown her out of the convent school, hadn't they? Condemned her to. . . .

She shook her head fiercely, holding Tolliver all the harder. That wasn't a profitable way to look at things at all. No, her only salvation was in not looking back, at anything, ever. All the old life she'd led, the easy existence, protected, sheltered, that was gone forever. What lay ahead was everything. The present, the future

29

(whatever that might turn out to be), these were all she had, all she would ever have. She clamped her jaw down on the thought. She'd never look back. There was too much pain in doing that. All her sustenance, all her comfort, they'd have to come from what she had at any given moment and from the dreams she could put into practice.

But what vain thoughts! Here she was, a fugitive, an escaped slave—what hope of a future could she have? Unless. . . .

Tolliver had told her he was heading north to Illinois, to free territory. He'd even spoken of manumitting her and Josh formally. If he could do this, if she could count on his strong arm to protect her while she found a new place in life. . . .

As they rode she closed her eyes to be able to feel, even through her fright, her first enjoyable close physical encounter with this most dashing man. She'd had a sense of awe and mystery about sex until Thiebaud had tried to cast stones of filth at it. With her eyes closed, with her body so close to Beau Tolliver, she allowed her arch-Romantic, mystical imagination free reign. She was feeling a gamut of emotions which ran from passionate and chaste to amorous and reserved. Thiebaud had raped her but psychologically she was still a virgin. She had loathed being pawed and panted over in the heat of Thiebaud's fornication, but if this handsome Beau Tolliver were ever to try to make amorous advances toward her, she wondered if she could resist what she had heard called "the soft sweet swoon of sin."

She shivered, and felt Tolliver suddenly shushing the animal under them, felt the horse's gait slowing perceptibly. She held on hard and looked around to see Josh pull up even with Tolliver, his head turned their way.

"Josh!" Tolliver said in his strong voice over the drumming of the horses' hoofs. "Up ahead . . . light on the road. You see it?"

"Yes sir," Josh said, his voice higher-pitched but carrying easily. "I don't like it."

"Neither do I. Pull up here." The two pulled to a dusty halt and Tolliver, leaning forward, patted the horse's neck with his free hand. "Josh," he said. "I can't tell you why, damn it, but it doesn't feel right. I think

30

we'd be running into a roadblock up there." He stared through the darkness at the dancing flame of the camp-fire far ahead up the road. "I don't know what it'd be for. There's no chance Thiebaud or anyone else would have gotten any message out about us this quickly. But there's something wrong about it." His hand, sweeping around to his side, brushed Graciela's bare leg and sent a delicious, uncontrollable shiver through her. If he no-ticed this he gave no sign. It was as if he'd decided not to notice her at all. "I wonder how far the levee is."

"Not far, sir, I think," Josh said, his eyes still far down the road. "And if you'll pardon my saying so. . . ." He hesitated. It wasn't an enforced deference, Graciela was sure of that. If he deferred to Beau Tolliver it was out of a respect few men had ever earned from him in his life-time.

"No, go ahead. You've ridden these roads. You prob-ably know the country better than I do."

"Thank you, sir. It's just that I think I know a place where we might be welcome. If we can find our way to the levees, and perhaps, ah, find a spare boat we might make free with. . . ." He left it hanging.

"Huh," Tolliver said. "I'll admit I could use a bit of rest, and perhaps a bit of doctoring. These friends of yours—up the River, perhaps?"

"No, sir. Down. There's an island some miles down-river from here. It's closer to the far shore than to this one. It was a hideout for runaways. The owners are Tockos. They don't have much to do with the mainland-ers. Few of them speak English. They don't hold with slaveholding. They do their own work the way they did it back in the old country. I escaped there once, across the River, and they kept me for two months. I'd still be free except that I tried to make it to the Gulf, and a priva-teer's longboat chased me down." He paused. It was, she gathered, a speech of unusual length for Josh.

"Tockos, eh?" Tolliver's voice was showing some strain now. "Well, let's see. You may have a good idea, at that. I'm getting weaker. If we can find a boat. . . ."

She felt him straighten up and nod vigorously. "Yes, yes. Good, Josh. Lead the way. There's got to be some sugar factor's landing nearby where we can find a *ba-*

teau nobody's using. Hang on, Graciela." She barely had time to renew her death-grip on his slim waist when he spurred the horse beneath them to action again. She watched wide-eyed as Josh pulled up alongside them, checked Tolliver's condition, and then spurred his mount to pass them on the first wagon track that led off to their left into the thick underbrush.

Chapter 5

There was fog down on the River: heavy, impenetrable fog that hung close to the water and sent shivers up and down Graciela's spine once the damp chill got to her. Looking out across the River she could see no more than a few yards: the very surface of the water itself seemed to fade imperceptibly into nothingness no more than a few boatlengths out into the sluggish current.

"Graciela," Tolliver said. "I'm afraid you'll have to get down for yourself. Ordinarily I'd dismount and hand you down, but. . . ." His voice had finally begun to show his exhaustion.

"Here, Miss," Josh said beside her. He held up his strong hands and she gratefully let herself fall into them. He set her feet down on the damp earth and turned to Tolliver. "Mr. Tolliver? Mr. Tolli—"

But then it took both of them to help Beau Tolliver. The mere act of leaning forward was too much for him. As he slumped in his saddle Graciela could see the broad red stain that marred his waistcoat. And as she reached up to catch him she could see that the hands she'd held his middle with during that long ride were themselves stained with blood. She and Josh barely caught him before his big body could hit the ground.

By the time Josh had located a rowboat and stolen four oars and two pairs of oarlocks for it, Tolliver was sitting up again, cursing himself for his uncharacteristic weakness. Once Josh had the oarlocks seated Tolliver managed to stand and lower himself precariously into the bow seat of the little boat. Josh then handed Graciela aboard and, casting off, set himself amidships. As he pushed them away from the little dock Graciela once again experienced the strange feeling—almost a ghostly one, it made her shiver all over—that in leaving the mainland now she was bidding farewell forever to a whole part of her life. To her childhood, perhaps. Well, she'd become a woman tonight, she thought bitterly. She'd hoped for a better initiation, but now . . . well, what could a runaway slave have expected, anyhow?

The current remained sluggish for many yards. Then the main current of the great River began to make its presence felt. There was a strong tow downstream, toward the Gulf. She watched Josh, his powerful shoulder muscles bulging, pull strongly on the oars. Tolliver sat up, his hands on the gunwales. "Josh," he said. "This is going to take two of us."

"No, sir," Josh said resolutely. "You're hurt. I can't let you—"

Then both of them stopped.

All of them heard the sound at the same time: a short-breathed, unmusical keening that came from at least three hoarse, nonhuman throats. A yelping, annoying, thoroughly frightening sound that once again sent chills down Graciela's spine. Looking into Josh's eyes she saw the duplicate of her own fear there.

"Bloodhounds?" she said in a small voice.

"Yes," Josh said. "Once you've heard that song you'll never forget it. Oh, I doubt it's for us. But God alone knows, one poor devil after another tries to run away from the plantations and thinks he's made it, only to hear that sound. . . ." He kept the oars in the water; she could see him shiver. "Miss Graciela," he said. "Change seats with me, will you please? It'll take the two of us to row, I'm afraid. Mr. Tolliver will only hurt himself worse if he tries to help. If I sit with my back to you you can do it just by watching me and following suit. Can you do that, please?"

"Oh, yes," Graciela said. "Just show me how to hold them." She scrambled forward in the bottom of the little vessel, hearing the echoing ululations of the hounds far behind her in the deepening fog.

Several hours passed. After a while she felt she was beginning to get used to it, although her muscles ached and her hands felt raw and painful. When she missed the water with a mighty heave—almost depositing herself backside down on the planks in the process—Josh turned and gave her a quick good-humored glance and told her she'd "caught a crab." Getting up again she looked around at Tolliver; his eyes were closed and his breathing was coming in slow even breaths. Biting her lip, she raised the oars again and tried to get in rhythm with Josh.

She was succeeding at this when the next sound came from behind her. Strangely, it wasn't until she heard the new voice, high-pitched and penetrating, that she realized it had been some time since she'd heard any sounds at all. This time it was a human voice, and it made sounds she'd never heard before.

"*Ko je tamo?*" the voice said. It waited for a moment and then said again, "*Ko je tamo?*"

"Keep pulling on the oars, Miss," Josh said. Then he raised his voice and said haltingly: "*Ja sam vas prijatelj. Vas prijatelj.*" He turned and craned his neck through the thick fog. He said louder yet: "*Prijatelj.*"

There was no answer for a moment. Graciela said in a stage whisper: "What are you saying?"

"I'm telling him we're friends," Josh said. Then he raised his voice again. "*Zdravo, prijatelj. Mi smo . . . mi smo ranjeni. Mi smo . . . uh . . . gladni, Mi smo. . . .*" He frowned. "Confound it, I'm running out of words. I was trying to tell them one of us was hungry and had been wounded."

"*Pricekajte jedan minut,*" said the voice ashore. They could hear the unseen speaker talking low with someone. Then the voice was raised again, but not at them. "*Mirko! Dodjite brzo!*" As Graciela, still pulling valiantly on the oars with blistered hands, sneaked a glance over her shoulder, she began to see through the fog the ghostly bulk of an island. She looked up at Josh; he smiled at her reassuringly.

"It's all right," he said. "He's calling Mirko. That's one of my friends here. Mirko speaks English. I think we're safe for now." He put his oars back in the water and began pulling heavily on them. Immediately Graciela could feel the difference. Josh began slowly turning the boat downstream, heading for a landing no one but himself could see.

*   *   *

Mirko turned out to be a hulking, dark-haired man with huge shoulders, a fierce black mustache that turned down sharply at the corners of his mouth, and eyes that burned right into Graciela's soul. His English was serviceable, it appeared, but he found no occasion to use it in ordering three of his friends to tie up the stolen boat and carry Tolliver ashore. His barked commands were monosyllabic and harsh, in a voice pitched lower than Graciela had ever heard a human voice speak before. His nod to her as he handed her up onto the dock was friendly enough, though, and when he looked her up and down, taking in the borrowed man's coat and her bare feet, he jerked his head at one of the men who stood beside him and fairly bellowed an order. In a moment the man reappeared from the bushes into which he had quickly vanished, carrying a woman's flowered linsey-woolsey dress in one hand. He handed it to Mirko and Mirko gave it to Graciela. "Here," he said. "You will need this." He turned to Josh. "I remember you. Come. We have food and place to sleep."

"Thank you," Josh said. "Rest assured I'll never forget *you*. Look, our friend, he's taken a knife wound. He's lost a lot of blood."

"I can see," Mirko said. "Do you think we have no eyes? We will heal him. Come. There is still food. This way." Not pausing to see if anyone was following him, he turned briskly on one black-booted heel and struck out confidently along the narrow catwalk. One of his men picked up Tolliver and tossed him over his shoulder as if Beau had been a child. Josh shot Graciela a look, shaking his head, and made a semicircular motion with one hand over the other bicep. His lips formed the word *strong!*

"My goodness," Graciela said, licking her spoon. "I had no idea I was so hungry." She watched Josh digging happily into the dish he called "oyster salad": cooked oysters, grated onion, black pepper, vinegar and olive oil.

"This is not true of Joshua," Mirko said, sloshing the wine in his cup to stir up the sediment before draining the vessel. They were Dalmatians, Josh had explained with some help from Mirko. They drank wine cut with river water, and it was difficult to tell where sediment began and silt ended. "Joshua eat oyster like drumfish eat oyster." He raised one black eyebrow—not disapprovingly; it seemed to be a compliment—at Josh. "Is good. Is plenty oyster in River mouth."

"It's wonderful," Graciela said. "I'm stuffed. I was thinking of looking in on Mr. Tolliver."

Mirko held up a heavy hand. "No," he said. The single syllable carried immense authority. "Let him sleep. He will be all right in morning. Sore, hurt, but all right. Lose blood, need sleep. I know. I fight in war once. Take saber right here." He indicated his heavy deltoid muscle. "Let him sleep. He is strong, young. Heal quickly." He nodded at Josh. "Joshua," he said. "You want pipe? Smoke?" Josh shook his close-cropped head. "Then I go to bed. You, lady, you sleep there." He pointed to a ramshackle cabin perched high atop four pilings. "Josh sleep across dock. You remember?" He looked at Josh, who nodded. "Then good night. We talk in morning." He stood up—they'd been sitting cross-legged before the open fire—and nodded, not unfriendly, at both of them as he went away.

Graciela took a sip of the red wine. "Josh," she said. "Mr. Tolliver. . . have you been with him for long?"

"Not long," the black man said. He sighed. "I tell you, ma'am, if I didn't have a wife and child waiting for me up across the Line in free territory I'd follow that man through hell and back. In a way you might say I have already. It was Mr. Tolliver that bought my family free and set them on Illinois soil. He came back—well, he has his own business, to be sure, but he came back as much to get me as anything. I really believe that. I've been with him for a year now. He took it upon himself to have my wife and boy traced through the markets. He went for them and bid on them. He would have manumitted me six months ago except that—well, we've been down here all that time. And it's just not something you can do easily down here. Not when you still technically belong to another man the way I do."

"And me too," she said. "You forget I'm a slave too."

"Yes," he said. "I can't get used to that. But the institution, as Mr. Tolliver says, doesn't play favorites. It

37

makes beasts out of everyone who has anything to do with it, rich and poor, master and slave." He took a scrap of the rough, delicious black bread the Tockos had given them and wiped up the rich oil in the bottom of his bowl. "You'll pardon my saying so, ma'am, but this society down here, maybe it's beyond redemption. I've met perhaps two men who haven't been made into beasts by it. No, make that three. Two white men, both of whom hated slavery and fought it, and one black man who was killed by it. Everyone else. . . ." He frowned. "But no. I'm forgetting Mirko here, and the Tockos. They're good, all of them, with all their faults. And they live off their own labor, not off someone else's. They. . . ." He let it trail off. His eyes clouded over; he was thinking of something else. "Uh, I'm sorry," he said, coming to himself. "Where was I?"

"The Tockos?" she said.

"Oh, by the way, that's a derogatory name the Creoles gave them. The first thing a Dalmatian says when he runs into a friend is *Kako ste*? That means 'how are you?' After a while people started calling them Cockos. Then Tockos. They don't mind, really, unless you mean to insult them. I wouldn't try that."

"They certainly look fierce enough."

"Indeed they are. A *man* always is. Mr. Tolliver, for instance. I saw him once take on three men, armed only with a bowie knife. Cool as ice. Tender as a spring tomato. Loyal. Strong. Compassionate."

"You speak beautifully, Josh," she said. "Better than most Creoles do. How—?" She blushed. "I mean—I didn't mean to—"

"No, it's all right. If people get to thinking of you as black they'll start wondering how you came to hold *your* head so high and carry yourself with such grace, Miss."

"Not Miss anymore, Josh. Graciela." She sighed. "I'm property. I'm a slave like you."

"You hush now!" he said almost savagely. "Don't you ever let me hear you talking about yourself that way. Don't you dare go accepting those people's valuation of you. You keep right on valuing yourself your own way, regardless of circumstances. Don't you let up doing that for one minute. If you ever get to believing those people you're lost. Look," he said, quieting down a bit, "I know you didn't mean it wrong. I was taught to read and write by my first master. He had it in mind to free me as soon as he had me trained. I can keep accounts, do business correspondence. But he died. I was sold for his debts."

"I understand. Father meant well by me too, but. . . ."

"Yes. Well, you're as good as anyone. White or black. Don't you forget that. Ever. My first master tried to teach me that. My next—the one I ran away from—he tried to take that away from me. Mr. Tolliver put it back where it'd been in the first place. He said 'Josh, you ever get to acting like you thought you were a slave, and so help me God, I'll make one of you. You ever act like a stupid darky and I'll sell you South.' " He shook his head fiercely. "That was strong medicine, but perhaps that was what it took. And what he told me I'm telling you. Don't you forget it."

She watched the fire in his dark eyes and thought of Beau Tolliver. *Cool. Tender. Loyal. Strong. Compassionate.* Yes, yes. And more than that. A man who made others as strong as himself. A man who could give you strength and still keep it. Above all, a *man.* . . .

Chapter 6

*Run! Escape! They're after you! The streets are full of
them! No place to hide! Run, run! They're coming!
Don't turn the corner—they'll be waiting for you down
every side street! Keep to the middle of the street—
away from the hands that clutch, away from the horrid
faces that watch, and laugh, and make sport of you—
just run, run like the wind . . . What's that up ahead?
The faces! The hateful faces! The hands, the brutal
hands waiting to grasp, and maul, and bind . . . and
the eyes—dark, hate-filled, red-rimmed with lust. . . .*

"Miss! Miss!"

The soft voice woke her instantly. Graciela sat up in a
cold sweat, pushing the featherbed away from her body
in its drenched linsey-woolsey sheath. A woman with
long dark hair leaned over her in the chill of dawn. As
her hands sought Graciela's she could feel the roughness
of the woman's fingers, her palms, hard-callused, almost
painful for Graciela's own oar-blistered hands.

"Please, Miss. You cry loud. You afraid?"

The voice was harsh and unmusical, but there was a
note of such concern in it that Graciela forced a wan
smile. Now, in the soft morning light, she could see the
woman's face. Its bone structure was strong and proud,
particularly in the cheeks. The nose was hooked, almost
a beak, but the effect was somehow handsome and
pleasing. The lips were full and red, and the head was
held high. The woman would perhaps have been a
beauty among her own people a few years earlier; but
now her face showed the signs of toil, and exposure to
the strong Delta sun, and weathering. She couldn't be
much over thirty, but she was already hardening into an

old woman. Graciela sighed and smiled again, this time more deeply. "I'm sorry," she said. "I had a bad dream. I was. . . ."

"No, no," the woman said decisively. "No tell about." Her hands waggled before Graciela's eyes to underscore her words. "Come, I fix you hot coffee. Wake. Not think of dream."

"I suppose you're right," Graciela said. She allowed the woman to help her up and went out of the little cabin they'd given her onto the mazelike nest of plank walkways they'd built out from the island. It seemed to be a nest of marsh-covered hummocks. Now she could see that their "town" was nothing more than a camp, a string of cabins on long pilings like the legs of a giant crane. The little patch of dry land they'd landed on the night before, the place where they'd sat before the fire and talked, was virtually the only dry land for some distance around. Elsewhere the Tockos had built up patches of "land" on the mudbanks by piling up oyster shells to stabilize the mud. It made a solid surface you could walk on if you wore thick-soled boots like Mirko's.

But not without! She tried stepping on the oyster-shell "ground" and cried out in pain. The shells were razor-sharp to her bare soles, and shifted uncomfortably underfoot. She stepped back onto the planking and followed the dark-haired woman along the boards to the patch of dry land where they'd landed the night before. A small fire was burning, and she could smell the strong scent of coffee.

The hummock stood perhaps six feet above the river's edge at its high point. The oystermen's cabins towered above this on their stilts, and a ring of pilings driven deep into the mud and strung together with catwalks formed the walls of their little settlement, a bulwark against intruders. Against all intruders, she could see, but the River itself: the whole settlement was obviously designed to allow high water to sweep by underneath the stilt-supported cabins and leave them standing high and dry. It was a precarious way to live, she thought, but they certainly seemed healthy enough.

There were several of them clustered around the small fire now, and to her delight their number included

41

Beau Tolliver. He'd done what he could to rinse out his shirt in River water; she could see it hanging to dry from a wire stretched between two pilings. He sat bare-chested beneath the same heavy coat she'd worn on their long and arduous ride the night before.

He looked up now, a stone coffee mug in his hand. "Graciela!" he said. His smile was courtly and welcoming. "Come over here, child, and sit by me. Don't stand on ceremony." He made a place for her on a patch of compacted marsh grass beside him, and handed her, very carefully, a steaming cup of coffee. "Easy, now," he said. "These good people don't make their coffee the way we do, with chicory. This is Turkish stuff. Don't jiggle the cup, and don't drink deeply. Sip." He smiled at the wry face she made. "There. You'll get the knack of it in a while. I'm developing a taste for it."

Graciela shot a quick glance at him. *She* wasn't developing a taste for it, that was a sure thing. But it was hot and strong, and it did help her wake up. Perhaps it was helping Beau Tolliver. Certainly something was. He looked a lot better this morning, dirty and bedraggled though he was. "How are you feeling?" she asked.

"Oh, much better," he said. "These folk have the healing touch." He grinned over at Mirko, who was striding forward to the fire, his face animated and friendly under those beetling brows. "Mirko! I was telling Miss McGee that no one could stay ill for long here."

Mirko chewed his lip under the covering mustache. "You are young. A knife wound, what is that? You will heal." He spat into the marsh grass beside them. "Look," he said. "Towboat come by soon. You flag down. You go up River, arrange passage."

"Splendid," Tolliver said. "I'll need man's clothing for Miss McGee."

"No. You go alone. Leave girl here. You come back for her when passage all right." Mirko looked at her now. "Not safe. Slave escape across River last night. People out to try to find. Come up and down River with boats." Seeing the sudden fear in her eyes, he waved a thick hand. "No. You dark. You look like Tocko woman. You stay with us. Joshua, we hide him in marshes. Tolliver go ashore alone." His words carried

42

great authority; perhaps it was just his own immense presence. He left no room for argument.

"Well," Tolliver said, standing, "I'm in your hands, Mirko, my friend. I'm sure you know best." He helped Graciela to her feet as the other oystermen rose and slipped away, down to the flat-bottomed oysterboats. He stepped forward to shake Mirko's hard hand and clap the dark oysterman on the shoulder. "I can't say how grateful we are to have met you and your people. All I can say is that there'll come a time when I can return the favor."

"Favor?" Mirko said. "What is favor?" But there was a small smile on his face as he turned to go down the bank to where the boats were tied up.

Graciela stood beside Tolliver, watching the men and women go. "Goodness," she said. "Do the women go out with them?"

"Yes," Tolliver said. "I've been up since before daylight talking with them. The women work right beside the men until they have children. There are few women in this settlement. When the men here have finished building up the oyster beds they've been working on for these three years now, they'll send down to the settlements farther downriver for women. Tockos only marry Tockos. Well, there are Serbs and Croats and Macedonians among them, but the bond is like to like. They're splendid people. It's a splendid life they've chosen: free and proud and beholden to no man. And," he said, looking gravely down into her eyes now, "using no man's labor but their own."

"I never appreciated that before," she said. "I don't know what I thought about things. I suppose I thought what people told me to think. But I'm learning to look at things in new ways." She sighed.

"Ah, yes," Tolliver said. His arm went round her waist for a moment, and she could not find it in herself to resent the distinct touch of fatherliness in his caress. It was enough to feel that protective arm touching her, and that gentle but strong hand clasping her waist for a second or two.

"You've had a rough awakening, haven't you, my dear? Well, it comes to everyone sooner or later. One would have wished for a few more years of childhood for you, but . . . well, here we are, and we have to make the best of what we have, don't we? Just remember there are some men who aren't as rotten as Thiebaud." He shook his red-haired head. "You heard what Mirko said. I'm going to catch a ride on one of the towboats going up past New Orleans. I'll see if I can arrange passage for us under an assumed name and then come back for you two. I managed to bring some cash with me, and once we've landed for a few hours' stopover at Memphis, say, I can get hold of more money." His hand dismissed the difficulty of touching a new source of funds. "You know: credit, gambling, whatever. There are people there who owe me favors, and others who owe me money. Meanwhile we'll be on our way North—to safety and a new life for you."

"And you?" she asked, her large eyes seeking his. "What will happen to you? You can't come back to New Orleans, can you?"

"Well. . . ." Again his idle wave of the hand dismissed all problems. "It doesn't matter. Things will cool down there in a while. A cash payment to the right magistrate, a word to the right politician." He saw the look on her face and grinned. "You don't believe me, do you?" He chuckled: a rich low laugh, an Irishman's laugh. "Look, Graciela, it doesn't matter. It's all temporary. What's permanent is that I have it in me to get back anything I lose. Look at me. I'm all over mud. My shirt is wilted and gray with River sediment and my coat looks as though a dog had slept on it. Do you think that makes a damn to me? Put me ashore and I'll be as dandified as ever in a day. In the meantime, I'm among valued friends, I'm safe from harm. . . ."

He stopped and looked down at her. His eyes grew more solemn. "I don't think you believe any of this yet. That's all right. Just remember my words and think about them from time to time. You feel as though you've lost everything and your life is in ruins. Well, I understand the feeling. But understanding it is not the same as agreeing with it. There are people who are born to be pawns. If I thought you were one of them I wouldn't have wasted any time on you—any more than I'd have wasted time on Josh if he'd turned out to be a

44

weak-spined chattel like so many of the blacks down here, content to eat another man's food and wear another man's shackle. The fact that I've concerned myself with both of you proves that I think otherwise."

"But—"

"Now don't interrupt. Look at you, now. You're cold, damp, dirty, scuffed and scratched. You're tatty-haired, shiny-nosed, barefoot, and reduced to one item of clothing in the world—a rough shift you borrowed from Maritza, an oysterman's woman. But damn it all, Graciela, under the dirt you're a beautiful young woman, and the difference between a pauper and a duchess is not in what they are so much as in how people look at them."

"I don't understand." But she did, and her heart was pounding. He'd called her beautiful!

"Now don't play stupid on me. Of course you understand. You know what it is I'm trying to tell you: that you're a strong and resilient young woman who's survived experiences in the last twenty-four hours that would have driven half the women in New Orleans into insanity or suicide. But you haven't cracked. Instead you've got fire in your eye and you're still holding your head high, just as you were doing the moment I met you. If you have that kind of spirit and self-esteem in the first place no amount of adversity can subdue you, girl, and if you don't have it nothing can put it in you."

He put his big kind hands on her shoulders, and the touch sent hot flashes through her. "Graciela, when you work on the gaming tables as I do for your living you get to be able to tell in a moment who's a winner and who's a loser. Me, I'm a winner. Your pa, God rest, was a loser. He had himself beat before he started. All I can think is that your mother, whoever she was, must have been a winner and she must have passed it on to you. You'll always be a winner, even when it appears you're losing. Early or late you'll win. Don't believe any evidence to the contrary. You remember that, girl, and you can never go far wrong. And nothing that ever happens to you, short of death, can touch you. Nothing."

She looked up at him and saw the light in his eyes change and his gaze went to her hair—her poor scarecrow hair, all full of knots and dirt—and down to her shoulders and her breasts. His chest filled; his sharp blade of a nose sniffed appreciatively at the strong scents of the marsh air, and a fierce smile spread across his fair face below that shock of flaming red hair. "That mother of yours," he said. "She must have been very lovely. I'd like to have known her. . . ."

Chapter 7

Tolliver's towboat stood off Mirko's island around noon. By that time Graciela was safely changed into men's clothes, borrowed from a Tocko oysterman's sea chest, and her dark hair had been hacked into a boy's shaggy mop with a sharp knife that had last been used to open oyster shells. She sat in the boat as Josh rowed Tolliver out to the towboat that stood backing water in the sluggish water two hundred feet out from the shore.

"I'll be back in a day," Tolliver was saying. "Perhaps two at the most. When I come I'll have false papers for the two of you if I'm lucky. I'll also have servant's livery for you, Josh, and boy's clothing for you, Graciela. It's not the way of traveling that I'd have chosen, but it's the safest. The thing to remember is that right now none of us is safe until we've put Southern soil behind us. Slaver soil. Or until formal manumission papers can be filed."

He frowned. Taking one of Graciela's hands in his own, he said, "The one thing that must be bothering you the most is what if something happens to me?"

"Oh, no," she said.

"Now, it has to have occurred to you. And don't think I haven't thought of it. Things can go wrong, you know. And one has to have contingency plans for when they do."

"Oh, dear God," Graciela said. "If. . . ."

"Oh, come now," Tolliver said. His voice was stern and harsh. "Try the vapors on some other man, Graciela. That shrinking violet business won't work with me. If you're going to turn into a sniveler. . . ."

"Oh, no. Really. But. . . ."

"I know what you mean. You don't want to think

47

about it." Tolliver's eyes left hers and swept out over the broad expanse of the great River. Somehow she could tell that his gaze was fixed far away, farther than the eye could see. "Well, neither do I. But look, both of you." His eye went to Josh now, sitting amidships and hauling hard on the long oars. "That may happen. *Anything* may happen. If it does you have to be ready for it. And the thing to remember is that you don't need me, either of you."

Josh lost a stroke. He sat erect and looked at Tolliver as if his master had suddenly lost his mind. "Don't need you? But sir. . . ."

"Mind your oars. You know what I'm talking about. The fact that both of you have come this far proves you have the stuff it takes to survive independently. Both of you chose to run away and made good your escape. No matter that you had the good luck to run into me in the process. A good gambler makes his own luck, the saying goes. Something made you turn your steps my way. If it hadn't been me it would have been someone else whose help you'd have used. Well, you can do that again."

He smiled at them now, and the smile was benevolent, confident, and winning. "Just remember: when the chips are down you'll know what to do, both of you. You'll find a way. And even if we're separated, well, I have the feeling that we'll see one another again." Impulsively he took Graciela's hand and squeezed it, once. It was like a wave of intense heat running through her, and she looked at him, her mouth open, her eyes wide. But he . . . he'd felt nothing, nothing at all. He was looking at Josh now with the same eyes, with that same friendly air about him. She sighed and tried to look away, but found she couldn't.

Josh was pulling the shallow-draft pirogue up beside the larger boat. Tolliver sat up and shot his cuffs, dingy as they were. There was something about him that seemed to give immense dignity to his bedraggled ensemble; it was not difficult to imagine him, dirty and tousled as he was, striding confidently into any drawing room in New Orleans, totally at his ease. Graciela sighed again, deeply, looking him up and down as he stood to grasp the boathook proffered to him by a deckhand on the towboat.

And then, for one glorious moment, a quick flash of hope swept through her. He stood close to her; his eyes went to her, to her bare legs below the tattered knee-pants, to the young breasts that filled out the rough man's shirt. He smiled, and there was real warmth in it for her now; he raised his hands chest-high, and she thought—she just *knew*—he was going to take her in his arms. Her heart was beating fast: even if his feelings were only fatherly, protective; even if he only felt. . . .

And then the moment passed.

His hands took hers between them; he squeezed; he let them go. "Goodbye for now, my dear," he said. "I'll return as soon as I possibly can." He stretched one hand out to the young black man in the boat. "Josh: you'll take care of her for me, now, won't you? Good man." With that quick handshake, the white hand encircling the black one, he turned and stepped up easily onto the deck of the towboat.

Graciela settled back into her seat as Josh pushed off and began rowing strongly back out into the stream. As she watched, Tolliver waved once and then stepped behind a pair of deckhands, out of her line of view. The big stern wheel of the towboat reversed itself and began slowly, powerfully, tugging at the strong current of the Mississippi, taking the big boat upstream.

Mirko Jovicic, besides being the acknowledged leader of the Dalmatian colony, was its official interpreter to the Slav oystermen's neighbors. Mirko's emigration from the old country, unlike that of his friends, had been in stages, with lengthy stopovers in various countries. He'd had false starts in the French possessions of the Caribbean—Martinique, Saint-Domingue—and on the Georgia coast before settling around ten years ago in the Tidewater area of the great Mississippi delta. In the process he'd discovered in himself a natural gift for languages. Not that he could read or write in any of them, Slovenian or Croat included; but he did have a knack for understanding other men and making himself understood, even among the hypercritical French. "*Il sait se faire comprendre*," they said grudgingly.

Rivermen of other nationalities tended to give the Dalmatians a wide berth, while remaining as friendly with them as the Tockos allowed them to be. Sometimes the French fishermen, approaching a Tocko oyster bed, would call out greetings, always in French. Most of the time this brought no more than an answering wave, but when the boats of Etienne Marchand's tiny fleet approached the oyster reefs Marchand could always count on passing a friendly word or two with Mirko.

This morning, Marchand, sitting at the tiller of his sailboat, bellowed his usual greetings at Mirko and got more than his usual monosyllabic reply. Jovicic stood in the muddy shallows perhaps twenty feet from him, his legs wet up to the crotch, and said in bad French: "Hey, Frenchman. How is the fishing?"

"Not bad," yelled Marchand. "You will have a visitor soon, I think."

"Visitor?" the heavy-set man said in his bass rumble. "Who would visit the Tocko?"

"Land people," Marchand said. "Kaintocks. Looking for lost slaves. There was a boat with ten of them, carrying guns and dogs. They are scouring the islands."

"Let them look somewhere else," Jovicic said. "We have work to do." He nodded, indicating the men at work around him in the shallow water. "Hey, Frenchman. Tell your friend Thiebaud I will buy wine from him next Tuesday."

"Good. The last shipment? You drank it all up on St. John's Day, eh?" Marchand grinned. The Tockos worked like demons every day of the year, dropping their grueling labors only on the twenty-fourth of June for a saint's festival day on which they ate, drank, fought and sang with single-minded compulsiveness.

"Yes," Mirko Jovicic said, raising his voice as Marchand's boat drew farther away from the oyster beds. "Tocko blood is half wine, half olive oil." He gave Marchand the closest thing to a grin the French fisherman had ever seen from a Tocko. "You tell him to come see me Tuesday, eh? Sundown?" As he waved his big hand a flight of small shore birds rose as one behind him, their wings whirring. Marchand's last glimpse of him came as Mirko turned to a comrade and bellowed a command in that impenetrable tongue of theirs, his hand pointing to the row of oyster skiffs anchored near them in the shallows. There was a more than usually peremptory tone in that order, Marchand thought, sailing briskly along on the port tack, the tiller pressing hard against his callused hand. For a moment he wondered why; then the wind changed, and the business of reacting to this drove further thoughts from his mind.

"Josh," Graciela said, "there's someone coming." Standing barefoot on the weathered planks, she held onto a tall piling and pointed with one hand.

The Negro man, instantly alert, tied off the hand fishing line he'd had in the water and stood to look where she pointed. "Yes," he said. "I'm not sure. It looks like Mirko. Yes, it is. He seems to be saying something. I can't make it out." He threw his head back and yelled at the approaching rowboat. Mirko sat at the tiller while two of his friends rowed amidships. "Mirko!" Josh bellowed. "*Molim ponovite. Govorite lagano. Ne razumem. . . .*"

"What's he saying?" Graciela asked. "Can you make out any of it?"

Josh frowned. "I made out '*pazite.*' That means 'watch out.' Now what the devil does *zaklonite se* mean?" He turned to look at Graciela. There was worry on his dark face. "I'll have to ask him in English. I've run out of Croatian words." He shook his head and looked back at the approaching skiff. "Mirko!" he said in a stronger voice. "I can't understand you. What's the matter?"

The Dalmatian's head went back and his dark eyes fixed on them. "Quick," he said. "Men looking for runaways. They look in the islands. You must go." He guided the little boat into shallow water. "Get in boat." His hand indicated the seat before him. "Quick. No time to lose. There are ten of them. They carry guns."

"My God," Josh said. "Graciela—Miss McGee—he's right. Get in the boat, please. There's no time to lose."

"But Mr. Tolliver," Graciela said. "He'll be coming back for us."

"I know," Josh said. "But what else can we do? If the slavers find me here before he returns. . . ." He let it die out and looked at her. "Look. There'll be a reward

51

out for you, too. Had you forgotten that? Do you want to fall into Thiebaud's hands again? After escaping him? And after we've killed several of his men?"

"My God, no!" Graciela said. Her hands went to her open mouth. She looked at him helplessly.

Below her, in the skiff, Mirko barked out a curt command in his own language; then he switched back to English. "Joshua," he said. "Put girl in boat. No time. Questions later."

❧ BOOK TWO ❧

Chapter 8

Back straight. Head high. Don't give the bastards an inch. Stare 'em down. Stare 'em in the eye until they flinch and give way. And keep smiling. Smiling all the way. No matter that the smile never reaches your eyes. That doesn't matter. What matters is panache. What matters is not letting a damn one of them see through your bluff.

There was more than bluff in Colonel Wesley Falligant's firm, cat-footed step as he walked, easy and relaxed-looking like a dancer, through the line of tables to the bar at Monsieur Ude's tavern and ordered a glass of Nongely rye. There was arrogance as well: arrogance born of a firm knowledge of his lineage and of his proper place in the world into which he'd been spawned some sixty years before; arrogance made doubly strong by the knowledge that despite his years he was as good a man as any in the room, as deadly with any weapon from the pistol to the foil, as sharp-eyed and quick-wristed as any stripling. Arrogance, finally, made inevitable by the fact that every step cost him pain; stabbing pain, the kind that would have made a lesser man faint by now.

Even now, as he stood at the bar, the touch of the glass against his palm reassured him, and he hastened to reinforce that reassurance with a quick shot of the raw Pennsylvania whiskey. "Here," he said, dropping a gold coin on the oak bar. "Leave the bottle." And he poured himself another draught, tossing it off as quickly as the first.

There, now. That felt a bit better. That'd hold him all the way down Market to Silver and then down the sloping path below the bluffs to Natchez-under-the-Hill—and safety. Or as much safety as there was right now for a man in his position. There he'd find a place to lay his head for a while, perhaps. But not for long. . . . The damned trouble was, he had bit off a little too much this time.

As he reached for the bottle again, the stabbing pain hit him, way up under the short ribs. He'd barely had time to bandage it; he hadn't even seen the wound clearly in the light of day. There hadn't been time for that. There'd only been time for fighting off the attack, killing one of them and hightailing it down the Trace to the River before the brigands caught up with him again. And, damn it, he knew they would, eventually. In the first struggle the man he'd later killed had called out to the rest of them about the fat poke he'd found in Falligant's pocket, and about the bulging saddlebags his horse was carrying. Well, the saddlebags had been more bluff—but the poke had been the real thing, all right: the results of a week's hard gambling in Nashville, in which he'd swindled a rich merchant out of a small fortune and the deeds to a couple of ripe properties.

No matter that the properties would revert now, now that he'd been caught cheating. He still had that fat poke and he had no intention whatsoever of giving it up to any Natchez Trace roadagent. So when the gang's leader had lifted that bulging purse from Falligant's vest with the hand that wasn't holding the pistol the Colonel had suddenly lunged forward with a stiletto he'd sneaked out of one sleeve and pinked his man neatly in the guts.

It hadn't come quickly enough, though. Perhaps he was losing his edge, after all. Well, people grew older. At any rate that cocked pistol had gone off and nicked him in the side, and although he'd spurred his horse and run the animal to the death coming down the forest road to Natchez he knew he'd been followed all the way. And now the only place to hide was the one place a light-fingered gentleman of the evening like himself could find safe lodging for a day or so this far upriver from New Orleans. That was on the Landing, in Natchez-under-the-Hill, the toughest waterfront north of the Swamp on Tchoupitoulas Levee.

Well, he'd be there in a few moments, he was thinking now, as soon as he had another drink or two in him to take away the pain. The truth was, nobody could find you under the Hill if you didn't want to be found, not in a half-landlocked, half-floating jungle where the flatboats tied up sometimes as many as fourteen deep on a stretch of waterfront two miles wide. A jungle populated with worse than lions and tigers, he was thinking: wild beasts from the Dark Continent would hold no terrors for the flatboatmen, Indians, gamblers, crimps, whoremongers, cutthroats, runaway slaves and pirates who populated the lower Mississippi's "nucleus of vice." Hell, they were his kind of people; he'd be perfectly at home there, with a bottle in one hand and a slut on one knee.

He winced and threw down another drink. Ah, yes. Women. That was another matter. He'd have to put that off for a bit, having picked up a nice dose of the Spanish Onion somewhere between Memphis and Nashville a month before. Well, all in good time. He'd had the clap before and he'd doubtless have it again before he was planted, him with his irresistible attraction for the gutter. His eyes on the mirror, where his own drawn face grinned humorlessly back at him, he threw down a last draught and chuckled softly.

"Keep the rest," he told the barkeep as he strolled back through the crowd, his step lively, his eye wary. Once, just once, he let one hand pat first the poke in his vest, then the tiny hideout pistol stowed in his left sleeve before he opened the door and stepped out into the gloom outside.

It was foggy on the River bottom, and there was a distinct chill in the air. He looked up and down the street before proceeding, and—better safe than sorry, after all—slipped the little derringer into his business hand before moving down toward Broadway.

Could they have followed him here already? Well, the damned horse had given out back along the Trace, and he'd finished his long haul on foot, cursing every step. Mounted, they'd easily have made time on him.

Suddenly someone moved out of the shadows toward him. "Who's there?" he said in a steely whisper, his old body still quick and alert as he stepped back and leveled the little gun. But the walker passed, staggering uneasily on unsteady feet, taking no heed of him. He lowered the pistol and continued toward the River.

Perhaps it was a combination of his sudden relaxation and the recent false alarm and the pain he still felt, even after five or six belts of Monongahela firewater; but when the next passer-by broke out from behind a warehouse wall and headed his way, he reacted wrong—reacted in a way he'd not have done a day, even an hour, before. Before, he'd been wary; now he felt sudden fear, panic. As the man lurched toward him he pointed the little weapon and, before he had time to think about it, fired point-blank.

"What . . . ?" the other said in a constricted voice. Then he pitched forward on his face.

Falligant sighed. *Damn!* A bad thing to do. Stooping (again to stabbing pains), he turned the body over. The face wasn't a familiar one; that much he could make out in the dim light. Identification? He reached for the man's coat and felt inside for the pockets. A thick wallet of morocco leather met his hand; he pocketed it, unthinking. Well, the poor devil wouldn't need the money, or whatever it was that made the purse bulge so. Now to make haste down the Hill before someone. . . .

Footsteps. Footsteps heading his way. Down the street to the west of him.

He stood up, this time ignoring the sharp pain that greeted the quick movement. Down Canal Street for a block to the corner where Silver Street took off down the Hill. Limping, he moved quickly down the side street, cursing himself for a senile fool. *Now you've done it,* he told himself savagely. *You've killed the wrong man.*

Below the Bluff, on the soft, rockless strip of land they called the Batture, the fog was thicker than before; nevertheless, Under-the-Hill was like day: brightly lit, loud, roistering. He walked perhaps a block in bright light, visible to any onlooker from above, before slipping down a row of houses into the comforting obscurity of the gaming quarter of the city. Only when he found himself in the thick of the crowd that surged forth into the streets, singing and bellowing, did he begin to relax. His eyes searched the crowd for unfriendly faces and

58

found none. With a savage grin he walked with that same light dancer's step into the first saloon that presented itself.

Another coin produced a bottle; he didn't bother with a glass. He moved to a table under an overhead light, waved away two aging, heavily painted doxies, and drank strongly from the mouth of the bottle before putting it down. He looked at it. The bottle wasn't marked. Why should it be? Enough that it was as good a painkiller as he'd found so far—so good a painkiller that it managed somehow to blot out the deafening din that he knew was going on around him.

On a quick impulse he reached inside his coat and pulled out the wallet. He glanced inside at one paper, then two. Then, his face white, he shoved the wallet back inside his coat. *God*, he was thinking. *The magistrate's son?* He took another drink and put the bottle down.

Across from him, suddenly, a man sat down. Instantly alert, Falligant sat up and looked across at him with wary eyes. "You weren't invited," he said. But there was something familiar about the face, with its great slanting scar crossing the sallow cheek. "Wait," he said. "I remember you. It'll take me a moment. . . ."

The man grinned, and Falligant saw the broken teeth and the curious way a second scar on the other side of the man's face drew his lip upward in a kind of involuntary sneer. "Matt Cooper," he said. "I used to shill for Peter Naylor, at the Golden Horn."

"Ah," Falligant said with a wan smile. "Matt. Of course. Yes. It's been a long time between drinks, my friend. Here." He proffered the bottle.

"No, no," Matt Cooper said. His eyes stayed fixed on Falligant's face. "Look, Colonel. There's a man I owe a favor to, and, well, it's as if he'd called the favor in. And you can help me with it. God knows, it may even be someone you owe a favor to yourself."

"Hmmm," Falligant said. "Well, if you won't drink then I will. God knows. . . ." When he put the bottle down again he shook his head. It was beginning to get to him. Better secure a place for the night. He looked at Matt Cooper again. "Favor? And to whom?" he said.

"Mr. Tolliver, sir."

59

"Tolliver? *Beau* Tolliver?"

"Yes, sir. Red hair, he has, and—"

"Ah," Falligant said. "Favors? Well, I can't remember owing Beau any favors. Matter of fact, he took me for six hundred last time I played cards with him. Why? What do I owe him? And where do I fit in all this?"

Cooper smiled again. Despite good intentions the effect wasn't ingratiating. The scars robbed him of any trace of that. "Well, sir, it's as if—"

"Oh, come on, man. Get to the point."

"Well, then, if you don't owe Mr. Tolliver any favors, I hate to remind you of it, but you owe me one."

"You? When was this?"

"Please, sir, I. . . . there was a night on the *Captain Shreve*, a quarter of an hour above Cape Girardeau, five years back it was. You were dealing, sir, and—"

Falligant settled back, his eyes hard and cold now. "By damn," he said. "You're right. You tipped me off that the table was on to me. If you hadn't slipped me the signal it's very likely I'd have been put ashore on a bar at low tide to drown. Somehow I'd forgotten the face, but I remember the act."

"It was before I got this scar, sir."

"All right," Falligant said. He took another slug, smaller this time. "Maybe we can both do each other a favor tonight, Matt. Look, I need to get upriver in a hurry. And, well, without any fanfare. If you could. . . ."

"Yes, sir. If you'd just come this way."

"Oh, all right." As Falligant stood up he noted with some surprise that the pain was almost all gone now. "Lead on. And if you could get me passage to. . . ."

"No problem, sir."

The lights in the hall were bright and glaring. As they opened the door to the unlit room at the end of the building, the sudden flash all but blinded its two occupants. They stood pressed against the far wall, a black boy and a white one, their two pairs of eyes mirroring the same fear and distrust.

"What's here?" Falligant said in an impatient voice. "Is this all you had to show me?"

"Yes, sir," Matt Cooper said, handing him the spirit

lantern. "If you'll stay here, sir, I'll arrange your passage upriver on the first boat that's leaving."

"Look here. . . ." Falligant began, but Cooper was gone. He leaned back against the near wall himself, looking across at the two boys. "God damn it," he said. "What do you want of me? I don't owe Beau Tolliver any favors. What makes you think. . . ?"

"Pardon me," the white boy said now. "It's not Mr. Tolliver. Mr. Cooper just said that because Josh, here, is Mr. Tolliver's man. It's. . . ." He hesitated, his eyes full of indecision.

"Please," Falligant said. "Get it out."

"Yes sir," the boy said. "I'm . . . I'm Tom McGee's child."

Falligant reacted, recovered, then reacted again. "Well, why didn't you say so in the first place? Any child of Tom McGee's. . . ." But he stopped now and looked incredulously at the boy's dark face. "But . . . Tom only had one child. A girl."

"Yes sir," the boy said. "He died a little while back. I've nobody, sir. He said if. . . ."

"My God," Falligant said, looking the "boy" up and down. "I think I know what he said. Sit down, both of you. Sit down, please. . . ."

Chapter 9

An hour later, Falligant, his wound expertly bandaged by Josh, sat watching the two young people mop up the last remains of a pair of heaping plates of red beans and rice. The frown on his face hadn't changed a whit in the last ten minutes, as Graciela told the story of their journey upriver. *Hell's fire and damnation*, he thought. *Now I'm harboring runaway slaves, am I? . . .*

He took a pull at the brown bottle the tavernkeeper had sent back with the food, wincing as the fiery liquid went down his already overworked throat. Returning the bottle to the table before him provoked another, more pained grimace: the wound in his side had been less serious than he'd thought it at first, but the glancing blow of the ball had broken a rib for him, and the wrong change of position invariably reminded him of the fact.

Well, damnation. Stealing another man's property—that was, after all, what harboring a runaway meant down here in cornpone country, wasn't it?—*was* a hanging offense, given the right jurisdiction and the right magistrate. No doubt about that. But then so was causing the wrongful death of a magistrate's son. Particularly in a town like Natchez, where the only thing it was worse to be than a thief, swindler and murderer (and he was, he reflected, all of these) was to be a member of the gentry with a taste for the gutter. A traitor to one's class, they'd call it. He was damned from the start; and, once having admitted that, he might as well hang for a hundredweight as hang for a groat.

Besides, damn it all, there was . . . well, if she was telling the truth she *was* Tom McGee's girl, and she *did* resemble Tom's wife, whom he'd met briefly in Memphis once. Damned handsome woman. Big dark flashing eyes, full of passion. He'd wondered at the time what sort of a ride she was, and how a weak man like Tom had handled a filly with that kind of spirit.

Hah. Weak? Well, that weakling had saved his life once, and at great danger to himself. No doubt about that. And a debt was a debt. He shook his head exasperatedly. It was all right on the River to swindle a fool, a gull, a mark. It was the worst sort of sin to welsh on a fellow gambler, and if anyone were ever to find out that you'd refused to honor a debt when it was called in . . . Besides, damn it, he did have his own rules to live by, and they didn't include leaving a friend high and dry when he'd risked his neck for you. *Damn!* With a hoarse curse Falligant reached for the bottle of strong Taos arwardenty again.

He was about to take another drink, an even stronger one this time, when Matt Cooper opened the door without knocking. Falligant's hand instantly went to the horse pistol he'd dug out of his grouchbag moments before, and before Cooper had the door open a full ten inches the big barrel of the gun was staring him balefully in the eye. "God's teeth, man," Falligant said in an angry voice, "don't you ever knock on a door?" Then he set the gun down and sighed. "All right, all right. Did you find out anything?"

There was something distinctly odd about Cooper all of a sudden. His eye wouldn't quite meet Falligant's. "Uh, no, sir," he said. "I mean, yes. But. . . ."

"Something's wrong?" The answer didn't come immediately. The question became its own answer. "Something *is* wrong."

"Well. . . ." Cooper hesitated again. He looked at the two young people, the white "boy" and the black man. Then he sighed himself. He looked down at Falligant's bottle. Falligant shoved the beaker across at him and watched him take a stiff drink. "I think it's trouble, Colonel. And I think . . . well, you'd better not go looking for passage on any upriver steamer right now. Matter of fact, sir, I'd lay low for a bit."

Falligant reached forward with a hand that moved like a rattlesnake's head, striking. His brown fingers grasped Cooper's thick wrist in a grip of iron. "Get it out, man." His face was drawn from the quick pain his movement had brought on, but his eyes bored into Cooper's hypnotically. "There's trouble, is there? What kind?"

"Well," Cooper said, drawing back a little, his eyes wary, "these two over here, the boy and the nigger—"

"They're none of your damned business."

"Well, yes, sir, but—well, there's a party of men down on the waterfront. Two parties of men, to be exact. One of 'em's lookin' for runaways." His eyes went to Josh, then back to Falligant. "Runaway niggers. And if you're thinkin'—"

"What I'm thinking is likewise none of your business," Falligant said in a steely voice. But he let go Cooper's hand. "You're right. Both of them are runaways. And I'm not giving them up to anybody. Go on." He sat back, wincing again at the pain of moving.

"Well, the other party. . . ." Cooper's eyes were still guarded. "Seems that someone killed Judge Cartwright's son up in Natchez-on-top-of-the-Hill a couple of hours ago. Shot him dead. Before he died he give the constable a description of the man who shot him."

"I see." Falligant sat up slowly, moving with great care. Then—the motion was so quick and smooth that it could hardly be followed—the hand with the big gun in it came up, and before Cooper could think twice the big pistol was thumb-busted and that deadly blue-black hole was pressed hard against the bulb of his misshapen nose. "Now," Falligant said in an icy voice. "It wouldn't have possibly occurred to you to put one or the other of these bastards on my trail, would it now? Or even both? Come now, Cooper. Think a moment before you answer. I've killed my man tonight, I have, and it didn't quite satisfy me. I'm not sure what will satisfy me, come to think of it. Maybe killing someone else for a chaser."

"No," Cooper said in a very small voice. "Please. I . . . I told nobody. I came back here as fast as I could come. Please. Don't. . . ." His eyes, seeking Falligant's trigger finger and settling for his steady hand, crossed ludicrously.

"Hah," Falligant said. The tone was contemptuous, dismissive. He eased the hammer forward on the big pistol. "Well, all right. I suppose there's no reason to suspect you." He reached for the bottle again, but his hand stopped halfway to the brown cylinder of glass. "Sorry, Cooper. I'm touchy. I haven't slept in a bit and I'm bone-tired." He frowned at the wall, then turned his head and looked at Josh and Graciela. "As you can see, some problems have developed."

He turned to Cooper again. "These *gens d'armes* you mentioned: where are they now? Are they coming this way? How much time have I got to clear out?"

"Other end of the docks, sir. Both parties. But I wouldn't stay around long, Colonel. Not with . . . well. . . ." His eyes went briefly to the runaways.

"God damn," Falligant said. "Well, who the hell's tied up here now, anyhow? Any towboats heading upstream? Is there anyone around who could be talked into making some quick coin taking us across the River, perhaps?"

"Please, Mr.—Colonel Falligant," Graciela said. "We—we had no idea—we don't want to get you in trouble."

Falligant turned upon her almost angrily. "Confound it, girl, an obligation is an obligation. And how the devil were you going to ask me the favor of seeing that you make your way upstream to free-nigger territory without risking my neck, pray tell me?" His exasperation was half buried under a thick layer of fatigue, but there was no mistaking it. "Well, no matter. I owed my life to your father. That's enough. We're together until your foot touches Illinois soil, or wherever you first feel safe. After that you're on your own, you understand? Now," he added with an exquisite irony, "please do me the favor of holding off your interruptions for a while until I can figure out a way of keeping myself from getting lynched."

Graciela shrank back, losing perhaps six inches of an already unimposing stature. "Yes, sir," she said in a small voice. Her eyes went to Cooper, then back to Falligant again.

"All right," he said, ignoring her. "I was asking who was tied up here, Cooper. And you were saying?"

"Yes," Cooper said. "Well, there's a boat full of bargemen down the way. But they're drunk and mean, and. . . ." His eyes went to Graciela. "I think you

65

won't want to have anything to do with them." Falligant nodded.

"All right," Cooper said. "You can be sure the *Andrew Jackson* and the two other commercial steamers in port will be searched before they cast off. I think that's out, Colonel." Falligant nodded again. Cooper frowned and continued. "Then there's the show steamer, and a couple of fishing boats, and—"

"Hold," Falligant said. "You said a show steamer? You're not talking about Will Chapman's Floating Theatre, are you?" His eye had a sudden keen glint in it as he leaned forward, this time ignoring the pain.

"No," Cooper said. "Nobody that fancy. I don't know this crowd. It's some sort of nigger minstrel. Nothing important. But as I was saying—"

Cooper stopped right there. He looked hard at Falligant. Neither of them said anything for a moment. Then Cooper said, "You know, Colonel, it might work out. It might just work out at that." He held up a cautionary finger. "I'll wager it'll cost you a bit."

"*Everything'll* cost me a bit," Falligant said. "It might be someone I know. But no matter. Hell, man, I've put in good years under the burnt cork in my youth. I can play the banjo better than Daddy Rice does, and I'm the best goddamned Mr. Interlocutor you ever saw. And"— that gleam in his eye was brighter than ever—"what better place to hide a couple of runaways than under lampblack? Eh?" A savage grin sliced its way across his narrow face. "Yes, yes. It might just work." He stood and faced Cooper. "Where did you say this wandering nigger showboat was moored?"

"I didn't say," Cooper said, standing up. "But it's at the end of the next slip. First show ought to be over by now." He smiled, and the scar on his face turned the smile into a hideous grimace. "Would you like me to go ask around down there?"

"No," Falligant said. "I'll have to do this myself." He handed over the big pistol. "Here, Cooper, you mind these two for me. Anybody comes in the door, shoot the bastard. Either one of these two tries to run away, same thing." He looked hard at Graciela. "I mean that, girl. You've gone and got me involved, for better or for worse. That means neither of us gets to back out until

66

your foot's on free soil, whatever the reason. You stay here with Cooper. He'll look out for you until I'm back. He knows good and well that if he does, there's a substantial sum awaiting him the moment we're lying off Natchez in a boat heading upstream."

His eye, cool and impersonal, went to Cooper once again for a moment. "He also knows," Falligant added, still addressing Graciela but with his eye drilling its message straight into Cooper's brain, "that if he fails me—or you either—I'll cut out his tripes with a dull knife, nice and slow." He looked back at Graciela, but his words were directed at Cooper. "Lie low. I'll be back as soon as I've found out something." He nodded curtly and slipped out the door.

Cooper watched him go. Then he looked at his two wards. He shook his head doubtfully. "I hope he's being careful," he said to no one in particular. "Those people back on the other end of the docks—they mean business. And every one of 'em is armed to the teeth."

"G-goodness," Graciela said. "I hope so too."

That was all she said. Her eyes went to Josh's, then to Cooper's. That single sound, cutting through her words, had stopped their breath, their speech, everything but their hearts—and Graciela couldn't have sworn to that, either. The sound was throaty, hollow, echoing. It was well up into the treble, but had more body to it than any human throat, pitched that high, could have mustered. It was a bay, a yammer, a yelp. It was the kind of sound that would carry for miles on the river bottoms.

Cooper shook his head with a shiver. He'd heard it too. "Bloodhounds," he said in a low voice. "I hate that sound. . . ."

Chapter 10

Miraculously, the moment didn't last. The baying stopped, and did not start again. Where was it going? Was it upstream or down? It didn't seem to matter. Cutting through the routine sounds of the waterfront for a moment, it had served to rivet their attention on the problem that faced them—all of them, since Cooper himself was now harboring runaways, and his own neck was in the same noose as Falligant's was.

Now the sound was gone, but the memory of it did not fade. It hung in Graciela's ear, and at the very thought of it a cold chill ran up her spine. It conjured up images of the maddened animals, their great yellow teeth bared, grasping her, rending her flesh. She shuddered, feeling in her mind the pain, smelling their foul breath.

What else? It brought images to mind that were worse than these, images she'd done her best in the last three days to erase, but had found she could not remove from the back of her mind. At the thought her hand stole to her lap and lay there, palm down, protectively.

God, she'd been . . . she'd been dirtied. She'd been raped, and by a man lower and meaner and dirtier than the dogs she'd just been thinking of. She wasn't a virgin anymore, and her deflowering hadn't been at the hands of a man who loved her and cared for her. There'd been nothing tender or thoughtful about it at all. There'd just been the battering she'd taken, and then someone brutally shoving something hard up inside of her until it hurt, hurt. . . .

She lowered her face, hoping neither Josh nor Cooper would see the shame that must certainly be reflected on it. If only Josh didn't know about it all! If only nobody knew about it—even Mr. Tolliver.

At the thought of Beau Tolliver something happened in her mind, and she brightened and raised her head to look around her. It was as if a bright, warm sunbeam had broken through dark clouds, and something swept away all the self-hatred and self-doubt that had begun to creep in. Thinking this, she knew that there'd always be something in her feeling for Tolliver that would make her feel good about herself, whatever her circumstances. It was as if his name, or the idea of him, was some sort of magic talisman she could always call upon, draw strength from, whenever she needed it.

Then the thought hit her: but she'd never see him again. She'd left him behind forever, and with him all her hope of emerging from this terrible mess. She was a slave, Tolliver's slave, just as Josh was, and their only hope of changing this had been Tolliver's brave and generous plan to take them to free soil and formally manumit them. But now that dream was ashes.

Now, without that paper Tolliver had volunteered to get for her once they reached Cairo, both she and Josh were still property. She knew all too well by now the terrible finality of this. To be sure, while Tolliver lived she was sure he'd never assert his claim to her. But what if he were to die? Then she'd be in the same shape she'd been in when her father had died, leaving her status perilously in doubt. She'd be part of the settlement. Title to her body and soul would revert to his creditors, or be transferred to one or the other of those relatives he'd repudiated, and that he hated so. And who knew what sort they were, these nameless Tollivers that Beau had held in such low esteem?

At the thought her heart sank. She looked over at Josh, and for a moment her eye engaged his, and she picked up for a fleeting second the glint of rock-hard determination she found there. "Josh," she said quietly. "I know what you're thinking. And you're right. The only solution is to. . . ." She looked over at Cooper. He had risen and walked over to the rude window of the cabin and was peering out of a crack in the painted-over glass. She lowered her voice. "Our only hope is to get across the River. If Colonel Falligant can get us upriver a bit on this showboat, maybe we can jump ship in . . . well, in Iowa Territory or somewhere."

"And light out for somewhere where we'll be safe?" Josh asked. There was the smallest edge of bitterness in his voice. "Well, Miss, that might work for you. The moment you're across the Line you're a white girl again. But me? I'm what I am. And without papers. . . ."

She reached out and impulsively touched his arm. "I'm sorry, Josh," she said. "I forgot. You can't just up and go anywhere, can you? You have family. . . ." She sighed. "Well, *that's* a burden I won't have to carry, anyway. I haven't a soul left in the world. Perhaps I do have it easier, after all."

"No, no," Josh said. "I'm the one who ought to be sorry. Look, I apologize. We're both in the same boat. It's just that—well, I was feeling sorry for myself, I guess." He tried to smile at her but there was a bitter turn to the edge of his surprisingly thin-lipped mouth, and there was hurt in his dark eyes.

"I understand," she said. But she looked into his eyes again and knew that he didn't believe her. No matter that, technically, she was black like him, a slave like him, a fugitive like him. He was the prisoner of that dark skin of his, and the fact was a wall between them. What she could understand, now, was his bitterness about the fact. It was the way she'd felt—her in her boy's clothes, with her hair hacked off to the length only boys wore—when they'd stood on the deck of the towboat the Tockos had hailed for them and watched the *Winfield Scott* pass them in all its gaily painted finery—and seen the free white women standing by the rail in beautiful clothes, looking down at them with scorn. The sound of soft but gay music rang in her ears as they passed them sailing under the radiant blue sky. Oh! How she wished she were safely on board a ship such as that, for that ship was tranquil and unconcerned with the turmoil in the lives of those who watched her.

If things had gone differently, wouldn't she have been one of them? Wouldn't she have been up there on the cabin deck, looking down her nose at slaves and ragamuffins? She frowned. That was idle thinking. It led nowhere, nowhere at all. The only thing worth thinking

70

about was what she was going to do right now: how she was going to save herself, and what she was going to do once she'd accomplished that.

"Here, now," Cooper was saying from the window in a tense voice. "They're on the next dock. They're going from door to door, damn them. They're breaking up into twos. And my God, they've got somebody. A nigger boy from the Blue Lion. God almighty, they don't fool around, either. One of them knocked him cold at the first sign of a struggle. Jesus Christ, what a blow."

"Are they coming over here?" Graciela said, crossing the room to stand behind him. She peered through the gloom but could make out nothing.

"Well, I reckon eventually," Cooper said. "Look, if the Colonel doesn't come back in a couple of minutes, you'd better start thinking about what to do. There's more of them than I'm prepared to handle, whatever the Colonel says. Look: there's a back way out. Likely you could slip out on the dock and climb down the pilings to the water without making too much noise. Water's pretty warm this time of year."

Graciela shuddered. "Please," she said. "Colonel Falligant will be back in time. I just know he will." Even as she said it, though, she could feel the cold hand of fear upon her. As if to confirm this, she heard the dogs again. "Lord in heaven!" she said. "The hounds. Can you see them?"

"Yes," Cooper said. "They're bringing them on the next dock. I guess they figure that if they managed to find one nigger on the dock they'll find another. There's a man with two hounds. Big dogs too: he can barely hold them back."

Oh, no, Graciela thought. *Please, God. . . .*

But the moment the thought entered her mind a wave of sick anger overcame her. God? What God? The God who'd orphaned her, and then made a pauper and slave of her? The God who'd separated Josh and his children—and then removed the one man who'd stood between him and safety? Who'd left the two of them to the bitter fate that awaited them here? What God indeed?

"Josh," she said. "Mr. Cooper's right. If the Colonel isn't here by the time they're ready to leave the next dock, I think we ought to try making a run for it. Or

71

going over the side, like Mr. Cooper says. What do you think?" As her eyes flashed past Cooper she caught a glimpse of the astonished look on his face: Imagine asking a nigger boy his opinion about anything! Well, damn Cooper. What did he know, anyway?

"Maybe you're right," Josh said. "Let's give it another couple of minutes, though."

The matter was made moot halfway through his sentence. Falligant, rapping once first in warning, opened the door and slipped inside. He bore a pair of long cloaks in one hand; the other was pressed to his side. His face showed the pain he was in.

"Here," he said. "Put these on. I borrowed them from the actors' slop chest. Costumes, for when they do Shakespeare. Here, Graciela. I think this is Portia's. And you, Josh. Prospero wears this one in *The Tempest*." He went to the window. "They're getting closer. We haven't much time. Eh? Yes, yes. Damned hounds. Well, a touch of greasepaint ought to cover up natural body odors. Especially over water."

He turned back to them after a single glance out the painted-over window. "We hit a patch of luck, I think. They can use an end man or two, and I can fill in on one instrument or another in the band until I can outflank the poor old dodo who's Mr. Interlocutor in this show. As soon as I can get you down the dock to the boat I'll slap some burnt cork on the both of you and we can start rehearsing our Mr. Tambo number. By the time they're halfway down the dock you'll be able to fool anyone but an old trouper." He looked Graciela in the eye. "Courage, my dear. I intend to keep the both of you so damned busy you'll not have time to be frightened. And the boat'll be in Cairo in a week."

Graciela drew what comfort she could from his bleak smile, and let him herd her and Josh ahead of him out the door. "Look you," he said to Cooper on the way out. "Here's something for your trouble. You cover for us and there'll be more tomorrow morning when we cast off. If anyone gets some funny ideas tell them you did see a runaway but he went over the side into the River rather than get caught. I have a feeling the dogs will find some trace, so it's better to have a story prepared in

72

advance. Just make sure they're put off our trail. You get me?"

"Yes, sir," Cooper said, his hand hefting the poke Falligant had pressed upon him. "Now, while there's time."

Falligant nodded and slipped out into the muted light and shadow of the docks. "Follow me," he said. "It's the old sternwheeler down at the end. Watch your step."

The ship was called the *Pleasure Palace*, but the name was the only thing palatial about it. The paint was visibly peeling, the brass needed polishing, and there was a general look of malaise about it. For all that, Graciela's bare soles felt the touch of the planking with an immense feeling of relief as she stepped down from the long gangway onto the broad deck of the old boat. "Here," Falligant said. "I think we'll make up below decks." He slipped a gratuity to a silently watching deckhand and motioned to his two wards to precede him down a dark companionway. "Go ahead," he said reassuringly. "Just watch your step when you get to the bottom. Wait for me. I know my way around and you don't."

Only when the hatch had been closed after them did Falligant open the closed lantern the deckhand had given him at the top of the stairs. When Falligant was sure the hatch was secure, he set the lamp high on a projecting timber and motioned to the two of them. "Here," he said, pointing to an open trunk. "Drop those cloaks in here. The other trunk's the one we want. I saw a couple of darky outfits there that ought to fit you. But first come here, Graciela."

Graciela complied, raising an eyebrow at the little pot of grease-base lampblack he held in one hand. But in a moment he had smeared the stuff liberally over her face and neck, and followed this by doing her wrists and forearms up to the elbow, and the backs of her hands. Then he tossed her a black stocking cap. "Here," he said. "Your own hair's dark enough, God knows, but this'll be more in character. Pull it on tight, like a wig. You want it to look like Josh's hair here." He looked her up and down. "Well, that'd fool most people," he said. "You're a regular Mr. Bones. Now get into that outfit over there, and quick. I'll smear some of this stuff on Joshua here."

"On me, sir?" Josh said. "But—"

"No matter," Falligant said. "The main thing here is misdirection and covering up the scent of you. No offense, now, but a black man does smell different to a hound than a white man does. Anything I can do to disguise the face has to be a step in the right direction."

"I understand," Josh said. "Look, if you don't want to touch me—"

"Hell's fire," Falligant said. "It doesn't matter a damn to me. And you can't afford black palms. My hands are already dirty. Here." And he smeared the black goo on Josh's black face with a heavy hand. As he did one of the dogs, down the way, let out another yelp. "Here," Falligant said. "Don't fidget or I'll get this stuff in your eye. Forget the dogs. By the time they're here you'll both be beyond recognition. I've got a bottle of the vilest damned excuse for cologne you ever smelled in your life, and I'm going to douse you down with it until you reek like a couple of Tchoupitoulas whores." He chuckled. "If that doesn't stop up their noses, nothing will."

Graciela caught his eye. For the first time there was a twinkle of enjoyment in it, despite the pain that still registered on his drawn face.

Chapter 11

Graciela and Josh spent an anxious hour below deck as the slavers came on board the *Pleasure Palace*. Graciela winced as the first set of hobnailed boots stepped down onto the steamer's deck, and shuddered visibly as the soft feet of the dogs followed it. Her eye sought Falligant's in the dim light of the covered lantern, and found reassurance in his slow shake of the head and contemptuous sneer; finding comfort in his attitude, however, required ignoring the cocked pistol in his hand.

When the last of them had left Josh made as if to head topside. Falligant's hand, however, gestured to him to hold. "No, no. Wait until someone from the ship itself comes down to give the high sign. They'll knock four times—two long, two short." Sure enough, the knock came only moments after his words, and was followed by the creak of the hatch as strong hands lifted it. "Colonel?" a voice said. "You can come up now."

"It's all right, Graciela," Falligant said. "The Captain's an old friend of mine. After you, my dear." Shooing Graciela and Josh ahead of him, he followed them more slowly up the steep companionway, holding his side.

"Ah, you're wounded!" the bewhiskered man on the deck said. "I'll have someone look at that."

"No, never mind," Falligant said. "These two have tended to me quite well enough as it is. I'm just feeling my age, Jeremy. Miss McGee, meet my friend Captain Jeremy Waterhouse, your new employer."

"Miss?" the captain said. He stepped back to get a better look at Graciela, holding his lantern high. "Well, yes. My stars. Miss McGee, you said?" He turned to Falligant. "I suppose that was pretty quick thinking, Wes. Let a couple of those scum have a look at the two of them and you'd swear they were just another couple of members of the troupe. Ugh! They reek like merry hell. What is that stuff you put on them, anyhow?"

"Falligant's Patent Cologne," the Colonel said, "and I'll thank you to speak well of it. It's earned me many a dishonest dollar in its day. Guaranteed to charm the saints from their niches if applied externally, and it makes a fine horse liniment in a pinch. A carminative and restorative too. A ten thousand dollar warranty behind our claim that repeated application of this incredible hair-restoring mixture, on an ordinary billiard ball—"

"God almighty," the captain said. "Wes, you haven't lost your touch. Look, we could use a talker with this show. If you'd like—"

"Heaven forfend," Falligant said. "This face must not see the light of day south of the Illinois line. There's a magistrate in Natchez, a widow in Vicksburg, a young woman in Memphis with . . . hm, yes, I think it was twins, wasn't it? And there's a. . . ."

"Enough," said the captain. As he moved forward Graciela caught a glimpse of his face, round and merry and framed in white hair and chin whiskers. He wore the uniform of a steamboat captain, but didn't look at all businesslike. "Wes, you're sure I can't do something for that wound of yours, now? I think you've opened it again."

"No, no," Falligant said. "If the slop chest has a spare shirt, perhaps, and I'd give a lot right now for a bottle of something authoritative. I was on the verge of drinking a few drams of the Patent Cologne when you knocked. Not that I haven't drunk a damn sight worse, mind you, but the alcoholic content isn't a patch on Old Nongely, and the damned smell of the stuff. . . ."

"I understand," the captain said. "Come along to my cabin after we've put these two up for the night and I'll split a jug of painter's piss with you. Ugh! What a smell. Let's get these two some cold cream to wash it all off."

Falligant winced. "I'll bet you're still using the same damned goose-grease you always did. Well, before we've

76

stood off Memphis I'm going to mix you up a batch of Falligant's Miracle Cream: one ounce of pure white wax melted in four ounces of oil of sweet almonds over a slow fire, and add a quarter pint of distilled rosewater, stirring until cold. It's also just fine for greasing a watch or oiling a pistol."

Graciela marveled at the sudden change that had come over Falligant the moment danger had departed. The years had fallen off his drawn face; his smile had become a surprisingly youthful grin. She exchanged looks with Josh, brows raised in astonishment, as the two were bustled into two unoccupied cabins for the night, each no bigger than a horse's stall.

In the morning it was "Everybody out!" and she stepped out on deck, feeling the unsteady thumping of the big engine under her bare feet, to see Natchez—twin towns separated by the steep bluff—receding behind her as the decrepit old steamer chugged phthisically upriver. A fellow trouper, taking her for the boy she looked, herded her along ahead of him toward the galley. She smelled cooking and suddenly remembered she hadn't had a square meal since the Tocko camp days before.

Breakfast was huge, heavy, filling, the biggest breakfast she remembered ever eating. When she made as if to stop in mid-meal the young man next to her said, "Better not do that. The rule is, you eat what's put in front of you. Besides, if you're new here you'll find you need it. They're going to work you so hard you'll be starving by lunchtime."

So it was. Even as a beginner she was showing an aptitude for dancing. Although she was thought to be small for a boy, they allowed her to join the hoofers in the back line. They practiced as they sailed for the next port, Vicksburg, where they aimed to unveil the new show. But she quickly learned there was more to showboat life than putting on a series of blackface skits and dancing. For one thing, there was hard work. And since she'd come on board as a boy she couldn't use the usual excuses that, if she'd been known to be a girl, would have had the rough physical labor assigned to someone else. The work came her way and she did it; and by and by she began to find herself as proud of her endurance as she was tired from the work.

Rehearsing the dance routine and scene changing wasn't the only work, though. The stage had to be scrubbed, the scenery repainted, the costumes washed and pressed. Men and women alike in the cast shared all of this work equally, and she found herself, boy's garb and all, ironing trousers just as she'd done at home when living with her father. She found that many of her household skills served her well.

She didn't see Colonel Falligant until the showboat's first stop at Bruinsburg Landing, where Bayou Pierre met the great River in two broad arms that spread themselves wide to embrace a stand of thick cypress woodland hanging heavy with grey Spanish moss. Here, at the cotton market, they could pick up the lively traffic from Port Gibson, nearby, but at cheaper dockage rates. When the seats were full and the overture began on the scraggly, out-of-tune band (Colonel Falligant, already in blackface, made his borrowed banjo do service for two or three instruments; he was, as he'd said, proficient), yes, she thought to herself, there is beauty in all kinds of music. It made her heart temporarily feel light. A sort of magical spell seemed to settle on the ratty boat and its threadbare scenery and scarred stage, and the audience sat rapt throughout a long and varied show, applauding and laughing in all the right places. Moreover, as they filed out at the end their faces were happy and animated, and in their mouths were words of appreciation and affection for the entertainment they'd received on Captain Jeremy's *Pleasure Palace*.

Graciela found the blackface business and the crooked card games thoroughly incomprehensible, and confided as much to Falligant when she met him that evening between shows. He was standing pensively by the boiler deck rail and smoking a huge cigar, the kind her father had called a "long nine."

"Why do they laugh at blackface?" Falligant said. "You know, my dear, I never figured that out. I think the jokes are terrible, some of the worst lines I've ever had." He leaned forward, elbows on the rail, looking out over the River. "Not *the* worst, mind you. There was a circus show I worked with once . . . but no matter. Still, in both cases, well, the creation of these extravaganzas was never my job. I was always content to learn my lines and deliver them the way I'd been taught. As long as the marks came in the door to gamble. . . ." He looked at her for a moment. "Well, it's not the same as playing Shakespeare, let me tell you. And a good stock swindle, or a patent-medicine formula, say, are of an altogether different order. Now that's creative. But as for this blackface stuff and crooked card games. . . ." He blew smoke and looked away, and then looked back at her again.

"Look here," he said. "You're an intelligent girl—ah, I mean lad." Her secret had remained safe with him and with Captain Jeremy so far. "What does it matter to you? All you have to do is your job, and lay low, and keep the word about your proper sex quiet enough to keep the deckhands out of your furbelows. Then, the moment we dock at Cairo. . . ."

She didn't answer, for a moment. "It's just interesting, I guess. I mean the music and dancing is fun but why do they keep coming back for that snake oil you sell between shows? Don't they know better?"

Falligant chewed on the big cigar for a moment. "I clean forgot, didn't I? You're your father's daughter, after all. It's in the blood. For all that Tom was, well, no more than intermittently successful in his trade, God rest him, he *was* one of the brotherhood."

"The brotherhood?" Graciela said. "I don't understand."

Falligant stood erect, wincing slightly at the quick stabbing pain in his broken rib. "Why, the brotherhood and sisterhood of those who learn very early in life—with me, it must have come in my mother's milk, for all that she was horrified when she found out what sort I was—who learn, I say, that they don't give a damn about respectability, consider social custom a sham, and have not the smallest intention of ever doing so much as an honest day's work."

"Oh." Graciela found his hyperbolic turn of speech—it was getting worse almost by the hour, as he settled into the role he'd assumed—hard to follow exactly, but something in the thicket of words seemed to strike a responsive chord in her. "You mean my father was a wastrel?"

"Wastrel? Where the pluperfect hell did you come up with a word like that? That convent school you told me about? For the love of Christ, your father was a wise man, just like me. The principal difference was not in basic inclination; there we were as alike as two peas in a pod. It was in the matter of experience, and in—my blushes, my dear—in the magnitude of the talent." He nodded sagely at himself. "Yes, yes. I'm better at it all than your father was, but we were a lot alike. With him it was Natchez-on-top-of-the-Hill that threw him out. With me it was Charleston. Or," he said, a wary look on his old face, "perhaps it was Savannah. No matter. We were both remittance men, black sheep, a blot on the family scutcheon."

His grin was sardonic now and he was enjoying himself hugely. He turned and looked her in the eye. "Look," he said. "I know you were a convent girl a week or so ago. I know you were raised gently, and before this Thiebaud swine got hold of you, I'll wager you'd never been alone with a man other than your pa."

"N-no," she said in a small voice, wondering what he was getting at. Then, when a random thought crossed her mind and drew the right response, she drew back a bit. "Please, I. . . ."

"Oh, hell," Falligant said. "I'm not propositioning you, girl. You're not my type anyhow. I like them fat and vicious. Besides, I've got a dose of—I'm incapacitated for the moment. You're safe with me. No, that's not your problem." He grinned and looked back out over the River.

"Problem?" she said. "I don't understand."

"You don't?" he said, amused. "Well, perhaps you will. I see it in your eye, I think. Maybe I'm wrong. I don't think so, but maybe I am. It doesn't matter in the long run whether I am or not. People will become what they have to become, what the voice in their guts tells them to become. And you. . . ." He looked her in the eye now, and despite his cynical words his gaze was respectful, sympathetic, even fatherly.

"Yes?" she said. "What do you think about me?"

His grin was the same cynical one, but there was only

concern in his eyes. "I've had a few drinks, and that loosens the lip," he said. "Probably I ought to shut up, but what the hell. You? What do I think about you? I think that down inside you're an evil angel. I'll bet you could be unscrupulous as hell and corrupted by a love of fame or 'filthy lucre.' No damn good, just like your father."

As he walked away, he took one last drag off the big cigar and threw it into the Mississippi and added, "Just like me."

The paddlewheel steamer sailed on calmly. Rather than retire below Graciela preferred to remain on deck in the dark, admiring the steamer's phosphorescent wake and listening to the helmsman's melancholy chant as he sang to keep himself from dozing off. She wanted these few private minutes to try to forget Falligant's assessment of her and to figure out who she was and where she was heading—most of all she wanted this quiet time to herself for she had a headful of dreams . . . dreams of the magnetic Beau Tolliver. When you feel this way about someone distance has no meaning.

She would try not to permit herself to feel Thiebaud had sullied her body by his contact. She would not let him vilify, in her eyes, what she dreamed must be the most respectable and holiest thing in creation, the divine mystery, the most serious of living acts, the most sublime in the universe. She must not separate her spirit from her flesh. She would allow her adolescent face to feel the breeze as the steamer chugged its way. There was a moment of hallucination during which she could see Beau Tolliver embrace her and she tried to imagine what it would be like to abandon herself to him as feverishly as she had resisted Thiebaud.

Oh! How sweet it was to have this very noble man to think about, to have him occupy her mind. But these thoughts, born of a soul hungry for love, made her knees tremble with a desire that was new to her, awakening feelings that were like the sap of life in the universe. She must stop this imagining, but she was glad she had treated herself to these moments on deck alone, for thought has its own raptures, ecstasies, and soft celestial bliss.

Chapter 12

By the time the *Pleasure Palace* tied up at Vicksburg, Graciela had a new identity—"Mick" McGee, dancer and boy-of-all-work for the minstrel show—and, thanks to the cornucopia-like slop chest, the makings of a sort of wardrobe. It was shabby, threadbare and thoroughly masculine, but she was grateful to get it, patched linsey-woolsey shirts and all. There were two pairs of pants, a much-mended jacket, and a woven straw hat to keep the sun from burning her any darker than she already was. Best of all, there was a pair of leftover boots in a size somewhere near hers—boots of soft and well-worn leather, relics of a long-gone actor who'd skipped the show in Baton Rouge, leaving his trunk behind him.

Thus, while it was difficult thinking of herself as a boy and maintaining the imposture, the very idea of having some sort of identity in which people accepted her as, if not an equal, a fellow trouper, gave her a kind of pleasure that made all the backbreaking labor she was given to do well worth it. And she felt a certain satisfaction in having brought some merriment into the lives of the people who came to the *Pleasure Palace*.

That morning, before the early show, she was in the galley with Josh, peeling potatoes for the crew's lunch. It was easy work, and pleasant: she hadn't seen much of Josh since the troupe's initial assumptions as to her color had separated her and her companion and relegated him to an improvised sleeping room in the hold. To her surprise she found she'd missed him. He was a link with the past she'd left behind . . . but no, that wasn't it, was it? After all, she had precious little past to look back on that did not fill her with an immense sense of sadness and loss.

No, she thought suddenly. Josh was a link to Beau Tolliver. That was the only past she cared to look back on. Tolliver . . .

Angrily she shut the thought out of her mind. *Don't look back!* she told herself. *The only thing that matters is the present and the better life to come.* Although she knew it was hypocrisy the moment the thought had formed, she stuck with her resolution. *Think about now.* There was a grim set to her jaw as she tore into the potatoes, digging the eyes out with her knife, laying into her work with a singleminded enthusiasm she could hardly have bettered if her knife were digging into Thiebaud's entrails.

"Miss McGee," Josh said.

"Please, Josh," she said. "Mick. You daren't forget."

"I'm sorry," Josh said. "I was going to ask what you were going to do when we reached free soil."

"I don't know," she said. "I—I don't dare think that far ahead. For now it seems to be enough to survive, and to keep my head about me. Why?"

Josh paused, a half-peeled potato still in his hand. "Well," he said, "me, I got folks. I got problems, particularly if Mr. Beau is delayed getting up to Cairo. But I got people too, and I figure if I can get back with 'em I got blessings enough. I can figure out what to do. But you, you're awful young, if you'll pardon my saying so. And you'll be all alone. That is, unless Mr. Beau finds his way upriver and turns out to be waiting for us when we step down off the gangway."

Graciela sighed long and hard. "I—I guess I'm hoping that he *will* be there, Josh. I mean, it'd be the best thing that could happen to me. But. . . ." Her voice stopped in something suspiciously like a sob, but she caught herself and went on. "What if it doesn't happen, Josh? Something could happen to him. And if he doesn't. . . ." She set her little chin firmly and bore on, her eyes flashing. "Well, you remember what he told us. If that happens, we'll just have to figure out something to do."

Josh looked at her, and for the first time she could see

the real reserves of strength in him, a strength that had brought him this far down the long road toward freedom despite disadvantages she'd—thank God!—never know. "Well, of course you're right. But we've come this far together, and I have to confess that . . . well, if anything happened to you—I mean after we dock in Cairo. . . ."

Graciela's eyes filled with quick tears. "Josh," she said. "Thank you. I mean, it's so nice to know somebody'd worry about me if. . . ." She stopped and couldn't go on. Impulsively she laid her white hand across his black one, only to have him snatch it back almost indignantly, his eyes darting from side to side.

"Please," he said. "I *know* we're friends. We got to keep up appearances."

"I understand," she said. She hefted the potato in her hand and went back to peeling. "But it'd be nice if folks could just be friends, without all of this white and black stuff getting in the way."

Josh's eyes blazed with an inner fury. "Well, that ain't the way it is," he said. "And don't you forget it. I—" He bit off his angry diatribe in mid-phrase. He sighed. He looked at her and his eyes softened. "You just have to remember. At least as far as Cairo, and maybe a lot farther. The one thing you're going to have to remember if you are compelled to survive on your own, up on free soil, is that every remnant of the past you're trying to escape—this business about your status—must be forgotten. It has to be ruthlessly done away with. That's the only way you're going to pass. It's the only way you're going to survive. You can't forget that for a moment. You're going to have to take on a new identity, one far removed from anything that could connect you and—"

He stopped abruptly as the cook strode through the galley, and continued in a much subdued voice when the coast was clear. "Well," he said. "If Mr. Beau finds us, and frees us, that's one thing. I'll be free to live my life with my family, and it'll be a life that'll suit me. I wasn't raised to the expectations you were raised to. I can always find work, and as long as I can support me and mine. . . ." He shook his head as he looked at her, his brown eyes full of compassion. "But you? Even if he frees us, you won't have the same status you were raised

84

to. You'll not be a free white girl anymore, fit to marry whomever you choose. You'll just be a freed nigger, and you'll be fit for marrying a black man, a man like me. Or you'll be fit to be some white man's mistress, kept over on the wrong side of town." He shook his head savagely. "No," he said. "Your only chance, whether Mr. Beau finds us or not, is to leave every trace of your old identity behind. To become someone new."

Graciela didn't say anything for a moment, but dug into the potato with a firm hand. Of course he was right. All her bridges were burned behind her. The only future she could possibly have was to become a new person. But how? What sort of person? And how would she live? What sort of community would take her in without asking after her background? What sort of people would accept her without having any idea of her pedigree? It was a vexing problem.

Again came the thought: Tolliver. If only he would . . . But no. To him she was a child, beneath his notice. He wouldn't be interested in her. Besides, you didn't marry someone you'd owned, bag and baggage, body and soul. You only married an equal. Bitterly, she tried to dismiss the thought from her mind.

She didn't look up at Josh again for some time. Her eyes remained on the potato she was peeling. For some reason her mind went back to the enigmatic statement Colonel Falligant had made to her up on the boiler deck: *You're no damn good. Just like me.*

What did he mean? Just because she'd expressed interest in why the "marks"—he never called the customers anything but this—kept coming back despite sure and certain knowledge that they had been gulled? Did that make her a ne'er-do-well in and of itself? Why? What could he have meant by this? She made a mental note to ask him herself, next time she had him alone. *Just like your father.*

But what had her father been like? It was a sure thing that she didn't know, for all that she'd thought she'd known the man all those years. The Tom McGee she'd thought she'd known had been a man who honored his promises to people—but look where she herself had landed, believing him.

Oh, to be sure she'd understood that he was a gambler. There had to be some explanation for the fact that, without an independent income, he didn't go to an office, didn't keep regular hours. He'd even spoken to her from time to time about the high-stakes games he'd been in, although he'd never mentioned the times he lost, only the times he'd won.

But as for being a card sharp like Colonel Falligant . . . well, that was another matter. Colonel Falligant, by his own admission, was a man who had no conscience about swindling another gambler—palming a card, say, or substituting a trick deck of cards, or dealing from the bottom. He excused this by saying that nobody without larceny in his heart could possibly be swindled in the first place, that in the act of cozening another person you had to get his attention in the first place by appealing to his own cupidity and crookedness: "You can't cheat an honest man."

But Colonel Falligant had spoken of her father as being precisely the same sort of person as he was: amoral, conscienceless, rapacious, and contemptuous of the framework of orderly laws that, in theory, stood between him and his prey. This, coming from a man who'd known not only her father but her mother as well, forced her to re-evaluate her father in her own mind.

Worse, he'd as much as accused her of being the same kind of person, at bottom. Could there be anything to this? Could his accusation have some basis in fact? Was it, in fact, possible for a person who'd known you no longer than he had to look inside you like that, and see the potential in you for being something so unlike your own picture of yourself?

It was a sobering and unsettling thought. As it truly struck home for the first time, Graciela shuddered involuntarily. It wasn't a picture of her real self that she wanted to see.

If only she'd known her mother! If only she had, now, another image to turn to when her heredity was impugned—some other person in whom to search for the secret of her own being! Instead, with no real notion of what kind of person her mother was, she either had to guess as to whom she took after, or she had to accept the cruel and demeaning picture Colonel Falligant had given her. *You're no damned good. Just like your father. Just like me.* How dare he say that? She, no good? She, who had been an honors student at the convent?

Heavy footsteps outside the galley interrupted her reverie just then, and she looked up, frightened, to see Colonel Falligant, dressed to the nines as he'd been when she'd first met him, throw open the door and stand in the opening. His jaw was fixed in a hard line and there was terror in his eye.

"Graciela—Josh," he said. "Round up whatever's yours. We've got to jump ship. I arranged for horses in town. Be prepared to leave in ten minutes. We have some hard riding to do."

Josh was on his feet before the first sentence was done. Graciela, the knife and potato still in her hand, stared up at him open-mouthed. "I—I don't understand," she said.

"For the love of God, girl, don't sit there letting a weed grow up your leg," he said in a tight voice. "It's a matter of life and death. And need I remind you that it's not just mine I'm talking about, but yours as well?"

This brought her to her feet. "Oh my God. Not again." Her small hands went to her mouth. "If only they'd just let us be!"

"What's the matter?" Josh asked. His eyes were wary rather than frightened. He'd seen too much trouble already to be much surprised by it.

"That bastard Cooper. He's sold us out. Thiebaud found him by chance, while passing through Natchez. Cooper told him—for a fat fee, I've no doubt—that two runaways of such and such a description passed through Under-the-Hill and got passage on the *Pleasure Palace*." He fairly spat out the words.

"We'd better get moving" Josh said. "I'm ready to go. Miss McGee?"

"But—but, Colonel," she said. "You don't need to come with us. We'll strike out together, perhaps across the River. You don't have to risk your life with us. I don't care what my father said."

"It's too late," Falligant said. "I was in town, and I overheard them all talking. Thiebaud's here—did you get that, girl? Here in town!—and so is a representative

87

of the law. It seems Cooper sold me out too, on the matter of that little killing in Natchez-on-top-of-the-Hill the night we met. Quick, now! We have at best only minutes."

Graciela's heart sank. Would there ever be a place to rest? A sanctuary from all this? Would she ever find a safe harbor in the midst of this incessant storm?

Chapter 13

Resourceful as ever, Josh had the good sense to steal food for the three of them before they took off; but for the first hour of their upstate journey there was no time to eat. Only when the thick forest north of town had begun to give way to cultivated land did Falligant, keeping the lead, call for a halt, and even then it was for the horses' sake. They pulled up in a clearing and tied up the animals before settling down on a fallen tree to the repast Josh had brought along: cheese, rolls, a tin of buttermilk.

Graciela, oblivious of everything but the fierce hunger that tore at her, ate ravenously. Falligant watched her, then watched Josh's sensible attack on the victuals. For his own part he tested the cheese, a sour expression on his face, then tossed the piece he'd cut into the bushes. Instead, he reached into his coat for a small bottle. The expression on his face as he drank was every bit as sour, but he made no move to throw away the bottle.

"How much lead do you think we have?" Josh asked, looking back the way they'd come.

"Oh, I think we're safe enough for right now," Falligant said. "Provided we keep moving. But I have reason to believe they know which way we've gone. What I'd really like to do is make it back to the River, and find our way across somehow." He stopped and leaned forward, peering intently at the trunk of a big oak tree nearby. "Here, what's this?" he said. "Well, I'll be damned."

"What do you see, Colonel?" Josh said. "I can't see anything."

"Well, look. Here. On the bark." He indicated a curious sign carved into the tree trunk, at a point where the bark had been stripped away.

"I don't understand," said Graciela. "It looks like somebody carved it there. But what does it mean? Who would make a sign like that? Indians?"

"No, no," Falligant said, smiling his small smile. He took another draught from the small brown bottle. "It's a lot older than the Indians, I'll wager. It means 'Look out—danger' and the source of the danger is indicated by an arrow." He dug into his shirt pocket and produced another long nine, lighting it with a lucifer. "As for the people who wrote it, well, I'm surprised to find their like here. It's been many years and many miles since I've run across sign of the Rom, and never so far south."

"The Rom?" Graciela said. "Who are they?"

"One of the oldest peoples in the world," Falligant said, inhaling and blowing forth a cloud of rich smoke. "The Gypsies. I think Circassian ones, by this sign. But I could be wrong. I'm growing old and forgetful." He searched the area around the roots of the tree. "No, I'm right. Here the sign's repeated in a patch of bare earth. That's Circassian, all right."

"How do you know all this, Colonel?" Josh said.

"Oh, in my youth, before either of you were born, I befriended a tribe of them and traveled with them. They made me a Romany Rye, a sort of official friend of the tribe. I learned a bit of the language, and many of the secret signs like this one, and a lot of the lore."

"Signs?" Graciela said, looking down at the hieroglyphic.

"Oh, yes. For instance, if the Rom passed on this road they left signs by the road to warn their friends— like this one, for instance—or to tell them where they were going and how to follow and catch up with them. They have their own signs for dates and places. They even have hand signs for telling each other how to bargain, when they're doing business. It's all done with the cigar, you know. Like this." He held his cigar between thumb and second finger, palm upward. "This means *Wait for an offer*. If I shift the cigar to thumb and forefinger it means *Caution*. If I hold it—still with the palm up—between all my fingers it means *It's a trap*. Here,

I'll show you." He reached for her hand and turned it palm upward—but then remained looking down at it. "Well, I'll be goddamned," he said again. "I'll be eternally goddamned. By heaven, we may have found our salvation, Graciela. And you may very well be the instrument."

"I don't understand," she said. "Was I holding my hand in a special way?"

"No, no," Falligant said. "It's—well, it's something I think I see in your hand. Extraordinary. Remarkable. If . . . But I'm getting old and forgetful. I'm probably dead wrong."

Josh stowed the provisions he'd purloined in the saddlebags of the nag Falligant had stolen for him. "At any rate, Colonel, maybe we'd better get moving again."

"No, it's all right," Falligant said. "The Rom are not too far ahead of us. Look, here's a message from one of them to any Gypsy caravan following them. The ideogram on the right tells the date they passed. That's two days ago. We're not far behind them. Ah, that settles it. Until I saw this I hadn't the smallest idea where we were going. Now. . . ."

Graciela caught his eye. There was a youthful gleam in it, and his mouth bore that same appreciative grin she'd seen there before. Wherever it was that they were going, it was someplace Falligant wanted to be, someplace about which he had nothing but good feelings.

Now the road began perceptibly to climb, and as they left the scraggly poor-white farms, with their starved-looking animals and their stunted grain crops, the road cut once again through thick forest, where in places the trees grew together overhead thickly enough to blot out the sun altogether. There was a lush and rotten smell about this part of the wood, and the ground under the trees sported not the choking underbrush they'd been used to, but fungi; mushrooms, toadstools, uglier growths than she'd ever seen. Falligant slowed their procession to a walk and kept a wary eye out on all sides. His hand stayed close to the big-barreled revolver in his belt.

Graciela nudged her horse suddenly and rode up to his side. "Colonel," she said. "I haven't seen anything. Have we lost them?"

91

"Not at all," Falligant said. "I've spotted half a dozen Romany signs by the side of the road. I could almost tell you which tribe they were, the signs are that specific. You just don't know what to look for. Why, look. Right there to my right. See the fork and the arrow? That tells me there are women of child-bearing age in the wagons. Well, at least one such woman anyhow. And she gave birth to a son here on the . . . uh, I'd say something like the twentieth of September. Very likely right here in the path. The birth of a son is a good occasion, and would be marked for other Rom to see. They'd celebrate a female birth, too. If it had been a girl there'd have been a target, not an arrow. Women help provide for the family as much as the men. They make great fortune tellers but sometimes they are forced, along with the men, to steal."

"Goodness," Graciela said, "did you say steal?"

"Oh, yes. Some consider themselves a tribe apart. They have a unity because of society's opposition to them. We, who have persecuted them and driven them away from time immemorial, are the *gaje* or the *gorgio*—a lower order of life. Stealing from the *gaje* is not really a misdeed as long as it is limited to taking basic necessities and not more than is needed for the moment. It is the intrusion of a sense of greed that makes stealing wrong, they feel, for greed makes men slaves to unnecessary appetites or to their desire for possessions. Perhaps that is why they took me to their hearts, many years ago. They recognized in me the same tendencies they were forced to develop themselves. And they recognized my nomad's itch for new places, and disrespect for the *gaje* laws. Oh, they spotted the taint, all right." He looked at her, one graying eyebrow raised, "And I suppose they'll find the same thing in you."

Graciela was glad, just then, of the darkness through which they were traveling; it hid the hot blush of shame which his words brought to her cheek. She tried to speak but couldn't. How could he go on in this callous and unfeeling way? Didn't he realize that he was insulting her?

"The ways of the Rom," he went on, "are rich in secrets. Look there, beneath that tree. Four acacia branches, stripped of their leaves all the way to the tips.

92

That means 'We shall stay for four days at our special place.' Now that's a sign meant only for the eyes of another Rom, and one whom the tribe knows. Now if I'm right there should be a sign coming up shortly to tell us which fork to take once the road has begun to come out of the woods. Watch carefully; it'll be on a bare patch by the side of the road, and the earth will have been cleared around it. That will mean the sign is to be read soon after it is made. Good, there it is! By heaven, we're not far behind them."

"What sign?" Graciela said. "I couldn't see a thing at all."

"The three clumps of earth in the clearing. They mean that we should take the third side road to the right. The clumps were spaced oddly, so I can only take that as a personal identification. It's as though they were signing their names. Now of course I don't know what the personal symbol means, or to whom it refers. But once I've met them I'll always be able to recognize their sign by the side of the road."

Josh had pulled up fairly closely behind them. "This is an old, old road," he said. "Look how it follows the natural curve of the land as the land rises."

"Oh, yes," Falligant said. "The white man's lazy. He seldom cuts a new path for a road, but uses the one laid out for him by people he mistakenly considers his inferiors. This was obviously laid out by the Choctaw or some other tribe, and—God knows—the Choctaw themselves aren't innovators in these matters. They probably followed a deer trail. Meanwhile, the only thing the white man provided was the labor required to widen the road so that a wagon could follow it." He looked around at Josh, a sardonic grin on his face. "Of course the labor they provided was black men's labor, not their own." He chuckled. "No matter. The Rom, these particular ones, we're following, provide no labor of their own and make no roads. The wagons ride high off the ground. If there was no road they would strike out across open lands. Free as the wind, they create their own pathways refusing to be penned in or tamed."

"Colonel," Graciela said. "You said we're following them. Why?"

"Right now we need friends, and I think we may well

93

find them among the Rom. They are fascinating devils and their mystery remains intact. I know the signs by which they'll accept me, and once they've seen that hand of yours. . . ." He half-frowned and nodded his head appreciatively. "We've been sold once by a man we trusted, a man we'd paid well to hide us. Now, it seems, our fortune may be changing. For the one people on the face of the earth who would never sell us to the *gaje* are the Rom."

They rode slowly past a fork to the right as the forest began imperceptibly to thin out. "Was there any sign there?" Graciela said. "I still couldn't see anything."

"I don't think so. I could have missed something. I'm a friend of the Rom and I know something of their ways, but I'm not a true Rom. Only a person born to it could understand all of it, because there's a great deal of it that you have to learn as a child, and that only your own blood kin will tell you. It's all right. We have two more forks to come to before we reach the one at which we're supposed to turn."

He smiled now, and his voice became thoughtful. "It's strange. Every time I've rejoined the Rom after my travels it's always felt as if I were returning home after a long absence. And yet it isn't my home, it can never be my home. I'll always be welcome among them—that is, unless I betray them in some way—but I'll never be one of them. And somehow, for me that has always been the source of an intense sadness."

"I think I understand some of that," Josh said. "It may be like the feeling I have around whites. I feel . . . well, among the two of you I feel as though I'm among friends, but I do feel left out."

Falligant turned and looked at him hard as if he'd talked out of turn. Then his eye softened. "Yes, yes," he said. "It must indeed be very like that. I'm sorry. I'm sure I must seem very insensitive at times."

"No, no," Josh said, flustered. "I didn't mean. . . ."

"It's all right," Falligant said. "And you're right. But—here, look. There's the second fork. We're getting close."

His voice took on a new excitement now, and it was communicated instantly to Graciela. Holding tightly to her horse's reins, she thought over her feelings as she'd

94

increasingly come to do in the recent, perilous days. There was a bit of fear in her, but also a boundless excitement, as if the world she was riding into were less a world of new dangers than one of new friends. Returning home after a long absence? No, that wasn't it at all. But there was something positive about it, something she couldn't adequately explain. Best of all, it was something new, and that was a comfort in itself in a world where everything old had turned sour for her, where familiarity had the constant ring of danger about it. She watched the road ahead with eager eyes. Her heart was beating fast.

Chapter 14

The shadows lengthened as they came out of the deep woods into a grove of widely spaced oaks, and Graciela, who'd lost touch with the passage of time, could see that their long day was mostly done. Worse, they now passed through a cloud of mosquitoes, who bit her unmercifully.

"Don't mind them," Falligant said. "Pick up the pace and you won't even notice them in a moment."

"They're terrible," Graciela said, slapping her arms.

"Nonsense. You should see the way the little devils grow down on the bottoms below the bluff in Memphis. Real gallon-nippers. Besides, that means it's mealtime. When we get to the Rom encampment it ought to be getting high on to dinnertime, and the Rom eat well."

"What does a bunch of skeeters have to do with dinnertime?" Josh said, trying to ward them away from his face.

"The Rom don't use watches," Falligant said, ignoring the pests. "They name the times of day after familiar events of nature, not after numbers. Dawn, for instance, is 'the hour when the horse neighs'; horses, of course, wake at the same time as men. Then there's the 'hour when the dog barks,' and so on. The 'hour when the duck flies overhead' signals the time to start the dinner fire, and the 'hour of the mosquitoes' is the first half of the evening, dusk. When it becomes the 'hour of the tree frog' it's night, and the stars are out. Then it's time to light the second fire of the night, the one you sit and look at until it's time to go to sleep. The first fire is utilitarian; the second is a real work of art, a thing of beauty. In every Rom camp there's one person who's

96

been trained at this, and whose job it is to make the night fire when the hour of the tree frog comes."

"Well, I hope that isn't far off," Josh said. "A good smoky fire ought to get rid of these little devils for us."

"Don't worry. For the most part the night itself will do it. Me, I'm immune to them. I got attacked by them unmercifully a few years ago, down off Barataria. I was sick for a week, but ever afterward they haven't bothered me at all."

"Look," Graciela said now. "The third fork."

"There's my sharp-eyed girl," Falligant said. "We'll just head down that way. Look, there's another sign reinforcing the original one. And there's yet another. See the strip of rag tied to three branches to form a triangle? That means 'Meet us at the next crossroad.' We're getting close."

The road they now followed wound up and over a low hill. From the top of the hill they could see the smoke from the cooking fires, and a random gathering of brightly painted wagons arranged loosely in a sort of circle, partly hiding the Gypsies from the road. Around the campfires sat women; most were dark-haired and olive skinned, wearing full-skirted, shockingly low-cut dresses and, everywhere, gold, shining gold that picked up the last rays of the sun and reflected them back in Graciela's fascinated eyes. Large numbers of small children ran about the camp, all of them wearing colorful but sometimes ragged garments. The smell of the camp-fires was strong and pungent, and mingled with this was the unmistakable smell of cooking food.

As they drew closer she could see the wagons themselves were gorgeous creations: the undercarriages were painted gold, and the sides and back were in gaudy colors so artfully chosen that they never seemed garish, only gay. There were double doors in front and single doors in the rear, and each end opened upon a kind of porchlike platform. There were three windows on each side, now open to the evening air. The horses, great-muscled draymen's hacks, were tethered farther away, and now for the first time she could see the men minding them: powerful, mustachioed, most of them dark-haired, with bulging arm muscles protruding from sleeveless vests. They wore no shirts at all, and there was a strangely alien weathered roughness about their looks, with the thick patches of hair on their bare torsos that she found oddly attractive.

Colonel Falligant rode ahead to meet one of the men, who walked out to confront them. He was evidently a person of some authority in the camp, and received Falligant cautiously at first, then courteously. His wave of the hand said it all, even to Graciela who could not hear his words clearly and could not have understood them if she had heard them: they were welcome. Falligant, dismounting with evident pain, waved to Graciela. "Come," he said. "There's someone I want you to meet."

She dismounted herself, and was surprised at how stiff she was after their all-day ride. As she approached them she was acutely conscious of the man's dark eyes on her, even dressed as she was in boy's clothing; she could not look him directly in the eye at first.

"This is Butsulo, Graciela," Falligant said in a tone that tokened respect for both the people he was introducing. "This encampment is of Butsulo's *kumpania*, and he is the patriarch here." He said a couple of words to the Gypsy in a language she could not make out, and switched to English. "This is Graciela. You see?"

The man looked her up and down again, this time the way one might look at a piece of horseflesh. "Let me see your hand, girl." Before she had time to think she had stuck her hand out and the Gypsy was looking it over, palm up, his hands rough and calloused. "Ah," he said, and looked her once in the eye. His gaze fairly burned into her! Then he held her hand up again, looking at her palm from various angles. "Ah," he said slowly once again.

"You see," Falligant said: "I am a friend of the Rom. I lie only to the *gaje*. I cheat only the *gaje*. Do I not speak truth to the Rom, who are my brothers?"

"You speak truth," Butsulo said. "But who is she?" It was almost as if she were not there, as if they were speaking about a cow one of them was considering purchasing.

"Her father was a *gajo*. He was a friend of mine and saved my life once. Her mother I met once. She was dark with sparkling eyes, and very spirited. She could well have been a Rom. Graciela knows nothing of her mother except that she was said to have come from the Islands, to the south. Her name is Spanish."

"Could be. Does she speak Spanish? Or better, *Caló*?"

"No," Graciela said. "I can speak for myself. I—"

"Quiet," Falligant said not ungently. "She speaks no foreign tongues except Latin, which she learned in the convent. Perhaps a little French. She knows nothing of her ancestry. I think her father was thrown out by his own people for the same sort of things my people threw me out for. He was not a real *gajo* at heart, and was naturally attracted to Graciela's mother."

"How did he live?" The deep voice was attentive.

"As I do. Swindling the *gaje*. He was what you call an Irishman. They are either red-haired or dark like a Rom."

"I have heard of them. Very well. This girl, she and you will live with us and travel with us as we go north. But what of the black man? He is your slave?"

"I am a Romany Rye and I do not believe in slaves. A friend asked me to take the black man north where no man is another man's property. I owed the friend a great debt." It was a little white lie, Graciela perceived, but it was evidently the sort of thing Butsulo would understand, for he nodded sagely. "He travels with me."

"This is as it should be," Butsulo said. "Come." And without further talk he turned on one booted heel and strode ahead of them into the circle of brightly painted wagons. Falligant ushered Josh and Graciela ahead of him, following the Gypsy chief. As they approached the nearest of the cookfires Graciela could make out the delicious smells of onions, peppers, tomatoes, meat. Suddenly she had never felt so hungry.

Butsulo's wife was named Tshaya, and she was stocky, coarse-skinned, nearly as dark as Josh, with a husky contralto voice. Her dark eyes kept going to Graciela, with more than a note of puzzlement in them. Nevertheless, when she served Graciela her dinner the girl noted that Tshaya gave her an extra portion of the delicious-smelling mixture, and handed her an extra piece of the hot, dark bread.

Well, so she was friendly, after all. This was a reassuring thought, and one which she could treasure all the way through dinner; she'd been more afraid of the Gypsy chief's woman than she had been of him.

The other Gypsy women were quite a mixture in looks, some lighter-skinned than others, some very beautiful; all were aloof toward the strangers, Josh and Falligant, but friendly toward Graciela. This aloofness toward strange men made the women appear enigmatic to her, like nuns of some unknown and mystical order.

Dinner was preceded by a Gypsy girl pouring water over everyone's hands. The unexpected daintiness of the act, coming from people who looked—well, untidy—came as a surprise to Graciela, but the surprise was allayed in a moment when it became evident that she was expected to eat the greasy mess in her bowl with her fingers.

Well, so be it, she thought, and pitched in hungrily. To her delight the dish, cooked in olive oil, was delicious. "Goodness," she said to Falligant, "It reminds me of something I had back at the Tocko camp."

"Tocko? Oh, you mean the Slavs downriver. Yes. As a matter of fact these Rom may originally have come from that part of the world in the first place. If not these, then their parents or grandparents. And much of the food in that part of the world is alike. This was roasted on a spit, the meat and vegetables together."

"It's splendid. And the coffee—"

"Turkish. I expect the Tockos served it that way too. It's an acquired taste, I suppose, but at any rate I did acquire it, some years ago, and I'm fond of it." He belched loudly. "Pardon me, but etiquette here demands that you do the same. Eructation is virtually the only thing that will keep the eternally generous Rom from continuing to refill your plate until you beg for mercy. Just belch in as ladylike manner as you can and say 'Tshailo sim.' That means 'I'm full.' They'll understand that." She complied, not without blushing.

"Colonel," she said, looking for a place to wipe her hands. "I don't understand this business about the hands. Why did Butsulo look at them so? And what was he talking about?"

"Here," Falligant said, and poured water from the jug over her outstretched fingers. "The Rom custom would

100

be to wipe your fingers in your hair for added shine. Well, it would be if you were a bit younger. No matter. They'll get used to the fact that you don't know their ways."

"But my hands. . . ."

"Oh, that. Haven't you guessed by now? I think, and Butsulo agrees, that you may very well be a Rom yourself. A true Rom, descended on the mother's side. Very likely your mother was a Spanish Gypsy even if she wasn't raised as one. After all, the Caribbean was originally settled by white people kidnapped in the port cities of Europe and sold into slavery in the island colonies of France, Spain and England. Theoretically there was an indenture paper, but if there was it was signed under duress and few slaves ever escaped their captors. The ones who did mostly became *boucaniers*, pirates who preyed on the Spanish fleets. Usually the women weren't so lucky. Your grandmother, whoever she was. . . ." He stopped and went into a violent fit of coughing. He tried to speak again in the middle of it, but once again had to stop. He held his handkerchief to his face, and when the paroxysm had ended Graciela could see spots of red on the white cloth.

"Sorry," he said. "An old illness of mine seems to have gotten a fresh start again with all this violent activity lately." He caught the concern in her eye now. "Oh," he said. "Don't mind that. I'm a lunger, of course, but I've been one for twenty-two years. It comes and goes. I have periods of as much as a year when it doesn't resurface at all, and then, all of a sudden it'll arise again to bother me for a while."

As he talked, though, she watched his face, with its unnatural flush—unnatural in a face that drawn. She suddenly saw, in his gaunt face and haunted eyes, the very visage of death. *He's dying*, she thought. *No matter that he's been dying for a long time. He's finally reached the age when that sort of thing catches up to you.*

This thought was interrupted by the advent of a younger man, the first man she'd seen near her own age since she'd arrived. He strode through the circle of faces around the fire, saluted Tshaya, and let her wash his hands before handing him a plate of food.

He was different—vastly different—from Butsulo. His

101

body was perhaps as powerful in its way, but it was slim, long-muscled, flat-bellied: an athlete's body, full of a crackling energy. His face was dark, Roman-nosed, hot-eyed; his teeth, as he smiled at a friend around the fire, were strong and white. The thing that struck her first about him, she thought suddenly, was his carriage: of only medium height, he stood as tall and straight as— as Beau Tolliver. His movements had a catlike grace about them without being anything but intensely masculine. There was a natural arrogance, a princeliness, about his bearing with that high-held head and that strong neck.

"Ah," Falligant said. "You've noticed young Shandor. Someone told me about him while I was taking a— while I was back looking at the horses. He's something of a black sheep around here, for all that he's the best horseman the tribe ever had. He's the son of the old chief of the tribe, Luluvo, but he and his father fell out before the old man's death and leadership of the tribe passed to Butsulo, the chief's brother. He's Butsulo's nephew. He ran away a while back to work with a circus as an acrobat and equestrian." He coughed some more and added, "Everyone seems to like him, but no one seems to trust him. They think him too close to the *gaje*, leaving the camp like that."

She was suddenly aware of someone standing at her shoulder and looked up suddenly. It was Butsulo. His own eyes followed Shandor as hers had done, but there was no friendliness in them for the young man. The look in his eyes was as cold as ice: they were, she thought suddenly, the eyes of a man who was looking at a person he might have to kill some day. It seemed a logical assumption to make, if the rule of succession in Gypsy camps was anything like that among the *gaje*.

"Come," he said. "There is someone who wants to see you."

She looked quickly over at Colonel Falligant; but he suddenly broke into another fit of coughing, which he interrupted only to nod vigorously to her: *Go with him. It'll be all right.*

Chapter 15

A few steps beyond the ring of people around the campfire Butsulo stopped and waited for her to catch up with him. His dark eyes regarded her impersonally, but not coldly. There was, if anything, something friendly in his manner, something welcoming. She couldn't put her finger on it: outwardly he was as undemonstrative and businesslike as ever, but at the same time she felt that he had accepted her the way she was, and that she was among friends.

She caught up to him now and stood looking up at him. "Butsulo," she said. "Who is it that wants to see me?"

"It is my mother, Pesha," he said in his deep voice. "She is very old and very wise. I have told her about you and she wishes to see for herself, to see if I have told her correctly about what I see in your hand."

"What *do* you see in my hand?" she said. "Nobody's told me very much of anything yet."

"Ah," Butsulo said. "I will let Pesha tell you. I could be wrong, although I do not think I am. She will know. She will speak with authority." He looked around, surveying his domain. "I am authority here in all matters of the day. Pesha speaks with authority of all things of the night. You will see."

"Butsulo," she said again. "My friend, the Colonel, I believe he is very ill."

"Yes," he said. "He has been very ill for many years, I think. He is like a horse who becomes ill in the middle of the race, but who has great heart and will not let himself fall until the race is done. While danger lay around him he did not cough into the white kerchief, making spots of blood. Now, when he finds the Rom, his friends, he will allow himself to be ill."

"Can he be cured?"

"I will see. If he is not too far along the road to death we can heal him with the hands by arts known to the Rom. If it is his will to die. . . ." He shrugged, but there was great concern in his eyes. "Perhaps it does not matter. He has lived long and faced many dangers. He has lived as a man lives and will die as a man dies. Here he would die among his friends and brothers."

"Oh," Graciela said, and her eyes filled with tears. "You speak as though you've known him a long time."

"No," Butsulo said. "I have never seen him before. But I have heard of him, and his name is great among the tribe of Bidshika, whom I met last summer. There was a time many summers ago, when the tribe of Bidshika did a monstrous thing—I will not say what thing this was—and the *gajo* who is not a *gajo*, Falligant, righted the wrong they had done and took away what could have become a great evil. The tribe of Bidshika is forever in his debt. All the Rom know his name and honor him. He is a man, and perhaps more than a man. In his youth, for instance, he is said to have been as good a horseman as any Rom. Myself, I do not know that I believe this, but Bidshika tells me it is the truth. And Falligant—he can fight with the knife, the sword, the pistol."

"He really is remarkable," she said. "I owe my life to him."

"I understand. It was good fortune for you to find him. He is old, but he still lives like one who is young. This is against the laws of nature, the laws of the body. It is time for him to live like one who is old. It is time for him to rest. He will do so among the Rom, his friends and brothers, and when he dies it will be with great honor. He will be buried the way a Rom is buried." He looked at her again. "You understand we will try to heal him. But even if he is healed he will not be the man he was, a grandfather who lives like a stripling."

"I understand. It's very sad in a way—but then perhaps it isn't. How fortunate of him to find friends now.

Friends who will love him and respect him and take care of him."

"Yes," Butsulo said. "Perhaps it is his destiny. Come. It is your own destiny we must learn." He nodded, still friendly, now somewhat fatherly, and led her to a gaily painted wagon with a gilt undercarriage and green and white trim. He handed her up as lightly as if she'd been a child in arms.

Inside, candles to either side of the central aisle lit the bed of an old, old woman who lay watching them enter. Her skin was dark and leathery, her hands, atop the coverlet, bony. Her eyes were the only thing about her that did not speak of immense age and decrepitude: they were dark and flashing, with immense depths in which low, banked fires glowed.

"This is the girl, Pesha," Butsulo said to the old woman. He turned to Graciela. "This is my mother, Pesha. Show her your hands, please."

Graciela obediently held out her hands; she'd learned by now to show them palm up. But the old woman, taking them in her own two fleshless hands, turned them over and over again, marking this and taking note of that, before finally turning them palms up again.

Her eyes fairly glowed as she looked into Graciela's palm, and she crooned soft and low in a cracked, aged voice. Once she chuckled and pointed to a configuration in Graciela's right palm, and when Graciela looked up she could see Butsulo nodding appreciatively.

Now the old woman began to speak in a low voice, and Graciela could not make out so much as a word. She understood that Butsulo's mother could not speak in English, and was if anything barely intelligible in Romany, since Butsulo asked her to repeat several times. She looked up and saw Butsulo nodding gravely, his eyes on the old woman's face.

Finally the old woman squeezed Graciela's hands weakly and released them. She whispered something that could well have been a goodbye, and when Graciela looked up she saw Butsulo motion her to the door. "Wait just outside the wagon for me," he said. "I must speak to Pesha." She obeyed and stood outside in the darkness, waiting for him.

There was a balmy summer breeze now, and the acrid smoke of the campfire wafted her way. It was not at all an unpleasant smell, mixed as it was with the smell of cooked food and of cigar smoke. There was a warm glow in the campfire area, and she could see the children and dogs running to and fro just outside the circle of light. Now she could hear the sound of music: a guitar, a low-pitched male voice singing a dark pentatonic lament that was not all lament, that burned with defiance at the same time it mourned loss.

It was strange. She felt as if she weren't among strangers at all. It wasn't even as if she were among new friends. It was something more than this, something subtler but at the same time something more elemental. A sudden chill went up and down her spine, a chill of—what? Recognition?

The music continued. Some of the group were dancing. Now Butsulo was beside her. He looked at the gay circle of light, watched the smoke curling upward in the firelight. "Yes," he said as if reading her thought. "It is a fine thing to see. I think you are seeing in it something more than just a fine sight, though. Do I speak the truth?"

"Yes," she said. "Oh, yes. I—I can't describe it."

"Well," he said, his eyes still on the scene before them, "think of it as what a weary traveler sees when he comes home after a great journey."

"Home," Graciela said. "I'm thinking—did I ever really have a home before?" She looked up at Butsulo, and felt his strong fatherly arm go around her waist. "Butsulo," she said, "what did Pesha say?"

Butsulo squeezed her gently, the bare touch of his hand sending an immense flow of strength flowing from his sturdy body into hers. "Pesha said that your hand is the hand of a Rom. More, she said it is a hand of immense strength and power. A hand that bears the Mystic Cross. It is the hand of one who will achieve great power and fame both among the Rom and among the *gaje*." He started to say something else, but stopped. "I must learn the time and date of your birth. Mala, the wife of Kore who minds the horses, is learned in the ways of the stars. Pesha says to learn what one can learn of you from Mala."

"Myself? A Gyps—a Rom?" Graciela said, catching herself. "Goodness. She's sure?"

"Pesha says that the hand does not lie. Falligant has said your mother may have been of Romany blood. You certainly have the look of a Romany woman, though you are little more than a child. And your hand . . . Pesha is certain of this. But come. We will rejoin your brothers and sisters at the fire. You have much to learn. But remember this: you are home. Home after a long journey." He hugged her again, and his rough touch was gentle and comforting.

Colonel Falligant looked up and smiled as Graciela once again entered the fire circle. His face was drawn and pale, but there was a look of immense content on it. "Here, Graciela," he said. "Sit down. I'm having a fine time. I'd forgotten how much I always loved a Rom encampment."

She settled herself beside him. "I'm glad," she said. "I like it too. I. . . ." She looked at him earnestly. "Pesha—that's Butsulo's mother—says I may be a Rom myself. She seems quite sure of it. It's something she found in my palm."

"Yes," he said. "I spotted it myself. It was one of the reasons I brought you here. I knew that when a Rom saw that palm of yours you'd find yourself some sanctuary." He reached out and patted her knee. The gesture was that of a favorite uncle.

These were people after his own heart. There was always a fiddler to play the wild, sometimes sad, sometimes gay music, and this in itself was intoxicating. The Gypsies never tired of dancing and could go on until the small hours of the morning. Graciela felt the bewitching violin music fall upon her ears like drops of some fiery, volatile essence.

Falligant sat up and held out a hand to a young man who held a guitar. "Here, Nanosh," he said. "If you'll loan me the guitar for a moment, I'll sing you a song I learned as a boy—a *gajo* song about the Rom." The boy passed the instrument across and Falligant, sitting up, snuggled one thigh into the curve of the guitar.

The instrument had gone slightly out of tune; he tuned it expertly and tested the intonation with a thunderous volley of strumming, using the backs of his nails.

As he did this someone down the line murmured in approval.

Graciela, looking up to see the source of the murmur, suddenly found herself looking squarely into the eyes of Shandor, the young man she'd noticed earlier. His gaze was straightforward, intense, frankly sexual. She tried to look away but found she couldn't.

"All right," Falligant said beside her, oblivious of her or of the young man. "This is an old Scots song, and it's about a great lady in a castle who falls in love with a Romany lad and runs off to live with him." He struck an introductory chord and began to sing in a clear voice in which there was the faintest trace of a Scots accent.

Graciela tried to look away; tried to blink; tried to free herself from the spell of the dark eyes that looked across at hers, across the firelight, from the far side of the circle of light; but she could not. Her heart was beating fast. The young man did not smile. His face remained immobile. His eyes burned into hers. Falligant's voice seemed far, far away.

Chapter 16

But the moment passed. The fire struck a green knot in the wood, and a dark cloud drifted up between their faces, and when the cloud had lifted Shandor was no longer there. Graciela blinked. Had he been there at all? Had she imagined the whole thing, under the spell of Falligant's song? She looked to the right and left, but there was no sign of the dark young man.

Falligant sang on. She turned to watch him. His strong fingers thrummed out an arpeggiated accompaniment for the song, and his voice was strong and clear. Yet there was the pall of death upon him, so strong and obvious that she wondered that she had not seen it before. She looked around. The eyes of the Rom people were upon him, and she saw several of them moving a hand or a foot in time to the strongly rhythmic music.

The song wound down to its tragic denouement. Falligant put down the guitar and reached inside his coat for the small brown bottle; he drank from it and then wiped his lips abstemiously on his kerchief. Graciela once again noted the red stains on the white cloth. "That was a lovely song," she said.

"Yes," he said. "It's a true story, too, so far as anyone knows. It happened some two hundred years ago. When the Earl of Cassilis, in Scotland, was away in Westminster signing the Covenant, the Gypsy leader John Faa carried away his lady. Yes, and died for it, I'll wager. The family Fall of Dunbar are descended from John Faa, the Gypsy king, and you can still get into a fight in that part of the world by singing that song to the wrong man, or in the wrong tavern."

"Goodness," she said. "You've been to Scotland?"

"I've been nearly everywhere," he said. "Gypsies traveled a path of legend and romance across Asia, Europe and America, footloose and free. Rom means 'a man of our own race'—from it comes the word Romany."

"I hope Gypsies never settle down and lose their zest for life," Graciela said. "It would be like harnessing a lion to a plow."

He started to say something else, but a fit of coughing halted his words. "Sorry," he said after he'd got it under control. "I—I think this damnable consumption's a bit worse with me this time around. It's all this living out of doors. What I need is to sleep in a bed, under clean sheets, and do nothing more strenuous than deal the pasteboards for a while. The autumn will be on us before long. I'm damned if I'm going to be living this sort of existence by the time the leaves are yellow. Oh," he said, looking at her reassuringly, "it isn't their way of life that I mind. Hell, girl, I'm as happy here as I've ever been anywhere, I suppose. There's always a feeling of welcome, of homecoming, when I meet a Gypsy band. But, well, there's a Gypsy legend about the wild goose, and I suppose that's what I am after all. When my time comes I've got to fly. Look, I've found you a safe place, haven't I? Wouldn't you say that qualifies to discharge the obligation I owed your father?"

"Oh, yes," Graciela said. "But if you'd only stay!"

"Well, perhaps I will. Yes, perhaps I'll stick around just to make sure, until the Rom wagons cross the line between free and slave state." This set off another barrage of deep, racking coughs, and out came the white kerchief again, to be spotted even more deeply. "Look, Graciela. It's too late to change my way of life. I'm locked into a rhythm that's of my own making. I can't help being what I am, maybe never could. My parents, they could never understand that. Damn few people I ever met could understand that. God knows I never found a woman who could undestand it; maybe if I could have found a Gypsy wench I . . . but that's another story."

He coughed long and hard again; guttural, racking, painful-sounding coughs that sounded as though he were bringing up his heart's blood. "As I was saying," he said in a weakened voice, "virtually nobody I ever met could understand or accept me on my own terms until I met these people. They're wiser than other people in some ways. They haven't lost their ability to be in tune with nature. Some of them are damn fools, but some of them have good horse sense. And there's a way in which they're like me. That counts for a lot."

"You told me the other night that I was—I was no good. Like you, you said."

"Ah. I didn't mean to hurt your feelings. I suppose I did hurt you inadvertently. I apologize. What I was trying to say was that you're a wild goose, too, and God help the man who tries to tame you or hold you down. Maybe a good Romany man could do it, but I doubt it. The only thing that will ever bind you to a man and a place will be yourself, and it'll be involuntary. That is, if I'm right about you."

"Goodness," Graciela said. "I—I don't know my own mind. Maybe you're right. But you're here among friends and you say they're people like you. Doesn't that make you want to stay?"

"Well, yes, it does," he said. "Somewhat. The trouble is, I have this strange notion that keeps haunting me, that the moment I relax I'm a dead man. And I could relax here. I could easily slip into this nomadic existence. But the moment I did. . . ." Here he was interrupted once again by a truly vicious spell of coughing. He kept trying to say something, but every time he opened his mouth the cough came back to plague him. "Goddamn it," he said at last, furious with himself, "that makes me mad as hell. I need a drink. Be a good girl and go over to the third wagon—over there behind the oak tree, the wagon with the red and yellow trim—and look in my saddlebags. There's a good bottle of rye I stole from Jeremy's larder in there. Could you get it for me? There's a good girl."

She patted his hand once and got up. Enroute to the wagon she ran into Butsulo. "Please," she said. "The Colonel, he's talking about leaving. I tried to talk to him, but I'm afraid he wasn't listening to me. Maybe you could."

"He will not go," Butsulo said. Then he thought about the matter a moment. "Or then again maybe he will. It is in God's hands. One cannot keep him. We

111

would enjoy having him, but it would be like keeping an eagle in a cage. The Rom have no use for cages. The bird must fly."

"Oh," she said. "Please, couldn't you just talk to him?" But as soon as she said it she knew Butsulo was not going to interfere. She looked at him with a mixture of disappointment and reproach and walked away toward the wagons.

A figure stepped out from the shadows and stood facing her. It was the young man Shandor, but his eyes, this time, regarded her with no more than usual interest. "Good evening," he said. "You are the Romany girl who knows nothing of her past."

"I—I think so. Pesha says I'm a Rom. She says she saw the signs in my hand and many other indications. I don't know. If I am, it would have to be through my mother, and I never knew her. She died when I was very young."

"This makes you even more of a Rom," he said in an even voice. "Among us all titles, all bloodlines, descend through the mother. A man with a Rom father and a *gajo* mother is not a true Rom." He looked her up and down, and there was more than a hint of appreciativeness in his expression when his eyes went back to hers. "I understand that you dress like a man to avoid the *gaje* laws. One of the women will give you clothing in the morning. Keja or Boti, perhaps. They are of a size with you."

"You're Shandor, aren't you?" she said with a boldness that surprised her. "Someone said you had lived among the *gaje*. What made you come back?"

His clear-eyed gaze told her quite clearly, *That's none of your damned business*. But he shrugged and said casually, "I come and go. Other members of the tribe don't understand this. You ask too many questions." But he grinned suddenly, and the flash of gleaming white teeth in his swarthy face softened the rebuke. "You have spirit. Perhaps you are of the Rom after all, for all that you know nothing of our customs."

"Perhaps I am," she said. "Now if you'll excuse me?" She stepped past him heading for the wagon, and there was a moment—a split second, really, no more—when she thought he was going to stretch out a hand to stop her. But he turned the motion of his hand into a courtly *gajo* "aprèz vous" gesture, smiling insolently, and let her pass.

She found the bottle easily and walked back with it to the campfire. But when she arrived Falligant was nowhere to be seen. She looked around and found Tshaya. "Please," she said. "Colonel Falligant—where did he go?"

Tshaya regarded her from under heavy lids, her face expressionless. "He went to see the horses. This is a Romany term for going out to make water. He went with Butsulo." She nodded over her shoulder. "That way. I would not follow him. It would not be proper."

Tshaya pushed past her, heading back toward the wagons. She stood looking around the fire circle. Some of the younger people were dancing as Nanosh played his guitar and sang a rousing dance song. A number of the older faces were gone, dispersed toward the wagons. The evening was winding down. Soon it would be time for her to go to sleep, once someone told her where to bed down.

She sighed and stood holding the bottle. It had been a day of surprises, she thought. But then what day hadn't, since that bitter day when she'd been called out of her class at the convent and told the bitter truth about her identity and her status? It would, she decided, be a good thing to have at least a few days—perhaps a matter of weeks, as the caravan wound its way slowly northward toward the Illinois line—of relative stability in her life, before she saw Tolliver again and he could right the great wrong that had been done to her.

Perhaps Falligant had done the best thing he could possibly have done under the circumstances, following the Rom camp and asking for sanctuary. At any rate she seemed to be safe—yes, and accepted too. That would do until she could get her feet underneath her. And then. . . .

Then? What? What *would* she do when she'd found her freedom at last?

There was something—something she dare not face, dare not even think about openly—lurking in the back of her mind whenever she thought about this subject. What was it? What could it be?

And then with a great rush of understanding she knew what it was that she had in mind. She found herself blushing, and giving thanks that she was not in the light and could not be seen by anyone.

You fool! she told herself. *You little fool!*

It was clear. There was something inside her that wanted, more than anything in the world, to make Beau Tolliver notice her, to show her love for him, to make him love her too.

What nonsense. He probably didn't care a thing for her! She was just another disadvantaged person for him to help, with his ingrained, deep-seated hatred of slavery and servitude and all they stood for. He had no more feelings for her than—than he had for Josh. If anything his feelings were fatherly ones, not those of a lover.

Besides, wasn't she his property? Bag and baggage? How could you love a woman who was no more than a chattel, whom you could own and buy and sell, like a horse or a cow?

Fool! she thought.

No, no. She'd better get that out of her mind, now and forever. She must dwell on her self-respect. Say only things to herself that would make her feel worthy of him. And somehow the one thing in the world that she wouldn't be able to stand—now or in the remotest future—was the idea of arousing Tolliver's laughter or contempt. The idea of exposing her feelings to him on a basis of anything but complete equality was repugnant in the extreme.

No, the best thing was to hold off until later, and make something of herself, by her own efforts, so that he would come to respect her. Once she'd won his respect—and somehow she knew that wouldn't come easy—then it'd be possible to go to work on making him interested in her.

Yes. Now that was more like it. With a place in society, with solid accomplishment behind her, she could meet him on his own terms, and make him come to her. Yes! Make him want her, so that she wouldn't have to do the chasing. Make him see the beauty in her soul, the person that nobody could buy or sell, who was the equal of anyone and maybe the superior of some.

Tolliver. Beau Tolliver.

Mrs. Beau Tolliver . . .

"Oh, stop that," she told herself aloud. Really, she'd have to get herself under control.

"Stop what?" a voice said. She turned suddenly to see Shandor standing behind her, his powerful arms crossed over his broad chest. "Or are you just talking to yourself?" His grin half mocked her, half accepted the foible as a legitimate, if ridiculous, human failing.

"None of your business," she said. Her face—she knew it, she just knew it—was red as a beet. She turned on one heel and walked away, her boot heels digging into the turf. Then she stopped as she heard the sound. Hoofbeats, close by. Settling into a trot, then a gallop. Receding into the distance.

She almost dropped the bottle. She turned and sought the ring of faces, looking for Butsulo's. She could not find him, and was making for the outer circle of wagons when he suddenly materialized at her elbow out of the darkness. "Butsulo," she said. "Colonel Falligant! I think—"

"Yes," Butsulo said. "That was him. I tried to talk to him. It was no use. You cannot hold back the wild goose. He has gone. I do not know where. Perhaps our paths will cross again sometime." He shrugged; but somehow, in his impassive face, Graciela felt she could detect a note of sadness.

"But he'll die!"

"Perhaps. That is in the hands of God. He has to find his own destiny. That destiny is not mine. I cannot understand it. But a man has to do what he has to do or he is no longer a man. That one," he said appreciatively, "is a man. He will die like one—and it may well be that he will die with his boots on, living as he always lived."

"Oh, dear," Graciela said. "Oh, dear. If only. . . ." She looked down at the brown bottle in her hand and shook her head. He hadn't wanted or needed a drink. He'd just sent her away so that she couldn't try to talk him out of leaving. And now she'd never see him again.

"Here," Butsulo said. "Let me show you where you will sleep tonight. Falligant has left you the bedding in his saddlebag. You can sleep here, just beyond the fire circle. The Rom sleep on the ground. It is healthful and good to feel the earth underneath you. In the morning the women will give you clothing of your own, clothing more befitting a girl of the Rom."

"Oh, dear," she said again. But then she straightened up and looked him in the eye. "Well," she said. "I suppose I can't do anything about it. Yes. Please show me where I'll be sleeping. And . . . Butsulo?"

"Yes?"

"I thank you. Thank you, all of you, for taking me in. It is very kind of you."

"No," Butsulo said. "Once we had seen the sign in your palm we could not have refused you. Not once we knew you to be one of us. The Rom don't turn a brother or a sister away from their fires. Not unless he commits some unforgivable offense. No, you are among your own now. You will learn Romany ways. You will learn the secrets that only the Rom know: secrets of earth, of life, of healing, of seeing the future, or seeing inside a person's soul and knowing what is in his mind."

"Yes," Graciela said, thinking only of Cairo, Illinois, and Beau Tolliver. "Yes, Butsulo, I'd like that." She'd made up her mind, very suddenly, about something. She'd stay with the caravan at least as long as necessary. And in the meantime she wouldn't discuss her plans with anyone. The more people you discussed your plans with, the likelier it was that you'd never put those plans into action. *No; keep your own counsel. Be polite, friendly, respectful . . . and confide in no one.* That was the way. It was the only way. She'd live each day as it came, and learn what these people who claimed she was one of them had to teach. She liked them.

And Beau Tolliver? She'd deal with him when the time came.

BOOK THREE

Chapter 17

In the morning the Rom struck camp, and the caravan began once again to move steadily north. Graciela, all decked out now in Gypsy garb—an ankle-length skirt given her by Tshaya, a shamelessly low-cut blouse borrowed from Mala, Kore's wife, and shoes of uncertain provenance—sat beside Tshaya on the seat of Butsulo's wagon as it jounced slowly down the long road. Far ahead she could see the horsemen riding point on the caravan: Butsulo's burly form, often joined by the athletic and lithe form of Shandor.

The two seldom spoke, though; no love was lost between them. This she could see plainly from their actions. No reason for this had been advanced so far, other than the Rom's general distaste for Shandor's wild-goose notions and disrespect for any Rom customs which happened to get in his way. No, there must be some reason other than these, she thought. Butsulo treated Shandor as a potential enemy, the nearest thing to a *gajo*. The grudging respect the tribal chief gave the boy was the kind of respect one accorded a powerful and dangerous foe.

It was perplexing; but Graciela, for some days, had little time to ponder the matter or ask questions about it. She was busy acquiring a basic education from a people whose view of the world was so different from the one in which she had been raised. There seemed at times something sweet about their ability to be free to roam, to witness the passing beauty of the landscape, the aroma of the flowers and trees. The Gypsies seemed so rich in heart and spirit. They might be outcasts but they could enjoy the blue sky and green grass. Perhaps, she

119

thought, when civilization burns itself out, Gypsy caravans will wind their way past crumbling cities because the Rom's way of life is that of nature.

Tshaya was her mentor for the most part. Atop the high seat on Butsulo's gaily painted wagon, the two women, matriarch and pupil, had plenty of time to talk. There were, after all, not only the language and customs of the Rom to be passed along, but also the legends and fairy tales and folkways of the wandering people, and the thousand signs they found in nature and in the symbols their brothers had left behind to guide and protect them.

The roadside signs she'd learned from Colonel Falligant, for instance, were augmented by a complex set of symbols the Rom called *patrin*. While simple, these managed to convey an amazing amount of information between passing tribes. Caravans passing through an area visited in recent months could learn much about a particular farmhouse and its inhabitants from the signs chalked on the wall of a nearby barn. The circle with a dot inside it signified extreme generosity; the same sign with two lines underneath it indicated that Gypsies were in disrepute here and were regarded as thieves.

Well, thieves they were, if one used the ethical standards of the *gajo* community. The *gajo* were fair game, it appeared. Natural enemies of the wanderers, they were seen as natural victims in any confidence game the Gypsies could work upon them. Barring the odd chicken or pig stolen for food, this larcenous disposition toward the *gaje* seldom took the form of outright theft. For the most part the Rom disdained such matters. But there was not only provender to be gained, but soul-balm and cachet as well, by swindling the unsuspecting *gajo* of his money in an unequal test of wits.

Passing an isolated farmhouse, for example, a Gypsy woman would first check the barn for signs. Then, fortified with the information an earlier Romany woman had gained in conversation with the housewife, she would approach the house and astonish the farmer's wife with information "divined" about her through "Gypsy magic."

Graciela could hardly believe what she was seeing at first. Tshaya, for instance, would approach a farmhouse and offer to sell charms against ill fortune such as the recent loss of the woman's mother. The woman, astonished that Tshaya knew about the matter, would invite her inside. Tshaya would then discuss the number of the woman's children and her plans for more (or, conversely, for an end to child-bearing). In no time, disarmed by Tshaya's seemingly miraculous knowledge, the woman would become a fit customer for her expensive services in predicting the future and in providing charms and amulets against bad luck.

Of course, Tshaya explained, all the information she had "divined" about the woman had been found chalked on an outbuilding. Deciphered, the message was clear. This household, it said, was generous to Gypsies, who had visited it recently. The mistress of the house, who was friendly to the idea of fortune-telling by cards, wanted another child, but her mother had died in recent months. Her husband had a roving eye, and that might well make her a customer for a charm against his infidelity.

Graciela was impressed—and appalled. It took a while for her to get over her shock at the casual attitude of the Rom toward confidence games. When she did, though, she found underneath her original disapproval a growing admiration for the Rom women's ingenuity.

Tshaya, it appeared, was a woman of some power in the Rom camp. The greatest power among the women still lodged in Butsulo's mother, Pesha, the *phuri dai* or Old Woman of the caravan. Pesha's power was considered to be pure wisdom, and her opinion was consulted in all matters involving the spirit and destiny of the inhabitants of the camp. But Pesha would die soon. Then her powers, temporal and occult, would pass to Tshaya, who already wielded temporal power through her husband.

The evenings Graciela loved most were when she was called in to see Pesha, who would look deeply into her eyes before pondering again the shape and lines of Graciela's pink palm. Her voice, now no more than a whisper, would mutter softly over Graciela's hand; but Graciela's slowly growing vocabulary of Romany phrases made it easier each day to decipher the slurred but wise words that Pesha spoke. Pesha tried to explain to Graciela that "not only the Rom but all people the world

121

over make their own destiny and then they call it fate. Character determines one's fate and by consciously changing one's character one can change her fate.

"My dear, use your imagination to change any part of your character you wish because imagination wins over will power one hundred percent of the time. This imaging ability we all have is our most powerful tool. When you realize this secret you can give readings that will help others, and therefore, you will be blessed."

Graciela wasn't sure she understood everything this very wise old woman told her but she knew somehow that it was the Truth and she wanted to learn as much as Pesha would share with her.

"Now the horoscope is like being dealt a deck of cards. Free will is how we choose to play the cards we are dealt.

"The palm, my dear one, has lines at birth but I want you to know that some of the lines may change. They change not because of what happens to us but because of our reaction to each experience, so our attitude is the real key.

"Most Rom," she told Graciela, "have kept their natural ability for precognition. Perhaps every race had it in the beginning, but because civilizations have ignored it most *gaje* or *gorgio* have lost this precious God-given gift. We Rom listen to it and, therefore, those of us who have kept it need not use any deception when we give a reading.

"Of course, there are those who have lost the gift and have not learned to 'read' so they must resort to being fakes, just as there are fakes in all professions. Because there are fakes doesn't mean the real doesn't also exist.

"My child, you will never have to resort to anything but an honest reading for you have kept your God-given gift intact. Listen to it always: it is the true inner guidance."

Pesha would tire after giving her ancient wisdom and she would slowly drop Graciela's hand as she fell into a calm sleep, a sweet smile on her lips. Then Graciela couldn't help but say one of the prayers she had learned at the convent. It seemed to fit the spiritual mood of these evenings.

Pesha, of course, was now *Bibi* (aunt) to Graciela, a

title that Tshaya would assume soon. Butsulo was *Kako*, "uncle." These were formal terms used in formal situations, and most of the time she called them by their given names. As the relationships grew, though, she found herself coming to lean upon Butsulo's rough authority and upon Tshaya's strength and intelligence; "aunt" and "uncle" seemed apt terms for them.

Graciela's duties kept her busy. The world of the Rom gave women a larger role than the *gajo* world did. Women did heavy, back-breaking labor right alongside the men, and, possibly since a woman represented less of a challenge to the *gaje*, it was usually the woman whose job it was to visit farmhouses and cadge, by whatever means, the food the caravan required. No matter that while the woman of the house was occupied with the Gypsy woman's fortune-telling, the men of the encampment might be busy making free in the farmer's pasture by letting the Gypsy horses graze, or thinning out the farmer's chicken-yard. Everyone in the camp acknowledged that the burden of the matter fell upon the women. A woman skilled at the art of separating the unwary *gajo* from his goods was highly respected. Graciela, eager to learn what the younger girls already knew, could hardly wait until Tshaya started teaching her the interesting life of living as a Rom.

Nights around the campfire were devoted to song and story, which brought merriment and novelty. Nanosh played not only the guitar but the violin, and the Rom danced to his music with great abandon. Gusts of Gypsy music mingled with the scent of the fresh outdoors. She found that not only their music had an exotic flavor, but the stories also were exciting and deliciously colorful.

In the Rom version of the Creation, for instance, good and evil were represented by God (*o Del*) and the devil (*o Bengh*). In the Gypsy version the two, God and devil, collaborated in the creation of Damo and Yena, the first man and the first woman. At the same time two trees were created which belonged to man and woman, the pear tree and the plum tree. Damo ate the fruit of his tree, but the Serpent unsuccessfully tried to keep Yena from eating the fruit of hers. When the two had eaten they made love: once, twice, thrice. From this moment the woman became sexually insatiable, though not promiscuous, and was so regarded to the present day.

At first the Rom's natural acceptance of sexual matters shocked Graciela, with her convent upbringing. Then, little by little, she came to regard this as natural. Children in the camp were raised to understand their bodies early, but the morals of the people of Butsulo's caravan were, if anything, even more rigid than those of the *gaje*. Courtship was a controlled process, with a fixed ritual, one which she could watch as the days passed and a growing love-interest developed between Balo, a nephew of Butsulo, and Graciela's new friend Liza. It seemed the more serious the two were about each other, the less often they got a chance to talk together. Liza complained about this, but complied. It was the custom.

Strangely, despite several incidents of spiritual surgery performed on the Scriptures, the Rom appeared to venerate Christ, or Yeshua ben Meriem, and the Virgin Mary, whom they called Bibi Meriem. Whether this made them Christians Graciela could not have said. Surely their divergence from the accepted Catholic faith of her own childhood tended to point to heresy; but in their simple animism and deeply held beliefs she found a piety and spirituality which in itself had been rare even among the nuns of her convent school.

The favorite saint of the Rom wasn't properly accepted by the *gaje* as a saint at all. This was Sara, the patroness of the Gypsies. Sara, a Gypsy, had a vision that the three Marys—Mary Salome, Mary Jacobe and Mary Magdalene—who had been present at the death of Yeshua ben Meriem would come to her and that she must help them. They arrived in a boat, and Sara, seeing their boat foundering, threw her dress on the waves. It became a raft, and on it she swam to them and saved them. In gratitude they baptized Sara and converted the Rom to their faith. Now, if a Gypsy prayed it was first to God, then not to Bibi Meriem but to Sara, *la Kali*, the Black Virgin, whose face in all Gypsy effigies was painted black, or, at best, a dark brown, a rich Gypsy color.

Graciela, whose natural dark good looks were daily enhanced by the Southern sun, saw herself growing darker and wondered about her own status. After all, by *gajo* laws, she was black, like Sara. The smallest touch of black blood made a person black, a non-person, a chattel without rights south of the Line. Well, that was all right with her as long as she had the Rom with her. After all, her coloring had if anything raised her status with them. And if she were an outcast, it was as one among a trible of outcasts, who fiercely protected their own against all assaults from outside. Now, for the first time since that terrible day when her father had died, she was no longer alone. It was a growing source of comfort to her as the caravan rolled steadily northward and passed over into Tennessee.

She mentioned this to Tshaya once over the evening coffee. Her words carried across the fire circle; she heard Shandor's curt laugh and looking up, she saw his hot eyes burning into her own across the ten feet that separated them. His strong teeth were bared in a smile of—what was it? Derision? Pride?

"A Rom who traveled with the circus," he said in his strong young voice, "once told me a story. He said that when God decided to make a man he took clay in the shape of a human being and baked it in the oven. But then he got busy and forgot—and when he took the man out of the oven he was overdone, burnt black." He looked at Josh. "I mean no offense," he said.

"No," Josh said. "Please go on."

"Thank you. Then God made another man. And this time he was so eager that he took him out of the oven too soon. The man was too white." He looked at Graciela again. "Then he tried a third time," he said, and his large dark eyes flashed with spirit. "And this time he took special care. And when he removed the man from the oven he was just right: baked to a turn, golden-brown." He smiled at her. "He was perfect. He was a Rom."

There was a murmur of approval all around the fire. Butsulo, however, scowled and threw another log on the fire, a green one which threw sparks high and spat viciously at the children sitting closest to the blaze. "A stupid story," he said. "Your friend made this one up. I would avoid such talk if I were you. It smells of sacrilege. Have you forgotten God's curse on the Rom? Do you want it to descend upon this caravan some day when you least expect it? Do you want the blight to fall upon us all? Do you want to be shoeing a horse one day and suddenly, when you least expect it, come upon the Nail?"

"The Nail!" someone said behind her. There was a sudden surge of low murmuring from the Gypsies gathered around the fire. Graciela did not look around. Her eyes were on Shandor's face.

"The Nail?" he said. "But that is an old wives' tale. Nobody seriously believes it." But he looked in Butsulo's eyes and saw that Butsulo did indeed believe it. The pallor of his usually dark face, and the look of stark, inescapable, ancestral fear in his own ordinarily fearless young eyes, told Graciela that he believed it himself, whatever it was.

And, in a gesture that startled her as much as anything he could have done, he crossed himself hastily. Like a Roman Catholic. Not in the least like a Rom.

Standing, he rushed from the circle of light around the fire into the darkness. Butsulo, still standing splaylegged before the fire, his heavy hands placed firmly on his hips, scowled unforgivingly after him.

Chapter 18

Graciela, who by this time was beginning to overcome her natural shyness with the Rom of Butsulo's wagons, might have spoken to Shandor about this if no more than a day had passed. He had continued to be friendly, after all, and sometimes the look in his dark eyes, as he passed her in the evening in camp, had spoken mutely of something more than friendship.

But in the morning Shandor was gone. So was his horse, a stunning black with an eye as fiery as his own. When Graciela tried to ask Tshaya about him her question was dismissed curtly. "He comes and goes," Butsulo's wife said with a scowl. "A wild goose." The phrase came out with such a contemptuous tone that Graciela decided to let it go at that. The last thing she wanted to do was anger Tshaya, who had been teaching her the Romany tongue. *"Tshatshimo Romano,"* as Butsulo put it, "The truth is best expressed in Romany." Her education continued.

First Tshaya taught her words; then short phrases, always by rote, emphasizing careful pronunciation. After a while the two, sitting on the high board before the wagon as Tshaya guided the horses down the dusty Southern roads, began to communicate only in Romany.

There came a night when one of the older girls, approaching Graciela at the campfire, unleased a long and fluent volley of Romany at her—and stopped in the middle of her speech, grinning that flashing Rom smile, white of tooth, dark of eye. "I'm sorry," the girl said. "I forget and speak to you in Romany."

"It is all right," Graciela told her in Romany. "That time I understood everything you said. And the look of

127

sheer astonishment on the girl's face was worth all the work she had put in.

"*Feri ando payi sitsholpe te nayuas*," Butsulo said beside her, lighting a long black cigar from a burning brand taken from the fire. "It is in the water that one learns to swim." Graciela smiled; she'd heard the truism before, but this time she understood not by rote remembrance, but rather by a direct comprehension of Butsulo's statement. To be sure, she had been tossed into the water, linguistically, and she had learned to swim. It was a magnificent feeling.

Mostly though, she delighted in her evening visits with Pesha, especially now that she could understand the language better. Pesha's thinking was so different from Tshaya's that she wanted to learn from both of them.

Her further questions to Tshaya about Shandor, though, were met with folk aphorisms drawn from centuries-old wisdom: *Na may kharunde kai tshi khal tut* (don't scratch where it doesn't itch). The message was unmistakable: don't meddle with things or people that don't concern you.

Yet the missing Gypsy lad continued to exercise a certain fascination for her. She kept telling herself that it wasn't man-woman attraction, but something else. After all, Shandor and she shared one thing in common: they were people caught between two worlds. And if she knew, deep down inside her, that despite the Rom's warm welcome to her she truly did not belong, would never be really one of them . . . well, she was not alone in this. There was another member of the traveling tribe who was not totally at home here, who had one hopelessly itchy foot in each of two camps. There was company for her sometimes confused feelings of displacement. So long as Shandor remained with the tribe there would be at least one person who understood from personal experience the Gypsy axiom that *yekka buliasa nashti beshes pe done grastende* (with one rear end you cannot sit on two horses).

But was Shandor still with the tribe? By now he had been gone nearly a week. Gathering up her courage one night, Graciela once again asked Tshaya where the young man could have gone. Had he gone to live among the *gaje*? Had he taken up their ways? If he could understand her, with her *gajo* way of looking at things. . . .

To her chagrin Tshaya lashed out at her with a fierce burst of Romany invective. Was she falling in love with Shandor? The all-but-outcast? Just as the tribe was beginning to accept her as a sister, a daughter? What was to become of her reputation? A prospective husband, among the Rom, knew well that a wife was best chosen *rode tshia bora le kanensa tai te na le yakensa* (with the ears and not with the eyes). It would not matter how beautiful she was if she were to lose her reputation. No matter that her dark good looks would turn many a head at a great encampment of the Rom. *May kali i muri may gugli avela,* the saying had it: the darker the berry, the sweeter the juice. "*Shuk tski khalpe la royasa,*" Tshaya said, her eyes flashing with anger. "Beauty cannot be eaten with a spoon." There were other values. She would do well not to forget them, or sacrifice them to other, less meaningful considerations.

In all this time the closest friend Graciela had was Josh. The black man had begun as someone without status among the Rom, an alien, an animal of another species, one to be considered of scarcely more value than a horse. But with his great gift for languages and his many useful knacks he soon won them over. Graciela came to perceive that Josh had almost the status of an honorary Rom. It was a status that, having won it in the hardest possible way, he took pains not to abuse.

The first knack Josh displayed was one certain to endear him to a Romany man's heart. He proved to be an excellent and accomplished blacksmith, even with the different and unfamiliar Romany tools. The Rom, a nation of horse-lovers and hereditary tinkers, were perfectly ready to value and cherish a man with high skills in these two areas. The work of his strong, nimble hands pleased them immediately; they assigned to him a couple of young boys whose task it was to keep the goatskin bellows pumping and the fire hot and high.

Josh reveled in this. Sitting crosslegged on the ground like a tailor at work, he directed the open front end of his goatskin bellows at the red coals inside an earthernware device which held them—a sort of ceramic stove not unlike the one which, he told Graciela, the Mongol ancestors of the Rom had used to cook soup in. Holding an iron horseshoe in a pair of hand-forged pincers, he plucked it white-hot from the fire and pounded it lustily with a handmade hammer on the curious stone anvil the Rom preferred in their primitive smithy.

"The Rom have been smiths for thousands of years," Josh said, punctuating his words with powerful strokes of his hammer. "Colonel Falligant told me they probably brought the art of working iron into Europe from the Caucasus Mountains a thousand years before the birth of Christ. And when they did they were very likely using a little forge like this one, and an anvil made of hard and polished stone."

Graciela watched him silently. His powerful forearms, bared by the tattered sleeves of the shirt he was wearing, glistened with a light sweat and his dark face, dripping with effort, looked like the polished ebony of a carved bust. His smile was warm and appreciative, with none of the exaggerated pride of the Rom. "You seem to be enjoying yourself," she said.

"Oh, I am," he agreed. He held up the shoe, looking at it this way and that. "For one thing, I'm working my way north." He looked into her eyes now, and there was a great seriousness in his expression. "Every day I'm another how-many miles closer to the Line, where I'm a free man. Where Mr. Beau can come get my papers for me, and where I can return to my wife and child." He turned back to his little forge. "Meantime, I got pleasant work to do, and I suppose I'm about as safe as I could get under the circumstances. The Rom, they're a lot like the Tockos. Maybe it's because they come from the same part of the world, more or less. Anyhow they take care of their own."

"They seem to," she said.

He looked at her again, a little more sharp-eyed this time. "You don't sound completely convinced," he said. "Is there something wrong?"

"No," she said. Then she thought about this for a moment. "Josh, I'm not sure what I think. The trouble is, these folks—Tshaya, Butsulo—they seem to have some sort of plans for me. And I don't understand. I don't know what they want of me. I mean, I'm going north

130

too, just like you. What I want is about the same thing you want, that is, without the family. I don't have any family. But. . . ." She let the sentence trail off, looking at him.

"Oh," Josh said. "Well, I don't know everything about these folks. I just got to the point last week or so where I could overhear a conversation and have any confidence that I was understanding what was going on. But I have heard this and that."

"Please tell me."

"Look here. I let this shoe get cold on me. Well, time enough. The horse isn't going anywhere." He grinned and put the horseshoe down. "You want to know what they want of you? Well, ma'am, it appears they think a lot of you. More than you know. Maybe more than they admit even to themselves. All of 'em but Pesha, maybe, and she understands most everything."

"Yes, I love her very much," said Graciela, "but what is it they want?"

He stood up, flexing his knees. "Body gets stiff sitting down there like that," he said. "Look, ma'am," he went on. "How does Tshaya treat you?"

"Pretty well," Graciela said. "Why? I mean, she gets mad at me now and then. Gets short with me. But that's just because I make mistakes sometimes."

"May be more than that," Josh said. "You see, ma'am, Tshaya is in line to become the *phuri dai* when Pesha dies. But Pesha doesn't want that to happen. She says Tshaya doesn't have the necessary . . . well, 'power' isn't the right word, but. . . ."

"I think I know what you're talking about," she said. "Please go on."

"All right. Pesha says that the *phuri dai* of this *kumpania* has to be a person with—well, with occult powers, but they must be used right. What they'd call a *mamaloi* down in New Orleans, maybe. The Old Woman of the tribe has to be—ought to be—somebody like Marie Laveau. You ever heard of Marie Laveau?"

"No. Who was she?"

"A magic woman. Mystic woman. She was a free black like her husband Jacques Paris. She was the *mamaloi* of the voudous. She threw strange, wild *gris-gris* parties down near Lake Pontchartrain. All the white ladies used to come to her to get a charm to make them have a child, or not have a child. She never used her powers for evil, though."

"Goodness," Graciela said. "And Pesha can do that?"

"No, Shandor told me Pesha knows there is only one source of power and that it can be used for good or evil. He said that all Pesha's life she has tried to keep the Rom using their powers for white magic, not black magic, although Butsulo won't listen to her."

"Yes, it is the difference between them that's important, Pesha says."

"White magic," Josh said, "is when we pray for something we feel is good for us or someone else, but black magic is only used to bring bad things to others."

"Now I understand more each day what Pesha has been trying to explain to me," said Graciela. "She warned me of the power and said if I used it to help others it would bring me luck, but if I used it wrongly, the bad fate I wished for others would bounce back on me. She said black magic is more dangerous for the sender than the receiver. She said Rom don't use black magic but she knows of the kind that they use in Haiti, and some bad cults in England, too."

Josh said frankly, "Pesha's been a very powerful woman in her day. *I* sure wish I had all her ancient wisdom. Let me tell you, you're lucky she is teaching you. Anyhow, she thinks that Tshaya hasn't learned to be powerful or wise enough, that she would be bad for the tribe because she and Butsulo aren't afraid of black magic."

"But I still don't understand."

"Don't you?" he said. "The person around here that's got the right power is you."

"Me?" The thought was so radical that she could think of nothing to say for a moment. "But . . ."

"I'm just telling you what I've overheard. So you represent some real competition for Tshaya. Has she been doing anything about your horoscope? Your birth chart?"

"Tshaya asked me about my birthday today. That was the first time, I think. Pesha asked a long time ago. Soon after I came with the wagons."

"Well, you can bet she'll soon find out whatever it is

that Pesha learned when she did your chart for you. The Rom don't draw charts, you know. But they figure out your stars, and they have a sixth sense for the kind of conclusions to draw."

"You mean. . . ?"

"I mean that you, and not Tshaya, are being trained to become the next *phuri dai* of the tribe. And Tshaya doesn't like it. Not one bit. Your stars are right, and hers aren't. You've got the Mystic Cross in your palm too, and she doesn't."

"Josh, do you believe in all this?"

"While I'm here among the Rom I do. It all seems to fit their way of life. Whether or not I'd believe it once I found myself settled up in Rock Island or Moline or Chicago, that's another matter. Down in New Orleans I watched it work with Marie Laveau, and *gris-gris,* and the *zombi* cult. Down there it worked, ma'am. It might not work away from its home earth, you know."

"But . . . I thought a *phuri dai* had to be old."

"No, she doesn't. What she has to be is the real leader of the tribe. And that means, among other things, the woman of the *man* who leads the tribe." He looked her hard in the eye.

"You mean . . . Tshaya thinks that I . . . that I'm going to . . . with Butsulo?"

"No," he said. "At least I don't think so. But Shandor. . . ."

She sat on a log, speechless, looking him in the eye. He wasn't funning with her at all. "Shandor?" she said. "What does Shandor have to do with it?"

"You forget who he is. Butsulo's not even in the main line of succession. Shandor is his nephew, but Shandor is Pesha's grandson, and the son of the old leader. No matter that he and his father quarreled, and Butsulo took over with the father's blessing. It's still not the normal line of succession. Shandor is the natural leader of the tribe. And while he's alive Butsulo doesn't have a real patent on the title."

"But that explains why Butsulo is so mean to Shandor. And why Tshaya keeps steering *me* away from him. As if I. . . ."

"You're blushing. Are you sure it's all that ridiculous an idea to you?"

Graciela, flustered, found she couldn't look Josh in the eye just now. "Josh," she said, searching wildly for a way out, "I—the other night, before Shandor left, Butsulo said something about a nail. What did he mean? What was it that he was saying?"

Josh bit his lip. "Oh, yes. Now that one—I have to admit it, when I heard about that one it kind of shook me up. I try to think of myself as not being too superstitious, but that story really bothered me some. It's kind of a combination of a Bible story and a *gris-gris* story. It's the kind of thing that gives you bad dreams. Are you sure you want to hear it?"

Graciela wasn't sure at all; but she knew that if she listened to it, Josh would probably forget his inquiry about her feelings for Shandor. She bit her lip and stared into the guttering flames inside Josh's tiny ceramic forge. "Please tell me," she said.

Chapter 19

"All right." Josh put down the hammer in his hand and sat down on a log opposite her. "You may know that some Rom claim that they're descended from Cain, the son of Adam who killed his brother. That's where they think the curse comes from, originally, the curse that lies on the Rom forever, and comes back to haunt them every so often through the Nail."

"Curse?" she asked.

Josh continued, "When Cain was cast out of the land east of the Garden of Eden, where his parents, the first man and woman, had settled after the Fall, God put a curse on him: 'When thou tillest the ground, it shall not henceforth yield unto thee her strength; a fugitive and a vagabond shalt thou be in the earth.'" He held up one black hand. "You hear: a fugitive and a vagabond. But then Cain said, 'This is more than I can bear; everyone I meet will kill me.' So God put a mark on him and said that the curse would descend sevenfold upon whoever killed Cain. And Cain went out and found a woman and married and built a city and named it after his son Enoch."

"But aren't we all descended from him then?"

"The story goes that Adam and Eve had another son named Seth. And we're all descended from Seth, whose line escaped the flood in Noah's Ark. But Cain's line . . . well, five generations down from Cain was a man named Lamech, who took two wives and had sons by both of them. By the first wife, Adah, he had twin sons named Jabal and Jubal, and Jabal was the father of those who dwell in tents, and of those who have cattle. And Jubal was the father of those who handle the harp

135

and organ. But Lamech, as I say, took a second wife, and she bore a son called Tubal-Cain, 'an instructor of every artificer in brass and iron.' " He smiled down at his little forge. "And there we are. Maybe the sons of Tubal-Cain are our friends the Rom. And I must say that they've taught me a lot since I've been with them."

"Yes," Graciela said. "Me too. But the Nail?"

"I'm coming to that," he said. "Now according to legend, everyone but the family of Noah died in the flood. Even Methuselah, the oldest man in the world, died in the flood at the age of nine hundred and sixty-nine. That was Noah's grandfather. But the legends say the Rom escaped the flood. They disagree as to how. There are several stories. But the years passed, and the Rom, fugitives and vagabonds, made a living as wandering tinkers, barred by the curse from settling, from tilling land, or from growing their own food."

He paused, looking at her with a strange light in his eye. "And then came into the world a man named Yeshua ben Meriem, whom the world later called Jesus. And he offended the Emperor of all the Romans. He was tried and sentenced to be crucified. The Roman soldiers were given money to go down into the city to buy nails, but they stopped at a tavern along the way, and when dusk approached it was getting too late to buy nails, and besides, they'd drunk up most of the money they had to buy nails with, for crucifying Yeshua ben Meriem who was to die the following morning."

Graciela, wide-eyed, crossed herself. When she looked back at Josh there was a darker, stranger gleam in his eye and his voice took on an odd and ominous richness. "Yes?" she said. "And then?"

"And then," Josh said, "they panicked. They went to a blacksmith and they asked him to make them some nails to pierce the flesh of Yeshua ben Meriem. But he was a pious old Jew and he said, 'He is a man of my people, and I will make no nails to crucify him with.' And they flew into a rage, and they killed him.

"The soldiers were beginning to get desperate now. It was sundown, and they still hadn't found someone to forge the nails, and Yeshua ben Meriem was to be crucified at dawn, and they'd drunk up all the money they had except forty copper pieces. So when they learned they'd just killed the last remaining smith in Jerusalem they rushed outside the city gates. And there they found a Gypsy, a man who'd just pitched his tent and set up his forge outside the city because Gypsies weren't allowed to practice a tinker's trade inside the city.

"And the Gypsy pocketed the money and said 'Sure, I'll make your nails for you,' not knowing what they wanted them for. He made the first nail, and the soldiers put it in their bag. And then he made the second nail, and they put it in their bag. And the same with the third nail. But when he began to make the fourth nail, he suddenly heard voices, the voices of men the soldiers had killed. The voices said, 'Please don't make the nails to crucify Yeshua ben Meriem. He is an innocent man.' So the Gypsy would not give them the fourth nail.

"Now it was night. The soldiers heard the voices, and they ran away, taking the three nails with them. The Gypsy finished making the nail, and when he was done he took it out of the fire and waited for it to grow cold, so he could use it for his next customer, perhaps.

"But the nail refused to grow cold. He poured water on it, and the water sizzled away. The nail began to glow, until you could see from its light as if it were daylight. He brought water from a nearby well until the well was dry, but no amount of water would cool the nail. Frightened, the Gypsy struck camp and went far out into the desert. But when he made camp he looked around again and saw a light. There in the sand before him was a glowing nail, white-hot—the same nail he'd left behind miles back, before the gates of Jerusalem.

"The next day, he set up camp at an Arab town, and a man came to ask him to patch up the iron wheel of his wagon. In the wheel, suddenly, a nail began to glow— the Nail. The Gypsy ran away again, and fled to a far country. The next place he stopped, a man came to him and asked him to repair a sword. When the Gypsy took up the sword he saw the Nail glowing in its hilt—"

"My dear God," Graciela said. Once again she crossed herself. "And this Nail—is it. . . ?"

"Some fear this is the Nail of the Curse. Ever after, the Gypsies find the Nail turning up in their camps from time to time. When it does it means the Curse is with them again, and they must move—ever onward, through strange lands, over mountains and rivers, always seeking a place where they will be safe from the Nail. But they will never be safe, because on that terrible day back in Jerusalem the other three nails the Gypsy had made were used to crucify Yeshua ben Meriem, with one nail for each hand and his feet crossed to take the only remaining nail. This is the Curse. And this is why the Gypsies wander, forever seeking a place where the terrible Nail will no longer haunt them.

"But whenever things begin to go wrong in a Rom encampment, whenever there is a clash of wills or whenever a Rom of the tribe has done something to bring shame on his people, a great disquiet comes over the members of the tribe, and the black wind blows, the hot wind that comes from the driest deserts and follows the Rom across the world, and then it is just a matter of time before the Nail appears. It may appear in a wheel of a Gypsy wagon, or it may appear in a piece of work some *gajo* brings for a Gypsy tinker to repair. But the Nail will come, and when it comes it will bring sorrow and death."

The story haunted Graciela for days. Worse, it haunted her nights, and several times in her dreams she saw the dread Nail itself, and awoke moaning with fear to find a haggard, displeased Tshaya standing over her, holding a shawl over her unbound hair, her eyes full of fear and—what? Hatred?

As her relations with Tshaya deteriorated, Graciela found she could speak to Pesha directly, and understand all of what the old woman said. As the language barrier between them vanished, she suddenly began, without warning, the next stage of her apprenticeship.

And apprenticeship it was. There was now no longer the smallest doubt in her mind about this. At no time did Pesha state her aims directly; but the very tone of her speech when she talked with Graciela in the evenings changed and became the tone not of a grandmother of the tribe speaking to an apprentice Rom but of a *phuri dai*, rich in both years and wisdom, speaking the words of truth and power to her successor.

Curiously, a new strength and power seemed to flow into the old woman as she taught Graciela the secrets of her wisdom—palmistry, astrology, magic, a powerful Rom form of *gris-gris* (as Josh insisted on calling it). The look of ancient and fragile age began to fall away from her. She asked Graciela to ride in her wagon as the Rom village moved steadily northward, and Graciela's apprenticeship began in earnest, with day-long recitations of the tribe's ancient secrets that flowed easily from the aged woman to the girl whom she had by now adopted in all but name.

Graciela, her mind all but overloaded by all this new wisdom, protested from time to time that she would never be able to remember all that Pesha taught her; but Pesha patted the girl's hand with her bony old fingers and said, "Do not fear. What you have heard but once will remain with you the rest of your days. Come now, child; we will work again on the Great Game."

The Great Game was divination, by means of a curious deck of cards Pesha called the Tarot. There were, she said, several different versions of the deck. Formerly the Rom had used the Egyptian deck, but in the course of their wanderings in Europe they had come to adopt the Tarot of Marseilles. Nevertheless, they used a special method called the *Etteilla,* which belonged to the Rom alone.

Sixty-six cards were set out. In the center of an imaginary triangle the cards were deployed one at a time. The triangle pointed downward, and the upper side represented the present. The right side stood for the past and the left side for the future. The first card in a deck shuffled by the questioner (or the eighth card, if the questioner was a woman) went in the center. Eleven cards were then placed on two sides of the triangle, and three more sets of eleven were arranged in a circle around the triangle. After that, all the cards were reshuffled and then twelve cards were arranged in a circle. These were drawn as sections of the zodiac, one at a time, and commented upon by the diviner. "The cards talk," Pesha said.

Graciela grew very fond of Pesha. From time to time, looking at the old woman, she fancied she could see under the wrinkles of age the vital young person she must once have been. The light had not gone from the old woman's eye, and as the two talked day after day Gra-

139

ciela could see the strength flowing from herself, bit by bit, into Pesha. Yet for some reason the flow did not impoverish her, but renewed her, as if the more she gave, the more she had to give away. She was beginning to understand the law of love that Pesha had explained so many times: the more you give the more you have to give away, the more you give the more you receive.

It was curious. Shandor had been gone for nearly two months, and she had almost forgotten him. But there came a night when Graciela, feeling a sudden stirring in her as Pesha paused in her recitation, suddenly let her hand fly to her mouth. "Pesha," she said. "I had the strangest feeling."

"Yes, my daughter?" the old woman said, leaning forward, aware and attentive.

"Shandor," she said. "Your grandson. He's near. I can feel it. Outside, in the dark."

"Yes," Pesha said. "I can feel it too. Flesh of my flesh, blood of my blood. I would have known myself, but you? You are not of Shandor's blood. Do you know what this means, my child? It means you have developed the Gift! It means that the power is going over from me to you, even as the youth flows from you into me." Her old face held a strange look, almost expressionless, that managed to convey even more pleasure than a smile would have done as Graciela kissed her. "Yes, he is out there. And you knew."

Graciela, excited and confused, stood. She opened the rear door of Pesha's wagon and stared out into the blackness, past the warm circle of the campfire into the moonless dark. If this were true, if the powers of the *phuri dai* were in fact flowing into her. . . .

A hollow, echoing shout from the darkness broke into her reverie. "*Na daran Romale wi ame sam Rom sthatshe*," a powerful young baritone—a familiar one—said. "Do not fear, you Gypsy men, for we too are Gypsies."

An answering call came from the camp: Butsulo's voice. "*Devlesa avilan?*" ("Who has brought you?")

The voice called back, "*Devlesa araklam tume.*" ("It is through God that we have found you.")

Graciela, recognizing the voice, stepped down onto the rear step of the wagon, her heart pounding fast despite herself. As she did three horsemen moved out of the deep shadows and pulled up just outside the ring of wagons. The first man dismounted and stepped down. Shandor . . . !

She didn't recognize him for a moment; he had grown a thick, dark mustache, like a Tocko's, and his dark hair had grown long and unruly over his ears. His arrogance had grown with it, and this could immediately be seen in his proud and straight-backed stride as he walked briskly through the circle of wagons toward the fire.

Graciela's hand went to her heart. Her mouth hung open. There was such a mixture of feelings in her that she could not have described them to save her life.

Chapter 20

Pesha called her back just then, and she lost her chance to see what Butsulo would do when Shandor returned to the camp after an absence that had spanned most of the summer. Pesha set her back to work immediately, learning the grammar and syntax of divination, and for well over an hour the old woman, spurred on by a fresh burst of energy, drove her onward. When Graciela complained, Pesha scowled at her: "There is so much to learn. So little time to learn it. I am afraid my time will come and catch us unaware."

Graciela bent again to her tasks, memorizing the meanings of the things Pesha told her: fate line, life line, health line, Ring of Solomon, Girdle of Venus, heart line, head line, texture of the skin. Then she heard Pesha's introduction to astrology: "And now we will leave the study of the hand and talk of the study of time. Yes, the importance of time, that is what astrology is. The study of time, astrology, is accepted by those who have studied it but disbelieved by others who know nothing about it. And those who haven't any knowledge of it are the first to attempt to deny it."

In the middle of all of it Graciela stopped. "Pesha," she said. "I must know. You are preparing me for something. What is it? I am scarcely a Rom at all, but you are teaching me things that none of the other women in the camp know. Secrets of divination, secrets of midwifery, secrets of—"

She stopped there, embarrassed. But Pesha looked hard at her and, softening, said, "Child, you know what I am training you for. Why ask a question when you know the answer?"

"But, Pesha, there is Tshaya."

"Tshaya does not have the Gift. She does not have the power or the wisdom or the interest. You do, my child. I knew it the moment I saw your hand. In Tshaya's hand, although she is older than you, all is limitations, here, there she gives herself limitations. In your hand, no limits anywhere. No fences, no boundaries. You let yourself go as far as you like in any direction." Her eye grew crafty; her voice lowered. "This is important. I have a responsibility to the tribe. If it is ruled by Butsulo, the weakest of all my sons—he will not allow me to teach him—if it tries to derive its power from a weak mind like Tshaya—it will die. One day the Nail will appear, and it will not go away. It will follow the tribe wherever it goes, and will haunt Butsulo or his successor. It will not matter how often the tribe moves, ill fortune will dog its tracks. It will be weak in all the places where it must be strong. It will die." She sighed a long, sorrowful sigh. "It will die," she repeated. "It will die. And all my hopes and dreams with it."

"But Butsulo *is* the chief, the leader of the tribe. And Tshaya will become the *phuri dai* when you—I mean—"

Flustered at her *faux pas*, she stopped again, her stricken eyes seeking Pesha's anxiously. "Grandmother, I'm sorry, I. . . ."

To her surprise Pesha did not grow angry. Instead a smile began to play suddenly over her wrinkled, beautiful old face, and love flowed into her warm brown eyes. "Ah," she said. "You call me grandmother. That is good. It is the proper way to speak to me. That is what I am to you, is it not? And a good thing, too." Her hand sought Graciela's face and caressed it softly. "Grandmother. Ah, yes. You will be a granddaughter to me. You will present me with fine children, which is a good thing for an old woman to have about her when she dies. You are a good child."

For a second or so the eyes went opaque and the face seemed far, far away, in a lost world from the far past. Then the light came back into them and the old face brightened. Graciela perceived that Pesha was looking past her, toward the door. She wheeled.

Shandor stood in the doorway. He seemed larger, taller, with broader shoulders. His unshorn head sat regally atop a strong neck. He seemed to fill the entire doorway, standing with hands on hips, looking at the two of them. His eyes rested on Graciela for a moment, looking her up and down, from the black hair she'd let grow to shoulder-length, down to her bare feet, peeking out from below the long colorful gown she wore. His gaze lingered longest on the low-cut blouse, and Graciela was suddenly conscious of the fact that only a thin layer of cloth kept her from being completely naked before him. The thought brought a hot surge of a feeling she could not define; her hand went to her bosom and felt her heart pounding there as her breath quickened.

"Greetings to my grandmother Pesha," he said, bowing slightly. He nodded a second time to Graciela, and the look he gave her, for no more than the blink of the eye, was—the look; the look every Gypsy man cultivated, the look that could calm a bucking horse, that could disarm an opponent, that could capture the heart of any woman. For that brief moment Graciela saw for the first time precisely what this phenomenon was, and she stood transfixed, her heart scarcely daring to beat. She could not tear her eyes away from him.

Then his eyes moved to his grandmother. Graciela looked at Pesha too, and saw the immense warmth she always showed for her young grandson. "Shandor," she said. "Come sit beside me, my heart." The fleshless old hands reached out for him, and suddenly Graciela might just as well not have been in the room.

Shaken by that moment of recognition, she suddenly found she needed fresh air. She inclined her head respectfully at Pesha and at Shandor's powerful back, but the two were no longer aware of her. With a sigh of relief, she slipped out into the night.

The wagons were drawn up under a grove of tall pines, and the soft needles were pleasant underfoot. There was a delicate flavor, a light scent in the air under the trees this far away from the fire and upwind of it. Dark as it was, it was a lovely evening, and she had no reason to regret leaving her shawl inside the wagon. She threw her shoulders back and breathed in the cool and balmy evening air, feeling as she did the rasp of the rough cloth against her suddenly aroused nipples.

Shandor. He didn't even seem to be the same person. Suddenly she knew why. It was his stance. Before, his posture had been that of a boy, a strong and full-grown one, but a boy. Now he walked like a man, erect and powerful and very conscious of his manhood. The set of his shoulders made you aware of the great strength in his broad chest and knotted arms. But more than this, it was the way he carried his head high, arrogantly, on that strong neck, as he strode forward into the world, unafraid, unyielding, bowing his head to no man, yet not too proud to bow to a woman.

The thought hit her suddenly. He walked like a king. Like a king! Like a chief, a leader. Like the leader he was born to be, back before he had quarreled with his father.

Well, no matter. A quarrel could have been patched up along the way—except that Shandor's father, the old leader of the tribe, had died before father and son could be reconciled. Shandor had been away when his father died, and Butsulo had been pressed to succeed his brother, despite the wishes of his mother, the *phuri dai* of the tribe. Shandor had returned to find his uncle running the tribe's affairs.

But now she saw it all clearly for the first time, and it was apparent that Butsulo was the lesser man. And he knew it, and hated and feared his nephew.

Did Butsulo walk like a leader? Was his carriage that of one you could follow? No, the very thought of Shandor in his place was enough to reduce Butsulo to nothing in her eyes. Now that she thought of it, she wondered very much what Butsulo was thinking of right now, as Shandor's two friends shared his fire and his bread.

A noise to her right, near the fire, caught her attention. She turned and saw Butsulo speaking to the two. Her curiosity piqued, she slipped forward, keeping out of the light and moving silently on tiptoe.

Standing before the wagons, in the half-light, Butsulo was confronting the two friends Shandor had brought with him. His voice was harsh and resentful, not regal and commanding, as a leader's should be.

"You are not welcome," he was saying. "No member

145

of the tribe of Pulika is welcome among us while Pulika refuses to discuss our differences under the law of the Rom. You must go."

The young man nearest Graciela must have caught the note of uncertainty in Butsulo's voice, for he gave no ground and his eyes flashed defiantly. "We are with Shandor. If he tells us to leave we will leave, and gladly."

"You will leave when I say so," Butsulo said, in the voice of a man who might back up his words with action—and then again who might not. Even without seeing his eyes, Graciela could visualize the look on his face. It would be one not of menace but of resentment. "And I say that Shandor. . . ."

His words were interrupted by a sudden cry from the circle of wagons. "Butsulo!" Shandor's voice, raised in distress, carried easily through the trees. "Come quickly! Pesha. . . ."

To his credit Butsulo wheeled, and on his face Graciela could see a sudden and genuine concern. He did, indeed, love and respect his mother. Without hesitation he rushed forward to the wagon. Graciela, holding her heavy skirts up above her ankles, ran after him, not knowing why she was running, but as they neared the wagon and could see the look on Shandor's stricken face, she knew and understood.

"Pesha," he said. "She—she has passed on. Her heart—"

Now Graciela, in her own shock, could see the two faces together, uncle and nephew. Where Shandor's face bore an expression of shocked concern, Butsulo's was a strange mixture of emotions. There was sorrow there, but there was also rage, and a fierce expression of triumph. With his mother dead, Butsulo now ruled the tribe.

Butsulo went inside the wagon and Graciela could hear his weeping from the outside. She stood beside Shandor, and something made her suddenly reach out to him and touch his arm. It was like a shock from static electricity. She was transfixed, and looked up into his suddenly aware eyes. "Shandor," she said. "I'm sorry. I thought she was getting better. I loved her very much."

His dark reddened eyes rested on her again, and there

was in them a new look: thoughtful, even tender. "Yes. She told me. She told me you had become her grand-daughter, her own flesh and blood." He sighed, long and hard. "Do you know the Romany phrase *Te aves yer-time mandar, te yertil tut o Del?*"

Graciela pondered it. "I can make out most of it. Something about *I forgive you, and—and may God for-give you as well.*" She realized with a shock that they were speaking English. She hadn't spoken English in the Rom encampment for over a month now.

"Yes," he said. "It is the phrase one says when dying. Pesha said it to me, after the attack began. I said it to her. We were reconciled. Then the second attack hit her, only moments after the first, and in a moment she was gone." His eyes tear-filled, stared unseeing past her into the darkness. "I am so glad I got the chance to speak to her before—before she went away."

"Shandor," Graciela said. She took his hand; it lay between her two palms, unfeeling. "Your grandmother never stopped loving you for a moment; she was very proud of you."

His hand, lying inert there, suddenly grew live again in her two hands. He gripped her hand tightly. His eyes burned into hers. "You mean this?" he said. "This is true? But Butsulo led me to believe. . . ."

His eyes suddenly burned with rage and hurt. His strong jaw set and his upper lip, covered now with that fierce black mustache, curled back in a quick and angry sneer. "Butsulo," he said. "Always Butsulo."

Chapter 21

It was her first experience of death among the Rom, and the first funeral she had ever attended. She would ordinarily have been drawn into the traditional women's duties of washing the body and preparing it for burial, but now she found that Tshaya contemptuously excluded her from this. As Tshaya passed her Graciela took note of a new attitude in the Gypsy leader's wife: one of arrogance and triumph. Her glance dismissed Graciela as one unworthy of concern, as an outsider, an outcast.

Riders went forth to put out the word, leaving signs on every road nearby to tell other bands of the Wanderers that a great and mighty person among the Rom had passed on to another life in the next dimension. By the second day of Pesha's wake two additional wagon trains of Rom had come to Butsulo's encampment, who had elected to stop and share the bereavement for Butsulo's great mother.

In the camp itself a big canvas roof had been erected on the top of Pesha's wagon, extending like a canopy over the space in which she lay in state. Under the canopy Pesha's aged face displayed an expression of peaceful repose. She had been dressed by the women in her finest dress and in all the golden ornaments she had collected in a long lifetime. Gold glittered on her wrists and ankles, on her fingers and on her bosom, where circles of golden coins hung from a golden chain. She looked as though she had lightly fallen asleep, and would wake at any moment.

Around her, however, the living acted out a strange and almost disquieting ritual. Women talked to their

God, singing, praying and sometimes even howling like banshees. Men beside them cursed loudly at their misfortune of having to give up their beloved Pesha, at the diabolic conspiracy of life which had deprived them of her. Yet as the first day wore on into the second, Graciela could feel the gradual attenuation of the people's feelings.

The Rom let go of their dead by inches, lamenting and cursing the unfairness of fate; but in the process they allowed themselves a healthy expression of their feelings; grief was recognized and solaced without dragging on for too long. On the fourth day of the fast the body would be buried and a great feast, the *Pomana*, would be held in the camp. After that the feast would be repeated at intervals of nine days, six weeks, six months, and one year. After one year no one would be allowed to mourn. Only in this way could the dead be freed to rest. At the end of the period of mourning the tribe would release her forever: "*Putrav lesko drom angle leste te na inkrav les mai but palpale mura brigasa.*" ("I open her way in the new life once again, and release her from the fetters of my sorrow.") *How wise! If only the* gaje *looked at life and death this way,* Graciela thought to herself.

During the wake all enmities were postponed or forgotten in the general sorrow over Pesha's passing. None of the men washed or shaved; instead, they drank wine steadily. None of the adults slept. None of Pesha's immediate family took nourishment. No one prepared food; the small children, howling with hunger, were solaced with dry bread and cold leftovers.

Dejection lay over the camp like a dark cloud for a second day, then a third. Then the Rom buried Pesha amid great honors in a field, under a spreading oak. Now the women began their screeching and howling again, like the spirits of the undead. They tore their hair, ripped their clothes, sobbed uncontrollably. Tshaya even tried to throw herself into the open grave with Pesha—but Graciela caught her expression as the men restrained her, and did not believe her theatrics for so much as a moment.

Finally, after the Rom had tossed gold pieces and other coins into the pit on the improvised coffin, they sat quietly around the grave. Graciela asked Shandor if she might read what Pesha had requested when this inevitable day arrived. Pesha had no fear of death, and Graciela loved her all the more as she read Pesha's last sharing of her wisdom, from the *Bhagavad Gita*:

> *Never the Spirit was born;*
> *The Spirit shall cease to be never;*
> *Never was time it was not;*
> *End and beginning are dreams!*
>
> *Birthless, and deathless, and changeless,*
> *Remaineth the Spirit for ever;*
> *Death hath not touched it at all,*
> *Dead though the house of it seems!*

After the burial, the Gypsies walked back to the wagons and to the sumptuous feast which was already simmering on the open fires awaiting their return. During the feast Graciela watched, worriedly, for signs of further strife between Butsulo and Shandor; but the two avoided each other studiously, conscious of the great ill that would fall upon the encampment if violence were to break out while the festival of Pesha's death was still in progress.

As the old woman's closest living relatives, however, Butsulo and Shandor were thrown together with Tshaya in the ritual of destroying all of Pesha's belongings. First the canopy was burned, then the wagon in which she had traveled so many miles. Her cups, plates, glasses were destroyed. Her bed and pillow were burned. This was to keep her from being earthbound. In the end nothing remained of her but memory. Shandor and Butsulo performed the melancholy tasks silently, not looking at each other. Butsulo seemed to be devoured by a secret sore.

At the end of the day's feasting the other Gypsies, who had come to share the tribe's sorrow, slowly drifted away, and the field where Butsulo's encampment had taken place was left a desolate shambles. Butsulo's own people made ready to strike camp and move on, away from the place of bereavement. Only on the road, the endless road down which the lives of the Rom would wind forever, would the feelings of bereavement lift and joy once again begin to flow into the tribe which had lost its *phuri dai*, its wise friend, its matriarch, its mother.

Shandor said to Graciela, "We press on forgetting what is behind and reaching out for that which lies ahead. The world throbs with life, but after staying put for a while it takes me about ten days in a caravan to begin feeling its rhythm again."

Graciela was carrying water from the stream to the horses when she happened upon Butsulo, standing before the last wagon, confronting the two young men of Pulika's tribe whom Shandor had brought along with him when he returned after his summer's absence. As she drew nearer she could hear their voices raised in mutually resentful anger.

" . . . while my mother's funeral was going on I could not refuse you the honor of paying her your respects. This is the law of the Rom. But now the *pomana* is over, and with it my patience has come to an end. You may not share our bread any longer. You may not travel with my tribe."

"But Shandor said—" one of them began. Graciela looked at him. He was a lad not quite grown, a boy with dark hair and a very dark face, darker than a mulatto's. He had the size and the evident strength of a full-grown man, but not the controlled force. His answer had a tentative ring to it.

"No matter what Shandor said. He must go too. He is not welcome among us." Butsulo's voice began to raise. He was evidently beginning, little by little, to work himself up into a rage. "Take your horses. Take all your belongings, we need nothing of yours here." Pesha was right, Butsulo's mind was sick, Graciela thought as she stood transfixed, watching. At that moment Josh wandered into Butsulo's view. "You!" Butsulo said. "Black man!"

Josh turned and said mildly, "Yes, Butsulo?" Josh, by now, spoke Rom as well as she did, and without an accent, where she would always have the smallest trace of a *gajo* tongue.

"You can leave!" Butsulo said. "We do not want you

151

here! Blacks are bad fortune in a Rom camp. Bad fortune," he lied, "which brings death and despair. Pack up your belongings. I want you away from my camp by nightfall."

"But, Butsulo," Josh began with a half-smile, not believing what he was hearing. "You yourself told me—"

"Quiet!" Butsulo ordered. "Away! All of you—before darkness falls. Or else—"

"Or else what?" one of the strangers said. "Will you call a *kriss* and discipline us? Will you invoke Romany law on us?"

The first boy spoke up now, and anger was beginning to show in his dark young eyes. "Is this the way a Rom— a leader of the Rom—treats a brother Rom, and at a time when the *phuri dai* of the tribe is scarcely cold in her grave?" He sneered and spat at Butsulo's feet. "*I* will leave. I do not know what the rest of you will do, but I will leave. Chains of iron could not keep me here any longer, in the camp of a leader who dishonors himself, who dishonors his mother and the laws of his tribe."

He turned to go; but Butsulo, a black rage already upon him, reached for the coiled horsewhip at his belt and spun it out to its full twelve-foot length. He raised it and would have sailed its deadly tip at the young man's retreating back—and Graciela knew you could kill a man with a Gypsy whip as easily as you could kill him with a gun—if Josh had not reached out and jogged his arm, spoiling his aim.

The young man wheeled, alert and on his guard now. Butsulo's anger did not fall upon him, though, but on Josh. The whip flashed; Josh's hand went to his face and came away covered with red blood. There was a line of red down his brown face, and a look of perplexity with it. His eyes showed hurt and then, slowly, anger. "Butsulo," he said. "I—"

The whip lashed out again. This time Josh dodged it and stepped nimbly aside. "Look," he said. "You made a promise. A Rom promise, which only you yourself can dishonor. You told Colonel Falligant you would shelter me and the girl all the way to the Line where the South ends."

"*Silence!*" Butsulo said. And the whip lashed out again. This time it wound around Josh's neck and the black man, his breath cut off, struggled to free himself. But Butsulo threw the other end of the whip, the loaded handle end, over a tree branch and caught it as it came down again. Then he jumped up and threw his whole weight on it. Josh's slender body, outweighed, rose into the air. His face was turning even darker; his eyes bulged. His brown hands tore at his neck, where the coiled whip end, half-knotted by the ferocity of Butsulo's fierce yank on the other end, was wound tightly around his neck.

Butsulo's feet touched the ground. He held onto the whip handle with one powerful hand. The other hand reached inside his belt and drew out a long, wicked-looking knife. "The first person who approaches me," he said in a dark and menacing voice, "will die."

Graciela stood, transfixed with horror, watching. Now she looked up at Josh's face. The light was dying in his dark eyes. His hands were pawing weakly at his neck, at the coiled leather thong that was strangling him. "Butsulo!" she said. "For God's sake *please*. . . ." And she stepped forward toward him.

The knife flashed. She looked down in disbelief to a thin line of blood flashing down her naked arm. "Butsulo—let him down, let him go!"

The knife flashed again, but this time, warned, she stepped back. Again her eyes went to Josh's stricken face. It was a dead man's. The hands fell by his side. The graceful brown body dangled from the tree at the end of Butsulo's long whiplash.

One of the two Gypsies moved forward. The other circled around to Butsulo's occupied hand. Butsulo suddenly released the handle and let it whip into the air as Josh's body fell to the ground. As the body rolled Butsulo stooped quickly to pick up the whip and yank it free. Josh's head swung to one side at an ugly, unrealistic angle.

Graciela rushed to Josh's side. "*Josh*," she said. Her eyes were full of tears as she rolled him onto his back and looked down at his face. There was no sign of life. She felt his wrist, his face. She rolled one eyelid back; the eye under it did not look at her. It stared sightlessly skyward.

"M-my God," she said. "He's dead. Josh is dead. Butsulo, you've killed him!" She sank down on her knees beside him, looking up at the Gypsy leader through eyes blurred with tears. "Butsulo, don't you understand? He's *dead*. Someone you . . . you promised shelter to. On the honor of the tribe. Don't you realize, you've broken a sacred promise. You've dishonored the whole tribe!"

"*Silence!*" Butsulo cried. He could hear nothing. A wild rage was upon him now, and he could think of nothing but the mood of destruction that dominated him. The whip lashed out and the young man on his left shrank back, his arm cut open to the bone. He readied the whip for another attack, when a new voice rang out.

"*Butsulo!*"

Graciela, rocking back and forth as she held Josh's inert head in her arms against her heart, looked up, her eyes still filled with uncontrollable tears.

Shandor stood at the edge of the clearing, a long coiled whip in his own hand. His feet were planted well apart; his whole body said in a language clearer than any words, *Here I stand, and heaven itself cannot move me from this spot!* His eyes were mad with rage, but it was a controlled and icy rage, quite unlike Butsulo's.

"I heard," he said. "The black man, the smith, you have killed him? After giving a promise on the honor of the tribe?"

"He was ill luck," Butsulo said. "As you have been. You have both brought bad fortune to the camp. Because of the two of you my mother is dead. Because of you—"

"Do you know what your mother said to me before she died?" Shandor said. He let the whip uncoil at his feet. He did nothing with it, just let it lie there. He looked down at its knotted tip. "She said, 'Butsulo has a twisted mind. You must—' "

"You lie!" Butsulo said. He flexed his own whip nervously.

"She said, 'In his hands the tribe will die. In his hands the Curse will return.' And look. The Curse *will* return. You *have* dishonored the tribe. You have killed a man you promised sanctuary. A good and useful man, too, one who trusted you. And you have broken your word to a man to whom the Rom owe much. Because of you the sickness will fall upon us, the plague, the aroused

154

anger of the *gaje*. Unless I cleanse the tribe of its ills by—"

"You? Cleanse the tribe?" Butsulo's voice was both mocking and menacing. "You will be dead yourself in a matter of moments."

"That is in God's hands," Shandor said. "If God chooses to kill me, so be it.. But I will not die at your hands. If you try to kill me it is you who will die." He jiggled the whip in his hand. There was ice in his glare.

"Then come kill me," Butsulo said, and drew back the long whip. But before either of them could strike the first blow, one of Shandor's friends, the one with the injured arm, cried out and pointed to the wagon nearest them. Graciela's eyes followed his.

There was an eerie light coming from one of the wagon's wheels. A thin trail of smoke rose upward from a tiny, smoldering fire. The wheel was held together by hand-forged nails. One of them was glowing. The fire smoldered fitfully around it.

The Gypsy lad said in a hoarse voice, "The Nail. The accursed Nail. . . ."

Chapter 22

For a moment there wasn't a sound to be heard in the little glade. If Graciela had listened hard enough, she might have found that the loudest noise was the beating of her own heart.

Her eyes went to Shandor's face, and she was appalled by what she saw there. The young man registered the greatest shock that she had ever seen on a human face. Shock, yes—and fear too. Tales of Shandor's reckless bravery in the face of adversity had come to her in the weeks before, but she could quite readily accept the look of sheer, unreasoning terror that she now saw in his eyes; his expression was no more than the mirror of her own.

She shot a quick glance at Butsulo, and saw to her horror that the Gypsy chief, while prey to the same primal fears, recovered from them more quickly than she or Shandor did. As Shandor stood, his whip at his side, his eyes still on the smoking wagon wheel, Butsulo, his own fear converted to rage, drew back his weapon and, cocking the braided leather behind his head, let fly.

"No—please!" Graciela screamed, but the warning came too late. The whip flashed; the deadly tip, moving so fast she could scarcely see it, lashed out and coiled itself around Shandor's right hand, the hand that held his own whip. Butsulo's hand, quick as lightning, jerked back strongly; the whip fell from Shandor's numbed and bleeding hand.

Shandor, jarred back to reality, reached down to retrieve the whip; but Butsulo, taking the initiative, lashed out at him again, driving him away from the grounded weapon. Again and again the whip sang out, and again and again Shandor was driven back before the onslaught. As Graciela watched, horror-struck, the whip cut singingly through the air and laid the back of Shandor's shoulder open; red blood stained that beautiful Gypsy skin.

"Please!" Graciela cried out. She looked around, but the Romany lads Shandor had brought into the camp with him, having decided that it was not right for them to join in this fight, had mounted and were watching the contest from the unsaddled backs of a pair of skittish horses. She ran to the younger of the two. "Please! Help him! He'll be killed!"

But the boy, looking once again at the smoking wagon wheel before casting another nervous glance at the two men circling each other at the periphery of the little glade, avoided her eyes—he knew she did not understand. "Come," he said in Romany. "We will go south. Perhaps we can catch the wagons." With that he nudged his mount into action with one booted leg.

In a panic, she looked back at the two men on the other side of the ring of trees. Shandor, ever circling, ever backing away, kept his eyes on Butsulo. As the lash swished out at him he stepped nimbly backward or moved behind a tree trunk, keeping its bulk always between himself and the weapon that sliced through the air at him.

"Shandor!" Graciela cried. "Can I do something?"

"Stay away," he said. "He is every bit as much afraid of you as he is of me. While either of us lives he has no real power here. If he kills me he will also kill you. His own mother told me. She warned me."

"Silence!" Butsulo said. "She told you nothing. You lie!"

But Graciela knew, as if the truth had suddenly appeared to her in some sort of mystic vision, that he had spoken the truth. She knew also that a Gypsy man, armed with such a formidable weapon as the long horsewhip, could indeed kill with it. If she didn't do something quickly. . . .

In a flash she remembered the little pistol Josh had carried with him ever since that terrrible day when he'd saved her from Thiebaud's men. She knew that she had to find it, and use it, or Shandor would be killed.

157

Now, as clearly as anything she'd ever felt in her whole life, she felt the surge of her own half Irish, half Gypsy blood. Suddenly she was filled with an emotion that ran through her as though the genes of her ancestors were seeking justice. She knew herself for what she was, a combination of two persecuted races: the Irish persecuted by the English and the Rom persecuted by everyone. No wonder she was born with tenacity and the ability to fight for her life. She rushed to Josh's inert body, pawing at the dead man's clothing, praying to herself: *let it be there, let it be there. . . .*

Then she happened to look up again. She saw the dark form materialize behind Shandor. And she saw the flash of the knife, the wild look in the woman's eye, and the whiteness of her bared teeth as she lunged forward. "No!" Graciela called out. "Please! Tshaya!"

The knife plunged. Shandor registered its impact with a sudden forward movement; then his face turned toward the woman who had stabbed him, and an expression of incomprehension swept across his face. Then this was replaced by a strange empty look as cold oblivion overcame him. He lay there and did not move.

Butsulo moved forward. "Give me the knife," he said in Romany. Tshaya, her face still flushed, handed the weapon over. Butsulo looked down at his rival, his finger testing the blade.

"Is he dead?" Tshaya said. The hot blood down in her now, she spoke with a quieter voice. She could not force herself to look at him.

"No," Butsulo said. "I see him breathing. But if he lives. . . ." He looked at her significantly.

"Yes," Tshaya said. Her voice carried a strange urgency. "If he lives you will only have to fight him again."

Butsulo reversed the knife in his hand. "Yes," he said slowly. The short word seemed to take a long time coming out. "Yes. . . ."

"No!" Graciela said, standing, the little pepperpot pistol in her hand. "Stand back, both of you. Neither of you is going to kill anybody. If there's any killing to be done around here—"

Butsulo's white teeth gleamed. He turned to face her and the next thing she knew the knife, reversed again in his hand, had flashed in the air beside his head and spun expertly at her. She ducked; it spun harmlessly over her head.

Something in her seemed to take over, to gain control of her body and its responses. The pistol in her hand turned his way and seemed to fire almost of itself. Butsulo cried out in pain. She saw the red hole in his forearm where her bullet had hit him. Tshaya shrank back against a spreading oak, her eyes wide.

"Tshaya," Graciela said in a voice clearly not her own. "Get me a wagon still under hitch. Hurry. If I can count the number of my fingers and toes five times before you have brought me a wagon I will shoot Butsulo again. And this time I will not stop at shooting him in the arm." It was a bravado performance, and she wondered where she was getting the sheer brass required. She'd never even held a pistol before, much less fired one. She had little or no hope of duplicating the unbelievable luck she'd displayed in hitting Butsulo on her first try. But something, once again, took over inside her and brazened it all out. "Quick!" she said. "I will shoot off his hand next, or put out an eye. Do you want this worthless man of yours maimed? Mutilated?"

It was as if the voice and the words were not her own. But they worked. Tshaya, her eyes as full of fear now as Graciela's had been when the fight had begun, moved through the trees to where the first wagon stood, four draft horses still in the traces. Butsulo, holding his arm and already weak from a considerable loss of blood, leaned back against the great bulging bole of the big live oak, his eyes on her, expressionless.

The problem was getting Shandor into the back of the wagon. Butsulo was near fainting when the wagon pulled up in the two-rut road and Tshaya stepped down from its high seat. Graciela, the gun still pointed at Butsulo's broad chest, ordered Nanosh and Balo, Liza's boyfriend, to lift Shandor gently up into the back of the gaily painted wagon. The other members of the tribe stood back, watching, their eyes wide, as Nanosh barred the door of the wagon and stepped down, looking at her with a combination of wonder and wounded pride.

"Thank you," Graciela said. "Now Butsulo will accompany me, and drive the wagon. I will sit behind him and watch what he does. If he does as I say I will let him leave the wagon where the dirt road meets the macadam road. There you will find him when I am done with him—if he has given me no trouble. But if he crosses me—he dies. If anyone tries to hinder me—he dies. And mark me: I was taught the use of this gun by my father. I can kill a squirrel at fifty paces." The lie came as easily to her as breathing. She could hardly believe the words she was hearing herself say. "Now everyone stand back. Butsulo: up on the high seat, before me."

It took him three tries before he managed to climb up onto the driver's seat. When he took his seat and held the reins in his good hand his face was drawn and weak. Looking about her on all sides, Graciela climbed onto the big seat and slipped easily into the half-seat behind him. "Butsulo," she said. "Let us go."

At the main road, as good as her word, she let him climb wearily down. Then, taking the reins herself, she faced him, the gun still in one hand. "Butsulo," she said. "The tribe is dead. You know that, don't you?"

He looked up at her. He was very unsteady on his feet by now. The blood seeping down his inert arm was dark and thick. His eyes remained on her but he did not speak.

"I'll take your silence as an answer," she said. "You know what's happened, don't you? Your mother did not leave the tribe to you. She left it to Shandor and to me. You know that, I'm sure. Otherwise you would not have been so afraid of us. She trained me to be the *phuri dai* and told Shandor, just before she died, that he was to take over the tribe. But you saw the omen just as I did. I don't pretend to know as much about this as Pesha did, but I do know when I have been spoken to, and decisively."

He watched her miserably, reeling slightly on his feet. He did not speak, but his eyes spoke more than his words could have done.

"The Nail," she said. "It means it all came too late, doesn't it?" She let the anger and contempt come into her voice for the first time. "It means that the tribe is accursed, that even Shandor could not save it. It means

160

that the tribe has fallen into unworthy hands, and is dishonored. Butsulo, it is a good thing that we are leaving. This means that we will not share the curse. It means that the curse is all yours, and it is you who will have to deal with it." Her voice took on an icy edge. "I leave the tribe to you. She left it to Shandor and to me.

"You think you know," Butsulo said now for the first time. His eyes were glassy and his words all but unintelligible. "You will learn. You will see. . . ."

"No," she said. Her voice was calm and collected now. There was a great core of peace inside her. Underneath the residual anger and contempt she felt for Butsulo she could also feel an amazing confidence in herself that she'd never felt before. Here she was, taking charge, taking the reins both literally and figuratively, and all of a sudden it no longer seemed a strange role for her to be fulfilling, but rather a natural one. Suddenly she could hear Beau Tolliver's words, as clearly as if he were sitting here beside her, speaking to her: *When the chips are down you'll know what to do . . . you'll find a way. . . ."*

"No," she said. "It is you who will have to do the learning." Her lips curved in a triumphant smile. "Goodbye, Butsulo. I will try to learn to forgive you . . . but later. Much later."

And without another word, she shook the reins. The big horses pulled powerfully at the traces. The wagon moved slowly forward, creaking musically as its weight shifted to and fro. Her only thought was to flee as fast as they could.

Chapter 23

Some miles down the road she pulled the horses to a halt. A quite predictable reaction had set in, and she found herself unable to stop the frenzied trembling of her hands on the reins or the ague-like chills that swept through her. Once the animals were quieted, Graciela held her hands to her face and bawled like a baby.

The thoughts that ran through her mind came too thick and fast for sifting. Nor did she particularly want to face any of the events of the last hour individually, or consider their implications. Given better present circumstances she would have retreated into safer and more consoling thoughts—anything rather than remember the frightful and barbarous scenes she'd lived through.

But the shadows were lengthening, and nightfall was no more than an hour away. Nightfall—and on the Bloody Way, the traditional northward route of flatboatmen and bargemen walking northward from New Orleans to the Ohio River ports from which they had come. Colonel Falligant had told her something of this sanguinary trail: a road as steeped in blood as the Natchez Trace, and the scene of as many robberies and murders, for highwaymen and footpads lurked at every fork awaiting the unwary boatman heading north with the proceeds of downriver sales in his pockets. It was a bitter and frightening place to be in the first place, even with a wagon train of wise and resourceful Gypsies around you. A single woman driving a wagon and team, armed only with a small pistol and with no companion but a gravely wounded man, was alone indeed in this territory.

She shook her dark curls angrily. *No!* she thought.

She wouldn't give in to defeatism and fear. She couldn't. She had survived this far, and she would survive all the way.

She was ready to shake the reins again and jolt the animals back into their patient, unhurried gait northward when she stopped herself. *Shandor!* She had to find out how he was. She had no idea whether he was alive or dead. If Tshaya's knife had killed him. . . .

She quickly jumped down from the high seat and ran frantically back to the rear of the wagon. Unbarring the door, she stuck her head inside.

Shandor lay on the floor, his body outlined in a pool of his own blood. She gasped at that first sight of him but was rewarded when she saw his dark eyes open and his head rise.

"Graciela," he said. "I. . . ."

She did not wait for more. She climbed up into the wagon, her eyes on his face, and ignored the bloody mess she was crawling through. She did not stop until she had reached his side. "Oh, my God," she said. "I thought you were dead."

"What happened?" he said. "The last I remember, I was . . . oh, yes. The woman. With the knife." He tried to sit up, but she held him down. "Please," he said. "I must. . . ."

"No!" she said in a firm voice. And once again it was the voice of the new woman within her, the competent one who took over when trouble arose and acted decisively. "No. I will get us to safety. You lie here and rest. I don't know how badly you're hurt. The bleeding seems to have stopped. At least most of the blood on the wound seems dry. If you get to moving right now, before I've found a good place to make camp. . . ." She held his good hand and squeezed it. "Trust me, Shandor. I know what I'm doing." This newfound independence was intoxicating.

His dark eyes shone as he looked up at her. "Yes," he said, this time in English. "Yes, you do. My grandmother told me about you. She was right. And Butsulo? And the Rom of Butsulo's camp? What of them?"

"I shot Butsulo," she said. At the look in his eyes she hastened to explain. "I mean I shot him in the arm. I made him come with me and drive the wagon as far as

163

the road. He was bleeding very badly. Perhaps worse than you. I told the others if they followed me I would kill him. I left him at the place where the wagons turned off. I don't think they're following us. But I still have to get us to safety. I'll have to drive on now. It's almost dark—too dark to see the Romany signs by the side of the road. I'll have to take my chances and pull off somewhere on my own. Then I can make a fire and have a better look at you. Perhaps I can even find us something to eat."

"It is all right," he said. He was speaking to her exclusively in English now, as if the two of them had left their Rom identities behind the moment they left Butsulo's encampment. "There is some food in the wagon. This is Laetshi's wagon whose woman died last winter. Laetshi has not found a new wife and lives by himself. There is summer sausage on the shelf, and some bread." His hand, still weak, squeezed hers back. "Even if you find Romany signs by the side of the road ignore them. We must avoid the Rom now, unless you want a taste of Rom justice at the hands of the *kriss*. We are outcasts, you and I. I am sorry, but. . . ."

"Shandor," she said. "I was already an outcast. I have no identity of my own. Until the Rom took me in I was a slave, with nothing and no one in the world to call my own. I thought I had found a family until things began to go bad between Butsulo and Tshaya and me. I had no one but your grandmother. I loved Pesha."

"Yes, he said. "Outcasts. The two of us. But now. . . ." His hand squeezed hers again, and now she could feel the strength in it. "Now you have me. Do not worry. I will be better. I will rest, as you say. But leave the back door of the wagon open so that I can get out if I have to. This is dangerous ground. I think that when the wagon stops next I will be able to get up and you will be able to bind my wounds for me. I do not think I am hurt too badly. I am young and strong. I heal quickly."

"Don't talk," she said. "I'll help you heal. I will take care of you, good care. I need you with me, healthy and strong. You remember, we're still south of the Line. As long as I'm down here I'm in trouble. You'll help me when you're better, Shandor. You'll help me get back north where I'll be safe."

"Yes," he said, smiling up at her. And the hand that touched her thigh, softly enough, but with authority, was not the hand of a dying man. There was great strength in it, but the strength was of a man resting, healing, biding his time.

Graciela, stepping down onto the dusty road again, was unable to explain the strange feeling of simultaneous calmness and eager anticipation that came over her. It was as if something very big, and very wonderful, was about to happen, something she'd never known before.

As she climbed back up into the seat of the big wagon and started the horses forward again, her mood of expectation dissipated into the rapidly chilling evening air. A cool night fog was rising, and she shivered against the cold, wishing she had a heavy shawl or a pair of shoes to keep out the chill. It was almost dark now, and only a moon which peeked in and out behind the clouds lit the dark road. Even that was scarcely sufficient as the fog thickened. Clearly she had to find a place to pull off, but this would be difficult now, when she could barely see beyond the dappled nose of the first pair of horses in the wagon's rig. She shivered and drove on.

Now, for the first time—until now she hadn't had the time to think of him—she found herself mourning Josh. Poor Josh, with his proud independent spirit and his great intelligence. In a better world he would have found a place of some distinction in the realm of business. He had a knack for learning things, and a head for the sort of commonsense things that would have made him a fine merchant or tradesman. But now that wife and family he talked so much about would never see him again. And Josh had died still a slave, still technically a man's property, just as she was. No matter that the man who owned him—yes, and her too—was Beau Tolliver, a kind and upright man whose only concern had been to get Josh north to safety where he could be legally manumitted. It was the institution itself. Slavery, even being the slave of a person who treated you as an equal, was a terrible and degrading thing, and it marked you all through this life.

Graciela shuddered, as much from the thought as from the cold. She flicked the reins, trying to stir the horses to greater speed. The patient animals plodded wearily along, paying her little mind. And the fog grew thicker, colder.

The horses actually passed the first turnout before she saw it. She stopped them and, getting down, backed them to the fork and calmed them before getting back into the seat and guiding them down the side road. She actually drove another quarter of a mile or so before daring to stop. Miraculously, there was a broad clearing by the side of the road, a sheltered one with a grove of trees around it. She got down and, stepping carefully, had a look around just as the moon came out from behind a cloud. Wonderful! There was even dead wood to burn. She took advantage of the moon's sudden reappearance to gather a stack of dead branches, fallen from the hardwood trees around the clearing, before going back to unhitch and tether the horses.

Then she set about making a fire. And no ordinary fire would do. It had to be a great roaring one to warm the heart of a real Rom of the road, the central patch of light and warmth around which a Gypsy encampment gathered nightly and from which it drew its sustenance and strength.

Starting the fire was a problem. Her tiny flame, made Indian-fashion, guttered and died three or four times before she got it going. After nursing and coddling it along, though, it caught, and the flames leaped high into the foggy air. Still shivering, she crouched before it and warmed herself.

As the warmth crept into her thoroughly chilled bones, she discovered a new feeling inside: a feeling of pride. The feeling warmed her more than the fire did.

She'd done it! She'd saved Shandor, and saved herself as well. She had the courage to stand up to Butsulo, and she'd dominated him and then made good her escape.

She'd survived! Beau Tolliver had been right about her. *You haven't cracked*, Beau had said. *Instead you've got fire in your eye and you're holding your head high . . . if you have that kind of spirit in the first place no amount of adversity can subdue you.*

Yes! Yes, it was true! She *did* have it in her. Whatever it was that was required to save the situation, she did have it and could draw upon it when she needed it. Tolliver had seen it, and had made her conscious of it herself: *All I can think is that your mother, whoever she was, must have been a winner and she must have passed it on to you. You'll always be a winner, even when it appears you're losing. Early or late you'll win. Don't believe any evidence to the contrary. You remember that, girl, and you can never go far wrong. And nothing that ever happens to you, short of death, can touch you. Nothing. . . .*

Something made her turn around just then, hunkered down on bare heels before the roaring fire. Her eyes peered through the dappled semi-darkness at the edge of the circle of light the fire cast.

Shandor stood there, leaning against a tree bole, watching her. His dark face was drawn and wan, but his eyes burned like red-hot coals in the reflected firelight. She could not see his mouth, with its sensual lips, behind the fierce, drooping black mustache he'd grown.

"Shandor!" she said. "You'll hurt yourself."

But she saw the look in his eye now, and knew that he knew exactly what he was doing. The Gypsy in him needed the evening fire more than he needed rest, and he had to make it all the way to the fireside without any help from her. She smiled. "Come. Walk slowly. Come sit by the fire. I'll take your shirt off and see what I can do for you. You'll be warm here." She made room for him beside her on the fallen log she was sitting on. And the look of gratitude in his eyes, gratitude for her understanding as well as for her valor and presence of mind, was ample reward for everything she'd done and more.

"Come," she said in Romany. "Come, my darling."

Chapter 24

"Here," she said. "Your shirt."

"No," he said. "A moment. The fire." He stretched his hands out to the fire, wincing slightly at the pain the motion cost him. "Ah," he said. "How wise you have grown in the ways of the Rom. A Gypsy needs the evening campfire the way the flowers need the rain. This heals me as much as any physic you could feed me." Pain or no, he turned a smiling face toward her, showing strong white teeth below the dark mustache.

It seemed she had never seen him before this day. She looked into the dark eyes, so impenetrable until now, and found them not mysterious at all. They were warm and understanding and appreciative, filled with an immense sweetness and strength. And inside her, for all her excitement, there was an unusual calm. Her own answering smile was ardent and accepting.

"Come," she said. "Sit beside me. I'll have a look at your back." She turned, straddling the log, and sat him down, his back to her. The shirt was stuck to his body in several places, but it came free without too much pain when she dampened it. When she had washed his wound, with wine from a bottle in the wagon, she saw that the cut was painful but not too deep. The knife had struck bone and stopped. The wound was an ugly one, but not as serious as she'd thought. Very likely the shock to his system had accounted for the initial weakness he'd shown when Tshaya had stabbed him.

For she could find no other weakness in him now, as God was her witness. Indeed, as her hands touched his broad and knotted back she fairly felt the strength flowing out from his body into her fingers. "Shandor," she said. "It's going to be all right. It's not serious."

"Good," he said. "I must go easy now. This must heal quickly. An acrobat needs to be in the peak of condition if he is to find work. And the autumn and winter are coming."

"Acrobat?" she asked.

"The best place for us now is the circus," he replied. "When we reach St. Louis, or perhaps even before that, I can ask where the traveling shows are. I have a good name with the circus people. I once had a letter from Hackaliah Bailey praising my work." He grinned back over his shoulder at her and swung his legs over the log to face the fire again. "The devil alone knows where that letter is now," he said. "No matter. A circus man needs no letters. With these two hands"—he held them up—"I can earn our way anywhere." His smile was confident and reassuring. "And," he said, "circus people accept you as you are, if you show the right spirit. They ask no questions."

"Good," she said. "But St. Louis—that's a long way away. I have to get to Cairo first. I have to get across the Line. And," she said, a note of tension creeping into her voice, "far enough across the Line to feel secure."

"I understand. And you will not feel secure until the Line has been passed. Well, we will see what we can do. You know, there are other signs than the ones the Rom leave by the side of a major road. Vagabonds of all kinds leave signs. But so do the traveling shows. They say much the same things Romany signs do: here there is shelter, there the people do not like strangers, here the people are generous. Circuses, like the Rom, are dependent upon the bounty of strangers for a place to stop for the night. I will look for the signs as we go north."

The night—she hadn't thought of that. How would they spend the night? It was a delicate question. "Shandor, inside the wagon—I didn't notice. Are there beds?"

"Yes," he said. "But who needs a bed when there is the good earth beneath us? I will get the bedding and spread it here before the fire. We. . . ." He winced as he tried to stand.

"No," she said. "I . . . I'll get it."

She had to find her way in pitch blackness, and she was annoyed at herself for not having looked for a candle. Finally she found a pair of blankets and dragged them across the floor to the door. She was still wondering about sleeping out here, with a man, alone.

Then as she moved into the circle of light around the roaring fire she saw him standing, waiting for her. He was naked, warming himself by the flames, and the firelight played crazily over his brown body with its powerful muscles. He turned and nodded at her, a look of intense pleasure on his face. "Come," he said. "Come to me, Graciela." She'd never seen a man naked before, and the sight of him standing there unashamed before her was the most exciting thing she'd ever seen.

Then she was in his arms, burrowing her face into his broad chest, feeling the power flow from him into her body, and when he released her to slip her dress up over her head it seemed the most perfectly natural thing in the world. She shivered, but not from the cold. It was a strange mixture of residual fear and reserve and eager anticipation, and excitement, and pleasure. She felt the delicious contact of naked flesh against naked flesh all up and down her bare body, and could not resist the temptation to run her hands up and down his back (taking care to avoid his wounds) and feel at last the hard globes of his buttocks as he pressed himself to her.

He held her at arm's length for a moment. His eyes swept over her. "God! You are beautiful! You are a queen! Yes! It is as Pesha said. A queen indeed." His arms went around her again, and with his bare foot he kicked the blankets into a pile by the fire. "Come. Come. . . ."

The first time was all power and conquest. With his strong hands holding her like that, his hard brown body riding above her as proud as a centaur's, she felt like a queen indeed—a conquered queen submitting to an invading king. Strangely enough, it was the loveliest feeling she'd ever had, and as he entered her she found herself trembling all over as she looked up into his brown eyes. Then she felt the real strength of him, and as he skillfully brought her along to one delicious new feeling after another she was content to let him call all the turns, direct the action, be the aggressor.

Then a great surge of warmth flowed into her, and a new person took over inside. It was again that new woman in her who had replaced the frightened girl. And the new woman said, "Shandor . . . Shandor, my dear one . . . yes . . . *yes*. . . ." Then as the excitement mounted she no longer knew, or cared, who it was that was experiencing this. It didn't matter. Nothing mattered but the experience itself, and it was savage and tender and holy above all things.

Afterward there was a time of lying on the blankets by the fire and letting the warm flames play on their nude bodies, and talking quietly. It was a time of getting to know each other, of letting down the barriers. It was, for good and all, a kind of mating. She'd never been so happy. Even though she was apprehensive about her future, she could still tonight enjoy the hidden magic of love.

"Pesha," he said, his hand idly cupping her round breast. "She told me about you. She said you were a woman of great power. Perhaps greater than herself. That you were the real *phuri dai* to come. But she had read the portents. She said you would not live and die among the Rom. She said that it was up to me to follow you when you left, and care for you. That it did not matter if we lived among the *gaje*, we would still be the king and queen of the Rom wherever we were."

"She wanted us to come together?"

"Yes. It was fated. And look at us. Yes," he said, smiling a calm and satisfied smile, "It is good, as she said it would be. I love you. Know this." His hand went to her wrist and held it. "It is not a quick fancy. We were meant to do this. We were born to come together like this. You are my woman and I am your man."

"Yes," she said. And the calm in her passed over into something else, and it passed over into him as well, and in a moment they were in each other's arms again. This time there was no tension in it, no fear, no reserve. Just a mutual giving and taking. *Oh, dear God in heaven*, she thought. *Hold this moment for me. Never let me forget it.*

171

She awoke in his arms to see his laughing eyes smiling down at her. "Good morning," he said. "Time to break camp. Time for a Romany couple to be on the road."

"Heavens," she said. "It's freezing." She burrowed deeper under the blankets, snuggling next to him.

"Yes," he said. He squeezed her playfully. "Come. Let us see if I can find a shirt inside the wagon. And if we are lucky, a coat for you."

They were, as it turned out, in luck. Laetshi, who had owned the wagon, had left all of his clothing in a big trunk beside the door. Shandor found a complete outfit there, clean pants and all. Best of all, Laetshi had left some of his wife's clothing in the box, and Graciela found three dresses, a shawl, and a pair of shoes.

As Shandor said, there was a small amount of food stored in the wagon, including sausage and the dried beef the *gaje* called jerky. It was more than enough to deal with the fierce hunger they felt after their first night together, and, gnawing on the tough meat, they caught each other's eyes and grinned happily as they ate.

She took stock of the remaining items in the wagon while Shandor hitched the animals. Then, with the sun still low in the east, they turned the wagon and found their way back to the main road. Heading northward, heading toward safety—and a new home.

Around midday they found a deserted farm where the barn held stored oats and hay, and there was food and water for the horses. Graciela wanted to stop and stay the night in the house, but Shandor, ever watchful, said no: there was no telling when the owner, or his heir, would return and find them. Better to sleep under the stars, far from settlements.

A fresh stream ran through the farm, and someone had dammed it for a swimming hole beneath a fine stand of sheltering trees. Graciela took the opportunity to wash out the clothing they'd worn away from the camp, beating the cloth against a rock in the rushing stream. Then what was more natural than to take a refreshing swim in the cool water, and wash her hair?

When Shandor, returning from the barn, found her standing nude and thigh-deep in the running water, what was more natural than to join her in the stream—and then on the sun-warmed grass above the pool, where the still-strong Indian summer sun beat down lustily on their bare and aroused bodies?

It was a day of pleasure. It was a day of sharing. It was a day of glorious epiphany, as the new love between them grew and deepened. It was a day she'd remember, and treasure, until the moment of her death.

In the afternoon it was time to get to work. Graciela found herself earning her keep, stopping at a farmhouse to talk a housewife into letting her read her palm. As she and the farm woman sat at the kitchen table, Graciela held the woman's hands. First, she observed the left hand and palm, turning it this way and that, then the right one. The woman's life became an open book to her as she studied the hand.

Graciela closed her eyes for a moment to become in tune with the Universal Intelligence. She hoped to be able to tap the power that would enable her to give a good and true reading. She felt almost dizzy for a moment as she began. She felt herself actually experiencing some of the feelings of grief from the woman's past. "You have had a small child . . . about two years old . . . named Jimmy . . . pass on into the spirit world. The child is happy there . . . you have always worked hard but felt lonely on this farm. I can see you will be finding yourself dancing . . . entertaining. . . . and picnicking soon . . . for I see many prosperous, loved ones visiting you and they will be here often. So much happiness, working and playing together. This new phase of your life starts very soon."

After the reading, the woman hugged Graciela for it was all so believable. She'd had a child named Jimmy who had passed on at the age of two. She was glad to hear that he was happy in the spirit world, and yes, she would no longer be lonely, for next month her sister and all her family were moving nearby. They would not only be working together but taking time out for fun, too, for her brother-in-law loved to play the fiddle, and they planned many good times ahead. "They are warm, gen-

173

erous, loving people and my husband and I adore them. But, tell me, how could you see all this just in my palm?"

"The palm is the mirror of the soul," Graciela said. Silently, she thanked God for helping her give such a good reading and she knew that Pesha must be smiling down upon her for being such an apt student.

Yes, she thought to herself, just because there are fake diamonds doesn't mean that the real thing doesn't exist. She knew she would never have to resort to giving a fake reading.

The days passed. Their wagon slowly moved northward, following the flatboatmen's trail, moving into hardscrabble rolling country as the path led away from the Mississippi into Piedmont territory. The nights passed, and with every one of them the bond between Graciela and Shandor grew. They traveled from Tennessee into Kentucky. Then one day there were only fifty miles or so between them and the eagerly awaited point where the Ohio River joined the Mississippi. Two days later they pulled the horses up atop a knoll and looked out across the Ohio at the first free state she'd ever seen—the first place where it was illegal to own a man or a woman the way you owned a horse or a cow, the first place of refuge she'd seen since the day Thiebaud had taken possession of her, only to lose her to Beau Tolliver.

At the sudden thought a cold fear ran through her. Tolliver! In the sudden joy of self-discovery, of falling in love with Shandor, she'd almost forgotten about him— the man who owned her! The thought entered her mind, and wouldn't go away: what would she do about Beau? Would she wait for him, and take the chance of incurring his disapproval when he met Shandor?

Biting her lip, she drove the thought from her mind. The main thing was to get across that river. There was the ferry, down below. In an hour or so she'd be on free soil.

"Now that you are mine, completely mine, what is my mercurial little Gemini pondering about?" Shandor asked, slipping his arm around her. "What are you thinking? Is it of freedom, of love?"

A wave of joy went through her, and she hugged him back fiercely. "Yes," she said, "of love *and* freedom. The better we feel about ourselves the more we can love, the more we can give each other."

But, there was a cloud on her happiness, for all that the happiness was genuine and unforced. There would always be a cloud on any joy she would ever know, as long as a single person in the world owned title to her that she was not free to revoke on her own.

"Come," she said, shaking the reins. And the wagon started on the slow, winding trail down the hill to the banks of the Ohio and the state of Illinois, toward a safety she still had a hard time believing in.

Chapter 25

On closer inspection, Cairo turned out to be a dismal little failure of a town perched precariously on a spit of land between the two great rivers, hedged in miserably with tall levees against the floods of the spring thaw, its scattered pattern of houses already looking half-occupied and threadbare after the failure of the Cairo City and Canal Company's ill-starred venture of 1840.

No matter. That unpromising, muddy little gore, with its tall flood walls and its grubby streets, was the southernmost patch of land above the Line. Graciela's heart beat fast and hard as she sat high on the wagon aboard the ferry, watching the Illinois shore approach one precious inch at a time. Shandor, holding the horses down on the ferry's hand-hewn planks, grinned happily up at her, feeling her anticipation almost as keenly as she did.

When the boatman tied up she urged the animals forward; then, when the wagon was firmly settled on solid ground, she jumped nimbly down into Shandor's arms. She didn't know which was the greater pleasure: touching free soil for the first time and digging her bare toes into the dusty Illinois earth, or feeling Shandor's strong arms holding her, welcoming her to the North and to safety.

"Now," he said, his mustache nuzzling her ear. "Now you are safe and I will protect you."

"I wish it were that simple," she said. "Josh explained the Dred Scott decision to me. I'm safe as long as Beau Tolliver owns the paper he won from Thiebaud. If Tolliver died before registering the paper, God forbid, I'm still technically Thiebaud's. And if he did register the paper, and died afterward, I would belong to his heirs.

Either way I could legally be pursued onto free soil and returned. My only real hope is if Beau Tolliver is alive and can take the papers down to the county courthouse here and free me legally. Otherwise. . . ." She looked ruefully back across the river.

"Then we shall hope Mr. Tolliver is still alive," he said, "and still wants to free you."

She pulled back from him and looked up into his dark eyes. "Oh, God, Shandor. He has to. He just has to. He couldn't have changed his mind."

"Do not worry," Shandor said. "If he changes his mind I will kill him." His eyes flashed hot lights. His mouth was grim. "No, I know. You have told me he is a duellist and had to kill others. Myself, I know nothing of duels. Duels are for gentlemen"—the phrase was sour on his lips—"and I am a Rom. If he changes his mind on you, though. . . ."

"Yes," she said, hugging him happily. "Yes, I know you would, and you'd succeed, too, whatever it took. But I don't think you'll have to. Tolliver is—well, he's an honorable man."

"Honor? Among the *gaje*? Bah. *Tshatshimo Romano*."

"Yes. Romany is the tongue for telling the truth. But as we have learned lately there can be treachery even among the Rom." She put one diplomatic hand on his broad chest, thrilling as she did so at the bands of powerful muscle. "And it follows that there are honorable men among the *gaje*. But I thank you for thinking that way about me."

"But if Tolliver—"

"*Na may kharunde kai tshi khal tut*," she said. "Don't scratch where it doesn't itch. Save your anger and your hot Gypsy blood for real enemies, not imaginary ones. God knows we have enough real ones to last us the rest of our lives."

"Yes," he said, mollified. "You are right. Let us go." He handed her back up into the wagon, his powerful hands making no more of her weight than if she were a child. Feeling the strength in him, she reflected that he might well be a match, in his own way, for Beau Tolliver or for anyone else who might oppose him. She only hoped that in Tolliver's case no such occasion ever arose.

Once across the levee they drove the wagon slowly down Washington Street, looking at the shabby aftermath of failure in the little town. A few years hence, at the height of speculation, the population had swollen to over a thousand, and building had tripled to meet the sudden demand. Two years after the bubble burst the population had fallen to a tenth of its high water mark, and had stabilized at that level. The houses looked dingy, with flaking paint and broken windows.

"It is a poor excuse for a town," Shandor said. "And mind you, I do not like towns much in the first place."

"That's all right," Graciela said. "My father said the railroads were coming to Illinois. Can you imagine what it'd be like if the railroad came right down this spit into Cairo? And connected up not only with New Orleans and St. Louis, but with all the Ohio River ports as well? It'll be an important town some day. But right now I have to agree with you."

"Where are we going?" he said. She turned the wagon on Jefferson and headed west, turning roughly north again on Walnut.

"Josh told me there's a tavern where Beau Tolliver goes when he's in town. They ought to have news of him there." Sure enough, a block up the dismal street stood a woebegone ordinary with a faded sign, "Tavern." "We'll pull up here," she said. "You'll have to go in with me. I don't know how they'll take to having a single woman in there asking questions."

"Do you want to be seen with a Rom?" he said.

"Why not?" she said. "I am one, after all." She squeezed his hand affectionately. "Do you want to be seen with a black woman? Technically I'm one of those, too. See? It doesn't matter. Besides," she grinned playfully, "we're Romany royalty. You're a chief and I'm a *phuri dai* but, for all that, we'll probably never reign over any tribe. Pesha said we were. That's all that matters."

"Yes," he said. "Here, I'll help you down." *My*, she thought, *some Rom have nice manners*. There were advantages to his double background, after all. Gypsy spirit and Gypsy ardor, but some of the more pleasing *gajo* ways as well. She was, it was beginning to seem, a lucky woman indeed.

As they stepped inside Graciela took a quick look around. There were two men at the bar, and over in one corner a third man slumbered, his head cradled on his arms atop a table. "Stand by the door," she whispered. "I'll go ask." She walked briskly over to the bar, where the host stood having a glass of his own wares, looking her up and down. He did not speak.

"Pardon me," she said. "I'm looking for news about a man who passes through here now and then."

One of the drinkers turned her way. "I'm a man who passes through here now and then," he said. His eyes looked right through her red Gypsy blouse.

Ignoring him, she said, "I'm looking for news of a man named Beau Tolliver. He's tall, red-haired—"

"Tolliver?" the barkeep said. "And what would you want with Beau Tolliver?" He tossed his drink down and looked her in the eye, neither friendly nor unfriendly. "It pays to ask. A woman looking for him might want any one of a number of things. She might, for instance, have a little surprise waiting for him outside in a wagon, something she'd a mind to have him put his name to."

"It's nothing like that," she said. "He's a friend of my father's. I have a message for him."

"Yes?" the man said. "And what might that message be?"

"That's for him alone to hear," she said. "I mean no offense. Have you seen him?"

The barkeep finished off his glass and looked at her, his eyes showing he'd made up his mind about her, once and for all. "Beau?" he said. "Hasn't been in since . . . oh, it must have been last winter. He was working the *Pride of St. Louis* then, and he stopped over for a day to free his nigger woman and boy, it was. He's not big on people keeping niggers."

"The more fool him," one of the drinkers said. "I seen the nigger woman. She can keep house for me any day."

"Mind your mouth," the barkeep said. "Miss, I'm sorry. I haven't seen Beau. I haven't heard of him in quite some time. Tell you what, though. Boat from New

179

Orleans docks here tomorrow. The *Captain Shreve*. Surely someone aboard her will have news of Beau. He's well enough known on the water. Although why we haven't seen him in all that time, I surely couldn't tell you. He usually works the boats north and south of here all summer. First time in years I've missed him."

"Thank you," she said. She was ready to go when a sudden thought struck here. "Oh, say," she said. "I was wondering if you'd heard any news of a man named Tom McGee."

"McGee?" he said. "Ah, yes. Poor devil. I did hear of him. He died earlier this year. Deeply in debt. They sold all his possessions to pay off the bills, including, I hear, a nigger wench he'd raised like a child of his own." The man crossed himself, an uncharacteristic gesture this far north on the River. "Ah, Tom had a taste for the spirits, he did. There but for the grace of God—"

"Thank you," she said. She wheeled and turned toward the door; it wouldn't do to have him see the terrible flush on her face just now. She didn't turn until she was halfway to the door. "Excuse me . . . this black woman he freed. Is she still in the area? I thought if she was I might ask if she'd heard news of Mr. Tolliver."

"Down by the Jefferson levee," he said. "She and her boy have a little shack there. She takes in washing, way I hear it. She might know something. You take care, now."

"Thank you," she said. As she turned to go she saw one of the men at the bar rise to follow her; but he stopped when he saw Shandor standing by the door, thick arms crossed across his burly chest.

"What did they say?" Shandor said, out in the street.

"They haven't heard from him. But there's a New Orleans boat passing through tomorrow, bound for St. Louis. I can ask there. Someone's sure to have heard of him."

"No," Shandor said. "I do not like this."

"I agree it's chancy," she said, "but. . . ."

"No," he said. "I have bad feelings." She looked in his eyes and saw there something of the same blind, unreasoning fear that she'd seen there when the Nail had appeared in Butsulo's camp. "It was a quick flash inside me. I think it may have been the spirit of Pesha."

180

"Shandor," she said. "It's all right. I'm on Northern soil. Besides, I have you here to protect me. And meanwhile, there's somebody I have to see here."

"Who?" he said. His eyes were still wary, like a trapped animal's.

"Someone who knows Tolliver."

"All right. But I will go with you. I will watch out for you."

"Of course." She looked around and made sure nobody was looking; then she stood up on tiptoe and kissed him. "I want you to go with me. Come." She climbed back up onto the wagon, and once again they turned the horses southward, toward the tall levee at the tip of the Delta town.

The house she sought was a shack all right. It had never seen paint. But there was a neat fence around it, made of scrap wood, and somebody had planted a small garden for growing flowers as well as tomatoes and a little row of sweet corn. Approaching from the street she could see a small black boy playing in the rear yard.

She opened the gate and walked in, with Shandor just behind her. As she did, the front door of the little house opened and a small black woman in her twenties came out. Her eyes were as dark as a Rom's and her face was expressionless.

"Hello," Graciela said. "I—"

"I don't want anything," the woman said. "I don't want any charms and I don't want you to read my fortune. I don't have anything you'd possibly want, and I'll thank you to go along. I mind my own business here." She stood immobile on the tiny porch, barring her front door.

"Please," Graciela said. "I'll only be a minute. I'm looking for Beau Tolliver."

"Tolliver?" the woman said. "Did you say Beau Tolliver?" Her thin lips curved in a wry smile. "God almighty, girl, if I knew where Beau Tolliver was I'd—"

Then a strange thing happened. Graciela and the black woman looked each other in the eye. And in an instant they knew each other. And all of a sudden they had gone from strangers to a pair of women who shared

181

a strange and terrible secret, and a fearful, if unequal, loss.

"Oh, my God," the black woman said in a changed voice. "I've been waiting for you to come. And praying you wouldn't."

"Please," Graciela said. "I had to. I—"

"He's dead, isn't he? Isn't that what you're going to tell me? My man Josh—he's dead?"

Graciela, biting her lip, forced herself to hold the woman's eyes, forced herself to look into those dark and terrifying depths. She sighed. "Yes," she said. "He was my friend. I owe my life to him. I saw him die."

The iron control came back now. The woman stepped aside. "Won't you come in, please?" she said. "Both of you?"

Chapter 26

There was no question of making camp in town: a Gypsy wagon never passed the night in an occupied settlement. Centuries of tradition and countless terrible experiences had made this decision inevitable. Graciela and Shandor, after a look at the inhospitable lowland between the break in the levee and the twin ferry slips serving Missouri on the one side and Kentucky on the other, turned the wagon north and camped in a thick grove of magnolias near the small settlement called Burkeville.

Even in her grief, Josh's widow, Mame, had pressed food upon them: a sack full of sweet potatoes and cold fried chicken. When the fire was made and blazing high, casting leaping shadows on the trees around them, they sat and ate. There didn't seem much to say that wouldn't bring back the terrible memory of having to tell Mame and her boy that Josh wouldn't be making it North to them now.

The worst part of it all had been the icy control Mame had maintained over herself throughout the whole bitter, melancholy story. Graciela could have taken tears, or anger, or even the sort of unrestrained, theatrical grief the Rom customarily indulged themselves in, once a loved one had passed on. That at least would be natural. But Mame's was a bitter, hopeless sort of acceptance of the fact—a fact that she had anticipated so many times in nights past that she had come to expect it. She even welcomed it in a way; the final delivery of the news of Josh's death freed her of the awful burden of waiting, freed her of dread.

Graciela put down her chicken wing and looked at

183

Shandor, her face expressionless. "The Rom are wiser than they know," she said. "They know the proper way to handle grief."

"God gave the Rom self-knowledge and cunning when he gave the rest of the world possessions and power," Shandor said. "There are fools among us, fools whose errors are as bad as any man's. But our foolishness hurts no one but us, and when the hurt has come and gone even our fools are wise enough to know how to live with it and let it go." He looked into the fire, and in his eyes was a great compassion for the folly of *gajo* and Rom alike. "Because this woman does not acknowledge her loss she will hold on to it longer, far longer than the year every Gypsy is allowed for mourning."

She nodded sadly and, looking down at the food in her hand, tossed it into the fire. She was suddenly feeling a little sick, and the idea of food made her even sicker. "Yes," she said. "And if the dead still exist, as Pesha said, and the personality is eternal . . ."

"I see you understand. It is wicked to hold the dead. It is better to let them go, let them progress." Shandor shuddered. "I do not like this place. I would like to leave tomorrow morning. I would like to head north again."

"Please," she said. "Just this one morning. The boat docks early, before noon. If we wait that long perhaps someone will have news of Tolliver. There's always a chance that he'll be on it himself, you know."

Shandor turned sad, almost resentful eyes upon her. "You do not believe that," he said.

She looked him in the eye and could not dissemble. "No. I don't, really," she said. "But there's just the outside chance. Please, Shandor. Please, darling. Just this once. I think I understand why you're uncomfortable here. I am too, in a way. But if I did go on, and he showed up just after I left, and I missed the chance of knowing—of seeing—"

"Enough," he said. "We will stay for the boat. Then we will head north." He got up and went out beyond the circle of light to relieve himself. When he returned his demeanor was matter-of-fact, slightly distant. He was courteous and solicitous of her, but when they put down the bedrolls he did not attempt to make love to her. He

184

rolled over and feigned sleep for a long time, looking with half-closed eyes into the fire.

In the morning she awoke early, nauseated. She stood up, trying to clear her head, and built a small fire to make coffee for the two of them. Suddenly the nausea came over her in waves, one after the other, and she found herself standing miserably under a big magnolia, dry-heaving. She hadn't eaten enough the night before to account for this. She was sick as a dog.

Shandor's head came up off the ground, tousle-haired, bleary-eyed. "Graciela," he said. "What is the matter?" He blinked once, twice, and was on his feet in a moment, at her side, all tender care and concern.

She did not answer, crouching there over the vomit-stained bushes, feeling the waves of sick dizziness wash over her. "I . . . must be something I ate."

"Here," he said. "Sit down. I will make some herb tea. Let me put the blanket over you." Distant as he'd been the night before, he was all protectiveness and caring now. He sat her down and tucked the thick blanket around her, covering even her bare feet, and threw dry branches on the fire until it burned high and hot. Then he busied himself with preparing a concoction of dried leaves in a pot of water, straining the mixture through a clean rag before handing it to her. It tasted vile, but it did clean the acid taste out of her throat, and after some minutes had passed she did feel soothed in a way, although she still felt sick.

Now he came and sat down facing her, astraddle a tree stump. "Look," he said. "It is no time for you to go wandering into town. I will look there myself. You stay in the wagon. I will ask around. I will ask after Falligant and while I am at it I will also ask after this man Tolliver. I want you to stay in bed. When I have asked the questions and got the answers, we will head north. I have seen marks on the trees. Not Rom marks, circus marks. I think we will be safest with the circus. I can always find work there. My back is healed, or almost so. Enough, at any rate, that I can work. I am well enough for work in the hippodrome, or on the high wire. I know all circus skills. Circus people are protective. They ask no questions but whether you are fit people to live among them. If you are, they will shelter you while they live."

It was a longer speech than he was accustomed to making. Finished, he closed his mouth tight under that bushy mustache and looked at her, his eyes simultaneously full of hurt and concern. She wondered idly why he was acting this way, what she had done to hurt him or drive him away from her.

"Shandor," she said. "I don't mind if you're the one to ask. Maybe it's the right thing. I understand. You're afraid someone I don't want to see will. . . . Yes. I'm still a fugitive, after all, and I suppose the New Orleans authorities still want me for—for what happened to Thiebaud's men. Thank you for being so protective. Frankly, I *don't* feel good. I feel terrible. If you *would* ask for me. . . ."

New warmth broke the chill in his detached and lonely manner. He didn't smile, though, and his eyes were still wary and distant. "All right. We will go back into Cairo with the wagon, but you will stay inside. I will go down to the docks. No one will know me there. I will learn what I can. You will stay in bed until you are better. This is probably some fever one contracts from sleeping down on the bottoms like this. I have aches and chills in my back, too."

"Oh, dear," she said. She handed him the cup, still half-empty. "Then you'd better drink the rest of this yourself." As she said it, though, another wave of nausea swept over her, and she had to fight the dizzy spell that accompanied it to keep from slipping off into a sick faint.

Morning fog lay over Cairo well toward midday, and there was a distinct chill in the air as they neared the point of land between the two great rivers. Graciela opened the front windows of the big wagon and, looking through Shandor's legs, watched their slow progress through the town's all but deserted streets. There were a few more people about. The boat was docking, and she could see its tall stacks on the other side of the levee, belching dark smoke into the foggy morning sky.

Shandor pulled the horses up near the little tavern and bent over to speak to her through the open window. "Wait here," he said. "I will go down to the dock and see what I can learn there." He stepped down and strode away briskly, his motions graceful and athletic.

Graciela sat back on the narrow bed Laetshi had built for his sick wife. She still felt bad: her head swam, her stomach continued to double her over with cramps at odd intervals, and, in truth, she was relieved to have Shandor do the asking. She was in no shape to go poking about and stirring up questions.

On the other hand, something in her desperately wanted to see Tolliver, and not just because he held the key to her freedom. Even without that, there was something about the yearning that arose in her whenever she thought of him, something she could not put a word or name to.

And then it hit her. Of course! That was why Shandor had acted so strangely last night, so distant, so cold. He was jealous! Jealous of Tolliver, and of the hold Beau still seemed to have over her! Poor Shandor. She'd have to reassure him, and soon. She was beginning to learn which were the best ways to do this, and happily enough, they all turned out to be ways that would provide her with every bit as much pleasure as she was giving him at the same time.

A secret smile played over her lips. Imagine, having a man jealous over you! And it wasn't hard, either. Once you had made that one decisive step into womanhood, the whole book of secrets women had to depend upon for survival opened up for you, and somehow you knew what to do. Men, for all that they had the greater strength and held the reins of power in society, were easy enough to manage if they loved you. And—she knew this now—you could always make a man love you if you wanted him to. Particularly after the tutoring she'd had from old Pesha, with her decades-old experience of life and the natural intelligence she'd always brought to everything and, not least, the centuries-old wisdom of the *phuri dai*, passed on from one wise woman to the next over a period longer than recorded history. What an arsenal of weapons she had, for getting

187

by in the world! What power—real power, stronger than the show of power men made—she could wield in this world!

A sudden thought, though, stopped her short. Power? Would she have power over Beau Tolliver now if she were to meet him, with her bare summer's apprenticeship in the arts of womanhood? Would the tenderness of love that worked so beautifully on Shandor, who, despite his maturity, was hardly more than an unfledged boy, work as well on an experienced and sophisticated man like Tolliver? Or would he still treat her like a girl—a promising pupil, perhaps, but a pupil nonetheless? But she had given herself to Shandor and she must not allow herself to think of Beau Tolliver this way.

She pondered the question as the street around her began to fill with steamship passengers taking an hour's constitutional on dry land while the dockside workers loaded cargo aboard the moored steamboat. From the dismal quiet of the morning, the streets filled with the voice of people, most of them men, and most of them, from the sound of things, headed for the little tavern where she'd asked about Beau Tolliver the night before. Rough voices, cultured voices, tenors, baritones, basses; voices speaking English, voices speaking French—

Voices speaking French. And one of them was a harsh and husky voice, a voice full of power and pique. A voice that said coarse things like *"Cela m'emmerde"* as if coarseness were more natural than manners. A voice full of haughtiness and cruelty and selfishness. A voice that came from a man who stopped to talk with his companion no more than a few feet from the window of her wagon.

Her heart pounding with a mixture of emotions, Graciela moved to the window and, screening her face with one tanned arm, peeped out into the street.

The speaker was well dressed. A black frock coat of expensive cut over a white waistcoat and lilac plaid trousers; silk hat and yellow gloves; black silk cravat. The figure was burly, the hair curly, unruly. The shoulders under that black coat were powerfully muscled, and the body thick and chunky.

Thiebaud!

Chapter 27

Graciela shrank back from the window, horrified. Thiebaud, here! Her first inclination was to panic, to throw open the door of the wagon and run, no matter where. The sudden fear inside her simply told her that remaining here was danger itself, that any place she could possibly run to would be safer than remaining right here.

Then she regained control of herself, and mastered her panic. That assured and competent self in her, which had emerged some weeks before, suddenly took command of her and calmed her unreasoning terror. Instead of running, she reached under the pillow of Laetshi's wife's bed and felt for the little pistol she'd shot Butsulo with. It still had several bullets in its barrels. If danger came she would sell her life and freedom dearly.

Now, with fear giving way to a cold and reckless anger, she approached the open window again and peeped out from behind a curtain. She was sure they couldn't see in, but still she made no move to expose her face to the light of day. She listened, piecing out their words from the gradually increasing noise in the streets. Her convent-school days had made her reasonably adept at French, and it was no problem understanding the gist of the conversation from Thiebaud's coarse Creole French and his companion's crisp Parisian speech.

". . . markets are down. Frankly, investment there is a poor bargain, depressed prices or no. Remember the Panic of '37? Believe me, all of us got taken, large and small. I lost a bundle then myself. And I can tell you it's no time to go chasing after some wild scheme. . . ."

"All right, all right," Thiebaud said harshly. "Perhaps

189

you're right. But if someone were to. . . ." He stopped and turned her way. Graciela, secure behind the curtain and out of sight, still shrank back, feeling those piercing eyes on the wagon. "Here, what's this? Good God, is Cairo letting Gypsy wagons park inside the town limits these days?"

"I don't know. It's just a single one. Usually they travel in caravans. Perhaps this one got separated from the tribe. Well, no harm done. If it's still there by nightfall I'll have the dogs on them. One Gypsy, well, we can handle that. A whole train of them, well, I'd have them out of town in a moment."

"Filthy scum. Worse than niggers. I'd have the hounds out." Thiebaud spat into the street.

"Matter of fact, I think I heard something of the Gypsy Davy who must own this thing. He was inquiring down at the dock about a 'friend' of yours, Monsieur Thiebaud."

"Friend? What friend of mine would have anything to do with some greasy-haired, snot-nosed *manouche*?"

The other man's tone was amused, supercilious. "Why, Beau Tolliver. The gambler. I think you know him."

"Tolliver?" Thiebaud's voice was caustic. "Why, Tolliver has a warrant out on him. I swore it out myself. Battery, murder, and grand larceny. Stole a nigger wench of mine. Tolliver's no friend of mine. And stop that damned smiling. It's not funny at all."

"Someone came through Vicksburg a while back with news of Beau, word has it. The claim is that Tolliver plans to file a countersuit. He has the notion that the wench was his, and that he was simply resisting an attempted theft. Well, of course one doesn't credit every story one hears this far upriver, but—"

"Well, this is one time that lying Irish tongue of his won't save him. Not if he comes to earth somewhere and I get my hands on him. Besides, I have witnesses. And let me tell you, he's a dead man if he shows his face in New Orleans. A dead man." Thiebaud's eyes went back to the wagon. "I wonder what a Gypsy beggar would be doing asking after him, though."

"Well, you know Beau. His reputation is that of a

man who makes strange bedfellows. Very strange bedfellows indeed."

"Damned right. I have it on the best authority that he's been running niggers North to free soil. That's going to get him hanged one of these days. I had a report, matter of fact, that my runaway was seen in Natchez some time back. In the company of another nigger Tolliver stole from a big planter in the area. And you won't believe who was running the bastards north for Tolliver."

"Who?"

"Wes Falligant, that's who."

"You don't mean to tell me."

"I do. Well, a bad penny always turns up. Although I have to say that's one offense I never heard charged to his account before this. Swindling, yes. Even murder. He shot some young man of the town this summer in Natchez-on-Top-of-the-Hill. But running niggers—aiding and abetting runaways. . . ." His eyes went straight for Graciela's curtained window. She shrank back again, the little pistol clutched tightly in her hand. "Look, I think I'd like to have a chat with this Gypsy tinker of yours before the dogs run him out of town. You couldn't detain him for me, could you?"

"Look, my friend, you're not going to be in town more than a few hours."

"I'll stay over. I can transfer my fare. The *Creole Belle* will be through here tomorrow afternoon. Cairo's a pesthole, but I can stay over an extra day, business in St. Louis or not, if there's a chance of getting a lead on Tolliver and that stolen nigger of mine."

"Look, let things go. I realize I'm being officious. But my advice to you is to cut your losses. If Tolliver turns up the authorities will take him in hand soon enough. Legal means take longer, to be sure, but they work out best in the long run. If you intervene in the process yourself you could wind up with more trouble than you bargained for. Beau's a dead shot, for one thing. And if he's on the run he's a desperate man."

"Just do me a favor; have the Gypsy picked up. Don't let him get out of town. If you find him I'll be at the tavern."

"Well, if you insist. I'll stop off at the magistrate's office. I may drop by the tavern looking for you after. And if you do stay over, I'd be pleased to have you stay at my place."

"I'm obliged." The tone was curt, ungrateful. Thiebaud's manners were no better than ever. "*Au 'voir.*"

Graciela watched as the man—he seemed to be some sort of official—walked to the curb, head high, shoulders back. Thiebaud stared, annoyed, at the wagon for a moment; then he turned on one heel and strode across the dusty street to the open door of the tavern.

There was no getting around it. Her mind was made up for her. She had to get out of town, and fast, and she had to pick up Shandor before he wandered into a trap. She cracked a side window and looked at the open door of the tavern, then she opened the door of the wagon and stepped down barefooted into the street, the little gun held by her side. Her heart was beating fast; at any moment Thiebaud could look out through that open door and recognize her. But no: he'd have to see her up close to recognize her, she was sure of that. She'd changed too much since then to be easily identified with the frightened girl he'd seen last; her hair was longer, and her skin darkened by constant exposure to the sun. And who would go looking for a convent-bred girl in a Gypsy dress?

Glancing back at the tavern door again, she climbed up into the high seat and took the reins. As she did someone came out of the open door, and her heart almost stopped. It was a stranger, though, and he paid no attention to her at all. *Please,* she thought. *Please don't let Thiebaud notice me.* Jiggling the reins, she urged the animals forward slowly.

Up ahead Walnut joined Jefferson for half a block; then Jefferson took a half-turn to the left to become Second Street. Washington, crossing Second, bored along through the gap in the levee to connect with the dockside area. If she could make it that far without anyone noticing her. . . .

To her great relief things continued calm all the way to Jefferson. She turned east, and then turned east again. So far, so good.

Now, guiding the wagon through the town's half-filled

streets, she took the time to think of the implications of what Thiebaud had said. And they were horrifying. For one thing, Thiebaud's words had implied as clearly as if the fact had been stated aloud that she was still a slave, and still his property. Beau Tolliver had not been able to get papers on her from Thiebaud, even through his lawyers. Since no reliable witness existed to testify to Beau's winning her on the turn of a card, and since Thiebaud himself repudiated his debt, Thiebaud was still technically her owner, her master. And the Fugitive Slave Laws made it quite legal, in most states, for a slave-territory citizen to pursue runaways onto free territory to regain his property.

She wasn't safe. Perhaps she'd never be.

Turning right onto Washington now, she made for the break in the levee. As she did she became aware of a hue and cry behind her: loud voices raised in anger saying words she could not make out, but whose meaning she could easily guess. They'd caught on to the fact that the wagon was gone.

She urged the animals forward; the horses broke into a trot, nearly bowling over an elderly gentleman crossing the street before her. Shandor! Where was Shandor? He had to be close by; he simply had to be.

There he was! As he came down the gangway of the big steamer she could see his head rise and his face register surprise at seeing her here, spurring the wagon through the crowd. He stopped, then broke into an easy jogging dog-trot, headed her way.

She swung the animals round in a great turn, her wheels skidding precariously. As she passed him, still running, he increased his speed and grabbed a wooden hand rail and pulled himself up onto the seat beside her.

"What's the matter?" he said.

"Thiebaud," she said. "He's in town. And there's an order out to stop our wagon and bring you in for questioning. Someone heard you inquiring about Tolliver. There's a warrant out for him, and for me too, as an escaped slave."

"Escaped? But I thought—"

"I did too," she said, driving the animals back through the gap in the levee again at a full gallop. Pedestrians, dogs, farm animals scattered before them. But now, from a side street, members of a hastily assembled posse comitatus (gathered, like as not, from the on-lookers fresh off the boat itself) moved out into the street to head them off. "Hold on," she said. "I'm not going to stop."

Instead, she gave the horses their head. The men blocking the street at first didn't think she was serious. They held their ground. Then, at the last possible moment, when her intentions became evident, they dived for safety to the left and right of her. She heard shouts of rage behind her as she drove the wagon along at a breakneck clip. "Hey! Stop that wagon! Runaway! Runaway!"

"Here," she said. She handed Shandor the little pistol. "There's no time for us to change places. Do you know how to use one of these?"

"Yes," he said. "A man with the circus taught me. I learned to shoot quite well."

"If anyone tries to stop us, let him get close enough to be a problem—then kill him. If I'm taken now. . . ."

"I understand," he said. She turned briefly to catch him grinning appreciatively at her. "You drive like a man. Perhaps better than a man." She smiled at his words.

"Do not worry," he said. "No one will stop us. Not alive."

"Fine," she said. The town itself was behind them now; to the right and left, farmhouses jutted out from cleared land between patches of thick underbrush. The road was rutted but brick-hard. *Thank God for that*, she thought. "Where am I going?" she said. "Do you know?"

"I have not been this way, exactly. But I spoke with a man back at the docks about the road. What you want to do is always take the left-hand fork of everything. If you do so the road will stay near the Mississippi. Before many miles there will be a ferry slip for crossing it. It is a large enough ferry to take the wagon and the horses."

"Good," she said. "Is anyone following us?"

He turned and looked back; then he stood up on the seat and peered over the top of the wagon itself. "Yes," he said. "Three horsemen. They are catching up with us." He set his feet and braced himself, taking a bead. "One of them is coming up alongside us on your side. I think he does not see me yet. Here he comes—yes—"

There was a sharp explosion above her head, just as she turned her eyes left to see the rider draw alongside her—and suddenly go into a sharp convulsion and drop his reins. Rider and horse alike disappeared. "I think you got him," she said. "God forgive us."

"Yes, I got him," Shandor said. "The others are falling back. They were not armed, I think."

"They weren't used to the idea of runaways bearing arms, I'll bet," Graciela said. "Look, there's the first fork." Up ahead the road cut sharply away to the left. She guided the careening wagon wildly around the curve without losing speed. Shandor jumped nimbly down onto the seat beside her and patted her thigh appreciatively. "Now," he said. "The River!"

They crossed the Mississippi without incident on the ferry, paying their way with money she'd earned reading fortunes in Kentucky. The crossing made, they stopped to lunch on summer sausage, goat cheese, and spring water some miles west of the road that led north to Cape Girardeau.

Halfway through the meal she suddenly found herself ill again. She vomited up the meager lunch she'd eaten and continued to heave long after the only food she'd taken had been eliminated from her system.

"I'm sorry," she said when she finally got her breath. "It must have been the excitement. I'll be all right in a day or so."

But suddenly she knew she wouldn't be all right. Not the way she'd said. And suddenly, just as surely as if angelic voices had spoken the words inside her head, she knew what was wrong with her now. As she looked into his eyes she knew he knew. "Oh, Shandor," she said. "I—I think I'm pregnant. And God. I'm still a slave, with a price on my head. We've just crossed over into Missouri, and it's a slave state."

Chapter 28

To her surprise, however, the look of comprehension in his dark eyes did not turn to a look of horror. Instead a broad, warm, accepting smile spread across his swarthy face, and the corners of that fierce mustache lifted to show strong white teeth. The next thing she knew she was in his arms and he was hugging the breath out of her. "But, Shandor," she said.

He hugged her again, then stepped back to hold her at arm's length, looking her happily in the eye. "Can it be," he said, "that you have lived with the Rom for a whole summer and not learned what joy it is to a Gypsy man to learn he is about to become a father?" He squeezed her hands. As she looked him in the eye, quite taken aback, she was astonished to find tears of joy there. This was just what it took to open the floodgates in her too. Diving into his open arms, she sobbed like a baby.

"Here, here," he said, patting her back. "Perhaps among the *gaje* a man does not welcome the news of a child?"

She turned a tear-stained face up to him. "But winter's coming. We're fugitives. We have no money."

"What do we need?" he said. "I have two hands. I am healthy. A Rom does not need much. The *gajo* needs land, and money in the bank, and power, and a place in the community. All these things can be taken away from him. All these things he can lose. And if he loses them he is nothing. A Rom has nothing to lose, and he is something special even with nothing in his pocket. Look. The good God gave you and me everything we need here"—he tapped his head—"and here"—he held up his two strong hands. "With these we can find everything we need and make it ours. If we do not lose our hands and heads there is nothing the *gaje* can take away from us."

"You're very encouraging," she said. She burrowed her face into his chest, seeking once again the solace of his strong grip. "You're more than that. You're my strength. You're. . . ." She could not say any more for a moment. "God," she said at last. "You can't imagine how good it is to have someone you can lean on, someone you can trust."

"Yes," he said. "I can imagine this. It is the way I feel myself." His hands on her back were gentle, protective. "Graciela, I have had women. I have lived with women. I have left women and been left by them. Never have I found an equal, a woman as strong and proud and independent as I. Manhood is not equated with one's sexual proficiency, Pesha used to tell me, nor with the number of one's conquests. Now I know why none of those earlier women lasted with me. Without knowing it, without thinking of it, I was seeking you and not finding you. Always." His voice was low and as calm as the midnight hour. "And now I find you are mine, doubly mine carrying our child. Oh, perhaps it is you who cannot imagine. . . ." He let the words trail off. Graciela didn't mind. She had never in all her life been so deliriously happy, in the middle of all that very real fear and apprehension and sorrow.

The good weather could not last. Now, down from Canada came the first dark clouds they had seen in many days, bringing with them the first chill rains of the approaching fall. The roads in the rolling country they passed through on their way north turned slick and treacherous; travel was wet and cold and miserable for both of them, although in wet weather Shandor insisted she remain inside the wagon. She kept the little front window open, though, and he chatted with her in a half-shout over the noise of the horses' hoofs as they made their way slowly north.

"How many days is it to St. Louis?" she said, talking to his stout legs in their homespun trousers.

"Perhaps two, three," he answered. It was raining

lightly, a chill drizzle, and the wagon was fishtailing on a muddy stretch of curving road at the top of a long hill. "I talked with someone back at the last settlement. The road will improve in a while. There should be no problem crossing back into Illinois there."

"I've been thinking about that," she said. "I think we should cross earlier. Thiebaud was heading for St. Louis. We don't want to run into him."

"I agree." At the top of the hill the wagon wheels bit into gravel and the wagon straightened out. She fancied she could hear the relief in his voice. "I asked about that too. There is a crossing downriver from St. Louis, at a place called Sainte Genevieve. It might be a good place to go back across into Illinois."

He stopped to yell at the horses, a nice round satisfying Romany curse. "Look," he said. "There are other things we could do." The wagon lurched crazily to one side in the slippery mud, then straightened out again. But now the rain came down hard, in heavy driving sheets, and he could no longer be heard. Graciela, seeing the water sloshing in, soaking her curtains, closed the little window and listened, sitting in the dark wagon, to the sound of the rain pounding on the roof. The groaning, creaking carriage under her rolled and pitched and swayed from side to side, and she was shudderingly ill again and again. But in her heart there was health and happiness and a feeling of belonging and of being loved and cared for. And in her belly there was life.

After a time she lay down on the narrow bed in the wagon and dozed. The rain drummed on the roof; the wagon rocked her like a cradle. She dreamed: a restless, fearful, unhappy dream, with people chasing her, with no place to hide, with nameless and unspeakable fears dogging her footsteps down a long and dreary road through a phantom forest in which horrid hands reached out from the shadows beside the road to pull at her, restrain her. . . .

She awoke with a start, sitting up suddenly in near darkness. The wagon was still. The rain had stopped, and there were voices outside.

She opened the little window behind Shandor's seat and called out to him. "Shandor?" There was no answer. As she looked out into the foggy post-rain gloom she could see people moving to and fro. But they didn't seem to be in a settlement. There were no houses, no buildings. They were standing in a grove of trees, and there were other wagons standing to one side. The horses had been unhitched and were no longer visible, trailing out before her at the end of their harnesses.

She stood up suddenly, bumping her head on an interior beam. The pain almost made her forget the wave of nausea which swept through her again the moment she stood erect—almost, but not quite. She felt dizzy, and sat down again before the back door of the wagon. In a moment, when her head had cleared, she reached down and pulled the latch that opened the rear door.

Seeing the brightly painted wagons, her first thought was of another Rom encampment. But the people gathered under the trees were not Gypsies. Although the Rom did not all tend to look alike, because in their wanderings throughout the world they had generated gray, green, and blue eyes and various shades of hair, the majority she had seen were usually of dark hair and olive skin. This group did not have the speech or the clothing of the Rom. Nor was it that of the workaday *gaje*. The thing that set them apart was not their looks, nor their clothing. It was what they were doing. She leaned forward to watch, fascinated.

There was a man juggling red and blue balls in the air: eight, nine, ten. He changed rhythm, changed hands, changed the very pattern of the balls in the air.

There was a man throwing knives at a tree trunk: one, two, three. They made the outline of a human being.

There were four men balancing on the shoulders of a fifth. As she watched a sixth leapt from a height onto a teeter-totter, throwing a seventh man high into the air to land, after two somersaults in the air, atop the grotesque pyramid.

There was a tiny man who stood no higher than her thigh, with ridiculously short arms and legs and a huge barrel head, who did back-flips and cartwheels, as agile as a normal person. Seeing her watching, he turned three flips and landed on his tiny feet just before her door. "Good afternoon," he said, smiling. And his smile, crooked teeth and all, was so warm, so winning, that she smiled back at him in spite of herself.

There was nothing else to do. She stood up, queasy stomach and all, and stepped out onto the rear platform of the wagon. "Hello," she said. "Excuse me—but where am I?"

The little man grinned confidently. "I haven't the faintest idea," he said. "Somewhere in Missouri, a day or so away from St. Louis, where we have an engagement tomorrow night." He bowed elaborately, in a genial caricature of formal manners. "Allow me to introduce myself. I am Marco the Magnificent, star of the Putnam and Frye Greater Combined Shows."

"Shows?" she said. "But I don't understand."

"The circus, Miss. You're with the circus. And we've stopped for the night. And we're glad to have you."

"Circus?" she said, stepping down onto the ground. "But how . . . ?"

"I don't know. Did you come here with someone?"

"Why, yes. But—" It was a good question. "Have you seen Shandor? My man? He's dark, and has black hair, and a black mustache, and—"

"Oh, yes!" the little man said. His eyes lit up with recognition. "Bruno! He's right over there. Don't get too close to him right now, though. He's practicing something. And if you're not used to that sort of thing. . . ."

"Thank you," she said, moving forward. Rounding the corner of a neighboring caravan, she came upon him: he was bare to the waist, barefoot, and to her great surprise had shaved off his black mustache. In a moment she saw why. He stood looking at her, his face breaking out into a mischievous grin. He held a pair of blazing firebrands in his two hands.

"Watch," he said. Without waiting for a reaction he opened his mouth wide and, as she stared open-mouthed, shocked, took one of the firebrands inside his mouth. Then he blew out, and a roaring burst of flame billowed forth from his open lips!

Graciela leaned back against one of the wagons, gasping. "My God," she said. "My God."

Shandor, laughing, put down the firebrands, dunking the lit ends in a bucket of water; they sizzled and hissed loudly. "Graciela," he said. "Welcome! Welcome to the circus!" He walked to her unhurriedly and threw his arms around her. "Here," he said. "Sit down. This must come as something of a surprise to you."

"I . . . I thought we were heading for the ford," she said. "I mean the ferry."

"My dear," he said, "we will not be safe anywhere we go, until we are new people. Here I am among my own. I have known these people, and others like them, since I was a boy, running away from my father's domineering ways. Here I am among friends. I am no longer Shandor, who is wanted by the *gajo* law for stealing a wagon. God knows, Butsulo is just enough of a fool to report me to the *gaje*. Here I am the Great Bruno, who knows every job on the circus lot."

"But. . . ." she said.

"Graciela," he said. "You still do not understand. No one here knows who you are. No one cares. Here you will prove yourself, or you will be asked to leave. If you prove yourself—and I will make sure you do—no one wants to know who you are. You are whatever, and whoever, you choose to be."

She stared at him, a small smile playing over her lips. In his excitement he'd switched back to Romany. *"Tshatshimo Romano,"* she said. Truly, the tongue of the Rom was the tongue for telling the truth. "Oh, God," she said, falling into his arms. "I hope you're right. I only hope you're right."

❧ BOOK FOUR ❧

Chapter 29

They made that engagement next night in St. Louis and then, to her astonishment (and not a little to her chagrin), they crossed the great River again and headed east: across Illinois, town by town, to Indiana, where they played Terre Haute, on its high plateau above the Wabash. Here, in a thriving boomtown where flatboats, steamboats, and the newly completed terminal of the National Railroad met to disgorge not only cargo but passengers as well, the circus flourished, and played a ten-day engagement, filling its small tent virtually every night.

Graciela had never been so happy in all her young life, nor as proud of anyone, ever, as she was of Shandor. He was totally in his element here, much more so than he'd ever been among the Rom wagons.

As the Great Bruno he turned out to be as good as his word. He did indeed seem to have virtually every skill required to perform every function in a traveling show. He could ride three galloping white horses at a time, nimbly leaping from one broad back to the next or doing a forward somersault through a flaming hoop to land on the horses' surging backs. He could walk a thin tightrope from one end of the rigging high above to the other, frightening Graciela every bit as much as he frightened the patrons in their safe seats. He could eat fire, juggle brightly colored balls, and balance atop a human pyramid or—his great muscles straining visibly, his eyes full of fire—support that same pyramid himself, at its bottom.

All of this, and more, he did with assurance, grace, and flair. And Graciela, despite her early pregnancy, found her love for him growing in intensity with every passing night as, flush from the encouraging and flattering applause, he strode directly from the make-up tent to their wagon to make tender and passionate love to her even before the evening meal.

There was something about applause, it appeared, that revivified the sort of person who performed for a living. She could see and feel the difference in Shandor. Something in his nightly conquests of the crowds stimulated him, intensified his lust and his tenderness alike. His youthful vigor had already surprised her before this; coming almost a virgin to him, she'd had nothing to compare him with, and the strength and enthusiasm with which he used her young body had thrilled and delighted her.

But this had been nothing at all, compared to the new man who came home to her bed every night, with the heady sound of the crowd's applause still in his ears, with his own skin still atingle from the eyes of the crowd—and particularly the eyes of the women in the crowd, whose voices were among the loudest raised when Shandor defied death on the high wire.

Graciela could well have given way to growing jealousy now, seeing the women's eyes on him. But, thinking it over as she stood by an entrance gate, watching his performance and running her own equally lustful eyes up and down his lithe and powerful young body, more than half bared by the performer's tights he wore, she found herself smiling a secret smile: *He loves me. It's me he's coming home to tonight. Look all you like.* But, being a true Gemini, she was not jealous and possessive. Pesha had told her how lucky she was to be a Gemini, because jealousy is the fear of a loss of love, which destroys that very love.

Even though there was apprehension of the future, she was enjoying the undiscovered marvels of this heretofore hidden magic of love. She studied the book on astrology Shandor had given her. It helped her to understand him. He, a Sagittarian, she read, "longs to play hookey from life's demanding karmic school. To cover his constant restlessness of spirit he adopts the pose of the actor, the thespian, which enables him to entertain others with a mixture of funny and tragic farces, while

206

he remains free to pursue the Socratic method of inquiry with his own soul, behind his theatrical mask. Meanwhile, he is optimistic, cheerful, daring and full of enthusiasm." Yes, that certainly seemed to apply to Shandor.

Once Shandor's routine had been established and there was no longer need for her help in setting up for his acts, Graciela found herself wanting to be more useful. One night, as the two of them lay in bed talking over the evening's performance, she brought up the subject of her own unproductive existence.

"Unproductive?" he said, sitting up suddenly, a small smile on his face in the candlelight. "But you are going to have a child. What could be more productive?"

"You know what I mean," she said. Still nude, she sat back defiantly on the little bed, modestly trying to hold a blanket over the breasts he'd kissed no more than fifteen minutes before. "I'm still not a circus girl. There ought to be some way for me to fit in here."

"What do you want to do?" he asked, puzzled. "All of the circus's trades require skill, great skill. And most of them are more athletic than would be proper for a woman who is expecting a child."

"I don't need to perform. Not that way, anyhow."

He smiled lovingly and put a comforting and exciting hand on her naked thigh. "I understand," he acknowledged, his eyes reflecting love. "But wanting to 'fit in' here. . . ." He stopped. "Look," he said suddenly. "What about a 'mitt camp'? I can buy canvas for a small single-0 top for you here in town. That's something you can do right now."

"Mitt camp?" she asked, puzzled.

"Reading palms. They call it a mitt camp because they don't know any better. You've been reading palms for some time now. And you know you are really good at seeing the truth."

"But Mr. Frye . . . I understand he hired someone."

"It's all right. Come to think of it, I talked to her this morning. She's a Rom, and she prefers to read the cards instead of palms. Her name is Lyuba. She speaks an odd form of Romany I've never heard before, but one can understand her. You'll have to make friends with her."

"Then we won't be competing?"

207

"No. Somehow the people who are interested in learning about themselves don't mind spending their money twice on the same night."

"Oh! I'll enjoy giving the readings, Shandor. I can't explain it completely but . . . it's not only the money I get for giving the reading but I also get a psychic compensation from knowing that I am helping someone."

"Yes, Graciela, you are a true *phuri dai*, a fascinating blend of earth and sky. You will help many. But first we must prepare a place to work from." He thought, then said, "Dear, can you sew? I mean, canvas, with a curved needle? Like sailmaking?"

"I can learn."

"I'll make you a top tomorrow, some of the others and I." He took her hands in his and pulled her to him. She looked his bare, brown body up and down and sighed happily, surrendering delightedly to his dominant urges. And the rest of the evening was just one long climax.

In the morning, after breakfast, Shandor and a number of the circus folk went to work sewing Graciela's single-0 top. She joined them, shoving the thick curved needle again and again through the heavy canvas with thimbled fingers. That night Graciela opened her "mitt-camp"—oh how she hated that name—and suddenly found herself doing a roaring business. A real live Gyspy, reading your palm? In authentic Gypsy dress? Why, there were men—and boys, too—who lined up before her modest tent as much for the privilege of having their hands held by an attractive young woman as to learn about themselves. She did so with gusto and with a flair that the other circus people, passing, could not miss. Nor was the size of the lines before her tent lost on them.

By slough time, as the entire turnout of circus personnel ringed the Big Top for teardown and folding and storing the big tent, Graciela had earned the respect of the entire show. And Shandor, catching the new light in the eyes of his associates as they watched Graciela walk modestly back to their wagon, was a new man as he followed her home in the chill morning hours. That night, his Gypsy ardor aroused by proprietary pride, he

208

renewed their liaison with a passion that fairly took her breath away.

She'd never been happier. Why, then, was it that the nagging feeling kept aching away at the inside of her? The feeling that it couldn't last? That her days of loneliness and fear and suffering had not come to an end, after all, but stretched much farther ahead of her than behind her? Why couldn't she relax and enjoy it? Why couldn't she believe her good fortune, and take it for granted the way another woman would?

And why did she keep waking in the middle of the night in a cold sweat, her body shivering and goosepimply under a thick eiderdown, her mind still haunted by frightening dreams, dreams of running . . . running . . . of being pursued endlessly down a lonely and desolate road by people whose faces she couldn't see? Why couldn't they leave her alone?

Chapter 30

Oscar Frye's advance man had been busy in Indiana. That next day their wagons crossed the Eel River by mid-afternoon and they played Bowling Green. Here Shandor stopped the show by walking the high wire with a midget perched precariously on his shoulders, and Graciela's palmist's tent did brisk business all the way to closing time.

Deeper into Hoosier country, Oscar Frye, as "patch" for the little show, found it harder and harder to buy compliance from the Indiana authorities; the two men who ran the tent with its new game called poker, fresh from the Mississippi riverboats, were dispatched instead to work as advance men down along the Ohio River, in Louisville. The thimblerigger game had disappeared from Frye's lot the moment they'd crossed the Indiana line.

They played Spencer, with its log courthouse, and delighted an audience of farmers and quarry workers. For a change Graciela found the action moving away from her mitt camp, and decided to close down for an hour to walk around the lot and take notice of popularity of the variout other single-0 attractions around the big ten-in-one.

To her surprise she found Lyuba, the Romany card-reader who had joined the show a few days earlier, standing in front of her own small top, smoking a black cigar. Graciela looked her up and down; her dress was not quite that of the Rom of Butsulo's camp, although the basics were there: low-cut blouse, very colorful full skirt, golden jewelry gleaming here and there at fingers and throat.

Her face was a Rom face, however, and the eyes in particular were Gypsy eyes: almost black, with unfathomable depths, and with virtually no trace of humor visible in them at all. She greeted Graciela in Romany, with a strange accent Graciela had never heard before. "Come," she said. "We will have a glass of wine."

Graciela followed her inside the little tent and sat down across from the Gypsy woman. "I'm sorry," she said, "I haven't had a chance to come see you before this. I am—"

"I know who you are," Lyuba said. She brought out two glasses and poured wine from a leather bota by squeezing its sides, fairly shooting the wine into the two glasses without spilling a drop. She sat down and picked up one of the glasses. "You are the girl of the Rom who was raised as a *gajo*."

"That's true," Graciela said. "I did not know my mother. There is still much I have to learn. Pesha— Bruno's grandmother and a *phuri dai* among her own people—had begun to train me, but died before she could finish."

"Ah," the woman said. "Let me see your hand." Graciela stuck out her palm. "Yes, yes," the woman said. "I see. This is a hand of great power. You will be great among the Rom. You will be a *phuri dai* yourself. But . . ." She suddenly bent over Graciela's palm again and looked hard. Then she straightened and looked Graciela in the eye, releasing her hand. "What do you know of palmistry?" she asked. "Is it just a game that one plays on the *gaje* with you?"

"Well," Graciela said, "Pesha wanted to teach me more but she died and so I am still eager to learn, but she did teach me much and I try to help those for whom I 'read.' She taught me that the lines of the palm change with the attitude of the person. She said over and over to me, 'We tend to move toward that upon which we dwell.' She also taught me that the secret of the universe is balance, and we are a reflection of that universe, subject to its laws inasmuch as we are a part of it. By looking at the palm we can detect inward disharmonies or faulty attunement, which if allowed to mature will throw the individual out of balance within himself and therefore out of balance with life. So, when I give a reading I try to help the person shape a good destiny. But there is so much more to the art that I would like to learn. If only Pesha had lived. . . ."

"Ah," Lyuba said. "Look. Come to my tent every night for, oh, perhaps half an hour. I will teach you what I know. It will not be enough, of course, for a girl who has the hand of a *phuri dai*. But you must learn everything, and perhaps it is your fate to learn some of it from me."

"I would be greatly obliged," Graciela said in her courtliest Romany. "And greatly honored. And Lyuba. . . ."

"Yes?" The black eyes bore into her own expressionlessly.

"Would you . . . I mean, I'm expecting a child. I have been in great danger. Would you read the cards for me, please?"

Lyuba did not answer for a moment. Then she nodded, and tossed her head back to drink the wine in her glass in one gulp. She wiped her mouth with one hand and stared at Graciela unblinkingly. "Yes," she said. "I will read the cards. Come tonight."

"Thank you," Graciela said, drinking her own wine and putting her glass down. She rose and dipped slightly in a respectful bow. "And Lyuba, would you read the cards for Shan—for Bruno?"

"Bruno?" the woman said. She pushed her chair back from the table that separated them. "I will think about that. For now, come tonight alone." She nodded and turned to go out. The interview was over.

Graciela went back to her own tent and continued to amaze the customers by first telling them something of their pasts that no one else could know. Then she would help them understand that they could shape their own destiny. "Knowledge is the power by which we control, direct, and shape the individual destiny, so use and apply the knowledge at your disposal, however unorthodox that may be." Then she would observe and tell them their own particular needs according to their palms. There was always great joy for her in helping to relieve some pain, be it physical or mental, that would otherwise not have been relieved.

After four women came two men. The first had a

farmer's broad hand and Graciela made some startling observations about his life and suggested those attitudes that must be changed, and that he could expect a "windfall" in about two and a half years. He was a nice man and she was glad she saw such a good change for him.

The second . . .

She did not look up; she had no need to look into the person's eyes, preferring to do as much of her work as possible by being sensitive to the palm and tuning in to the person. But this man simply laid his lean hand on the table before her, the cuffs at his bony wrists immaculately starched. He did not speak.

She looked up—and dropped his hand. She stared open-mouthed.

His face was gaunt, even more than before. The eyes were deep-set, haunted. But there was a winning, devilish grin on his face, and a recently acquired gold tooth gleamed in his lined face. The gray hair at his temples was cut and combed to perfection. Even at his age, in his precarious health, he remained the dandy.

"Graciela," he said. "Hello, my dear."

"Colonel Falligant!"

He'd been on the road, he said. The South was closed to him for a time, now: his collusion in her escape and Josh's had made him *persona non grata* below the Mason-Dixon. Murder, rape, larceny, incest—all these the Southerners would eventually forgive, but acquiescence with the Underground Railroad remained the one unforgivable sin.

So, his itchy foot calling the shots for him as usual, he'd ordered some labels from a print shop, made himself up a batch of the Universal Restorative and worked his way north selling snake oil. He'd stopped off in Warsaw, Illinois, with a young widow of some means and considerable charm; then, his interest waning, had worked his way across Illinois, one tiny hamlet at a time.

She told him about Butsulo, and about Josh—and saw the hurt cross his face, then the anger. "Damnation! I could kill the bastard myself. Put Butsulo's neck right here between these fingers." The hot flash of hatred receded, though, to be replaced by a look of sadness. "God," he said. He reached in a back pocket for the omnipresent bottle and, having vainly offered her a drink, took a quick snifter himself. "Ah," he said with a sigh. "The one true palliative. By God and by Christ, that's bad news. He was a strong and intelligent lad. In a better world he could have made anything he chose of himself. Now you said his wife and child are in Cairo? I've a mind to send them something."

"They'll likely be gone now," she said. "They were only waiting for Josh. I'm sure—well, Mame had relatives farther North. The only reason she'd have waited that close to the Line was the hope that. . . ." She couldn't finish the sentence; the words broke in her throat.

"My God," Falligant said, taking another drink. "And you say you saw Thiebaud? And heard news of Beau?"

"Not really news of him," she said. "Only that he'd apparently disappeared. Like you."

"Ah," Falligant said. "Well, he'll turn up anon. Like me. We're a pair of bad pennies. No damn good, either of us. I'm old enough to be his father, but we're as alike as brothers in some ways."

He looked her over now. "My God, you've changed. And in so little a time. This Gypsy garb looks good on you, girl. You're a grown woman now, it appears. And there's something else, isn't there? Did I hear you'd taken up with some young buck who does tricks on the high wire?"

"Bruno!" she said. "I mean . . . you remember Shandor, of course?"

"Ah, yes! The outcast. Another one of us bad pennies—only a bad penny among bad pennies. An outcast among the Rom."

"A chief among the Rom." She told him the tale of her apprenticeship with Pesha. "So you see, perhaps we didn't just drift into this."

"I think you were pushed into it. But he's a fine lad. I hope you're happy?" The look in his eyes was protective, paternal.

"Oh, yes," she said. "And we're expecting a child."

"Wonderful," he said. "I'm glad for you. But you're going to stay with the circus? Considering fall is already

214

here? You know, of course, what'll happen when all the leaves have gone."

She shuddered. "I've been trying not to think about that. I know the show goes south, running away from the winter."

"Well," he said, leaning forward. "It *is* a problem. And you with a child due, I'd say, in the spring. You'll be at your biggest in the dead of winter. And every place you can go that's warm will be south of the Line."

"What else can I do?" she said. "I've thought about everything."

"You could—but no," he said. "It's a foolish idea."

"No, please," she said. "What?"

"Well, I went west once, in a ship 'round the Horn. I've talked to folks recently who've been there since. There's a little community there now, in a town called Yerba Buena, on San Francisco Bay. It's mild the whole year round. There's a thriving little town a-building, led by a young friend of mine named Sam Brannan. Sam claims to be a Mormon, but he doesn't seem to let that stop him from having a good time, nor from making money either. He's going to own the whole area some day. Word has it that American troops have entered Mexico City to restore order. The Yanks will own California one of these days. They've got the Spaniards over a barrel, and I expect to see them extort the whole damned shebang away from Spanish rule before this time next year."

"But California?" She hadn't any idea what sort of a place it was. "What would we do?"

"Oh, hell," Falligant said, taking another drink from the bottle. "You're a couple of resourceful young folk. You'll figure out some way to turn the tip. You'll have your hands in a lot of pockets before the first season's over. Never you worry. The main thing is raising the fare and perhaps having a trifling sum to live on for the first six months or so, while you're learning the territory and getting a line on the local marks."

"You make it sound so easy," she said. "But going around Cape Horn in winter? Expecting a child?"

"Damn," he said. "You women and your unshakable logic. Let a man start painting pictures in the air for you and what do you do? You blow it all away with your damnable common sense." His grin was almost boyish, and had a lot of avuncular affection in it. "Come on," he said. "The last show's just beginning. You haven't any more customers. Let's go see that young man of yours and his death-defying feats of derring-do." He pronounced the bombastic words with relish. "By God. It's nice to walk on sawdust again, so help me it is. I've half a mind to talk Oscar Frye into letting me frame a joint here and start parting these Hoosier marks from their hard-earned cash." He rose to go, taking one last swig from the bottle before corking it securely. "After you, my dear."

Shandor was wonderful, as usual, and Falligant applauded as loudly as anyone. "Louder, my dear," he said. "We're part of the claque. He's depending on us to create enough interest for a blow-off. Let's do it for him."

"All right," she said, increasing her own part in the clamor. She knew what a blow-off was—a second show, done by request after a second payment, in which the performer attempted even more difficult and dangerous stunts. Sure enough, the applause, led by them, continued for a long time. Shandor came out again and again to take bow after bow. Finally Oscar Frye, resplendent in his fox-hunting outfit as the ringmaster, stepped forward and made his pitch. "Ladies and gentlemen, your attention, your attention please!"

Graciela, sitting beside Wesley Falligant on the bottom row of risers, felt a tug at her arm. She turned to see Lyuba, her face expressionless as usual, her dark eyes enigmatic. "Here," the Gypsy woman said. "You come now. I will read the cards for you."

Graciela touched Falligant's hand. "Excuse me," she said. "I'll be only a few minutes." She rose and followed Lyuba out into the night.

Chapter 31

Once again Graciela sat down opposite Lyuba in the little tent. This time Lyuba pulled the curtain that blocked the open doorflap of the little top. "I am done with the *gaje* for the night," she said.

Graciela looked at Lyuba's face, and saw the cold and distant mask replaced by lines of worry and concern. "Lyuba," she said. "What's the matter?"

The older woman sat back and looked at her. Now those dark eyes held only fear and sympathy. "I read the cards for you a while ago. While you were not here. Then I read the cards for Bruno. Then I read the cards for you again."

"And?"

"And I would like to read them for you again. While you are with me. I hope . . . I hope I may be wrong."

"Wrong?" Graciela leaned forward, suddenly tense. "Wrong about what? What did the cards say?"

"Please," Lyuba said. She leaned over the table, her eyes fixed on the red tablecloth. "Pick a card. Do not look at it."

Graciela did so. As she did Lyuba traced with her finger an invisible triangle on the tablecloth. She laid out the cards to the right and left of the one Graciela had chosen. Then came the three circles of eleven cards each, in a ritualistic pattern determined by the *Etteilla*, the centuries-old tradition the Rom used. Once the pattern was complete Lyuba placed the remaining cards under the one Graciela had chosen.

Now, however, instead of turning over the cards in order she leaned back, her eyes closed, and began rocking slowly back and forth from the waist, crooning softly

217

to herself. "Lyuba," Graciela said softly, but it was obvious that the trancelike state Lyuba was seeking had been achieved. She could no longer hear Graciela.

As her body continued its rhythmical rocking, her lips opened and words came forth. Graciela was surprised. The voice was not Lyuba's. It was deep, rasping, like a man's.

Graciela sat transfixed, her eyes on Lyuba. Her breath came in short halting gasps. She knew better than to interrupt or, worse, to awaken Lyuba in the middle of the seance. Pesha had made that plain. Her hands were shaking uncontrollably; she placed them on the table in an attempt to bring her nerves under some sort of rein.

"Hear now," the strange voice said. "Hear now the message. Hear the voice of the spirit.

"*One*: You have traveled far. You have worn many names and been many persons in a short time."

So far, so good. Graciela leaned forward, her eyes on Lyuba's wooden face.

"*Two*: Your wandering has not ended. You will wear other names, other faces.

"*Three*: You will live long, and will gain the world and lose the world and gain it again.

"*Four*: You will rise and fall and rise."

Graciela, in spite of herself, could not resist breaking in. "But Lyuba," she said. "You repeat yourself." She looked at the impassive face and knew she would get no answer. The face was that of a woman who could hardly be said to be alive, much less attentive.

"*Five*: A great city will lie at your feet. You will conquer it alone, with nothing but your own mind for a weapon.

"*Six*: You will be every man's goddess, one man's queen.

"*Seven*: What you have lost, you will win again. What you have won, you will lose.

"*Eight*. . . ."

Graciela's eyes bored into the expressionless face. There would be thirteen statements, she knew: one for each card in the pile at the middle of the pattern. The first one was merely the identifier, the card she had chosen and which had bound the cards beneath it to her and to her alone.

"*Eight*: What you shall gain is far away. What you shall lose is close by. Death is close by. Beware. . . ."

Death? "Lyuba, please! What do you mean?"

"*Nine*: If you would find what your heart most desires you must seek what your heart most fears.

"*Ten*: The Great Game will fall to your hand. You must learn it and cherish it.

"*Eleven*: You are a queen but will not reign as one. You are a slave but will not live as one. You are all things. You have lived many lives before.

"*Twelve*: You will know when death is near. The blood of the Rom, inside you, will tell you."

Graciela, shaking, waited for the thirteenth statement. But Lyuba's impassive face, its eyes still tightly closed, continued to face the upper panels of the tent. The lips did not open. "Please," she said. "Lyuba?"

"Speak," the strange voice said. The eyes did not open; the face did not turn her way. "Ask."

"Lyuba," Graciela said. "This death you speak of. Whose is it? Is it mine? Is it Shandor's?"

Just then the panel was pushed open and a *gajo*, a farmer from the looks of him, stuck his face inside. "Par'n me, lady, is this the—?" He looked at Lyuba, gulped, and retreated.

Lyuba's face twisted. Her lips opened. Her eyes opened.

"No!" Graciela said. "No, please!"

But the face came back to life again, and the voice was Lyuba's as she said, "That's odd. I was just going to read the cards."

"You did read the cards," Graciela said, her voice taut and tense. "But you were asleep at the time."

Lyuba's eyes flashed. "Nonsense. Come, we will read. Now, would you take a card?"

But Graciela could take no more of this. Pressing her hands to her burning cheeks, she scrambled to her feet and lurched unsteadily out of the little tent into the night.

The Niccolinis, an equestrian troupe, were just finishing their blow-off act as she walked back into the main tent. She sat down beside Falligant, her eyes staring, unseeing.

"Graciela!" Falligant said, leaning her way. "You're

white as a sheet! What's the matter, my dear?" He put one bony hand on her arm. "My God, you're shaking like an autumn leaf. Here, come outside with me." He led her out into the night again, to hold her in strong arms and croon quietly and soothingly to her. "There, there, my dear. If you saw something or heard something, it's all right. Just tell me."

"Lyuba," she said. Her voice was phlegmy and choked with salt tears. "She said. . . . she said. . . ."

"Lyuba? Who's Lyuba?" His voice was conciliatory, calming. She couldn't tell whether he was listening or not. It was enough to feel his arms holding her, protecting her from harm, his fatherly hands patting her quaking back.

"She—she read the cards. The Tarot. She said—she said death was near. She said I would know, and oh, God, I know; *I know*. . . ."

"Know what, my dear?"

But she *did* know. And suddenly it all became clear to her. Shandor! The death she could feel in the air, in her mind, in her very bones—it was Shandor's! She had to warn him! "Please," she said, pulling away. "Shandor—where is he?"

"Why, he's just getting ready to go on," Falligant said. "I saw him adjusting his rigging."

She couldn't wait. She broke away and dashed across the half-dark ring, avoiding the pounding hoofs of the big horses with a practiced ease, as if nothing could harm her. *Shandor!* Where was he? But he was nowhere to be found under the main top. She dashed out through the far flap into the near-darkness outside.

There! She saw him, standing just outside the warm light from the tent. He was doing deep knee-bends and alternately touching his toes, limbering up in the cool evening air. As he looked up he saw her, and his dark face opened up in a broad grin. "Graciela!" he said. His arms opened wide; she rushed into them, sobbing.

"What is the matter? What is bothering you, my own?" His arms were stronger than Falligant's, but they brought her no more comfort. He made soft, low, calming sounds close to her ear. "Look, my darling. I have to go on in a moment. But then when I am done we will

220

go to the cook tent and eat. The women are making a feast for us. I told them about the child."

"Shandor!" she screamed with the little breath that she could muster. "You can't go on! I have a feeling—Lyuba—she told me. . . ."

"But my darling," Shandor said, his voice strong and confident. "This is the blow-off. It is the first one we have had since we joined the show. Wait until I am done."

"But Lyuba, she said. . . ."

"Never mind Lyuba," he said. "She just makes up superstitions for the *gaje*. She doesn't give readings as you do. Pay no attention to her. Now we have a child to look forward to, a family to raise. And if it is among the *gaje* that we must live, it is as a *gajo* man that I must conduct myself. You and I, we can choose our worlds. We can raise our child as we choose. Please, do not be afraid. I am invincible. Invulnerable. Did you see the way they applauded? Did you see?"

As his strong arms held her and the soft, low words caressed her ears, she suddenly felt the fear leaving her. She felt the strength flow from his powerful, rock-hard young body into her own. She knew, once again and this time with a certainty that shocked her, how wonderful, how miraculous a thing it was to have someone who loved you truly, utterly, with an absolute abandon and with a fierce protectiveness that stood always between you and the things you feared and dreaded. "Oh, Shandor," she said. "I'm sorry. I'm such a fool. I just felt suddenly frightened."

"This is the way a woman feels when she is with child," he said. "You must pay no mind to it. I am with you. I am always with you." He turned her face up to his, and his kiss was hot and lusty. Confidence filled her, his own boundless confidence, born of a matchless bravery. "Now," he said. "Sit right here and watch me. Wish me well." His smile was warm and winning; he kissed her again and released her to stride majestically into the tent just as Frye finished the hyperbolic spiel that preceded the star attraction.

The applause that greeted him was strong, appreciative. He'd pleased them before, and enormously; they expected even more of him this time. Graciela, her heart pounding with pride in her man, dried her tears and stepped through the open sideflap to watch as he clambered up the rigging to his perch atop the tent. When at last he stood at the near end of the tightrope, his body gleaming in the light of the star candles, and acknowledged the applause, Graciela thought she'd never in her whole life seen anyone so beautiful. The bright smile gleamed white in the middle of his dark face; his powerfully muscled arm rose high to wave to the crowd below.

The crowd quieted as Frye stepped into the middle of the ring, his chunky body managing to look quite dashing in the riding outfit, his round face framed in prematurely white hair. "Thank you, thank you, ladies and gentlemen, thank you. And now, the Great Bruno will attempt a feat never before completed successfully on the American continent. Risking life and limb, he will attempt to cross the wire in all but total darkness."

"No," Graciela said in a small voice. "No."

"Please, *Signor* Niccolini, would you douse the sidelights? Thank you. And now, ladies and gentlemen, only the lights at the two ends of the wire remain, to guide the steps of the Great Bruno as he walks the wire forty feet above the ground!"

"Please," she said, looking up, her hand over her mouth. "*Please. . . .*"

"Mr. Bandmaster!" Frye said. The term was a foolish one: the band was a fife and drum unit of perhaps six people on a good night. "A drum roll, please!" And the slow, exciting roll of a pair of sidedrums filled the air.

"Don't do it," Graciela said. Her voice broke. She could say no more. She knew he couldn't hear her.

Shandor stepped confidently out upon the wire, which was by now totally invisible to him. He walked slowly forward.

There was a sudden gasp from the crowd, and a hubbub which became a low roar.

Graciela looked at the middle of the tent.

A bright glow came from the center pole.

A single nail held the rope that braced the centerpole. The nail glowed red-hot. There was a wisp of smoke

222

from the rope as the heat singed it, scorched it, slowly set it on fire.

The Nail! The Nail of the Rom!

Shandor, on the wire, looked down and saw it. His steps faltered. He tried to regain his balance. His arms flapped like the wings of a mighty bird. He wobbled to and fro on the invisible wire.

The rope, aflame now, burned brightly. The crowd's growing panic became audible. A woman screamed. Shandor righted himself on the wire. Just as he did, the rope burned all the way through. The burned end flew heavenward. The canvas above them dipped, struck the tight wire.

Shandor, in that last moment, stood erect on the wire. His body tensed, then relaxed. He bent his knees and reached for the invisible wire with both hands. . . .

. . . and missed.

His body plummeted to the ground and hit, hit hard. He lay still.

"Oh, dear God," Graciela said in a broken voice. "Oh, dear God."

Chapter 32

The drums rattled. The fife shrieked away crazily. The Niccolinis, quick thinking as always, shooed the joeys into center ring as young Aldo, star of the act, lit two candles and, one in each hand, his arms held high, leapt on the back of Peppone, the troupe's venerable dapple grey, and guided the old animal into the hippodrome at a walk which became a trot as soon as the old horse's hoofs touched sawdust.

Amid all this frantic activity Falligant and Ettore Niccolini, patriarch of the tribe, managed to drag Shandor out of the ring into the shadows, where they lay him flat on the ground on his back. Graciela, looking down at him, could not speak. Her eyes filled with tears as she heard Frye's voice, inside the tent, quieting the skittish crowd: ". . . the Great Bruno just had the wind knocked out of him, folks, he'll be all right in a few minutes, he'll be back to entertain you. In the meantime, we are proud to present the Clowns of Clown Alley, led by Marco the Magnificent!" The audience roared with nervous laughter. "And, in the center ring, the dashing young star of one of the greatest acts of the European continent: the incomparable, the magnificent, the death-defying *Aldo Niccolini!*"

There was a huge roar of applause. The audience, scared out of its wits by the events of a moment before, wanted desperately to be entertained, and the Putnam and Frye Greater Combined Shows was determined to give them what they wanted. The laughs came thick and fast. The fife and drum kept up their inane blather: a *prestissimo* galop, played with a mad end-of-the-world brio, as fast as the flutist could play and at the very edge of the drummer's capabilities. The nervous edge in the audience's laughter gradually dropped away, and became instead a tone of warm appreciation.

And outside, in the shadows . . .

"Oh, God," Graciela said again and again. "Oh, God. Is he. . . . ?"

Wes Falligant threw one arm around her and hugged her hard. "I couldn't tell. Look, I'll see what I can find out." He released her and knelt by Shandor's side. "Ettore!" he said. "Bring a blanket, quick!" Niccolini, crossing himself, went away, his face drawn under the white circus paint. "Now, let's see."

Graciela fell to her knees beside him. Something in her would not let her touch Shandor, not yet. Not until she knew, once and for all, whether he was alive or dead. Her eyes did not leave his face, calm and serene in the half-light that filtered through the canvas sidewall. "Please," she said. "Is there any sign of. . . ."

"I'm not sure. Yes . . . yes, there's a pulse! But it's weak, unsteady. But he's alive!"

"Oh, thank God!" And Graciela let one quaking hand snake forth from under her shawl and touch him. He was so cold! "Oh, he's freezing!"

"You're right," Falligant said. "Poor devil, he's in shock. Here!" He looked up and saw Niccolini approaching with a heavy horse blanket. He took it from the rider's hands and tenderly draped it over Shandor's body. "Yes," he said. "Ettore: has anyone gone for a doctor?"

"My son Ruggiero, he took one of the horses." Niccolini's face was haggard and his voice was low, fearful. "The boy, Bruno, he is alive?"

"Yes," Falligant said. "Gods! Did you see that—that thing? Inside? The glowing thing?"

"*Si, signore.*" Niccolini crossed himself again. "It was—I do not know what it was," he said. "A thing of the devil!"

"Graciela," Falligant said. "What was that? I have a strange feeling, you know." He laid one hand on the stricken man's cheek, his eyes on her.

"It was—" She started to tell him, but stopped. It sounded so ridiculous. But on the other hand everyone had seen it. Was that fact itself any more plausible than the story the Rom gave of its origin? "I don't know. There's a Rom legend, about—but no. I don't know."

"But you do," Falligant said calmly. "You do, don't you? Look, don't give me this nonsense about stupid Gypsy legends. There are more things in the world than you can measure with a scale or a dressmaker's tape, and you and I know it. You know something about this. What is it?"

Graciela's eyes went back to Shandor's strangely peaceful face. "You're right," she said in a flat voice, her face devoid of expression. "There's a Rom story. It's the fourth nail of the Crucifixion."

She looked up at them now, hesitant. Niccolini's face went blank; he crossed himself again. Falligant, on the contrary, showed some sign of recognition. He blew out, open-mouthed. "Ah," he said. "I think I've heard that one, years ago. But I never believed it. Until now. And even now I'm not sure."

"It's true," she said. "Shandor and I, we saw it the day Butsulo killed Josh. We thought it was an omen for Butsulo, an omen of the end of his reign over the tribe. Instead. . . ."

"Instead, it came to your young man." Falligant's voice carried a world-weary irony that somehow managed to hold a strong note of pity and compassion. "God, girl. What can I say? If he lives. . . ."

"Yes?" she said. Her eyes went to his. There was a great darkness in his face. "Yes? Go on."

"I'm not sure. He may be gone. He may have another hour left in him. I've seen a lot of people die, and I still can't say. But if he lives. . . ." He sighed, and all of a sudden the weight of his years hung heavy on him. "I don't know. I think his days as an acrobat may be over."

"Oh, God," she said. She took one of Shandor's ice-cold hands in hers: it was unresponsive, unfeeling. Then, as she looked down at him, she saw him open his eyes.

The eyelids fluttered. The eyes opened. They looked straight ahead. They did not look at her.

"Shandor," she said. Her voice was quivering, frightened.

The eyes turned her way and saw nothing. They

226

looked away, looked front and center. The head did not move at all. The lips trembled; they moved slightly. The jaw did not move with them. "Graciela . . ." he said. The voice was flat, dead.

Falligant looked at her and then down at the boy. He nodded to Niccolini; then he stood up and moved away, his hand on Niccolini's shoulder, steering the equestrian leader into the shadows. Now the man on the ground and the girl at his side were alone together. She could barely make out his face in the light of the candles.

"Shandor," she said.

"Graciela, you saw it?" His voice was strangled, soft. "The Nail—it was for me. . . ."

"My darling," she said. "Oh, my very own darling."

"I am going to die."

"Oh, please . . . oh, please, God, don't take him, not now, don't make him leave me!"

"I am going to die. I can feel it. I can feel . . . nothing else. I . . . I tried to move my hand. I can move nothing. I feel no pain. . . ."

She held his hand in both of hers, rocking back and forth on her knees beside him. The tears finally came and once they had come there was no stopping them. "Please, please," she said over and over. But the hand she held between hers was lifeless, inert. "Shandor, my precious. . . ."

"Please," he said. The lips moved. Nothing else of him moved with them, not even the sightless eyes. "Please. I must talk to you."

"Oh, yes," she said. She made a supreme effort and, gritting her teeth savagely, shut out the tears. "Yes, my darling. Please. Talk to me."

"The child. Raise the child away from the Rom. Raise it as a *gajo*. Do it for me. The curse might come to it if it remains among the Rom. Raise the child as a *gajo*."

"Oh, yes," she said. "Anything, anything you want."

"Remember I love you. I have never loved another woman. There was Pesha, who raised me as her child, and then there was you. I have known other women . . . but I never loved until you. . . ."

"Please," she said. "Stay with me."

"No, I am going. I cannot feel. I cannot see. I grow cold all over."

"Oh, my darling." She threw her body over his. If she could keep him warm, if she could give him the warmth of her own body. . . .

"My . . . my body is cold. Graciela . . . I love you . . . Graciela, goodbye. . . ."

Now her whole body was on his, and her arms went around him, even as she knew that the feeling had left his broken body and he could not even feel the weight of her upon him. No matter; logic had nothing to do with it. There was only the desperate, panic-stricken feeling that if somehow she could keep out the cold, could keep his poor body warm. . . .

There was a moment in which he was still alive—and then there was a moment when he wasn't. She knew it. She sat bolt upright and looked at him. Now there was a look of peace on his dark face, a look of rest. She knew that his face hadn't moved a muscle since his last words to her, but somehow she knew that in the moment he had slipped away from her he had managed to take something of her love with him, something to keep away the cold, to warm him as he slipped into the next dimension, into the new existence that lay before him in the next life.

After a while she stood up and looked around to see Wes Falligant standing beside her. His face was grave and serious. "He's gone, isn't he?" Falligant said.

"Yes."

"I knew it, damn it." He put one gaunt hand on her shoulder. "There isn't much to say, is there?"

"I . . . I guess not. Colonel . . ."

"Wes, my dear. For all that I'm a grandfatherly distance from you, we've been through enough together for first names, haven't we?"

"Yes," she said. And then it was the most natural thing in the world to seek comfort in his arms. She hugged him close and let him pat her back and croon low unintelligible things into her hair. "I . . . I can't cry. I just can't."

"You will," he said. "You've got to. But there are times when it takes a while to catch up. Your feelings have just had too many assaults on them lately to. . . . don't worry about it. Why, child, when you've had your heart broken as many times as I have. . . ." His voice turned sour, self-mocking for a moment. "But you haven't, have you? And you're feeling this kind of loss for the first time." His hand stroked the middle of her back; the feel of it was soothing and warming. "Ah, poor child, poor child. You've had a lot to deal with in your young life, haven't you?"

"I won't," she found herself saying suddenly. "I won't—I won't let myself—"

"Ah," he said. "Don't close up against it, now. You've an honest grief to go through, and come out the other side. Go ahead and experience it. Let yourself go."

"It's not that," she said. She stepped back and looked up at him, her face set, her mouth severe. "I can't let up now. I can't ease up. I have to keep together. I can't just come apart, like some protected young woman with a family to cushion her against harm. I . . . I've got Shandor's child inside me, and—for God's sake, I'm still a slave, still alone in the world, still on the run. I've got nobody—nobody to turn to."

"Ah," he said. "I was going to wait awhile to bring that up. Look, you're not going to stay with the show until it crosses the Line and then breaks up. You're strictly first-of-May, child, and you know it. What *are* you going to do?"

"I . . . I don't know. Strike out for the Coast, perhaps. New York. Boston. Someplace like that."

Falligant knelt beside Shandor and gently closed the staring eyes with two fingers. Then he pulled the blanket up over his handsome face. He nodded to Ettore Niccolini. "Would you have him taken to the wagon? We'd be much obliged. The young lady. . . ."

"*Capisco, signore,*" Niccolini said.

"*Grazie di molto,*" Falligant said with a courtly nod of the head. He stood and took Graciela by the arm, steering her away from the sideflap, away from the big tent itself.

"Look," he said. "We've got a friend to bury, you and I. After that, well, we'll figure out what's the best thing to do. If you want to cut out for the East, I can give you some names to look up in New York or Boston. And perhaps I might have some advice to give if you wanted to ask for it. But in the meantime, well, the offer I made the two of you—coming with me to California—well, it still goes."

His voice changed. "Don't get me wrong. I'm not proposing anything between you and me. I'm an old man, and I'm ill. Not just this stuff in my lungs; I've got another disease which will keep me away from women for a time, for perhaps all the time I have left. And, well, you bring out the father in me, I suppose. But that's all academic. The thing is, you'll get more of a new start there than anywhere else in the country. California'll be ours shortly, you can bet your bottom dollar on that. And we'll be in on the ground floor. There'll be fortunes made there. The land is rich and the weather mild, and you can grow truck-farm stuff around the seasons. And where there are fortunes to be made, by Christ, there'll be people like Wes Falligant to part the makers from their fortunes. Look you: you have the gift of gab just like the rest of us; you got it from the Irish and Gypsy sides alike. You'll be right at home out there."

His voice grew philosophical. "No hurry, now. But think it over. It may make sense to you in a day or so."

"I . . . I'll think about it," she said. But inside, she already knew. He was right. It was the only thing to do.

"You do so," he said. "And look, if you need anything in the meantime, please call on me. For anything I have to give." He turned and started to go; but then he thought of something. "We could book passage for you as my niece and ward," he said. "I know a man in New York who's damned good at forging papers. All kinds of papers. We can give you a new identity, a new name." He gave her the same courtly nod of the head she'd seen earlier, then turned smartly on one heel and walked slowly away. His carriage was erect, his head high. There was even a bit of the old swagger in his stance. She fancied she could almost read his mind: *a fresh start in a new land . . . new worlds to conquer . . . new gulls to fleece . . . new money to be made, and not an honest dollar in the lot.*

Yes. Yes, it was the only choice in the world she had.

Chapter 33

The circus turned out the next day to bury Shandor in a patch of woods, under a great spreading tree overlooking the meandering White River. There wasn't much ceremony. Circus people turned out to be superstitious—ever so much more than the Rom had been—and the thought of death, particularly death in the middle of a difficult and dangerous circus performance, cast a pall over the crowd gathered in the fall chill on the river bank.

They had all liked "Bruno," who could do so many circus things, who was, whatever his origins, a real circus boy, a real trouper. They had all respected him. All of them, at one time or another, had had cause to thank him: for sewing up a tattered top, helping out with an act, pitching in for an injured member of another troupe. As they gathered at the simple unmarked graveside, Graciela could see genuine grief on many faces, and tears in more than one pair of somber eyes.

One of the roughies patted the pile of dirt once more with the back of his shovel, "for luck," another said under his breath. Graciela stood by Falligant's side in her improvised widow's weeds and let her eyes drift to the overarching foliage of the great tree, at the banks and the beautiful river below. "Bury a Gypsy under a tree," she said. "It's a very Rom sort of place, isn't it?"

"Yes," Falligant said. "You insisted the burial, the funeral service, be kept simple, with no touch of the Rom rituals. Why?"

"He would have wanted it that way," she said. "He was a leader among the Rom, but they threw him out. He was a man with one foot permanently in both camps, and I know he had a divided mind. Torn, you might say."

"Then why repudiate the Rom half of him?"

"Because of the child I'm carrying," she said. "It's not that I want to insult the memory of his life among the Rom. But he told me to raise the child as a *gajo*. He said this was the only way to escape the curse. And, well, I think he saw the beginning of the end for the Wanderers. In the world we're entering there'll be less and less place for them, I'm sorry to say."

"You say them. Not us."

"You forget," she said wearily. "Butsulo threw me out too. As everyone has thrown me out." There was a bitter smile on her face as she looked down again at the packed dirt. "We were well matched."

"You were, in fact, a beautiful couple. It made my heart leap to look at you." Falligant's arm went out; she took it gratefully. "I'll confess," he said, "I thought—well, if I'd stayed around Butsulo's camp a while longer I might have done my best to steer the two of you together. As it was, I was delighted to learn you'd found each other in the normal sort of way." He turned to look down at her. "Your experiences in the past months have matured you—and damned handsomely, too. Whatever they've done to your heart, child, they certainly haven't harmed your looks. We'll have to give some thought to dressing you properly when we go West. Give you just the right sartorial touch, to set off that dark coloring of yours. Gods! You'll have half the gallants in Yerba Buena at your feet before the ship drops anchor in San Francisco Bay."

Oscar Frye came up just as she and Falligant were climbing into the light four-passenger family wagonette the Colonel had purchased in town that morning. "I heard you were going," he said.

"Oh," she said. "I'm sorry. I forgot. I did mean to say goodbye to everyone. Please, would you tell them all for me? And the wagon—Aldo Niccolini's wife is expecting. They can't stay with Ettore anymore. Would you ask them if they'd like the wagon? It ought to be just right for the three of them."

"That's very kind of you," Frye said. "I'll tell them. Here." He handed her an envelope. "Bruno hadn't col-

232

lected his salary for some time. You two apparently didn't have much immediate need for money. I put a bit of a bonus inside. I wish it could be more. He earned it and so did you. I'll miss you. So will the others. I'll be happy to say goodbye for you." He gave her a formal little half-bow. "You kept describing yourself as first-of-May. You're not. While you've been on the lot you've been with it and for it. You'll always be welcome on a lot of mine." He saluted her with the crop he held in one hand and turned smartly on one heel to leave.

As he did Graciela spotted another familiar figure standing by the last of the gaily painted circus wagons, a figure whose face bore an expression in which fear and sorrow were mixed. As Graciela's eye caught hers the woman turned to go. "No!" Graciela cried out, and ran after her, catching her by the hand. "Lyuba, don't go!"

"I—I was afraid something I had said. . . ."

"No," Graciela said. She grasped the Gypsy woman by the arms and then impulsively hugged her. "No, you didn't even know what you were saying. And besides, the spirit was upon you. You can't feel responsible for visions you have when you—please, please don't go away. I—I want to talk to you."

"You are not angry?"

"No, no. Please come with me. Over here. I . . . I'm leaving the circus. We were just getting ready to go."

"I am leaving the show too. I have brought bad luck, and to a fellow Rom."

"No, no."

"Graciela?" Falligant said. He was checking the bit in the horse's mouth. "We'd better get ready to leave." He stopped, looking at Lyuba. "I beg your pardon?" he said. "I think we haven't met."

"This is Lyuba," Graciela said. "She predicted Shandor's death. And much more. Wes, could we . . . could we take her along? She's leaving the show too."

"Huh," Falligant said. He looked at the two of them, standing there together arm in arm. "Well, if this is something you really want. Hmmm. Traveling as my 'niece' you could, in fact, use a duenna. If the lady'd be willing to go along with the act. It'd look better all around. But you know, we're traveling light. Living off the land, as you might say."

233

"She reads cards. She has all the skills of a Rom woman. She'll fit in just fine."

"But the wagon's rigged for one horse."

"Mr. Frye just gave me Shandor's pay. Here." She tossed the envelope; he caught it easily in one hand, his brow raised skeptically. As he opened the envelope and looked inside his expression changed. His lips pursed and blew, softly. "Ah," he said. "You knew just what it'd take to convince me. This is about half again what I had in my pocket to get us to New York. I'll buy horse and rig in Bloomington. This old nag will get us that far by herself. Miss Lyuba? Be our guest, please." And, courtly again, he helped the two women up onto the high seat.

As they rolled slowly away Graciela couldn't resist one last look back. She craned her neck and peered around the side wall, bracing herself with both hands. Already the circus was collected and ready to go. As she looked Oscar Frye stepped lightly, despite his portly bulk, into the seat of the first wagon and reached out with his quirt, flicking it lightly at the horses. The caravans moved along, down the dusty road. She stole one last glance at the grave site, sitting high on the bank. Then she looked once again at the train of wagons as they slowly moved away. They were taking a part of her life with them, she knew. Another part of her lay in the grave beside Shandor, her proud and beautiful lover of—how many weeks? No matter. The thing that bound a part of you to another person wasn't the length of time you'd known them, but the intensity. She knew she'd love again, but Shandor had been the first person to whom she'd given her heart.

Except . . . except. . . . But that thought she managed to quench before it had time to strike fire in her. Her face somber, her mouth grimly determined, she pulled herself back into the seat and let her gaze run far down the road ahead, as the old horse slowly *clip-clopped* along the pike through the lush rolling countryside of Owen County.

There was no time for looking back now. Only for looking ahead. There would be ample time to think of the past when she'd made provision for the present and the future. She had a place in life to make for herself,

234

and she was determined to make it. Where better than out on the new frontier of California, where, if Colonel Falligant's assessment was correct, most of the people had some sort of shady doings in their past, where nobody asked your real name and inquired into your background, provided you made no indiscreet inquiries into theirs.

And, too, she had a child on the way. She had another life to think of, one she had every intention of providing for, and a lot better than her father had provided for her.

Yes! *Her* child wouldn't have to suffer as she'd suffered. Her child would grow up in security, with a safe place in life, with an assured position nobody could take away. That, too, had been the message Shandor had given her just as he died. No unprotected Rom life, living under the stars with the *gajo* always after you. Who protected the Rom? No one!

Look at Shandor himself! A leader—but a leader of what? Of a bunch of wagons riding down a road someone else owned. Even that couldn't be defended, if someone wanted to throw you out. No, this was no life for a child of hers. Her child would grow up in a protected and secure home, one she'd made for herself, with her own skillful hands and sharp intelligence and ironbound determination. And nothing—nobody—would stand between her and her goal. Not for long, anyhow.

She'd show them! All of them!

❧ BOOK FIVE ❧

Chapter 34

Struggling through a crowd of drunken seamen to the corner of Dupont Street, Sam Brannan paused at the Washington Street marker to look back down the precipitous hill.

God, what a rathole, he thought. *And you've only yourself to blame for it all.*

When he'd landed with his shipload of Mormon emigrants from New York aboard the *Brooklyn* in 1846, the town had been called Yerba Buena; it had been a dozen or two peaceful, scattered houses dotting the rolling hills of the peninsula. He had hoped to bring the people who sailed with him to a new land, one they could make their own; but already the Stars and Stripes had flown from the flagpole over San Francisco Bay. It had been a bad omen. Already the United States, which had persecuted the Mormons endlessly since their prophet, Joseph Smith, had founded the Church in 1830, had begun moving West, for all that the land still technically belonged to Mexico.

Brannan had seen the beginning of the end then, and had started making plans. As leader of the Mormon community that dominated the town, he'd steadily fought virtually every innovation that had followed the first American ships West, from renaming the city San Francisco to the U.S. government opening customs and assay offices immediately following the cessation of hostilities with Mexico and the ratification, in March, 1848, of the Treaty of Guadalupe Hidalgo that officially ceded California to the United States. But as a businessman with an eye to future profits, he'd taken steps to make money from every one of those innovations. The good

Lord, he'd reasoned, had nothing against a Mormon's making money from a gentile, and if progress was inevitable the only thing for a sensible man to do was profit from it.

Recently the businessman in him had begun to gain a certain irreversible ascendance over the Mormon Elder. No surprise: the running battle he'd had with Brigham Young, leader of the main body of Mormons in Salt Lake City, had soured his stomach for Churchly dispute over dotted *i*'s and crossed *t*'s, over money, over the question of where the Saints were going to settle down for good now that they'd left Illinois forever. He'd said California; Young had said the high desert. After a fruitless debate Brannan left the Deseret colony in disgust and came back to San Francisco, eager to get back to making money and acquiring land.

Now, in June 1849, his acquisitiveness and single-mindedness had already paid off handsomely. He owned two hundred lots, a warehouse, two floating stores, and most of the small city of Sacramento, which he had founded with Dutch Sutter's son half a year before; he was well on his way to owning virtually the same kind of portion in San Francisco itself if he kept his wits about him a bit longer—and if he managed to get his hands on enough new cash. There was that block of property atop Fern Hill, for instance; in a few years it'd be the most desirable part of town, and then its value would appreciate enormously.

Well, he thought, looking down on the untidy crescent of Bay below him, laying hands on new investment cash shouldn't be too hard. Every day a thousand new gold seekers poured into town, either by the overland routes or on shipboard. Every day a hundred rich, thirsty, woman-starved miners came down from the Sierra foothills with pokes bulging with nuggets or gold dust, eager to drop a sizeable portion of their earnings in the city. And Sam Brannan could help them drop it. Sam's houses, even the cheapest hovels he could put up, rented for $800 a month. His stores sold eggs for $12 a dozen and bricks for the same price, a dollar apiece. The Chinese laundries he owned in town charged $8 a dozen just for washing shirts, down in Washerwoman's Lagoon, near Black's Point.

Funny, it was almost as if God himself had smiled down upon Sam Brannan's acquisitiveness. The discovery of gold on January 24, 1847, had taken place on Mormon land up the American River, and the first millionaires to come down from the pannings and diggings were all members of Sam's flock. It had been a simple matter then to hit every man Jack of them for the Lord's tithe: ten per cent of their winnings in the gold fields. After all, he'd told them, those who tithed to the Lord would continue to be rewarded by the Lord. He'd taken that tithe and invested it heavily in land, in property, in business. Now, with Brigham Young on the verge of disfellowshipping him, it became more and more of a sore point with him that Young was insisting, almost weekly, that he share those tithes with the Lord—as represented by Brigham Young.

Scowling, he reached into an inside pocket and withdrew once again the letter he'd read and reread since Amasa Lyman had left it at his house the night before. Lyman had come to town with that unkempt-looking brigand Porter Rockwell in tow and had delivered the letter personally. It was a letter in which Young's wheedling and kowtowing had suddenly opened a crack to show the threat of violence that lay just below the surface in everything Brigham did. He read the section again:

. . . if you deal justly with your fellows, and deal out with all liberal heart and open hands, making a righteous use of all your money, the Lord is willing you should accumulate the rich treasures of the earth and the good things of time in abundance. But should you withhold, when the Lord says give, your hopes and pleasing prospects will be blasted in an hour you think not of—and no arm can save. . . .

Why, the insolence of the bastard! This was an outright threat—a threat of murder! No matter that right after this Young's words went back to butter-wouldn't-melt-in-his-mouth. This was telling him right out that if he didn't cough up what Young said he owed, he'd have him used up, likely as not by a cutthroat like this Rockwell.

His eyes blazed as he looked down the street. The sight they saw wasn't the prettiest or the most reassuring. The damned city was a sinkhole, after all, a place where the worst sort of scum roamed the streets, the dregs of the world's seaports. There were thousands of them living in ramshackle hovels or even tents down in the mud at North Beach and on the fill that had begun to extend out below the Montgomery Street bluff into the Bay. Some of them were living in beached windjammers. One enterprising cove had commandeered an abandoned sloop and was renting it out as a hotel. The Bay itself was clogged with forgotten vessels rotting at anchor, some of them with valuable cargo inside that their crews had abandoned when they took off for the gold diggings.

Now he turned and looked at his building, the Alta building, which he'd constructed on the site of the first house he'd owned in San Francisco. Even here there was something to annoy him: the damnable Bella Union gambling hall, just downstairs from his own business office. He'd rented it on a long, virtually unbreakable lease to the first person to apply for space in the newly erected building, under the unspoken assumption that a conventional business would occupy the premises. Instead, open gambling had begun in the saloon from the first. Whores, dozens of them, worked the cafe, either employed by the management or as freelance operators. It was one of the scandals of the city that an upright and decorous businessman like Elder Brannan had rented property to a gambling hall and a whorehouse. Besides, there was the noise, the fights, and the general disrepair that everything had fallen into. Before long he'd have to find himself another site and build a new building, if only to make space for a new office for himself.

In the meantime . . . Brannan scowled at the marquee of the establishment and, scoring its always-open doors, entered the door to the second story, walking briskly up the stairs.

His own office door was already open, and two visitors, an elderly, white-haired man and a stylishly dressed young woman, were waiting in chairs by the door. He nodded curtly at them and glanced to his clerk, Sims, who sat at work on a great ledger.

"Mr. Brannan," Sims said, looking up. "Uh . . . these folks are waiting, and Mr. Lyman's in your office already."

"Thanks," Brannan said. He nodded again at the pair in the anteroom. "If you'll excuse me for a moment. . . ." He pushed the door open and strode into his office. There they were, in the two chairs that stood before his big desk. He gave Rockwell—bearded, unkempt, unwashed, his uncut hair tangled and tatted—no more than a curt nod of the head. Lyman, however, he greeted with normal courtesy. "Elder Lyman!" he said, shaking the older man by the hand. Then he went behind the desk and sat down. "What can I do for you?"

Lyman's face was impassive. "Let's not beat around the bush, Sam. You know why we're here. I left the letter with Liza last night. You must have read it by now. What have you to say?"

"Say?" Brannan said. The danger sign went up in his mind. He calculated the speed with which he could open the second drawer and get out the loaded Allen pepperpot pistol he had stowed there against just such occasions as this. Then he caught the light in Rockwell's pale blue eye and felt a sudden and uncontrollable twinge of abject fear.

He recovered himself, angry with his own momentary weakness. "Say? What do you expect me to say? Brigham wants me to build him a house out of my own pocket. He wants—what does he say? 'A present of twenty thousand dollars in gold dust, to help him in his labors.' Well, by heaven, I'm wondering how the devil it can cost twenty thousand dollars, in the present economy back in Deseret, with building materials cheap as dirt, to build Brig Young a house. Hah! Don't tell me now: he's added another forty or fifty wives, and he has to build a stable to hold them all."

Rockwell started forward at this, his lean hand digging inside his coat for something; but Lyman's hand on his arm stopped him. He sat back, eyes burning.

"Brother Brannan," Lyman said. "You collected tithes on money last year which, by the most conservative account, beggars description. Do you mean to sit here and tell me that, having collected these funds in the

243

name of the Lord, you intend to withhold them from the Lord?"

Brannan's eyes narrowed, for all that his mouth framed a wry smile. "The Lord, well, no. I'll make my own peace with the Lord in my own way, though. When He asks me Himself for the money, hell, Amasa, I'll give it all to Him. It's His anyway. That's not the same as saying it's Brig Young's. Tell you what: if you can get me a receipt for the money, signed by the Lord God Almighty himself and not by Brig Young or any other upstart. . . ."

"Why, you—" Rockwell's hand went inside his coat and came out with a long bowie knife. His hand reached out and grabbed Brannan's lapel and pulled him across the desk. "By God and by Christ, I'll cut your damned guts out for that, you foul-mouthed, cowardly swine." The voice was high-pitched, but it carried. There was real menace in it. Brannan's hand groped ineffectually for the top drawer but could not reach it.

"Easy, now," a voice said from behind Rockwell. Rockwell released Brannan, wheeled. Lyman stood erect, half turning toward the door. Brannan sank down into the chair again and his hand stole inside the second drawer and pulled the little revolver to him. He sat, gasping, with the gun in his lap.

He looked at the man in the doorway. It was the white-haired man he'd seen before in the outer office. Now, however, he didn't look old. He was lean and hard, and the long-barreled Colt pistol in his hand was leveled with deadly accuracy at Rockwell's middle. His eyes were cold and hard. The smile on his face was lopsided, mocking. "Pardon, Mr. Brannan. I couldn't help overhearing. Point of fact, I heard these two talking when I sat outside waiting for you to come in. They had some plans for you I think you might have not approved of. This one, the one with all the hair. . . ." His insulting glance indicated and dismissed Rockwell. "He had notions of killing you if you didn't pay up whatever it was they claimed you owed them. He probably still does. I'm a reliable witness. I'll be glad to testify if you have any idea of pressing charges."

"I . . . no," Brannan said, looking at Lyman. He shook his head. "But if Rockwell here. . . ."

"I get your drift," the white-haired man said. "You. That gun in your pocket. Pick it out with the wrong hand. Nice and slow." Rockwell, glaring, dropped his gun on the floor. "All right," the man with the gun said. "Out. And down the stairs. If I see you in town again. . . ."

"If you see me again," Rockwell rasped, "count your breaths. You won't have many of them."

"Talk, talk, talk," the old man said. "If you're worth anything more than talk, try picking the gun up. Go ahead. Bend over. Kill me if you can. I'll stick mine in my belt and await your pleasure."

"Now, now," Brannan said. He stood up, the pepper-pot in his own fist. "Amasa, I read the letter. I read the threat. I'm on my guard from now on. Tell him."

"He'll collect," Lyman said, his mouth a straight line.

"Perhaps," Brannan said. "I'd advise him not to stand on one leg until he does. Tell him I spit on his threats. Tell him that he can go whistle up a gumstump. Do you hear? Tell him."

The gun still in his hand, he watched the two of them go out the door. He did not place the little pistol on the desk until after he had listened to their footfalls all the way down the stairs.

Chapter 35

Brannan, breathing hard, started to sit down. Then he looked once again at the man before him, calmly tucking the big pistol in his hand into a well-concealed holster under his open frock coat. The older man's eyes were on him, keen, observant. There was the same hint of a wry smile on the gaunt face.

Brannan reached forward and stuck out his hand. "Your servant, sir," he said. "I am in your debt."

The old man took his hand, and Brannan marveled in the strength in his grip. "I'd be a poor citizen indeed," the stranger said, "if I couldn't intervene when murder and robbery were planned. Let me introduce myself. My name's J.W. Falligant. Colonel, Third Maryland Irregulars, retired. And I'm honored to meet, under whatever circumstances, San Francisco's most illustrious businessman."

Brannan, acknowledging the compliment, looked the man's ensemble up and down. Falligant, he had to admit, was impeccably turned out in tall silk stovepipe hat, fawn waistcoat with silken collar, a black silk cravat over which the collar tabs were rakishly turned down, and checked strap trousers over black boots of the softest and most pliable leather. Brannan wondered how he'd got this far uphill through the muddy streets without soiling either trousers or boots. "My pleasure, sir," he said. "Won't you sit down? I gather you've business with me."

"A moment," the older man said. "I've someone with me." He went out into the anteroom again and returned with the young woman Brannan had seen earlier outside. "This is Mr. Brannan, my dear," he said. "My niece and ward, Mrs. McGee."

Brannan looked—and looked again. Now this, he was thinking, was not your ordinary visitor to San Francisco. This might well be the most beautiful woman he'd ever seen.

The face was oval, the eyes dark and long-lashed. The coloring was excitingly dark, and set off the flashing white teeth she showed by her frank yet reserved smile. The hand she extended was exquisitely formed, petite, graceful. And her turnout was magnificent: rose velvet gown, lace collar and bertha, jeweled buttons, and a bonnet of shirred and corded silk with a lace veil that stood out handsomely against the coal-black curls that framed the delicate face.

"I'm charmed," he said, bending over her hand. "Please, won't you be seated and tell me what I can do for you now that I'm so completely your debtor."

Falligant seated his ward, then took the chair opposite her. "It may take a moment," he said. "Are you in a hurry?"

"Not for the man who may well have saved my life," Brannan said. "And for so charming a guest"—he nodded gallantly at the girl—"I'd cancel all obligations for the day." He smiled at both of them. "Please. I'm at your disposal."

"Splendid," Falligant said. "I must say it, although it's none of my business: do I gather that you've broken with the Mormon church?"

"Insofar as it's represented on earth by Brig Young, it appears I have," Brannan said. "Oh, don't fear that you've helped to precipitate something. I'd had my doubts for some time. You know the succession was hotly disputed at the time of Joseph Smith's murder. Well, at the time I tended to take the part of the Smith family, who insisted that the succession was hereditary—and who also insisted that the polygamous notions that the Church began developing around the time the main body moved to Illinois, ten or eleven years ago, were Young's, not Joseph's. I'd had my doubts about polygamy from the first." He nodded at the young woman, his face appropriately grave. "No," he concluded, "my conscience remains the same. But as to

247

whether I submit to Brig Young, or pay him blood money. . . ." He dismissed the thought with one hand.

"I see," Falligant said. "Well, I've studied Mormon history some. I know that the Mormons don't drink coffee or tea, but don't mind selling them to a gentile. Is that correct?"

"My warehouses are well stocked with both commodities. The good Lord has nothing against a man making money."

"And the Mormons—courtesy of the prophecy your people call the Word of Wisdom—don't drink strong drink, but you have nothing against selling the spirits to those who have need of them. Am I correct so far?"

"Right on target, sir," Brannan said with a smile. "Why, Joseph Smith himself once opened a saloon in his own home to cater to travelers. He ran it at a considerable profit, too—until his wife made him close it down." He chuckled. "Strong-minded woman, Emma Smith."

"I see. The Church recognizes human foibles, then— in the uninstructed, at any rate. And realizes that if a damn fool wants pizen, he's going to get it somehow, and the wise man gives it to him and charges him well for it."

"It is," Brannan said, "the nature of business. Pray, sir, what is the nature of yours?"

"I'll get to that in a moment, sir, with your kind indulgence. I have, in a word, taken your measure. You're well known in the city, sir. One might call you its first citizen—whatever the *alcalde* may think." He acknowledged Brannan's deprecatory nod. "One also knows your views concerning the lawlessness of the streets, the curse of prostitution and the unfortunate spread of social disease thereby, the"—his voice slowed considerably here—"the uncontrolled spread of gambling in low, uncultivated hells such as the. . . . ah . . . the one downstairs." His mouth turned sour, disapproving. "I regret to bring this up. It's a thorn in your side, from all I hear."

"You hear correctly," Brannan said. "I've nothing against gambling, mind you—not for gentiles, anyhow. One even might say it was my own profession. I gambled on Sacramento. I gambled on San Francisco. I gambled on real estate and on a string of stores and warehouses. I'm still in up to my neck at it. What I do object to is—damn it, Falligant, the confounded gall of these people! The damnable low tone of it all—and settling it right under my own nose, on my own property!" He pounded the desk with one broad-fingered hand. "Frankly, I'd give a lot to see that particular place driven out of town."

His eye caught Falligant's, and he took note of the small smile on Falligant's gaunt face, and the aroused interest in the dark eyes of Mrs. McGee. "Ah," he said. "We come at last to the point."

"We do," Falligant said. "I do agree, sir. Gambling needn't be a bedfellow with bawdy houses. It needn't take place on so debased a scale. I can tell you that I have taken the waters in the premier spas of continental Europe, and I can witness that sums far greater than those wagered here, in the abominable Bella Union, cross the tables there in an atmosphere of the greatest decorum. People *will* gamble, sir. And in an atmosphere of quick money the *nouveaux riches* will, if they have the money to pay for it, exchange grubbiness for quality virtually every time. In a word, sir, I am convinced that the new-rich miners who come to town and pay a king's ransom for hangtown fry or raw oysters will, in a relatively short time, come to the city for elegance rather than for the sort of disgusting rutting one sees nightly at the Bella Union."

"Ah," Brannan said, sitting back. "And you, sir, what do you propose to do about it?"

Falligant smiled. "My ward and I . . . we have been to the gold diggings for a year. We would like to propose a partnership with you, sir. We think we have a pretty accurate understanding, by now, of what it is that the miners want when they come to San Francisco. You will have noticed, for instance, that a year ago, you couldn't give away fine clothing in your stores. Well, today the latest styles, imported directly from France, are selling briskly."

"Yes, yes," Brannan said. "But down to business, please. I gather I'm to put up the money. What sort of skills have you to contribute to the enterprise, if we open a casino on the sort of lavish, high-class level I think you're talking about? Pardon my bluntness."

"Think nothing of it, sir," Falligant said with that small smile. "And do allow me to correct a misconception. We are not asking you to put up the money. If you will inquire in my name at the Merchants Bank of this city, you will find that my ward and I bring something more than mere solvency to the enterprise." He sat back and regarded Brannan. "We are fellow depositors there, I believe. Well, city gossip has it that you could make a bundle, as we say, on a certain piece of Fern Hill real estate if you had the ready cash. We are ready to lend you the cash for that particular deal, in exchange for a partnership in the enterprise . . . and for," he said with a cavalier expansiveness, "your continued cooperation, good will, and friendship."

Brannan sat up, his eyes wide. "You are? But that particular real estate deal—do you have any idea how much up-front money they're asking? Why, it's in six figures."

Falligant's tone was icily good-humored. "Feed for the chickens, Mr. Brannan," he said. "We propose a casino, on precisely that same Fern Hill property. The three of us will take home better than that in the first year of its operation. That's *each*, mind you. Each. And, well, we've a mind to make money in this town. We'll do so. Inquire into my account, Mr. Brannan. I have authorized you to do so. And when you do, take note that an equal sum is on deposit in the name of Mrs. McGee. Since the unfortunate death of her husband our family affairs have been on an equal-partners basis. We are offering you a third share in that family enterprise. We will make the money, you will invest it—in your usual judicious manner—in appropriate real estate, here and elsewhere around the Bay."

"But two hundred thousand. . . ."

"A trifle, Mr. Brannan, as you yourself well know. In a few years sums like that will be bid for a single lot in that parcel. There'll be handsome mansions there, and lavish hotels, and—"

"Agreed, agreed. But. . . ."

"—in short, we are prepared to offer as capital for the present project the sum of six hundred thousand dollars, on deposit in dust and nuggets, sir." He settled back and let that statement take effect. "And with your business sense and . . . ah . . . sensible acquisitiveness working for us all, sir, we are confident that our investment of this relatively insubstantial sum will—"

"Insubstantial!"

"—will in time make of us people of, let us say, truly comfortable and independent circumstances. Will, in fact, sir, make us rich."

"Rich!" Brannan stared at the two of them, openmouthed. "Six hundred thousand in dust and nuggets! You mean to tell me you made this in the diggings, sir? Do you own producing mines?"

"Not a square inch of land do we own up there," Falligant said. "No, that's not quite true. We did take a worthless piece of grazing land as settlement of a debt last fall. Brannan, we don't give a goddamn about land. Can you see the both of us grubbing away with a shovel? Hell, man, my hands are very nearly as tender as Mrs. McGee's, and hers are as soft as a baby's behind. They have to be."

"I . . . I don't understand."

"Mr. Brannan," Falligant said patiently. "If the casino we propose is to have the sort of high tone we seek, it has to take that tone from a single person. The host or hostess of an establishment of this kind has to be the sartorial equal of royalty, the equal in beauty of Helen of Troy, the peer in manners of Athénaïs de Montespan. As you come to know my ward you will come to agree that she has these qualities and—"

"Oh, of course, of course," Brannan said with a gallant nod of the head to the still silent Mrs. McGee. "But—"

"—and of course she has other qualities. She learned some of them from me. My dear, would you demonstrate, please?"

"Gladly," the young woman said in a thrillingly low voice, soft and melodious.

Those soft, gloveless hands went to work, and Brannan saw why she had come to his office barehanded. From her sleeve came a deck of cards. Her fingers fanned them, shuffled them faster than the eye could follow, fanned them again, picked out four aces, tore the aces to bits, then shuffled the rest of the deck, cut, shuffled again, fanned the deck once more, showed the mi-

251

raculously restored four aces in precisely the same places in the deck, palmed the deck in one hand, made it disappear, made it reappear in the other palm, and, for a finish, tossed the entire deck high in the air, one card at a time, in a graceful cascade that arched through the air like one of the little bridges in a Chinese ivory carving. Then it came to rest in one graceful hand and disappeared once again inside that voluminous sleeve.

"M-my God," Brannan said. "And . . . and this casino of ours . . . it'll have to have a name." His eyes remained on the woman's shapely hands, resting quietly and demurely in her lap.

"The miners have already named it, whether or not they know it. It'll be named after the city, the name the people have been calling it since the first real rush started last winter. A nickname for a city, mind you, is a sign of love. Why not ally oneself with that sort of love, identify oneself with it? In San Francisco—why, there's only one thing to call it."

"And that is?"

"Call it Frisco. Or, better, Frisco's." Falligant's grin was suddenly youthful, expansive. "And name it after its gracious proprietress. Mr. Brannan, meet Frisco McGee."

Chapter 36

Two weeks later, in Sam Brannan's office, the three of them signed the papers Sam's lawyer had drawn up. Under the terms of the contract, Falligant and "Frisco McGee" were to remain silent and—to the rest of the town, at any rate—unacknowledged partners in the new company. Brannan drew a red herring across their trail by starting, at the same time, another new firm, subordinate to this one: a new store in San Francisco, with a working partner named J.W. Osborn. To impress the new firm upon the consciousness of the San Francisco merchants in suitable fashion, Sam startled the community by cornering the city's entire tea market in a single transaction, purchasing a shipload of five hundred cases of choicest hyson and oolong teas from the Orient. Falligant watched from the sidelines, smiling his small smile, as Brannan, with his usual showmanship, told the merchants that from this moment he was going to be *the* San Francisco importer of Far Eastern goods.

The two of them had become almost inseparable companions in recent days; word had it that Amasa Lyman had returned to Salt Lake, alone, leaving Porter Rockwell behind. Falligant, protecting his investment, had decided to keep Sam company until news to the contrary had been received, or until Rockwell made good his threat of a second meeting.

Besides, another problem had developed, one that, unchecked, would destroy Brannan's recently announced campaign to keep the streets safe for women and children in the city. A block down the street from Sam's Alta Building stood the tent that served as headquarters for the Regulators, a self-proclaimed "unofficial

253

governing body" whose canvas meeting hall bore the crudely lettered sign "Tammany Hall."

The nucleus of the group—an ill-assorted troupe of roughs and rogues without fixed address or visible source of income—was a group of unruly ex-soldiers from a disbanded regiment of New York volunteers who had been brought around the Horn in four ships to fight in the Mexican War. Mustered out without means, they had landed in the Tenderloin district and, after failing to make their way in a brief foray into the gold country, had settled back into a routine of bullying and petty thievery, some of them into such darker arts as armed robbery and even murder.

By now, they ignored what law existed in San Francisco. A wagonload of miner's gear—shovels, picks, rucksacks—stolen from Brannan's store by Regulators; Brannan's complaints to *Alcalde* Leavenworth and to the sheriff's office had received the same inattention. "They're calling 'em the Hounds nowadays, Sam. I can't control 'em. Maybe nobody can. They're the real power in this town. Maybe Leavenworth has the title—but Sam Roberts, down at 'Tammany Hall,' actually runs this town these days." Brannan had stalked out of the sheriff's office in a huff, determined to do something. The first thing he did was to announce his candidacy for the Town Council.

People were beginning to notice a difference in Sam Brannan. Gone was the sobersides Mormon Elder. In his place was a nattily dressed young man of business, who dressed in the latest Continental fashions and sported a dashing little beard like any dandy. This Sam Brannan had conquered his former aversion to alcohol enough to make a nightly tour of the city's better saloons, plugging both his candidacy and the lavish new casino he was planning to erect on his new property atop Fern Hill. "Fern Hill, hell!" Brannan was saying. "It'll be the center of San Francisco society a decade from now. They'll be calling it Hoity-Toity Hill, or Nob Hill, or Toff Hill, or something like that, before I'm done with the place. That is, if we can do something about cleaning up the town."

For a time, then, with Brannan stirring up trouble, Sam Roberts steered his Hound raiding parties away from Sam's section of town. Instead, the marauding toughs under Roberts's direction began harassing the desolate and unprotected little community of Chilean immigrants who had begun to settle in the little valley west of Stockton and north of Jackson Street. Indeed, one night the sheriff's department, unable to collect a due bill from a *Chileno* named Pedro Cueto, actually hired the Hounds to collect it. The Hounds made an aimless stab at collection; then, on impulse, they ransacked all of the houses in the ramshackle settlement and, opposed by the inhabitants, fell into outright violence, killing one man and wounding two others, beating women and children and driving them into the streets before setting the little Latin village afire.

Brannan, the silent, dangerous-looking Falligant at his side, stormed into *Alcalde* Leavenworth's office the next morning. "Look here, damn it, if you won't do something I'm going to! This situation has got completely out of hand, and that damned sheriff's department of yours is hand in glove with these scum. You'd better take sides, and right now. Either you're for law and order in this town or you're against it. Which way is it going to go?"

Leavenworth looked mildly up at Brannan, real concern in his eyes. He looked down at the holster at Falligant's side. The word had already come down to him that this deceptively genteel-looking old gentleman who accompanied Brannan everywhere was a dead shot and fearless as the day was long. More: he was a lunger and hadn't long to live. That put him one up on anyone who chose to oppose him in a gunfight: he had nothing to lose, and a man who had nothing to lose had a fraction of a second's edge on a man who gave a damn whether he lived or died. Inwardly, Leavenworth shuddered; a former navy chaplain himself, he shrank from any show of violence. "What can I do, Sam? Issue a proclamation? That's about all the power that city charter of ours gives me."

"Then issue one," Brannan said. "I'll write you up an order summoning all the responsible men of the city to Portsmouth Square. I'll have it printed up and nailed to every wall and barn door in town. All you have to do is sign it. After that, I'll take over."

Leavenworth, one uneasy eye on that big pistol on Falligant's thigh, nodded his head wearily. "All right, Sam. I hope you know what you're doing."

Brannan did. At noon the next day, Falligant standing cross-armed at his side with the big gun prominent on his hip, Sam stood atop the old adobe custom house and addressed a crowd of over a thousand men. They were an oddly assorted lot: businessmen, merchants, miners, transients, and a surly contingent of Hounds, scattered at the fringes of the gathering.

Brannan didn't waste words. "The question is, are we men or cowards?" He waited a moment for that to sink in. "Night before last, somebody among us killed a man, beat up women and children, burned several blocks of our town. And every damned last man of us knows who did it. The dregs of the New York slums, augmented by the worst sort of scum Botany Bay could be bothered to send us. You all know who I'm talking about—the Hounds. Sam Roberts and that rag-tag army of spineless, yellow-livered—"

"You watch your mouth!" a voice from the crowd bellowed in a low-class New York accent. "You could stop a bullet!"

"Sure I could!" Brannan said, raising his voice. "But who's going to fire it? A chicken-livered wharf rat like you? Here!" he bellowed, throwing open his coat and sticking out his chest. "If you're going to do it, you might just as well do it now. Well? Go ahead! Shoot! Shoot while you can!"

It was a bravura performance. But the onlookers noticed that as Brannan said this the grim-looking, pasty-faced old man at his side stepped lightly to one side, his eyes glinting, his mouth an expressionless slash across his gaunt face. His hands fanned out, fingers relaxed and spread, only inches away from the lethal-looking long-barreled weapon at his side. There was a low murmur of awe.

"See?" Brannan said to the crowd in general. "That's what they're all like when you face them down. Cowards, every one. And here we've been letting 'em call the turn on us, when every minute we've had the remedy for this at our hands."

256

"What's that, Sam?" a voice came up from the men gathered below.

"*Posse comitatus,*" Brannan said. "An ad hoc force of military police. Volunteers. If we can't have law and order at the hands of our elected officials, then we'll have to take the law into our own hands. Come now, who'll join me in this? For let me tell you, I've had enough. Either we're living in a city or we're living in a jungle. Who'll join me in cleaning out the place? You, Will Howard—are you with us?"

"You bet I am!"

"Then you won't mind chairing a committee for law and order. You—Hiram Webb! You deal in firearms, and the militia'll need guns! Are you with us?"

"Count me in!" Webb said. "I'm good for sixty muskets if you've the men to man them!"

"All right!" Sam said. "Now let's get down to some *real* business: passing the hat for those poor devils they burned out down in 'Little Chile' the other night! Here!" he said theatrically, tossing down his brand-new beaver hat. "I'll provide the hat and the first donation. Tucked in the lining you'll find a check for five thousand dollars. If the lot of you can't match that by the time the hat's gone around once, I don't know my friends and neighbors at all."

The speech worked. Howard's volunteers numbered a hundred and thirty, and most of them were able to bring their own arms to the organizational meeting Sam called an hour or so later. The troops fanned out into the waterfront area, dragging Hound after Hound from their hiding places. Sam Russell they found cowering in the hold of a vessel bound upriver for Stockton, hiding behind a stack of flour bags. They dragged the prisoners to the docks and rowed them out to the war sloop *Warren*, where Navy personnel took them in charge. Brannan, surveying the transfer with a disgusted eye, was already planning a thick-walled, virtually impregnable jail for the town.

A hastily assembled grand jury of 24 citizens sat two days later, considering evidence against the arrested. It was obvious that most of the Hounds had escaped, most likely upriver, to bedevil the people of Stockton, Sacramento and the gold towns. But Brannan was confident that the ringleaders had been among those arrested, and when he walked out of the courtroom after giving his own testimony he had every intention of forgetting the matter. "It's all over but the shouting, Wes," he told Falligant. "Now we can get down to business, making money here, building a city."

Falligant, his eyes flinty, demurred. "I'm not so sure. That's an impressive sort of circus in there—but that's all it is. Two dozen prominent citizens sitting on the jury; three judges; the *alcalde* presiding; prosecutors, defense attorneys . . . what do you want to bet that most of your fish swim right past this net? Eh?"

Brannan started to reply but saw the cynical glint in Falligant's eye. "Bet? Against you? Not likely, my friend. You're probably right. And we'll probably have the same troubles again until there's decent provision for full-time law and order here, and enough police on hand to put down any sort of riot the scum of the streets can incite. No, you're right. It's just that I'm sick of the whole damned matter."

Falligant scowled; then he grinned his cynic's grin. "'. . . *and I will put this foot of mine as far as who goes farthest,*'" he said. "Everyone always says that. But you watch; they'll most of them get soft-hearted when the time comes to give a nice stiff sentence. Oh, perhaps Sam Roberts'll get his, I suppose. He'll make a good scapegoat, for all that there are people in that dock who make Roberts look like Jesus Christ himself. But where the hell are they going to incarcerate them? There isn't a *calabozo* left in all California now that the Mexicans have deserted the Presidios here and in Monterey. And you know the Navy isn't going to foot the bill for feeding the bastards aboard the *Warren* any longer than it takes to try them." He stopped before a tavern in Clay Street. "Well?" he said wryly. "Let's go in and toast the *posse comitatus* and the grand jury for upholding law and order."

Afterwards Sam was damned glad he hadn't placed that bet. Roberts got a ten-year sentence; eight others received shorter sentences. There being no legal place to incarcerate them, the town fathers had to settle for imposing a verbal exile on the convicted men. Brannan's disgust was as pointed as Falligant's snort of derision. They'd all be back, and worse trouble with them.

But in the meantime the two of them had made their point. It was time to clean up the city and make a better San Francisco. One fit to invest in. One fit to build in. And one fit to house the most elegant gambling hall west of Brittany.

Chapter 37

Graciela read all about it in the *Alta California*. She didn't have to, of course; she'd already heard about it from Falligant, four times over, in a highly colorful running account spiced with oaths, snorts of cynical laughter, and derogatory comments about the human species in general and about every single civic leader in San Francisco in particular.

When Falligant visited her for coffee one morning in the sitting-room of the lavish apartment she'd leased in Kearny Street, she thought about what he'd said. "Then you don't think the trouble's over?" she said, folding the little four-page paper and putting it down.

"Hell, no," Falligant said. "Ah—excuse me. I must get out of the habit of profanity in your presence. If we're to maintain that impeccable status of yours I'd better be the first to observe proper decorum." He grinned, reached for the omnipresent flask in his coat pocket and poured a liberal draught into his coffee. "There. Gives it a bit of authority. You were saying, my dear? Oh, yes. No chance, no chance at all that we won't have further trouble. Why, it's brewing right now. Most of the Hounds who got away are now ensconced up in the Australian settlement above Pacific Street, the one folks are beginning to call Sydney Town. Word has it that one or two of the convicted have already slipped back into town and joined them."

"Well, then why go to the bother of cleaning things up in the first place?" She looked with concern at his drawn face. He was pale, deadly pale. Worse, the telltale ruddy patches had begun to appear on his cheeks. If only he'd ease up a bit on that rugged and grueling schedule of his, roistering all night with the blades and bucks of the city, men a generation younger than he.

"Oh, to embarrass Leavenworth, of course. To make him look bad and make Sam look good. And you'll note we have a new *alcalde* as a result: John Geary, the postmaster. He's taken the lesson, all right: he's called for a gaming tax to raise money and he vows to spend some of it, at least, on a resident police force. He's already made arrangements to purchase an abandoned brig down at the Wharf to use as a city hoosegow. Next time the Sydney Ducks—those scurvy jailbait down along the Coast there—break out and steal a horse and wagon, one or another of them's going to wind up cooling his heels for a spell. And look you: I've got Sam all built up as Mr. Responsible Civic Leader. Next time he gets up on a stump to make a law and order speech, I wouldn't be surprised to see somebody get lynched." He took another sip of the coffee and, scowling, "sweetened" it again from the pocket flask.

"But a gaming tax? Won't that work against us?"

"How? Good God, I intend to press for an on-the-premises plainclothes policeman out of it, paid for at city expense. The biggest damned Mick in town, if I can get him. And of course while our honest assessment ought to be a pretty penny indeed, I think I can handle that with a bribe or two here and there." He grinned his cynical grin. "Trust me, Graciela. I've done extremely well for you so far, if I do say so myself. Trust me."

"Certainly you have," she said, suddenly feeling the pain she'd caused him by an apparent distrust. "Oh, Wes, if my own father had taken as good care of me as you have. . . ." She sighed and put one well-tended hand on his arm. "I only wish you'd let me—or some-one—take care of you. You're so pale. You've lost weight again, you look like a ghost."

"It's a strange thing, my dear. The Ducks are calling me that. 'The Ghost.' It's a good name for a lunger. Me, I don't give a damn what they call me as long as it's a name that shows they're frightened of me. And as for taking care of me, my dear, the ladies upstairs above the El Dorado are doing a fine job."

"Oh, come now. You know what I mean. And stop calling me Graciela. 'Call her Frisco,' you said. All right, if I'm to be identified with that name, let's make it unanimous, and run it right around the clock."

"Sorry," he said. "You're right, of course. I'll try to watch that. Meanwhile, what about that image of yours? What sort of capers have you been cutting while I've been out raising hell with Sam?"

Graciela smiled. "Capers? I don't know that I'd call them that, but it's been pretty much what you suggested. I took your man Wong and ran a wagonload of supplies down to Little Chile, dressed in my Sunday finest. I took care to establish myself as 'Señora Frisco,' and by the time I'd left I heard several of them using the name to talk about me."

"Good. Now make sure you follow up by appearing at the bullring Sunday, dressed to the nines, with a Sunday-go-to-meeting veil, just as if you were still a good Catholic. Matter of fact, I'll take you to church before that. Nine o'clock Mass, where everybody'll notice. And in the meantime I'll start some rumors second-hand, around town. Something about the mystery woman who is the angel of the Latin community. Let's make a saint out of you; it'll soften the sinner image when you open the saloon."

"Fine. Speaking of which: how's construction coming along?"

"Excellent. Sam's turned out a warehouse for the best in materials. I've ordered pearwood paneling from the East. You simply won't believe the bar, or the oak tables. Every damned last toothpick of it brought 'round the Horn, and if we hadn't insisted on it ourselves it was intended for the bank on Portsmouth Square. I'll have some swatches for you to look at tomorrow. The decorator's coming in."

"Send him by here." She looked at her desk calendar. "Hmm . . . make it ten a.m. sharp. And Sam? Has he cleared title to the Fern Hill property?"

"He says he has. You have to check him out though, every time. Thanks for reminding me. Sam's a great initiator, but he's uniformly poor at following up. It's a miracle he's done as well as he has. When we pull out on him I expect it to take maybe ten years, perhaps twenty, for him to lose everything he's got, but he will. Never fear about that. He's been able to manage here because he was the smartest of a poor and scurvy lot. But ten years from now the town'll be full of really sharp operators—people more of the calibre of your humble servant, madam—and they'll pick his bones for him. But he's a great man for innovative ideas, as far as he's able to take them. I'm not sorry we've tied in with him for a time. Neither will you be, when I'm gone."

He just tossed it off like that, with no particular expression, and would have gone on, but her hand on his arm again stopped him. "Wes," she said. "How bad is it? You used not to talk that way. Now hardly a day passes when something doesn't slip out."

"Oh, don't worry about me, my dear. Things will come when they come." He turned full-face to her, and now she could see something in his eye that in its own way chilled her worse than desperation might have done. It was resignation. He saw that she saw it, and he tried for a moment to look away but found he couldn't. "Look," he said. "That year in the mine country, and then coming here to Frisco, where it's cold and wet, well, any doctor would tell you. . . ."

"But you've got to leave! We've got to find a place where you can—"

"No!" he said gently but firmly. "Don't you understand? Last year was—well, I had to see that you were well-fixed when I pass on. It was worth it, putting in a year swindling those damn fools out of their dust and their chattels, if only for the bottom I've put on the next period of your life, child. And damn it, there was a way in which I enjoyed it on my own hook, for all that these damned lungs of mine got a lot worse up there. What better place for a worthless scoundrel like myself than a place where the towns are named Hangtown, Chicken Thief Flat, Cut Throat Bar, Poker Flat, Whiskey Bar?" He laughed, a short harsh sound. "By God, do you remember the camp they called Delirium Tremens? Now, there was a name for you, and they knew what they were doing when they called it that. You really know what you're in for when the best liquor you can buy in town is Mexican *mezcal*, with a red worm swimming around in it, and the second best is a foul-smelling *aguardiente* you could put to better use cleaning out an oven! But by Christ, I've drunk worse." He paid for the uncharacteristically long speech, though, with a fit of coughing. It went on longer than usual this time, and he covered his mouth with a handkerchief from his sleeve. When he had the coughing under control he looked down at the handkerchief and, scowling, balled it tightly in his fist.

"Wes," she said, her voice full of real concern. "If only I'd known. We didn't need to stay that long, or make that much money. Your health is more important."

"Please," he said. "Let me be the best judge of how important my health is. For God's sake, girl, can you imagine that a man might just get tired of life? Tired of this vile collection of gutter scum and unsuccessful thimble-riggers he has to live with and do business with? Tired of the shams and hypocrisy of it all? Tired of seeing his life settle into a routine of sterile fiddle-faddle, things he's done a million times and which had already begun to bore him to extinction years before? Tired of liquor and whores and cozenage and snake-oil politics and the whole damnable thing?" His eyes lost their bitterness for a moment. "I'm trying to think of how many things I've done or witnessed in the past few years that I actually enjoyed, that made me happy even in the smallest of ways. I'm counting them on one hand. One, watching you grow from a beautiful child into a beautiful and resourceful young woman, with heart and guts and intelligence to match her looks. Two . . . but there you are, goddamn it. There isn't any two."

"Oh, Wes. You've done it all for me, then?"

"Huh," he said, thinking it over. His eyes seemed far away. "Perhaps. As much for myself as for anyone. Graciela, one doesn't—"

"Frisco," she smiled, reaching out to take his cold hand. "Call me Frisco."

"All right. Frisco it is. But look, I could have just ridden away without declaring myself, that time I found you and Shandor at the circus. I'd had every intention of going off on my own the day I left the Rom camp. And hell, girl, I would have been dead a year ago. Instead, when I found you, and when Shandor died, leaving you unprovided for and with a child on the way, well, I just couldn't walk off and. . . ." His voice turned harsh and low. His eyes turned to hers again and there was an absolute candor in them now, of a kind she'd seldom experienced with him before this. "For a change," he said, "I had something to live for. For a while. . . ." And then he turned away, and suddenly she knew this part of the conversation was over. Instinctively she knew he was asking her, without words, never to bring it up again. It was the kind of candor that came only once between two proud and independent people. "Speaking of the child, how is he?"

"Come and see for yourself," she said. She rose and led him by the hand into the nursery, where year-old Alex McGee, a chubby, dark-haired boy, slept under the care of a uniformed *Chilena* Graciela had brought in from the little settlement the Hounds had burned. "He'll be sorry to have missed his Uncle Wes. Isn't he adorable, Wes? He loves you, too." She gently kissed the baby.

"Hah. It's probably that pocketful of comfits he's got used to." Falligant emptied his otherwise unoccupied watch pocket onto a table: a handful of candies. "By God," he said. "He's a swart little beggar. The spit and image of his father. And born on the damned boat, in the straits of Magellan. By God, I'd like to see that little devil's horoscope."

"Lyuba says he'll be a real Rom. And you forget, he's a chief by heredity. He'll own this town some day."

"Perhaps he will," Falligant said. "For all *that's* worth. Look you: is Lyuba going to work up at the casino?"

"Certainly. Telling fortunes. I'd be doing it myself if it weren't for that ladylike pose you've picked out for me. Frankly, I'm not sure what use I'm going to be. You've ruled out dealing, shilling. . . ."

"You're the lady of the house. You'll make a brief appearance one or two times a night, greeting everyone by name. Putting on the dog. Showing off your finery. Showing off that lovely face of yours. Showing off those fancy New Orleans manners they taught you back in the convent school. By God, if that doesn't have every man in town at your feet inside of six months I'm a Dutchman."

"Who says I want a man?" Graciela said. "Seems to me I'm perfectly happy as I am. Honestly, you men think you're indispensable. Can't a woman be happy by herself?"

"Don't be a damned little coquette. Sure, you're happy enough, as far as it goes. But I know you—about as well as a substitute father can know the girl he's raised, anyhow—and I know damned good and well you're not going to be satisfied with being single. Not for long. First there'll be beaux, and then you'll be damned picky about them and start weeding them out, and then some vigorous young devil will come breezing right on by the lot of them and sweep you off your feet and you'll suddenly find, for all your damned independence, that it was exactly what you wanted anyhow. Trouble is, it's going to be damned hard finding you a young man who's stronger than you are—or even as strong. I know *that* much about you, too."

"We'll see," she said, smiling. "*Volveré en un momento*," she said to the Latin girl as she showed Falligant out of the child's room. "You think you've got everything figured out, don't you?" she said to Falligant.

"Not everything," he admitted at the door. "I have this nagging feeling that there's something I've forgotten. Something damned important. Well, perhaps I'll remember later on. Sam's ill today. I think I'll go have a look at the construction site. Last time I was down there someone had stolen six hundred dollars' worth of bricks on me. I put an armed Paddy in charge of the site but word has it he's been slipping off after lunch for a touch of the old *uisquebaugh*. I'll put a stop to that."

"You do that," she said. Impulsively she stepped forward to kiss him gently on the cheek. "And Wes, take care. If you won't do it for yourself, remember we need you, Alex and I. I haven't any idea what we'd do without you." She squeezed his arm, releasing him, and was shocked at how the flesh had fallen away from the bone there. The man was a walking skeleton!

"Of course you know what to do," he said. "But it was a nice thing to say. Goodbye, Graciela."

"Frisco," she said.

"Frisco it is." She watched through the cracked door as he strode, back straight, head held high, to the stairway, a trace of the old arrogance already beginning to creep back into his stance. By the time he reached the

266

street, two floors down, he'd be his old sardonic, barely tolerant, all but insufferable self. His strong blade of a nose would be held high, his eyes would be haughty, daring any man to stare him down or stand in his way. And with it all there'd be charity for the needy, friendly regard for the unassuming, and gallantry for any woman worth the name (and for a few who weren't). He was a rare man, all right. Something inside her told her to fix this picture of him in her mind for good and all, to remember him as he still was, strong and proud and independent, asking no man's quarter, no man's favor, a man of vigor and force and power.

Chapter 38

In August, after much prodding from Sam Brannan, the city fathers organized the first standing volunteer guard organization, using the volunteers who had turned out to eradicate the Hounds as a nucleus. Sam's name, of course, was prominent among the members of the new California Light Guard—"Brannan's Guard," folks already had begun to call it, and for good reason: Sam's money and, less openly, Falligant's and Graciela's had financed the organization from the beginning. In due time Sam was made a captain in the Guard. It was small enough payment for the arms, the uniforms, even the band instruments his warehouses supplied.

Sam's activities carried him far and wide. By now, Graciela's urging had made a city-bound man of Falligant and he left Brannan's junkets to Sacramento and Coloma to other bodyguards. Only when Sam returned to San Francisco would Falligant go back to his pointed shadowing of Brannan.

Meantimes, he was seen on Graciela's arm, squiring her to various charity events or to the odd theatrical entertainment that was already beginning to visit the brawling little city by the Golden Gate. Every day, it seemed, the sloops and clippers disgorged new and ever more exotic passengers, and not all of them were bound for the gold fields. Some of them had decided, as Wes and Graciela had done, that the real money was not to be made in chunks of yellow metal but in rich black land instead. Now, as the new investors arrived, Sam, making one hasty real estate or construction deal after another, began to find the bidding harder, the bargaining tougher. He leaned more and more heavily on Wes

Falligant's whispered advice, in every area of their joint ventures.

Thus Brannan's only solo enterprises, the only part of his business that he could totally call his own, came more and more to be the part that remained rooted up the river, in Sacramento and in the gold towns. He maintained warehouses at Sutter's Fort and at the corner of Front and J Streets in Sacramento, and ran both retail and wholesale businesses in both locations. He also did a thriving business as an auction merchant and auctioneer, although imported talent from the East actually manned the gavel.

Doing business in California favored the California merchant. All goods shipped to San Francisco were shipped on consignment, and Brannan's warehouses had only storage problems; Sam seldom had to go out of pocket to corner the local market in Eastern or Far Eastern goods. Before the year was out, it was possible to say that if you wanted to do business in the area between Sacramento City and the Gate, you had to do it with Sam Brannan. He prospered. He opened a hotel in Sacramento. He was named to the town council in San Francisco. As the year drew to an end it became obvious that income from rents alone on Brannan's properties—the ones he held on his own, not the ones held in silent partnership with Falligant and Frisco McGee— would come to over a hundred thousand dollars.

Nevertheless, the real estate virus had gone through Sam Brannan, as Wes Falligant wryly put it, "like suet through a duck." With Falligant's all but infallible advice steering him to one faultless deal after another, the properties and businesses upriver became less and less interesting to him, and the trips he had to take in support of them became more and more burdensome. Sam's thoughts turned more and more to San Francisco, and when the Constitutional Convention took place in Monterey in October Sam was stuck on the partly completed Central Wharf at the foot of Clay Street, hastily auctioning off consignment merchandise that otherwise would have spoiled in the incipient rainy season. There simply wasn't room left in his warehouses to hold all the merchandise he had for sale.

The same month he sold all of his upriver holdings

but the hotel: the Coloma and Sutter's Fort stores, the Mormon Island partnership, the Sacramento stores, and the three warehouse ships he'd been using for overstocks on the Sacramento wharf. Sam breathed a sigh of relief when the papers were signed; this meant new money, money to spend on the real estate ventures Falligant was so astutely steering him to. There were twelve new business lots for sale downtown, on the choicest land. Rentals were soaring and showed no immediate sign of leveling off. Yes, San Francisco was the place to be, the place to put your money right now. And in the meantime it didn't hurt a damned bit to encourage this tendency folks had to start calling it "Sam Brannan's town."

The dry weather held right up to the opening of the casino. A good thing, too: Wes had plastered every flat space in town with handbills, put Portsmouth Square winos out in every alley with sandwich boards on front and back, and made every preparation his resources could provide. Officially Sam was listed only as landlord. It wouldn't pay, in some circles in which he did business, to put out the word that Sam Brannan, the one-time Mormon Elder, had allied himself with outright gambling (and God alone knew what else, in a rowdy city like San Francisco). But anyone with an eye to see, and with foreknowledge of Sam's methods, might have seen Sam's hand in the appointments up at Frisco's, on top of the hill. His warehouses had disgorged the finest in furnishings, upholstery, wallpapers; the catering was the best the new city could afford; and best of all, the word had been put out that the drinks were on the house ("the sky's the limit") and the drinks would be Brannan's best. For a month preceding, runners had gone forth to the gold fields to announce the opening, and every tree on public property had borne its handbill for weeks, inviting every miner who owned a clean shirt to come and try his hand against the best and most honest dealers the City could supply. (People had already begun calling it "The City"—capital letters, please—and were never to lose the habit.)

The handbills made much of one refinement Frisco McGee herself had made in the course of outfitting the casino that was to bear her name. All the dealers were

270

women: young, beautiful, well-spoken, and trained to her own exacting specifications. She and Falligant had placed their own advertisements in the New York papers and had hired girls for the casino through an old friend of Wes's who had agreed to act as their agent in the matter. The women had come 'round the Horn and upon their arrival had gone immediately into training. By the end of October there wasn't one of them who couldn't fan a deck, shuffle it with one dainty hand, or work any other trick nearly as well as Frisco herself.

Another rule, one which the handbills didn't advertise, was that there was to be no hanky-panky between dealer and player. If a girl met a man off the premises, what the two of them did was their own affair; but no assignations were to be made in the casino. "Keep in mind," Frisco had told them immediately upon their arrival and many times since, "that the eyes of the whole town are going to be on you. You can decide to take up with some drunken miner, and live in a high-priced pigsty with him for a month or two before I find out about it and fire you, but it won't last. The rest of us will still be back up here on the hill, holding out for something better. This town's going to be a playground for miners for a while. Then the best of them are going to come to town and invest in something solid, something that won't go away, like land or property. And they're the ones who are going to make the best husbands. If you have any sense at all you're going to hold out for that kind. You aren't going to be young and pretty forever. If your heads are screwed on right you'll be taking steps to provide for the future."

It made a nice speech. She knew it by heart now. She ought to: she'd had it, word for word, from Wes Falligant, who had drilled her in the same point of view for a year and a half now. Well, she guessed it made sense. She'd largely ignored it as the fatherly rantings of an old man who wished her well, right up until the time when she had twenty young charges in tow, teaching them the ins and outs of a trade. Then, when it came to advice, she found the advice she had been given was the best she herself had to give.

Not that in her case there'd been any time for men since Shandor's death. There had been the odd flirtation here and there, first in New York, then, after the baby's birth on shipboard, a brief and bittersweet affair with the young captain of the clipper that had brought them out here. But the New York liaisons she had never taken seriously, and her own pregnancy had kept her mind occupied. Besides, they'd all seemed such slight men after Shandor, with his powerful physical presence and his passionate intensity. The ship's captain had been another order of business altogether: a strong man of few but well-chosen words, a man of sensitivity and competence and inner power and integrity. He'd delivered Alex himself, on an oak table in his own cabin, while Wes stood by feeding the both of them whiskey and running whatever errand came to hand. . . . Well, the memory was a fine one, sweet and poignant, but his course had been set on another route than hers, and she'd sensed from the first that it wasn't in the cards. She'd given him up, and said no, and while everything in her had told her almost daily since then that she'd done the right thing, still, the memory of Captain Peter Clay of the Flying Horse Line had power to strike a bittersweet chord in her heart at the end of a long day, after Wes had left and Alex was in bed asleep.

She'd never expected to see him again. The word he'd given her was that he was being taken off the San Francisco and Sandwich Islands run, and would be working New York to New Orleans instead: a shorter run which would have allowed him more time in port, more time to settle down, find a wife, raise a family. A run which had the inside track, word had it, when it came time to retire from the tiller and take his place indoors, on dry land, in an executive's chair where all the real money was made in the shipping business. It had been a big promotion, and an important one in his young life; it had been just the sort of thing that, he'd said, would allow him to make a woman a serious offer for the first time in his life. But she'd written him off altogether.

Two days before her opening, however, she was taking a turn in Portsmouth Square in the morning, dressed in her best and most stylishly prim street clothes, with Juana Godoy and infant Alex in tow. Then her heart almost skipped a beat. She stopped, one hand to her breast. Then, crossing the square, he saw her, and paused himself, his sturdy figure trim and elegant in his captain's uniform, his neatly tended beard jaunty and stylish, his head held high. His smile was warm and delighted, for all his New England reserve. He came her way, his steps quick, purposeful.

"Mrs. McGee!" he said. "How wonderful to see you again!"

She looked around, but it was no time for reserve. "Captain Clay!" she said. She held out one elegantly gloved hand, but returned the pressure he gave it with warm frankness. "I thought never to see you again."

He smiled. Was it possible that she'd forgotten how handsome he was, with that high forehead and the strong chin and those sea-blue eyes? "I'm pleased you remember me," he said, the trace of a Down East brogue still strong in his deep voice. "The firm sent me west to open a new freight account with a merchant here. I'm a passenger this time." His eyes made a quick assessment of her. "If you'll pardon a personal remark, motherhood and a year's passing flatter you quite as much as everything else always did. I'm finding it hard to express the sort of pleasure it gives me, running into you like this."

"And me you," she said. She pressed his hand once again and then dropped it. "Look," she said. "We must see each other while you're here. You say you've business in the city?"

"Yes," he said. "With a man named Brannan. The word is that he draws a lot of water here."

"He does," she said. "I'll give you my own personal introduction. I'd keep it quiet, but Sam's a business partner of mine."

"Of yours? You must be doing well here."

"I've prospered. Matter of fact, you're here in time for the grand opening of a—of a business I'm just getting started here. You must come see it." She pointed to a handbill on a nearby tree. "The opening's tomorrow night. Won't you be our guest?"

"Ah," he said. "Frisco's. Did you know the place is already famous in New York, before it's even opened? I can see Wes Falligant's fine hand in this. But I hadn't made the connection. Who is Frisco McGee?"

"Me," she said, beaming. "And I'm going to own this

273

town one of these days. Oh, Peter, it's so good to see you. Come take a look at this big boy of mine. You'll never recognize him now."

Alex started crying just then, and bellowed lustily all through Juana's attempts to silence him. Clay grinned down at him, one hand on the tiny fingers. "Well," he said, "I recognize the voice, all right. Look, would it be too much to ask you to lunch, here on the Square? Or anywhere else?"

"Oh, dear," she said. "I'm due at Sam's warehouse at one, and I have letters to post before then. There's all sorts of last-minute things to do for the opening. Look, I'll tell Sam about you. If he doesn't give you the business you're seeking I'll pull his beard for him. Make no other plans for tomorrow night. Wes'll be so glad to see you." Her voice was warmly sincere as she added, "As I am myself."

"It would be hard to make me much happier than I am now," Clay said. His eyes crinkled delightedly in a way she'd all but forgotten. "Until tomorrow, then."

She turned to go, and knew in her heart that he'd be surprised beyond his imagining to know how hard her heart was beating.

Chapter 39

The day of the opening Wes took Frisco for a spin in a new buggy he'd bought her a week or so before right out of one of Sam's warehouses. It was an elegant conveyance for San Francisco, and sported not only a brake, a rarity on the buggies of the day, but a calash-style folding top of genuine leather. Under the seat there was a waterproof storm curtain with isinglass windows for the rainy season. "Nothing but the best," he said, "and besides, in two weeks or so the streets down here off the Hill will be impassable."

His prediction looked to be a true one, as they moved lazily down Clay Street behind Wes's grey gelding, Matty Van Buren. The morning fogs were growing thicker and staying longer, and the evening fog came in around four-thirty as thick as *cioppino*, the home-made bouillabaisse San Franciscans were beginning to serve in the better restaurants. Storm clouds hung over the crest of Mount Tamalpais, across the Gate, and the city was already making ready for another siege as bad as the one last year, when the land-fill area down below Montgomery Street had become such a mire that horses, mules, and some said a human being or two had drowned or smothered in the mud, unable to struggle out of the water-saturated muck of the streets.

Perhaps, she was thinking now, they were reclaiming too much of the Bay too quickly. Look at lower Clay Street, where the beached hulks of abandoned windjammers served as the first stories of office buildings, saloons, warehouses, and the upper floors of the buildings rose above the weathered timbers of the once-proud ships. There, in a single block, sandwiched between con-

275

ventional buildings, were the stranded freighter *Niantic*, now doubling as the Niantic Hotel, and another name-less hulk, two doors away, serving as a store ship on the hold floor and a Chinese laundry above decks. All of this was scattered among liquor stores, saloons, dentists' offices, general stores, notaries' offices, and the like.

"Well, it isn't New York," Falligant said wryly on the seat beside her. "Did you ever see the like of it? I haven't and I've been virtually everywhere between Edin-burgh and Canton." He chucked loudly at Matty, and then pulled the buggy up sharply as a ten-mule team, the skinner astraddle the near wheeler, the jerk line in his callused hand, pulled out into the street at the corner before him. "Hey!" he bellowed. "Easy there, skinner!"

The muleskinner started to let fly an oath or two—the teamsters' prowess at cussing was already famous in the city—but stopped when he saw Frisco, resplendent in a gray riding habit with velvet collar and black satin stock, smiling at him, amusement in her eyes. "Excuse me, ma'am," he said. "Didn't see you there." He looked at Falligant and apparently thought better of any man, of any age, who'd have such a filly in tow on a fine Friday afternoon. "Sorry," he said above the mules' noise. "Didn't mean to crowd you. Gettin' these devils started's enough trouble without having to get 'em stopped. They knows *hep* and *gee* and *haw* all right, but they ain't learned *whoa* yet. *Whoa! Whoa there!*"

"Your off eight's lame," Wes said, not unfriendly, holding Matty still. "You got a dog link fixing to come loose between wagons." He tipped his hat mock-gallantly, an insolent grin on his pale face. "Good luck." He drove on.

"Well," he said approvingly. "Any woman who can stop a muleskinner from cussing just by looking at him doesn't need any help from me anywhere. Perhaps I'd better let you drive this thing."

"The day will never come when I won't need, or wel-come, your help, Wes. And speaking of business, did we ever get delivery on clean linen for the refreshment ta-bles?"

"Stop fretting," Falligant said. "You've checked every-thing twice and I've checked it three times behind you. Everything's going to be fine."

"How about security?"

"Look. I finally figured out a use for a round dozen of the Sydney Ducks. Pay 'em well, promise 'em a case of liquor the moment the place closes tomorrow morning, wave the chance of busting a head or two under their noses, and you'll have the toughest damn set of bouncers a casino ever hired. That's not the problem. Getting 'em scrubbed down and into that fancy Frog livery we picked out for 'em was another thing. Damn good we bought the extra-large sizes. The only Ducks who could afford to take the job were the biggest, brawniest bruisers in Sydney Town. Anyone smaller and less bellicose, why, his friends'd laugh him out of town if they saw him in those outfits."

"But won't they be something of a disciplinary problem themselves?"

"The rule is, no liquor before the place closes. And I'm damned if I'll waste my own time doing the enforcing. Hell, I hired Sam Roberts to do it for me."

"Roberts! But the town council told him to get out of town!"

"Yes, I know, and it cost me a pretty penny in bribes to get the exile order lifted. But I figured that anybody who could control the Hounds the way Roberts did can handle a bunch of Botany Bay riffraff, no matter how damned big they are. Meanwhile, how are those girls of yours?"

"A little stage fright, but I'm going to give them all a good talking to an hour or so before opening."

"Splendid, my dear. And yourself?"

"Butterflies, but perhaps not as much as I expected. It's a funny thing, Wes. I was a lot more scared the first night I read palms, back with Putnam and Frye."

"You hadn't been through as much then. Look, you'll knock the lot of them out of the water. Forget it. And, Graciela?"

"Frisco."

"Frisco it is. That ship's captain of yours, Clay. Anything happening there? That is, if it's any of my damned business?"

"Peter? I don't know. I *am* glad to see him, and a little excited. More than I'd have thought I'd be. But. . . ."

"Sam said he's thrown the lad the bulk of his—of *our*—shipping for the next year. That'll make him look good back in New York." Wes whoa-ed Matty at the next street corner and turned to look at her. "Of course I told him to do it. I figured you could use something to keep young Captain Clay here in the City for a bit."

Frisco smiled affectionately at him. "That was kind of you, and observant, too. In truth, I would like some time to see him, and get to know him better."

Falligant pursed his lips, his face thoughtful. "He is, in point of fact, a cut above most of the . . . uh . . . gallants who've landed here. But give the town time, girl. In five years the pick of America will be here. It'll be *the* thing to do, going to San Francisco around the Horn. Or, God knows, maybe someone'll find a better and more sensible way across the Sierra. No matter. There'll be no shortage of beaux here soon." He cleared his throat sententiously. "That's in case the notion of haste had entered that pretty head of yours."

"No, no," she said. "But on the other hand, as you said some time back . . . well, it's been a long time between drinks. I haven't had a young man around in a while."

"Ah. Feminine vanity rears its charming head. Well, by Christ, girl, you're human. I've wondered for quite some time how you put up with the celibate life, knowing you for a normal young woman with normal needs. God knows I can't, for all that I'm old and decrepit and too damned cranky for any woman to spend more than an hour's time a day with. Well, then, have your fling. He's a handsome lad, and there's a bit of substance to him. I stood him a round of drinks last night, and chewed the fat with him for an hour or two. I liked a lot of what I heard. He's got a firm head on his shoulders, and ninety percent of the women in the world would count him a better than average catch." He sighed. "I almost regret the way you're going to break his heart."

"Me?" she said incredulously. "Break his heart?"

"Why, of course. The trouble is, he's serious about you. He didn't know he was until you sent him packing before. And then he spared no expense of spirit and honest sweat to work himself into a position where he

278

could come back, with a merchant's landlubber commission in his hand, and do you some serious wooing."

Frisco's face fell. "Oh, dear. And I was rather hoping, you know, no strings . . . just a nice friendly sort of. . . ."

"By God and by Christ, girl, the only place you'll ever find a nice friendly sort of liaison is one where the cash goes on the barrelhead. A nice friendly sort of liaison is what I get when I visit Mother Judge's, up above the El Dorado, and ask for Gertie or perhaps Maude. Unless you want to take yourself a gigolo, or take your place working the midnight shift in a parlor house, you'll not find a nice friendly no-strings-attached liaison this side of the grave. Let it get past the holding-hands-and-sparking stage, and there'll be no turning back. If you're the one that doesn't give a damn for him, he'll be your slave—and he'll cut the guts out of anyone who looks wall-eyed at you. If he's the one who wants to keep things nice and friendly, no strings attached, you'll be the one that'll walk barefoot over hot burning coals to claw the eyes out of the first filly that flashes an ankle at him, stepping down from a buggy on the Square. I'm sorry, but that's the way it is. The only way to find a nice friendly love affair, where nobody falls in love, is to by Christ get married, and settle down to being comfortably bored with each other." He paused to cough into his now ever-present handkerchief.

"Well," she said, "that was quite a harangue. You know, I *have* thought of getting married. It'd be a blessing for Alex, for one thing. But, Wes, my only experience of that sort of thing was with Shandor, and it was a happy one, short as it was."

"That's why it *was* happy," he rasped. "It was short."

"Come on, now. As I was saying, my only experience was with Shandor, and it was, well, *intense.* It was beautiful, powerful, all-consuming. Shandor . . . well, he had a way of using up a woman, all the way. The way she wants to be used up. When I was with him there wasn't anything else I wanted to think about, anyone else I wanted to be with."

"Ah, yes." Falligant's eyes were far away. "I can remember a few like that myself—a *very* few—and I know what you're talking about. But it can't be that way

279

all the time. There'll come a time when you'll desperately want to settle for the right kind of dull life, with the right kind of dull patches here and there. That sort of thing, well, it's comforting. It's like a nice broken-in pair of shoes, the kind you choose when you've got some serious walking to do."

"I understand. But Wes, for all that I've been through so far, well, I'm competent, and confident, and—" she smiled warmly at him, her hand on his stick-like arm— "for all that I'm the young woman you've all but raised, you know, independent and, well, I guess fearless enough as women go, the way you wanted me to be, the way you knew you had to make me be. . . ."

"Go on," he said, his voice low.

"Well, I'm . . . I'm still *young*. You can't make me a sensible woman of thirty or so. I'm a decade younger. The blood's still hot. And Wes, I'm my father's daughter, and my mother's too. I'm Irish, and a Gypsy, and it's going to take someone as intense as Shandor, as strong, as dynamic, as powerful and independent, as mercurial, as unpredictable. . . ."

"I know," Falligant said. "One couldn't tell me a goddamned thing at your age either. Well, no matter. I was just testing you. Playing the *advocatus diaboli*. Sounding you out. You know that, though. Look how many times you've steered me into doing it for you. I wouldn't be surprised if you'd been doing that right now."

She grinned that amused, devilish, white-toothed Gypsy smile of hers. Falligant melted. "Ah, God," he said. "I'm damned glad, at times like these, that it's the father's role I'm playing in this medicine show of ours and not the lover's. Smart and experienced old bastard that I am, you'd have me flimflammed in two blinks of an eye like any mark on the midway. Well, have your fun with young Clay. There's a way in which I almost wish he'd change your mind for you."

"There's a way in which I almost wish it too," she said. And suddenly her eyes were dark and somber and thoughtful. Her smile was a tentative one, full of indecisions and ambivalence. She sighed deeply. "Let's go up and look the place over one more time. Six hours to opening. . . ."

Chapter 40

Upstairs, before the great mirror in her own private room, Frisco fretted over her hair. Was every curl in place? Did it look right from the side?

"Here," Lyuba said, stepping forward to tuck in a stray strand. "You look lovely. You will bewitch every man in the house." Lyuba's dark features relaxed into a conspiratorial smile. "Ah," the Gypsy said, "if ever I had looked like that, for so much as one evening."

"Oh, go on with you," Frisco said. "What I want to know is how am I going to get downstairs in this gown? I can't even see the floor, much less the steps."

There was a knock on the door. "Come in," she said. She didn't bother to look around. The Ducks, downstairs, had strict orders as to who they let up the grand staircase.

The door opened. "I think I heard something about how you are going to negotiate the staircase," Wes Falligant said. "Why, on my arm, of course. Although, good God, I'm going to feel like a father giving away the bride." He looked her up and down, resplendent in her lace-trimmed black taffeta with the four-layered white organdie canezou billowing above the waist to end in enormous puffed sleeves. "My God," he said. "Just look at you. You could snub royalty in an outfit like that." He coughed lightly and covered his mouth with the ever-present kerchief.

"What does it look like downstairs?" she said, still fussing before the glass.

"Oh, you won't believe the business we're doing. I've got two men busy doing nothing but water the drinks. For a while it was so tight you could hardly get from

281

table to table, but they're down to some serious gambling by now. Everyone in town who owns a clean shirt or dress is here. Two new ships docked this afternoon, and if every passenger aboard hasn't found his or her way up here by now I'm an Indian."

She stepped forward to kiss his polished-ivory cheek, hiding her shock at how deathly cold he was. "Wes, is— is Peter here?"

"Why, yes. With the captains of the two ships that docked today. It appears young Mr. Clay is well thought of in New York shipping circles. He's risen a long way in a hurry, in point of fact. Coming ashore to run the company's affairs? And not forty yet? Admirable."

"I'm all aflutter," she said. "I keep thinking something's unbuttoned."

"Here," he said. "No more delays. Everyone in town has been waiting for this moment. It's time you made your appearance." He held out his hand, smiling. And with a small bow he led her to the door.

As they stepped down to the landing and turned, so that she could see the gay scene below, with the green tables and the flawless Louis Philippe decor, the string quartet struck up a stately tune and all eyes turned upward to her—to her!—and the action in the room stopped. One hand on Wes's arm, she put one foot slowly after the other, coming down the grand staircase, taking care to keep her smile small and enigmatic, to let her eyes sweep the crowd. Yes, there was Peter Clay, standing with a tall, handsome man with unruly blond hair and a burly, Napoleonic figure in a black captain's uniform. All of them were admiring her, and she was lovely, she knew it, the loveliest sight any of them had ever seen. It was the most thrilling moment of her life.

Sam Brannan dropped by an hour later, trying to make his appearance look as perfunctory as possible. Wes Falligant met him at the door, showed him around, and steered him to the punchbowl for drinks. "No, not that one, Sam. That's the watered one. I took care that this one has a bit more authority."

Brannan took a sip from his glass. "Authority! God in heaven, Wes, if it had any more authority it'd close down the place and arrest everyone here!" He gasped

282

and sipped again, more cautiously this time. "What in hell's name is that, anyhow?"

"Chatham Artillery punch," Falligant said. "An old Revolutionary War recipe. One of the early stops in my bleak career as a remittance man was Savannah, and the only thing of any utility I took away from the place, other than a pair of choice society maidenheads, was the secret of the punch. Here, what have you been up to today?"

"Well, Wes, I came to warn you. I had word from the waterfront. Porter Rockwell's back in town. No, no, I don't think I'm in trouble. Brigham knows damned good and well that if he kills me he won't get a cent. He's hoping to scare me into some sort of blood-money payment, forgetting that I know him of old and know precisely where and when his every move is going to be. But Wes. . . ."

"Yes?" Falligant smiled his small deadly smile. "You're going to tell me, I think, that Porter wants a hunk of *my* hide to nail to the barn door. Yes, I know Rockwell's type. He'll forget money, liquor, women or his hope of heaven to avenge the smallest slight. Good Christ, Sam, I've killed a round phalanx of Porter Rockwells in my day. One more of the tribe doesn't scare me." He took another drink of the powerful punch and smiled. "Well, by God, perhaps it's time. I can get my evening exercise, let off some anger that's been building up in me, and get Young's bloody brigand off your back in the same evening."

"Wes, no! You don't know the man."

"No, and I don't want to. But I know the type. Let me tell Frisco where I'm going. You skedaddle along home to Liza. You've compromised your reputation quite enough as it is by coming down to a gambling hall. I'll see you in the morning."

"But Wes. . . ."

It was no use. He was gone, threading his way expertly through the crowd below the tinkling crystal chandeliers.

The seafarers' names were Laurence Haupt, the tall, blond Adonis with the beguiling smile, and Anthony Donato the dark, brooding one who looked like Shan-

dor. They were charming, attentive, virile, attractive—
and Peter Clay was getting more and more visibly irri-
tated at their attentions as the moments passed.

She'd have to do something about this. "Look," she
said. "I'm the hostess here. Fascinated as I am with you
gentlemen, it's my duty to circulate. So if you'll let me
tear myself away for a moment. . . ." She compromised
her farewell, giving each man a radiant smile and touching Haupt's and Donato's hands lightly with her own
before pressing Peter's warmly between her two hands
and giving him an especially warm look—the Gypsy
"look" that could tie a man to your skirts as efficiently
as any physical tether.

"Ah," Wes said, coming forward. "Frisco, my dear—
see, I got the name right for a change. . . ."

"Wes. You've been back at the punchbowl. And the
Light Cavalry punch, at that."

"Artillery, my dear. *I'm* light horse, but it's gunners'
punch. Yes, I'm feeling no pain. It's a splendid evening.
Sam was here. I'm going out for a spell. The air's close
in here."

She looked at him with concern. The red spots were
back in his pasty cheeks. "You . . . you'll take care of
yourself? Bundle up against the fog? Be sure you take
your greatcoat. It may rain before the night's out."

"All the better. If they can't get home because of the
rain they'll spend more money here. Ah, God, the
money this place is going to make!" His smile was almost happy, through the alcoholic haze. "Look, have all
the fun you can. It's a good night, a good night."

And now courtly Wes Falligant, who was never forward with a woman, leaned forward to kiss her on the
cheek. "God, look at you!" he beamed. "I love you. I
haven't said that to anyone since I turned twenty-five,
back when Tom Jefferson was in the White House. I say
it to you. You're the daughter I always wished I had.
How kind of fate to give me a daughter so late in life,
when a man really needs a child of his own to care for."

"Wes," she said, her eyes filling with salt tears. But
he'd slipped away from her, through the crowd, and
here was a fresh contingent of them coming through the
front door now, people to be greeted. Remember, take
note of the name and the face. Make sure you don't

forget. The wise hostess learns to memorize these things instantaneously. People will come back again and again to a place where they're remembered, where they're treated like old friends from the first. It's that first impression that counts, and if you let that one slip by you you've let the person slip by you, forever. Now introduce yourself. Be very ladylike so the women won't be jealous. Circulate, circulate. . . .

Falligant touched his greatcoat on the hall tree, but decided against it. To be sure, it was cold as bloody hell out there, a wet unhealthy cold, the sort of thing a lunger could die of. He chuckled at the thought. Die? How did that quote from the Bard go? *We all owe God a death.* . . . God, his memory was fading day by day. He'd once had reams and reams of first-rate poetry at the tip of his tongue, and as much of second-rate or worse. Some of it had been his own, but a damned poor poet he'd been for all that he'd been a decent technician in his youth: Petrarchan sonnet, ballade, villanelle, all had tripped merrily from his tongue as he'd wooed the randy daughter, the errant wife. Now, how much of it was left? Damned little. None of it fitted his life anymore. Not much of it, anyhow:

That time of year thou may'st in me behold
When yellow leaves, or none, or few, do hang
Upon those boughs which shake against the cold:
Bare ruin'd choirs, where late the sweet birds
    sang. . . .

There, now. That was a verse of use for an old duffer like him, with one foot in the ground already. He strode out into the street and looked down the long hill at the city below. The moon came out from behind the clouds, big, round, gibbous. He could see the lights of the saloons and stews, the moonlight glinting on the forest of masts standing at anchor along the eight-hundred-foot Long Wharf they'd spent so much money on. No matter, it'd pay off its costs within the year, he was sure of that.

He strolled, light-hearted, down the steep hill, his steps light, his heart pounding. How about another drink?

He reached inside his coat, past the warming, comforting presence of the big gun there, and pulled out the omnipresent flask. He tipped it up and drank deeply. Ah, yes! Yes, that was something now. . . .

Ah, Shakespeare! He'd spent his time at that, too, in his checkered career, playing the mummer in sock and buskin. He'd understudied one of Kean's performances, playing Hotspur to Kean's Prince Hal. Ah, yes. Shakespeare. You could find anything, anything at all you wanted in him. Both sides of any question. Reasons to steal a crown, reasons to defend it. Reasons to live, reasons to die. . . .

Bah! A pox on all cowards! He turned the corner in Dupont Street, and turned his face toward Portsmouth Square. Here, in the flat, the fog hung heavy, but less heavy than the night before. There'd be plenty of light, if the moon held up, if the clouds continued their drift across the night sky. El Dorado, Sam had said? At the bar? But in a crowded room more than the man you sought could be slain by a stray bullet. He didn't mind killing a man who needed killing, but an innocent man? A man with wife and family dependent upon his life and labors? No, it'd be better to call the bastard out. He reached the Square and walked kitty-corner across the green grass, loosening the big gun in its holster. He stood in the street, facing the swinging doors of the first floor. Upstairs, on the balcony, two whores giggled down at him. "Wesley! Come up and buy us a drink!"

"Later, my doves," Falligant said. "I've got some business first." He threw back his head, standing defiantly in the middle of the street before the saloon doors. "*Rockwell!*" he bellowed above the din. "Porter Rockwell! Come out and play in the street, you mother's boy! Rockwell! Come out! I'll pull your beard for you, I will! Yoo-hoo! Porter!"

A face appeared above the swinging doors, but it wasn't Rockwell's. Falligant strained, trying to make out the face—and then something hit him from behind, and he gasped at the shock, and looked down to see three inches of razor-sharp steel protruding from his own belly. He half-turned. "You—" he said to the whiskered face with its mad eyes. His hand went to his chest, to the holster, but it was too late. The strength was flying from him in a great rush. He fell to one knee. "A pox on all cowards," he said, quoting Falstaff again. Falstaff, who died in his bed. A rough hand pulled the knife out of him, and his blood spilled on the ground. He tried to rise, but a cloud came over the moon and he couldn't tell which direction was up anymore. "Graciela," he said, and died.

Chapter 41

Frisco, radiantly happy, her face flushed with victorious pride, stopped Sally, the second-shift faro dealer, on her way to the ladies' room. The girl's face brightened. "Miz McGee!" she said. "I was just goin' to the—"

"It's all right," Frisco said. "I've been watching you, all of you. You're doing fine, and I'm proud of you. Just remember, everything the table makes above the limit we agreed upon, you two girls split ten per cent of the excess."

"Yes ma'am."

"Don't call me ma'am. I'm ten years younger than you." Frisco, holding her at arm's length, smiled at her. "Although God knows, nobody'd ever know it, looking at you. You look wonderful."

"Thank you, Miz—"

"Miz nothing. It's Frisco. Pass the word on about that. I don't want anyone who comes in this place ever to call me anything else. Do me a favor, Sally, and make a point of that. That word—Frisco—it's going to be one of the most famous place-names in the world one of these days. I want to be identified with the name, every inch of the way. Please. Make the effort."

"Yes ma'am." The girl grinned. "You're serious about that, aren't you? I mean about all of it. Getting rich. Owning half the town. Being a great lady."

"I was never more serious in my life. Look, you stick with me and the Colonel, and follow that good advice he's been giving all of you, and you'll do well by yourselves. There's a better class of men coming into town, little by little. Men you won't grow tired of in a hurry.

Do right by me and we'll both make a lot of money. And when Mr. Right comes along you'll have yourself a nice nest egg so you won't come to the marriage feeling you have to be dependent on him." Frisco smiled. "But you know all this."

"Yes ma'am." The girl grinned again. "Damn! I mean—"

"It's all right." Frisco squeezed her arm and walked away into the crowd. "Mr. Haupt! Captain Donato! Are you winning or losing?"

"Losing, ma'am," the blond giant said. "At least, we're worse off than we were. We've had the pleasure of meeting you, and a marvelous pleasure it is. But then again, we've had the displeasure of having to share you with the rest of the people in the room. Not to say the displeasure of having failed, so far, to secure your permission to call upon you while we're here in San Francisco."

"Please," Frisco laughed. "I'm making a rule: everyone who enters that door over there has to call both me and the city 'Frisco.' It certainly seems little enough to ask."

Donato, the quiet one, smiled that slow, dark Italian smile. How very like a quieter, slower version of Shandor he was! But there was fire in him, she knew that, even if the fires were banked. This was a man who chose his battlegrounds carefully, and fought like a cornered tiger when he had decided to stand. "Ask!" he said. "But that is the trouble. You ask far too little of us. Name what you want. We will get it all for you, whatever the cost." There was elegance and a curious sort of power in his half-mocking bow. This one would be no woman's fool, that was sure.

"All right," she said. "I'll ask something of you before the evening's over. Meanwhile, how long will the two of you be in town? A day? A couple of days? Oh, I forgot. You're leaving tomorrow, Captain Haupt? Tomorrow evening? If you call on me tomorrow morning, at eleven, you'll find me home. Captain Donato? I'll be pleased to receive you the following morning, if you're still interested." One look at their faces dispelled any lingering doubts she might have had as to their interest.

"Now, if you gentlemen will pardon me, I've got a couple of tables to visit. I do hope you're enjoying yourselves."

The tall man from the saloon bent over Falligant's body, felt the fallen man's wrist, and waited for a pulse. He found none. Softly, gently he turned the body over onto its back. "Poor devil," he said under his breath, to no one in particular, least of all to the small crowd that had gathered around him. "Curious . . . he was armed to the teeth. I wonder how . . . but damnation! Whoever it was got him in the back. You wouldn't think that would kill a man, though, that quickly." Half-kneeling, he called to the people around him. "Can anyone give me some light? A lantern? Anything?"

He lifted the dead man's arm, let it fall. "God, the man's skin and bones," he muttered. "He must have been ill in the first place—sick as a dog. Well, perhaps the shock. . . ." Quick footsteps; someone handed him a covered lantern. He opened one side of it. "Thanks," he said. "Now, let's see if there's anything to identify him." He frowned. There was something about that face, some lingering memory, jogged by the still-arrogant cut of the now peaceful features.

Someone, bolder than the rest, stepped forward and peered down. "By God!" he said in an awed voice. "The 'Ghost!' " He stepped back and called out to a friend. "Hey, Mert! Somebody's gone and killed the 'Ghost!' "

"Ghost?" the man kneeling by the body said in a musing voice, still talking to himself. "Well, he certainly looks like one, and I guess the name's appropriate now." He turned the face this way and that. There was something . . . something. . . .

"Here comes the constable," another voice said. "Make way! Make way there." The crowd parted to admit a puffing middle-aged man in street clothes.

The tall man stood up. "Here he is," he said, handing over the lantern. "Someone seems to have knifed him in the back. I'd say he was ill, badly ill at the time."

"Thank you," the constable said. "Look here, did any of you see anything? Anybody leaving the scene?"

The voices came thick and fast:

". . . man with a beard. . . ."

". . . look, he's dressed like a nob! Wonder who. . . ."

". . . stood outside the saloon and called somebody out. . . ."

". . . Jesus Christ, they like to of cut his guts out!"

The constable held up one hand. "Look," he said. "I want all of you in my office across the Square. Don't anybody leave. Two of you boys help me move him down." He turned to the tall man. "It is all right to move him, I reckon?"

"Oh, he's dead enough," the tall man said. "And come to think of it, I doubt there'll be much here in the way of evidence, after all these folks have finished fouling up any footprints. No, it's all right, I'm sure." He pursed his lips, thinking uncharitable thoughts about the kind of constable that would have to ask a stranger these questions. "On the other hand, one of these men seemed to think he knew who the dead man was. You might know yourself if you took a closer look."

"Oh? Oh, yes. Yes, I suppose if I. . . ." He opened a second side of the dark lantern. "Oh, by God! Oh, heaven!"

"You know him yourself? It's somebody well known here in town?"

The constable's face was shocked, wretched. It was obvious that his duties, whatever they were, hadn't included playing witness to the death of an acquaintance before this. "God almighty," he said. "Harvey, you run quick like a rabbit up the hill and get Sam Brannan. Quick! You tell him what you seen. You hear?" His face was full of distress as he searched the faces around him. He turned to the tall man. "Leading citizen," he said. "Sort of, anyhow. Oh, my God. Why did this have to happen on my shift?"

"It's unfortunate," the tall man said. "Look, could we go make our depositions now? I've got a packet leaving for Sacramento on the morning tide, and I had notions of getting some sleep. I came in on the clipper this afternoon, and all my business is upriver."

"Oh, yes, yes," the constable said absently. "Of course. Damn. Let me think. Now where is everybody? Where could I find—Charley? Charley Findlay! You

291

run up the hill and tell Miss Frisco! Tell her somebody's gone and killed Mr. Falligant!"

Frisco, with Peter Clay in tow, went from room to room, an anxious eye on the tables. She'd only had to invoke house limit once, and had had misgivings about it then. After all, there had to be a big winner now and then; it was good for business. It kept the marks hoping, hoping against all the odds that the Big Hit would happen to them, too.

"It all looks very much on the up and up," Peter said. "I'm much relieved."

"It is," she said smiling. "Rule one in this business is that the house doesn't have to be dishonest to win. The percentages are always firmly in our favor." She turned and looked up at him, her eyes friendly but reserved. "You don't really approve, do you?"

"Well, I'll be honest. All this, it's outside my experience. I'm out of my element." He smiled that delightful smile of his, warm and accepting. "You forget I'm new to *all* this landlubber business. I'm not even terribly used to the fact that the floor doesn't roll and pitch beneath my feet. I took up my Pa's trade, you know. At sixteen. We've all been sailors since—well, since the family landed here in the 1600s. Maybe earlier. There's a tradition in the family that one of my ancestors sailed with Drake." His smile changed to a knowing grin. "There were even a few pirates in the family, word has it. Although the distinction between pirate and privateer seems, for all practical purposes, to be the sort of thing only a lawyer can understand."

"Some people," she said, watching her girl Shirley expertly scoop up dice and cash alike in a game of Birdie, "have the same trouble making the legitimate distinction between an honest dealer and a three-card monte man."

"I confess I'm not sure myself."

"Stick around. I'll explain in a day or two. Meanwhile, don't be too alarmed at my choice of profession. I took up my father's line of work too, mind you, and he was an honest dealer just like I am. True, there are swindlers in every trade, and this is no exception. But the fact that there are ship's captains who wreck their firms' ships on the rocks, working in collusion with salvagemen, doesn't mean all ships' captains are crooked."

"A point well taken. What's this they're playing?"

"It's called Birdie here. My father ran a game of it on a boat going up and down the Mississippi. The name of it changed from one river town to the next: it'd be Ten-Spot here, and Dicey there, and Roll-Ten a hundred miles down the River. The French call it *passe-dix*, and that's the name my father called it when he worked New Orleans."

"Fascinating. Three dice. One player's the banker, right? And if the man with the dice rolls below ten, he and all the other players lose their stakes to the banker. If he rolls above ten . . . ah, yes, there's a winner . . . the banker has to—"

"Has to double the stakes all around. It's not as fast a game as roulette or Red Dog, perhaps, but it doesn't take long to win a fortune—or lose it."

"And you're taking the risks?"

"I am. It's a formidably independent lady you insist upon wooing, Peter."

"If only you'd let me. But every time I start getting serious with you, or even steer the conversation away from pleasant trivia. . . ."

"I'm sorry. I have to be honest with you." She put one hand on his for a moment. "Peter, I'm the girl I am, and that's the long and the short of it. I won't dissemble with you, and play games with you."

"I'd be disappointed in you if you did. And disappointed in my own poor judgment."

"Thank you. I appreciate your honesty. I only hope you appreciate mine as much. Peter, I *am* fond of you. You're handsome as Adonis, and brave and true and brilliant, and you'd be a catch for any woman in the country. I can't think how you've lasted as long as you have, being as successful as you are, without some woman catching you."

"They tried. But until recently I seldom got a chance to meet anyone but the daughters of shipowners and rich merchants. And they all seem to have voices like

293

squeaky wheels and figures like walruses. While you. . . ."

"Peter, can't we keep it more or less the way it is? For a time? While I make my pile here and make up my mind?"

"If only I thought that was what you were doing— making up your mind, that is. And as for money, well, I'm well paid. And I've an interest in the firm now. A fiftieth share, to be sure, but I'm in line for better. And the company is constantly expanding. We bought out a fast group of clipper ships two months ago. One of them landed here this morning. The sale's so new the captain doesn't even know he's working for me."

Frisco smiled. "I'm proud of you. But Peter, you know what I was worth when you delivered that lovely baby of mine on a table in your cabin, with the ship pitching back and forth like crazy—I was worth a trifle more than the price of my ticket West. That was a year and a half ago, I think. Do you know what I'm worth now? Guess."

"I couldn't begin to. Sixty thousand? Eighty? From the look of things you seem to be doing well. I assume you've a money partner."

"Peter, my dear, I *am* the money partner. By year's end I'll be worth three quarters of a million dollars, if I don't do anything stupid. Taking everything into account, I'm worth half a million right now, although I'd be hard pressed to lay my hands on half that in cash right now. You know how it is."

"My stars! No, my dear. I'm sure I *don't* know how it is. Half a million. . . ." He raised one arched brow high in surprise. "But how?"

"Stick around another few days and I'll explain that, too. Now do you see why I—"

She didn't finish the sentence. One of the Ducks touched her arm. She turned. "Par'n, ma'am, but Charlie Findlay, he's at the door, he says it's important."

"Peter? Will you pardon me?" She put one hand on his arm for a second again and smiled a quick goodbye at him. He watched her go, shaking his head in wonder. What a woman! And in a year and a half, starting from scratch.

He started to turn away, but something in her face

caught his eye as she stood at the door talking with a man in a brown workman's coat. Her hand went to her mouth and her face fell. He rushed through the crowd to her side. When she turned to look at him her face was wide-eyed with shock.

"Peter," she said dully. "It's Wes. He's been killed."

BOOK SIX

Chapter 42

They just had time to bury Wes Falligant—with no more ceremony than he'd wanted—before the rains came. As it was, there was a light drizzle when Frisco, Sam and a few friends stood at a simple gravesite on Wes's own property on Telegraph Hill, above Clark's Point. Watching the wet clods fall, Frisco let her mind reject the words flatly: they were from the English Book of Common Prayer, and Wes, by his own words a "life-long recusant," would have snorted all through the reading.

At the carriage Sam helped her up. "Funny, Frisco, I'd have expected to find one or the other of your young gallants to be here. Wasn't young Clay a friend of Wes?"

"Yes, he was," she said, adjusting the black veil. "But he had business upriver. When you sold out in Sacramento you opened a new and separate market for Peter's firm."

"I suppose so. Incidentally, this is a bad time to talk business, but there's a splendid opportunity coming up. I'm wondering if I've the legal right to act in Wes's name. He was a third partner, and. . . ."

"We signed over power-of-attorney papers for each other some time back. You never can tell when lightning is going to strike someone. 'In the midst of life we are in death,' as the parson was just reminding us."

"Fine. But the problem is—and it's a problem to everyone but us, I suppose—that the federal government has begun to claim title to a lot of land up Sacramento way. This includes land that a lot of folks have already paid high prices for, some of 'em to us, and think they have clear title to."

"And they don't?"

"Some do, some don't. But the point is, they'll have to defend it. And that's going to cost cash a lot of 'em don't have. If I can touch some of the funds on deposit in the bank under our three names, I can loan 'em money up there at whatever rates I choose. I can clean up."

"I don't think so," Frisco said. "Wes wouldn't have wanted to get into the usury business. He had some pretty salty things to say about that, as I remember."

"But if you'd like to invest in this yourself. . . ."

"I'm afraid I'll have to pass, Sam. I know you mean well, and it's good business, but, well, it's not my style either. You can lay hands on enough cash to become a loan shark up there without involving me. Meanwhile, as a Council member you stand a chance of being the first to know when the city puts up new land for sale. I'd appreciate all the vigilance you could give that sort of project."

"Oh, I will, of course. But Frisco—"

"Sam, ours is a limited partnership. You can do all the business of that kind that you like, and I won't think the worse of you. You're a fine man and a splendid business man, and you have my complete and unalloyed respect. But either something's my style or it isn't. I'm afraid I'll have to stand firm on this one."

"I understand," he said regretfully. "I do understand that some lots are due to be put up for sale in January. I'll be in the front row, with the right bids."

"You do that." Smiling through the veil, she gave him her lace-covered cheek to kiss. Then she nodded to Wong, Wes's man, whom she'd given work as her own driver. The carriage slowly turned and pulled back out into the street, leaving deep ruts in what had already begun to turn to slippery mud.

In a moment or two she was glad she'd had Wong put up the storm curtain and wear his own heavy greatcoat and big-billed cap. The drizzle became a regular rain, and if it hadn't been for the leather cover she'd have been soaked. As it was the pony's feet slipped and slid, and the wheels dragged in the slick rain-soaked clay.

The funny thing was, she'd known Wes was going to die. That day he'd told her he loved her, when they'd talked about the days up in the mining country . . . she'd known somehow, even then. The only thing she hadn't known was how long it was going to take for death to catch up with him.

But then, thinking this, she sat up with a sudden start. Of course! She'd also known that Shandor was going to die. And Lyuba had predicted that she would!

What had she said now? *"Twelve: You will know when Death is near. The blood of the Rom, inside you, will tell you."*

It was uncanny. Strange, though, how long it'd been since she'd thought of herself as a Rom. As Shandor had observed once, the moment you put aside Rom customs you stopped being a Rom. But there *was* something to the old ways. There was no doubting that. She'd had proof enough ten times over.

Lyuba! She'd fitted in perfectly at the casino, dealing any card game. When she felt like it she would let the customers know she could read palms or read the cards. But Frisco, self-absorbed in her quest for security and stability, had pretty much neglected her in recent months. While she knew Lyuba read the cards constantly, she hadn't consulted her. There were times when this was a smart thing to do. Like now, when—good heavens, she was on her own! There was no Wes Falligant to direct her affairs for her now, and she could flounder helplessly without that near-infallible rudder he'd provided since he'd decided, back in Indiana, to take her in hand and end her running and fear and worry once and for all.

What had Lyuba said, back on that terrible evening when Shandor died? She put her hands to her temples, thinking.

"One: You have traveled far. You have worn many names and been many persons in a short time.

"Two: Your wandering has not ended. You will wear other names, other faces. . . ."

Well, that was already proving to be true. She had gone wandering, first to New York, then to the gold fields, then to San Francisco. Halfway around the earth. And here she was, sporting a brand-new name of her own choosing. The rest?

"*Three*: You will live long, and will gain the world and lose the world and gain it again.

"*Four*: You will rise and fall and rise.

"*Five*: A great city will lie at your feet. You will conquer it alone, with nothing but your own mind for a weapon."

There! Here she was, the most prominent female citizen—not even excepting Sam's wife Eliza—in San Francisco, which she was sure was destined to become a great city in no more than a few years. She'd made her way more or less under her own steam, and her position was getting stronger with every passing day.

"*Six*: You will be every man's goddess, one man's queen.

"*Seven*: What you have lost, you will win again. What you have won, you will lose."

Well, enigmatic enough stuff—or perhaps it was transparent, if you wanted to read it a certain way. She and Shandor had been both master and slave, each of them. And this talk of winning and losing, that was no more than a reference to her profession, wasn't it? Wasn't it?

"*Eight*: What you shall gain is far away. What you shall lose is close by. Death is close by. Beware. . . .

"*Nine*: If you would find what your heart most desires you must seek what your heart most fears."

Curious that she should experience so little difficulty in remembering it all, when she hadn't consciously thought of Lyuba's words in months and months. Not since she'd come West, as a matter of fact. There was that prophecy again, the one about death being near. Well, it *had* been near. Poor Shandor! And poor Graciela. (Would she ever hear that name again, spoken in love the way Shandor spoke it, in the dark, between the sheets of a bed of her own?)

"*Ten*: The Great Game will fall to your hand. You must learn it and cherish it." Well, she had. When Wes died she'd been his equal in every way at every game of chance. He'd taken pains to make this so. And she'd had an obvious natural talent, far beyond her father's, he'd said.

"*Eleven*: You are a queen but will not reign as one. You are a slave but will not live as one. You are all

302

things. You have lived many lives before." Strange, the incantatory nature of automatic speech. There was a rough but soaring poetry in it: the rhetorical repetitions, the sing-song, litany-like, mesmeric quality of the long list. There was a Biblical cast to it too.

Well, she *was* a queen—if Pesha had in fact known what she was talking about, she was one by blood as well as by mating with a Gypsy king. But she had not reigned as one. And—well, there'd been that business in New Orleans and upriver. But surely that was behind her. After all, the prediction said: *a slave, but you will not live as one.* Well, she certainly wouldn't! She'd kill first—or, failing that, die first.

She shrugged it all away, sinking back against the padded seat, looking out the isinglass windows at the rain that pounded down deafeningly on the top of her carriage. It'd be New Year's soon, a time for new beginnings. And it was becoming painfully obvious that, whatever Sam Brannan's virtues—and they were many, especially if you considered him primarily as a man of business—he and she were simply not meant to wear the same yoke as a team. Not without Wes's moderating hand to smooth over the differences between their ways of looking at things. Sam wanted to go off like a shooting star in every direction. She, on the other hand, wanted to sleep on everything, and consider every move slowly.

Well, it was her style. And Wes, whose own way of doing things was backed by an uncannily strong instinct and intuition, had backed her up in her own way of doing things, again and again and again: "*Trust* your own way of doing things, once you've found out what it is. My way won't do it for you. Neither will anyone else's. Only your own will bring out your uniqueness. And don't let anyone tell you different. Merciful Christ, girl, what do *they* know? They're all floundering. They haven't a grain of your ability. They're all in trouble themselves. No, your apprenticeship's over. Forget it. You're the master of your own fate. Sooner you get that notion into your bones the better."

Suddenly the extent of her loss hit her, and she collapsed into great racking sobs. Behind the leather curtains, where no one could see her, the uncrowned Queen of San Francisco, as one of Sam's fellow Council members had called her two nights before, wept like a parentless child. Which in a way she was.

That night, however, she was her old self again. The rains kept back some of the crowds that might otherwise have filled Frisco's with high rollers; but the word was already out that business at the El Dorado and the Silver Slipper—and, to Sam's great delight, the Bella Union as well—was down. The same was true of every gambling hall in town. Most of them were subsisting on the profits from the whorehouses upstairs. Well, *let* them have that trade. She could make plenty of money in that business, but she knew what it was like to be a slave and she would never stoop to encouraging anyone to sell her body. She would never allow herself to profit by exploiting some disadvantaged soul—a life she herself might have had to turn to if dear Pesha hadn't made her realize the power she could have by *imaging*—From then on she was able to keep her head high and image herself being respected, and being capable of survival under any circumstance. Pesha had taught her to tune into the higher level of her mind, the part that was open to intuition and knew what was truly right for her. Pesha helped her to understand that knowing what was right for her was for her highest good, because her future good was in the seed of her own potential.

When the time came to get out of the gambling business, she could live off her investments, live down having been the proprietress of the biggest and cushiest gambling hall atop Fern Hill (or Nob Hill, as some folks were beginning to call it). But let the name *madam* be tagged onto her and she'd be a social pariah the rest of her days. No, she'd keep the standards high and the house percentage low. She'd still get rich, richer than all of them.

Chapter 43

Peter Clay went reluctantly back to New York in December. They had become off-and-on lovers, and Frisco enjoyed this part of his company every bit as much as the rest; but something still kept her from releasing her whole heart to him. What it was she could not explain, but whenever Peter threatened to make her lower her reserve and fall in love with him, she'd always manage to find occasion to put him off, or to play him off against another of the increasing number of "good catches" who had begun to appear in the rapidly expanding city.

Some of these she cultivated for a time and then passed on to one or another of her lovely young dealers, with advice and sometimes instructions. There was, she told them, enough for everyone.

The rains continued. It was the worst rain to fall since the Spaniards had left. The flatland fill below Montgomery Street became, in the words of a wag who planted a sign to that effect at the corner of Kearny Street, "impassable; not even jackassable." Montgomery itself, the main shopping street, had to be salvaged, and the merchants did so by planting stepping-stones in the mud-choked street. The stepping-stones were cases and crates of consignment goods for which no market existed. Crossing the street, they trod upon kegs of Connecticut nails, crates of Tidewater Virginia tobacco, and when the slow-market crates were *all* used up, cases of fast-market items would augment them, and the patrons of Sam's stores walked across Montgomery on tea and coffee.

At Christmas Sam's house burned down, in another of

the many fires that sprang up in a basically wooden city. Building materials here were mostly wood; there was something about the local soil that made brick manufacture impossible. He and a number of the other burned-out citizens erected ready-made houses Sam had shipped in from New York. Only this time Sam moved to Happy Valley, a newly developed area along Mission Street.

In January, well after his loan-sharking activities up the river were underway, Sam, Frisco's power of attorney securely in hand, purchased thirty-three more of the fifty lots offered by *Alcalde* Geary at open sale. As a Council member he got first choice, and he purchased wisely. Nevertheless, he was surprised at the opposition he received. "I could have bought forty more lots with money down, some of 'em bettern'n the ones I got. But there's a new syndicate. The front man's name is Wheeler, that's all I know. But he's got the money behind him, and he's outflanking me. I have a feeling he's out to stop me. I have a feeling he's under orders to do so."

Yet another group of investors joined Wheeler in the bidding next, and Sam found himself hard pressed to counter their double assault on the choice land he and Frisco had their eyes on. One of these groups must have had ties in local politics. In April, just when he needed his edge most, Sam lost it, and for good. The State Legislature met and passed a charter for the City of San Francisco. The old Mexican-style form of government was dropped altogether and Sam found himself out of office. Worse, the new Board of Aldermen turned out to be packed with men backed (and bribed) by the two new syndicates which were opposing him.

"I don't know who they are, Frisco," he said ruefully one day in May. "Frankly, I think I may be stymied. If it weren't for my loan-sharking up the river, I'd be stumped. I'm wondering if you wouldn't do better by yourself in this business. We seem to be at odds these days anyhow."

"Well, I'm sorry about that, Sam. But you've got the money to do what you want to do, including developing that spa over in—what did you call the place? Calistoga? Well, you know that's not really what I'm after. I want to make it here in the City. I hope you wind up owning the rest of California, frankly, but I don't want to operate out of the City just now."

"Seriously, Frisco, do you think we ought to dissolve the partnership?"

"Not yet, Sam. Unless you really want out, bad. If you want to go. . . ."

"Not actually. But. . . ."

"Then stay on top of things for me, Sam. I'm not solid enough here at the Casino just yet to hand over the reins to anyone else. I trust you. Keep me covered. You're still the best businessman in town. My affairs couldn't be in better hands, no matter what they've thrown against you here in town."

There was another big fire; the El Dorado burned. Frisco and Sam sent separate donations to the owners to help with the rebuilding. The idea of one casino-owner helping another after a natural disaster was so novel it shocked everyone. It seemed like a good tradition to start, however. When a second fire, only a month later, razed the entire area between Clay and California streets, all the way from Kearny down to the water, and Sam's store went up in smoke, Sam was surprised to see the hat passed by other merchants to help restore his property.

In July Sam was called away to Yuba City on business. He sent a note up to Frisco's:

I met the feller who's been crossing me up this way. He represents a syndicate out of Philadelphia. I told him about you; I figured you'd want to have a gander at him and size him up. He'll be by this evening or at the latest tomorrow night.

Wes's will finally cleared the courts. He'd left everything to her. "I haven't a relative left in the world that I'd speak to, and there isn't a damned city on earth that I'd endow a park bench in," he'd written in a note to her. "But if you'd like to please this iconoclastic shade of mine, my dear, you'll see to setting up— anonymously of course—some sort of retirement fund for the girls above the El Dorado. It's worth ten thousand or so just to set my old soul at ease. Seeing what the prospects are for an old sinner like myself when he's almost ready for the shelf, I'm struck by a sudden attack of sympathy for an old whore who's ready to be turned out to pasture. Let's buy 'em some green grass to feed on, at worst. . . ."

Now, she was worth . . . what was it? Well over a million, even if she couldn't put her hands on a fraction of that in cash. Never mind; she had plenty to borrow against. That wasn't the problem. This new move against Sam Brannan was. Maybe she should have taken him up on that offer to break up the partnership. But who would buy out whom? Both of them were cash-poor at the moment. Well, that was academic. This new group wasn't. She was looking forward to meeting this new man Sam had talked about, though. Very much so.

He didn't show the first night. Then, on the second, at the height of an evening of feverish activity in which two people had cashed in at the house limit and another man, playing Red Dog, had run the pot up to thirty thousand dollars before dropping the entire wad, double or nothing, on the turn of a single card, Frisco suddenly felt a sort of foreboding. Instantly alert, she looked around the room. The sea of faces were all familiar ones. She'd passed to and fro in the crowd often enough to have memorized every name in the room, and she knew most of them already. But. . . .

The feeling passed and came back again. Now she was beginning to feel a little uneasy. She searched her mind, her feelings. No, it wasn't the kind of foreboding she'd felt the night of Shandor's death—or even the less keen feeling she'd had the day she knew Wes was close to death. It was—well, call it a sixth sense.

She sought out Lyuba. The Gypsy woman was taking a break upstairs, having a cup of Rom-style coffee. Her dark eyes looked up at Frisco without surprise.

"Lyuba, I've had a premonition of sorts. I want you to read the cards for me."

"Why? You can read them yourself by now. I have taught you everything I know."

"Everything you *know*, yes. But, Lyuba, once you spoke to me. I don't think you remember all of it. Maybe none of it. It was the night. . . ."

"The night Bruno died. Yes, I know. I almost ran

away that night. I was afraid of what I might have told you." Lyuba's face remained expressionless, but there was something rather like doubt and more like fear in her voice as she said, "You want this again. I do not wish. . . ."

"Please. Please. I—I felt a premonition. Something is different—something's about to happen. Whether it's good or bad I don't know. But it'll be something that'll change my life. Lyuba, I have to know. This isn't something I can get from the cards myself. Whatever it is that you were able to do that night, you have to do it again."

Lyuba looked away. Then she looked back at Frisco. "All right," she said. "Come."

They went to Lyuba's room in the big house, sat down before a broad dressing-table, and took down the precious Tarot deck. Once again Frisco watched as the complicated Romany pattern was laid out on the imaginary geometric underpinning, and the drawn cards piled in the center of the great invisible triangle. "Now," Lyuba said, sitting back and touching the cards lightly with her outstretched fingers. "Now. . . ."

Frisco watched and waited. She noted that Lyuba's breathing settled slowly into the deep draughts of sleep. She heard once again the strange alien voice:

"*One*: Time is running out for you.

"*Two*: Life is closing in on you. Gone are the days of many choices. Now your choices will be few and you will be powerless to change them.

"*Three*: You have built a house of cards, which will fall. You have everything. You will have nothing.

"*Four*: You will—".

"Oh, please God, no," Frisco found herself saying. "Not now. Not when I'm just right on the edge of making it. Not when I'm so close."

"*Four*: You will know when the day of your ruin is upon you. You will know by the blood of the Rom inside you. The blood of the Rom will tell you.

"*Five*: Ruin is near. You are near the end of all present power and riches.

"*Six*: If you would find what your heart most desires you must seek what your heart most fears.

"*Seven*: From the ashes of one dream another dream will arise.

"*Eight*: You must lose all to gain all."

Just then a violent lateral shake rocked the whole building. It was as if the earth had suddenly moved to one side, leaving furniture, people, all solid objects where they were. The walls creaked. The chandeliers rattled uncontrollably. The earth underfoot and under her chair shook like aspen leaves in a strong breeze. There was a terrible thrill of fear inside her as she gripped the table and stared around her. Across the room a mirror crashed to the ground and shivered into a million pieces.

Lyuba's eyes opened. She was herself again. "What— I felt—"

Frisco waited until the aftertremors subsided. "An earthquake!" she said. "God! I'd better get downstairs and see that nobody's hurt and make sure everyone's in a safe place. That was a rather big one. There may be aftershocks. I thank you so much for the reading, Lyuba dear."

Lyuba shook her head and looked up at her as she stood, visibly shaken, and walked briskly to the door. "I—what did I say?" she asked, her eyes full of fear. But there was nobody to answer her.

Downstairs, the first panic had subsided. A pier glass and several windowpanes had shattered, and some of Frisco's expensive cut-glass cups had fallen to the floor beside the punchbowl and shattered. But little direct damage had been done from the looks of things. The crowd had apparently decided, on principle, to laugh off the whole thing. A shake was, after all, a common enough occurrence in San Francisco, and the proper response to it was a light-hearted one. She breathed a huge sigh of relief and walked down the great staircase, her hand on the rail, her eyes scanning the crowd.

She moved from party to party, bantering, joking lightly with each group of guests, and being reassured by them on all sides. Just as she was moving to the adjoining room Will Howard, dressed to the nines in his semiofficial finest, stepped forward with a stranger in tow. "Frisco!" he said. "I want you to meet someone.

310

This is Mr. Franklin Wheeler, of Philadelphia. He's representing a coalition of Philadelphia investors who have been making some mighty large purchases in the city recently. Mr. Wheeler, Miz Frisco McGee, one of the great ladies of our city."

She looked Wheeler over just once. He was a man of middle height, clear of eye, with thinning hair. His mouth had a humorless cut about it, but his greeting was courteous enough. There was something cold about him; she couldn't place it. He bent over her hand gallantly, if a trifle stiffly. "Philadelphia, and New Orleans and St. Louis as well, ma'am," Wheeler said. "We're a fairly large organization. We believe, though, as Mr. Howard does—and as he tells us you do—that San Francisco has a great future. We're willing to put our money where our mouth is."

"Well, there's enough success here for all of us," she said, smiling. She looked hard at his bland face, wondering: *Is this the one? The one I have to fear?* There was no telling. This was one of the best poker faces she'd ever seen. "Welcome to San Francisco, Mr. Wheeler. And I hope we see you again up here, sir."

"I would, under ordinary circumstances, tell you that was highly unlikely. My business is gambling on real estate. A teamster doesn't drive wagons for a hobby, ma'am. But with an invitation from so charming a lady, how could I refuse?" Oh, it all came out smoothly enough, but the eyes weren't in it. They were a shark's eyes, cold and distant. She made the usual small talk and moved off through the crowd. Strange, only now was the shock of the quake beginning to catch up with her. Or was it fear? Fear of the things Lyuba had said? Fear of the challenge Wheeler represented?

She stopped and took a few deep breaths until her heart quieted its furious pounding. God, if a tenth of the things Lyuba said were to come true, if Wheeler's crowd did, in fact, stand a chance of ruining her. . . .

She turned and stopped dead.

The man at the door was just handing over his coat. He stood tall, erect, arrogantly athletic. The face was long, sharp-boned, aristocratic, with a wide sensual mouth; the eyes were green and the hair red. The expression was quizzical, taking her in with obvious appreciation, but with something else as well. Incredulity. Surprise. Recognition.

"Well, I'll be damned," he said in the same deep, humorous, half-mocking voice she remembered so vividly. "I'll be eternally damned." His smile widened. He took in the whole sight of her, approvingly. His ruddy brow went up; he smiled delightedly at the—*was* it a disguise? Or was it just a new identity she'd assumed? No matter. His grin accepted it all, and the green Irish eye winked at her.

"Your servant, ma'am," he said. "My name's Tolliver. Beau Tolliver."

Chapter 44

Frisco recovered something of her composure after a moment's hesitation. "I've wondered for a long time what I'd do when this time came," she said. "I—I'm glad to see you."

"You'll pardon my saying so, but you don't look it. Perhaps it's the shock." His manner was as enigmatic as it had ever been, back at their first meeting: simultaneously courtly and mocking. "My God, I'm shocked myself. You've grown into a great beauty. But all this?" His hand indicated their lavish surroundings and somehow, without disrespect, managed to dismiss them. "Is this yours? Really?"

"It is. Look, we've got to talk. I'll make my rounds and check on the damage, and then. . . ."

"Certainly," he said. "I gather one can expect one of these earth-shaking evenings every few months in San Francisco. Well, go and check your windows and your china. I'll risk a few dollars on the tables. Really," he said, grinning appreciatively at her, "I'm quite taken aback. I'm terribly impressed. I want to hear all about it. You go do your business and get back to me, my dear. I'll be right here." He faked a tiny bow that was once again gallant and satirical, and waved her politely away. She went back to the kitchen in a flush, her head spinning.

Beau Tolliver here! It was unbelievable!

Well, she'd simply have to get hold of herself. She simply couldn't show him anything but her best side. She stopped now before another pier glass—this one had cracked slightly, but had not shattered like the one by the front door—and touched up her hair here and there.

313

Well, thank goodness she'd worn one of her most fetching—and most expensive—gowns tonight: a plain princess gown in ivory silk, which showed off her bosom and her small waist. If only there were time to go upstairs again, and change into the green gown, the one with the low-cut. . . .

But no. She didn't want to be obvious. She had to maintain some sort of dignity, for the last time she'd seen him she'd been a barefoot ragamuffin with stringy hair, a *gamine* from the streets of New Orleans, on the run.

Oh, this was all so stupid! How could it be that the moment she saw him again she'd turn into a stuttering, inarticulate child?

Get hold of yourself, she told herself savagely. He's just another man, if an extraordinary one. She'd dealt with his like before.

But had she? With the single exception of Wes, who was any man's intellectual equal, had she been dealing with her peers since Shandor's death? Why, even Sam Brannan, for all his business acumen, had been relatively easy for her to wrap around her finger most of the time. And—*But no*, she told herself. It was time to face up to the fact, on the most low-down level, that she was playing at world-class level now. She was no longer in the small time, playing penny poker. She was up at the rarefield level where Wes Falligant had taken her and left her, where the real high rollers operated. Beau Tolliver would simply have to see this, and recognize it. And get that slightly supercilious grin off his mocking face.

Now it was time to go back and face him. It was time to meet him on an equal level and get rid, once and for all, of this damnable tendency in herself to treat him as an elder, as a mentor, as a father. Why, he'd had her buffaloed from the moment he'd come in the door, with his mocking grin that said that if she was here, running Frisco's, it was clearly an imposture. Imposture! She'd show him! She'd force him to accept her for what she was, what she'd become.

He looked up from his poker hand, smiled, and nonchalantly folded his hand. He scooped up his chips and dropped them—there weren't many—into a pocket.

"I'm yours to command," he said, that same grin on his face.

"Come on upstairs," she said. She led the way, nodding at the big Sydney Duck who guarded the staircase and the second floor from intruders. "It's all right, Bill. He's with me."

Once in her room, she showed him in and shut the door behind him. "May I offer you a drink?" she said. "Or—well, help yourself. The bar's right over there."

"Splendid," he said. "You'll join me? Ah, cognac, and a good year too. Imported from France. Really, my dear, I'm impressed. The appointments, the service, the sheer professionalism of it all is staggering. It's the equal of many Continental establishments. I assume you had advice for some of this."

"The best," she said acidly. "I'll pass over the obvious fact that you don't think me capable of any of it."

"Ah, I've offended you. I apologize. I'm just taken aback by it all. If it makes a boor of me, I'm sorry. It's just that, well, I never expected to see you again, somehow. I had word that you were dead, you and Joshua."

"Josh is dead," she said. "Perhaps I'd better tell you all about it. But first, yes, I'll take a glass of brandy, please. This has been something of a shock for me, too."

"I'm sure it has," he said, conciliatorily. He handed her a big snifter and, swirling the liquor in his own, sniffed it appreciatively. "Please. Tell me everything. And did Wes Falligant have anything to do with this?"

"My partner," she said. "He was—he became something of a father to me, at a time when I needed one very badly. Why? How did you guess that?"

"I'm afraid I was the one to discover his body, down in Portsmouth Square. I was—passing through on the way to the country upriver. I had business there."

"Oh. Well, Wes was a friend of my father's, and. . . ."

It didn't take long to tell him the story of her wanderings, the more so since something in her kept making her censor her words at judicious places. There were parts of it that, for whatever reason, she simply didn't feel like telling him. But there was more than a little pride in her recounting of her quick and meteoric rise to fame and fortune in San Francisco. And, to give him credit, he nodded appreciatively from time to time at her account of her exploits. When it came to her arrangement with Sam, she kept quiet, though. Force of habit made her do so—that, and something else she could not name. Perhaps she was simply keeping her hole cards covered.

"Amazing!" Tolliver said at last. "What a story! It sounds like something out of—oh, *Gil Blas*. Tragedy, comedy, lots of local color, death, deeds of derring-do. . . ."

"You make it sound as if it were all exciting," she said. "Mostly I was frightened to death."

"And so weren't we all? I can tell you tales of my own wicked youth that would curl your hair." He took a slow sip of the brandy and looked at her hair, her face. "God in heaven, my dear. You'll pardon a personal statement, I hope, but you've grown into an enchanting creature. Incredible! I can't find a flaw in you anywhere. Of course, with Wes playing Pygmalion—but no. You were quite lovely as a schoolgirl, on the run from that swine Thiebaud. Wes couldn't have made this particular silk purse out of any sow's ear. All he could do was teach you how to polish what you had, to put you in line to find your proper place in life."

"Ah," she said. "After speaking of me as if I were horseflesh, to be judged by the tats in my mane or the smoothness of my coat, you'll perhaps begin to acknowledge that the place I'm finding for myself in San Francisco may be . . . ah, deserved?"

"No question about it," he said. "No question. But you're offended. I've been boorish again, just by not thinking. I must make it up to you. My apologies. Look, I've an appointment down the hill at nine, and I do have to go. I told a business associate I'd drop by after dinner. But may I see you tomorrow, perhaps? Would you like to go for a drive? I've the use of quite a handsome buckboard and pony while I'm here." He stood and held out his hands to her, smiling charmingly. "Come, I won't take no for an answer. I'll pack a lunch. No, I'll have one catered, with all the trimmings. I was taken out to a lovely spot on the cliffs above the Gate when I first got here, and I've been wishing ever since that I had precisely the right woman to take there."

She rose, holding his hands, looking up into his green

316

eyes. There was no mockery in them now, only a friendly and, yes, affectionate interest. And something else. Something else. . . . "Why, I suppose so. . . ." she began.

He started to say something, but stopped. His hands still held hers. Then, in a gesture too slow, too paced, to be mere impulse, he raised one of her gloved hands to his lips and kissed it. He turned it over to kiss the palm, and then briefly—ever so briefly—hold it to his cheek. "You're bewitchingly lovely," he said. "You're a dazzling and fascinating young woman. If you'll give me a little time to get used to the fact that the frightened child I gave shelter to back in New Orleans has grown beyond measure, has turned into one of the most beautiful women I've ever seen. . . ."

She could not tear her eyes away, could not speak to him to say yea or nay. But he must then have seen something in her eyes, for he bent forward unhurriedly and kissed her.

Then she found herself kissing him back. Her hands left his, and went around his neck and held him close. His own embrace closed around her, and the first powerful squeeze from those long arms of his almost took the breath out of her. The kiss became something else, a passionate and impetuous union of two souls, if only for a moment.

Then he was releasing her. He shook his head as if to clear it and held her at arm's length. The look in his eyes now was dead serious, as serious as he'd been the day he'd faced Thiebaud down, as serious as the time he'd told her, *"You'll always be a winner, even when it appears you're losing. Early or late you'll win. Don't believe any evidence to the contrary."*

His smile, now, was a different one altogether. There was no mockery in it at all, no condescension, no irony. "A lady as beautiful as you should get her beauty sleep. And I've got business both tonight and tomorrow morning. I wouldn't dream of waking you early. I'll call for you at noon. I took the liberty of bribing one of the Ducks for your address. And now, my dear, much as I regret it. . . ." His simple gesture of the hand told her he was leaving, albeit regretfully.

317

At the door he stopped and looked back at her as she stood there, silently watching him go. "I meant every word I said," he told her in that thrilling voice. "And a lot more that I didn't say. Perhaps I'll find time to say it all soon. *Au revoir*."

His parting bow was courtly this time: the full New Orleans treatment. He would have bowed this way to a duchess.

She stood looking at the door for some time. "Oh, my," she said. "Oh, my." Her hand, gloveless now (when had she taken off her gloves?) went to her cheek, hot and flushed; it went to the lips he'd kissed. God! She hadn't felt like this since—since Shandor.

There was a knock on the door. "I—come in," she said. Even her voice sounded different. She felt like a different woman. Changed. Shaken.

It was Bill, the Sydney Duck who'd guarded the stairs. "Par'n me, ma'am, but Mr. Brannan, he wants to see you."

"Oh . . . send him in. Thank you, Bill." She sat down, shaking her head. How curious! And tomorrow, tomorrow afternoon. . . . She sighed, long and hard. She'd have a hard time getting to sleep tonight, that was for sure.

Sam Brannan, coming through the door, was a different Sam Brannan than the one she'd known. "Frisco!" he said in an excited voice. He was rumpled, windblown; he still had the dust of the road on him. "There's something of a crisis, or I wouldn't—I apologize for barging in like this—"

"It's all right, Sam," she said. She stood up. "Sit down, please. You're all out of breath. Here, I'll get you a drink. And don't talk a lot of strait-laced Mormon nonsense at me; you haven't obeyed the Word of Wisdom in years."

"I—thank you. But—all that property Wes and I invested in up in Yuba City, well, some people have set up a rival town up there, called Marysville. It's across the river. Somehow, when the steamers started making their way up the river, somebody in the other camp got hold of the captains and talked 'em into making their stops at Marysville, not at Yuba City. Now all the travelers headed for the mines get off on the wrong side of

318

the river, in the wrong town. My store's bankrupt. The town's a ghost town."

"But Sam, we can always sell out."

"Damn it, Frisco, we paid down and have been paying in installments. We've got a payment coming due on each one of God almighty knows how many properties, and no cash in the account to pay it with. And we've got a pretty penny sunk in all this. If we default on the payments, we've lost a bundle, let me tell you."

Frisco frowned. This was one of Wes's pet projects, the only time he'd talked her into an out-of-town investment. And now, without Wes to watch over it. . . . "Sam, there's no crisis. We've plenty of property here in town that we can borrow against. We can raise the money. How much is it?"

"Ah . . . a total of . . . ah . . . just under three hundred and fifty thousand."

Frisco just stared. "My God," she said. "I've been leaving all of this up to Wes, and now you. I had no idea. A third of a million—in installment payments?"

"Yes. Of course this is, well, three months' payments. I've been making payments a quarter at a time. And now, well, if the stores were operational, if business was normal in Yuba City at all, well, I'd have the payments in hand just from rentals, and profits, and on new property sales in town. But now, with people leaving town in droves, and defaulting on their own loan payments and on payments on account to us—well, I'm not sure. I'll try to raise it here." He wiped his brow. His face was tight and drawn. "I'll keep you posted. But Frisco. . . ."

"Yes?"

"That business about the land titles being contested by the federal government? Well, they're doing the same sort of thing to a lot of the lots *we* own."

"Well? We have the money to fight it. Fight it."

"But—well, if the title's under a cloud, I'm not sure how easy it's going to be to borrow money on land we have to prove we own." He looked up. His eyes held real concern, even worry.

319

Chapter 45

She tossed and turned through the night, thinking of many things: Tolliver, Lyuba's predictions, finance. In the morning, breaking precedent, she dressed early and went down to Sam Brannan's office.

Sam hadn't slept either. His desk was a mess of jumbled papers, deeds, bankbooks. He looked up, smiled nervously, looked back at his work, then pushed his chair back and stood up. "Frisco! I'm glad you came but I wish I had more encouraging news for you." He held her chair while she sat down.

"Why, Sam?" she said. "Is it something new?"

"Well, no, but it's something I guess I didn't know about. You know I've sort of been working as an unofficial bank up north, in Sacramento. Well, I've got most of *my* money out in loans. That way I can't touch it to bail out *our* projects. And, frankly, I've had some defaults. I think I told you that last night."

"Well? So far we've looked mighty good at the bank here. And if we can't borrow more money on any of our local properties due to this title-challenge business, well, for God's sake we certainly ought to be able to raise money on our signatures. We've certainly shown an outstanding ability to generate new income so far."

"Yes, but . . . well, these new folks. Wheeler, and the people behind him. They've been here, keeping it quiet, for some months now. Since well before Wes's death. And they've been not only buying up this and that, nice and quiet, but—confound it, they've been playing politics too. And expertly. I have every reason to believe the government's challenge to our land titles came about through Wheeler and his friends. We're being squeezed out, little by little. It's the slickest thing I ever saw."

"But Sam, the bank. . . ."

"That's just it. Several of these groups are in cahoots with Wheeler. Some old friends of mine—or at least I thought they were friends until. . . ." He frowned anxiously. "I suppose they see me—and by extension us, although they still don't know of your connection with any of this—as a threat. If we're knocked out of the way, my 'friends' think they can deal with Wheeler. The more fool them; he'll eat them up for breakfast without even thinking. Besides, there seems to be some sort of *tertium quid* in there. I can't identify all the actors in this. There are so many *sociétés anonymes* springing up these days, with bogus front men the only visible agents. . . ."

"I still don't understand. The bank—"

"Frisco, the bank's been bought out by one of these groups! And they've refused me refinancing! And what's more, they're calling our loans!"

"Calling our loans!" Frisco said, sitting bolt upright. "Sam, have you got all the information here? I mean, in one place, where I can look it over? I need to find out where we are, right now, and what could happen if this goes on."

"It's not all here. Some of it's at my house."

"Then could you get it all together? I'd like to look it over bright and shiny tomorrow morning, if I can. There may be something we can do, properties we can sell to raise cash—"

"Well, maybe. But how can you sell something you have yet to prove you own? It's the same problem you have with borrowing on it."

"There may be other sources. I haven't had a real hard look yet at what Wes left me. There appears to be some property he held outside the corporation. He did some speculating on his own. And if any of that can be touched. . . ."

"Let's hope it can. Curious, isn't it, how you can be sitting on top of the world one day, and the next. . . ."

"Sam," she said, looking him dead in the eye. "What if it can't? What if no new sources of funds become available?"

321

"Well, you know I get my own funds with the New York banks at four percent for loaning out up Sacramento way at ten percent. . . ."

"Yes."

"*That* loan's being called. These folks have influence in New York, Washington. . . ."

"Sam, you haven't come to the bottom line. You haven't answered my question. Where do we stand if we can't lay our hands on any new money inside thirty days?"

"I swear to God," he said, tossing his hands up helplessly. "We're ruined."

Frisco just sat there, staring at him, remembering Lyuba's prediction. *Time is running out for you . . . you have built a house of cards, which will fall . . . you are near the end of all your dreams of power and riches.*

She walked back to her apartment a changed woman. Gone was the jaunty, half-arrogant carriage people had commented upon before. Her steps were those of a woman burdened by many cares, a woman suddenly older, wiser—and none the happier for the new wisdom. Climbing the stairs, she felt the weight of the ages upon her.

At the door Juana smiled at her. "*Señora*. The baby, little Alejandro. . . ."

"Yes, yes," Frisco said absently, taking off her coat. "Oh, I promised to bring him something, didn't I? Damn."

"Oh, no matter. He wanted to show you something."

"Oh." Frisco, her step heavy, let herself be led into the baby's room. Alex looked up from where he was sitting on the floor, playing with his blocks, and smiled his beguiling smile, like Shandor's.

"Mama," he said. "See what I made." He indicated the huge construction. He'd built a little city with blocks: houses, streets, warehouses. "I made it for you," he said. He got up, all haste and impulsiveness, and toddled over to hug her legs. "I love you."

She picked him up, feeling his solid sturdiness. Oh, he was his father's son all right. Made of oak, solid oak. Shandor's passing was hard to endure, but she was ever greatful that he had left her his son to care for. Part of her heart had gone into this precious soul. *How wonder-*

ful nature is, she thought, *to release in her this flood of love for her child.*

She gave him a loving hug. "I love you, Alex. It's lovely. And you made it all for me?"

"Yes. Mama, can we go to the park? Like you promised?"

Promised. Promised when? She searched her mind feverishly. "Oh, no, darling. I . . . I have to go somewhere. But tell you what. Tomorrow, why don't we go to the beach? You can play in the sand."

But it wasn't enough. She'd promised him today, and he'd been thinking about it all morning. He started to cry. This was more than Frisco could handle just now. "Juana, please, help me get him dressed and I'll take him to the park." His tears ceased immediately as she went to get her coat.

"*Sí, Señora,*" the girl said. She took the child, cooing soft Spanish words into his ear.

Enjoying her precious son in the park, she kept a smile on her face, so as not to interfere with what was most important to her—her son's happiness.

Later, at home, she came back to reality. She went into the bedroom and closed herself off from the rest of the apartment. Sitting on the bed, she stared at the wall, troubled. *Ruin is near.* And it had all come upon her so suddenly.

She shook her head. This wouldn't do. This wouldn't do at all. She'd write a note to Oscar Talbot, her lawyer, asking him to bring the file on Wes's estate to Sam's office tomorrow morning. It was perfectly obvious she'd better get into the habit of having Oscar present at every business meeting from now on. How could it all have gone on so long, gotten this far without her knowing? Without Sam suspecting?

Well, this was what she'd been telling the girls at Frisco's. Soon the day would come when San Francisco wouldn't be a small town with small-town people running things. The real operators would hit town, the really competent men of affairs. The whole complexion of the town would change. Its raw boomtown atmosphere was already disappearing. Soon the real high rollers would come in, and the fortunes made then would be made by people who would know how to keep what they'd won.

It was all true. Only she hadn't figured out that it would be at the expense of folks like her and Sam. She'd always thought of herself as one of those high rollers, one of those people of substance: the advance guard of the new regime in San Francisco. She'd never thought of herself, before this, as a small fish about to be eaten by a larger one.

Somehow she managed to pull herself together in time for Tolliver's arrival. When he called he found her exquisitely dressed in the gray riding habit with the velvet collar and satin stock. Her hair lay close around her face in dark ringlets. But the face it framed was troubled, preoccupied.

"Here!" Tolliver said, handing her up into the buggy. "One would think I was the devil coming for your soul. What can I do to change that somber look to smiles?" His own smile was just as she'd remembered it: warm and good-humored—for all that those green eyes didn't miss a thing.

"Please," she said. "I've had some disquieting news. I—I'll get over it." She smiled to reassure him, knowing very well that her eyes weren't in it any more than her heart was. "I'll be myself again before we've reached where we're going. You said the Gate?"

"Yes. Fog's lifting early these days. It should be warm and balmy by the time we get there, and there'll be a view the likes of which you couldn't find on Martinique or Capri. I've had a lunch packed that Monsieur Dumas, in Paris, would fight a duel over. And I intend that the two of us will get to know each other again, if it takes all afternoon."

She looked at him, her eyes still somber, and tried to smile. "You're very kind," she said. "I wish I could be better company."

"That's all right. Tell me more about those Gypsy days of yours. Can you really read fortunes? Palms? Can you do horoscopes?"

"I learned much about astrology from Lyuba, after I left the Rom camp. I'll have to do your chart one of these days. Josh told me your birthday once: you were born under the sign of Aquarius."

"Yes, I'm an Aquarian. But I don't want to hear about me. I want to hear about you."

"All right. Gemini, June 9. I'm restless, changeable, versatile, controversial."

"I gather then that I have rivals—quite a number of them. Go on, please." He drove the pony up a side street that came down between Nob and Russian Hills.

"All right. People born on this day have to learn by experience or they don't learn at all."

"That's true of everyone," he said. "Perhaps only people born under your sign have the good sense to admit it. Go on."

"Well, we tend to be good conversationalists, good hosts. I'm in the right trade, it appears. But Lyuba says that a person with my chart generally seems to have more friends when she's down and out. That's been the case with me. When I've needed a friend most desperately I've found one. First you, then. . . ."

He turned toward her, the reins still in his hand. "Is that the way you think of me, then? As a friend in need? A father like Wes?" The smile was as good-humored as ever, but the eyes were serious. "Because I'd like to change hats if I can. I want to take off that fatherly hat and put on altogether a new one. You've knocked me arse over teakettle, if you'll pardon the phrase. I've had to do some serious adjusting of my picture of you. I hope you don't have a fixed picture of me, one that can't be changed to fit changed circumstances."

She looked up into his green eyes, wondering. "I'll try to keep an open mind," she said.

Sam ran into Wheeler in Montgomery Street. He seemed to be a permanently changed Sam Brannan: nervous, volatile, even bellicose. "Look here, Wheeler," he said. "It won't work. I'll beat you people yet. You think you've got me boxed in, but if you think you can stop Sam Brannan you've got another think coming. Tell your bosses."

Wheeler looked at him with cold eyes. His face was expressionless, his voice low. "Brannan, I don't tell them. They tell me. I have my orders. There's nothing personal in it, you know. It's just business."

Brannan, an oath on his lips, turned away and stalked down the street. Business! Business indeed!

Chapter 46

Beau Tolliver steered the conversation to pleasantries that continued all the way to their destination, and Frisco found her spirits lifting. It was hard to think about heavy, depressing things when her companion was determined to keep everything light. She was realizing now that she'd never before seen the full extent of Tolliver's considerable charm. She watched with something not unlike awe. If this was the sort of spell he could cast any time he wished, what woman could resist him? And—this thought was more sobering—what woman could hold him?

Nevertheless, she found herself falling in step with his own lighthearted mood through the exquisite luncheon he'd had prepared for them: lean cold beef, a delicious smoked ham that must have come around the Horn (nobody out here seemed to know the secret of Tidewater Virginia ham), fresh fruit, imported wine. They sat near the cliff's edge, looking out at the far headland, the soaring gulls and white surf, the barren rocks of the Farallones far out to sea. Below them a clipper sailed close-hauled through the Gate, its sails a-billow, bound for the Port of San Francisco.

And somehow . . . afterward she was never quite sure how it had begun. But at some point in the conversation Beau leaned over to kiss her lightly, once, twice, and . . . and then it was no longer time for talk. His lips found her throat. His hand cupped her breast. The kisses rained upon her, growing more insistent, more pointed, more ardent. She looked into the green eyes and found them serious at last. "Beau," she found herself saying in a husky voice. "*Yes*, Beau." He took her up to those wordless realms of feeling that are impervious to logic, and where the very act of speech seems a frivolous intrusion. Rapture of ecstasy seemed eternal.

Later, passion gave way to play; he was the odd unconventional man who didn't turn silent or sad afterward, but wanted to talk small talk—even though they were half-naked in the open air under a bright blue sky, looking down on the darker blue of San Francisco Bay. He wanted to see her, touch her, all of her. The next thing she knew she was as naked as a child, and his big, gentle hands were running all over her smooth and aroused body.

"God," he said. "No statue could do you justice. By God, I owned you once. I should never have let you out of my hands. If I were your master now I'd keep you at home under lock and key, and I'd never let you put on a stitch. I'd never tire of looking at you like this." He smiled and reached over to kiss one full breast. "What a pity you had to give up that lovely name of yours, Graciela. It's beautiful, beautiful like you." His hand went to her cheek, caressing it softly, turning her head this way and that. "Now I've seen all of you, I'll say it. If you've flaw anywhere I haven't found it."

She let him go on like this for some time. Then she said reluctantly, "The sun's getting low. It's time to be getting back. Your work day may be over, but mine's just beginning. Beau, please. . . ."

"Oh, all right," he said reluctantly. He rose to dress, looking down at her, his eyes going over every bare and deliciously satisfied inch of her. "Look," he said. "Do you intend to keep this up forever? The casino? The—well, whatever other business you're involved in these days? I gather from the way you're treated around here that you're not just a casino owner. You'd have to have other irons in the fire to draw as much water as you seem to. You're well-fixed, then?"

She sat up, drawing her dress up over her shoulders, watching his raised-brow expression of mild chagrin as her breasts disappeared inside the gown. It was odd that the moment money and property and business entered the conversation, the slight touch of superciliousness entered his tone once more. Perhaps he wasn't aware of it. Well, she'd show him—but in her own good time.

"I'm doing fairly well," she said. "I had my own investments here, and of course I was Wes's heir."

"Oh? That's good. That's fine. Odd to see Wes Falligant settling down, even in his old age, and letting a weed grow up his leg like that. Of course he had the business sense to make any kind of money he wanted. But usually his itchy foot betrayed him. Usually, before he could consolidate his gains anywhere, he'd get the urge to ramble and he'd move on."

"You never said what sort of business you were in here," she said, holding up one long leg while, to his intense admiration, she slipped her stocking on. "You're not in the gambling business, that's for sure. I'd have heard about it if you were."

"Land, my darling," he said, tying his cravat expertly. "In New Orleans it was money, because in New Orleans the land isn't worth a damn unless you're patient enough to work it, and I didn't care much for trying to compete with the slaveholders at raising cotton or cane. Let them work the land over, then I'd work them over. Here the money's not worth much. The bottom is going to fall out of prices in a while, when the boom subsides a bit, but the land's going to be worth a great deal one of these years. It's already appreciating at a hell of a clip."

For some reason the poker player in her held back from disclosing her own interest in land speculation. "And you've already deep into investment here?"

"Partly here, partly up the river," he said, gathering up picnic basket and blanket deftly. "I'm in with a group of investors who've started a new town up there called Marysville. We've been bumping noses with some local bumpkin named Brannan, but it looks as though we have his number now."

"Brannan?" she said, instantly alert. She stood and adjusted her gown. "Sam Brannan?"

"Yes. I should have supposed you'd know him. You seem to know everyone here. At any rate, we've knocked the bottom out of his investments across the river in Yuba City, and he's a dead man in Sacramento. And down here—"

"Down here? What are you up to down here?"

"Easy." He talked with his back to her, rehitching the

pony. "You sound touchy. Look, I'm not doing anything that would decrease the value of a casino. Rather the opposite, as a matter of fact. Brannan's had a stranglehold on this town for a couple of years now. It can't go anywhere with a man like that acting as the unofficial power here. He controls perhaps a quarter of the best commercial real estate in the town right now, and he doesn't know how to develop it. He's content to settle for minimal rents. He should be building. Well, we won't be making that mistake once we've got him out of the way."

"Out of the way?" she said, putting on her heavy riding habit, feeling the afternoon chill beginning to settle. Already wisps of fog were blowing in off the Pacific, and a haze obscured the headland across the way. The Farallones had long since disappeared. "How do you propose to do that?"

"Ah . . . business attracts strange coalitions. Some of the people I'm associated with, back East, are people I might not have spoken to a year before. There are financiers, wildcatters, politicians, and members of a banking syndicate which has purchased controlling interest in the bank where Mr. Brannan has some apparently quite important—even crucial—loans. They're putting the squeeze on him. He's finding out that there's hardly any place left for him to turn. I almost feel sorry for him. Poor devil, he's seeing the stars wink out in the sky above him. But that's business," he shrugged.

She climbed up into the seat by herself, disdaining his helping hand. "Please," she said in a much altered voice. "Let's go. I have to be home."

"Here," he said, turning. "What's the matter? I haven't offended you, have I? I mean, you're a gambler. I gather you've become a businesswoman too, and a good one. You know how little room there is for sentiment and softheartedness in business. Why, Brannan's done the same with others, and he'd have done the same to me. You should see the usurious rates he's been charging the miners up the river. No, Brannan's no lily. It's not like fleecing the widows and orphans."

"Please," she said. "Let's go."

"Ah," he said, climbing up. "I *have* offended you. I'm

sorry. I should have known. Brannan's a friend of yours, I suppose. But yes, now I remember, someone told me he was pretty close with Wes, before he died. I was up here scouting the City briefly, but most of my business was up the river. I'm damned glad I didn't have to bump noses with Wes, if they were associates. He'd have been a tough customer. He'd have known how to head us off. Apparently Brannan doesn't."

She perked up at that. Down inside her, now, there was a core of the coldest Arctic ice. Beau Tolliver, the man who'd made love to her this afternoon, so tenderly and passionately, the man who was on the verge of ruining her! This was not to be borne! She'd show him!

She mastered her rage and said with a voice into which she tried desperately to inject some sort of friendly tone, "This is interesting. What *would* Wes do if he were to find himself in such a bind?"

"Well," he said, chucking under his breath at the pony and releasing the hand brake, "it would depend on whether he knew who we were, of course. Brannan may not be sure who's behind what. My man Wheeler, a cold fish, but a useful enough man in some circumstances, has something going under the table with an Eastern group that—well, in five years or so they'll be serious competition for us, and we'll have to scotch them then. But for now they're very useful." He let the pony have his head, going down the shallow grade.

"You see," he said, "the people we're using on Brannan, they've got a line into the U.S. Attorney's office. The present incumbent is a man not above a little under-the-table dealing. They've bribed the man to challenge the title to every piece of real property Brannan has. And Brannan doesn't know what to do about it. Wes would. Wes would have slipped the man twice as much money and perhaps paid the local newspaper publisher an equal sum, and he'd have simply placed every lot in San Francisco under challenge. He'd have left every title in the City in doubt. That'd have put everything back to square one. We'd be every bit as stymied as Brannan is. So would these Easterners we have this unholy little alliance with. And the only solution to that would be for everyone to get together somewhere in an alley and hash things out. In the meantime *all* those title challenges would have to be quietly dropped. Including Brannan's."

Oh, they would, would they? Inside Frisco was seething. Well, she'd show him. And she'd show him what a damned fool he was to go prattling on like this to her just because she was a woman, and because women weren't supposed to have any interest in, or understanding of, this sort of thing. "These Easterners," she said. "Do you know who they are?"

"No. *My* Eastern associates may know them. I understand one of their bigwigs is due out here shortly to take over their affairs in San Francisco. But I don't know any of them. Wheeler may, and then again he may not. Wheeler is smart enough at his own tactical level, but he's not the sort who would have much in the way of information or contacts at the strategic level."

"Yes, yes. Lead the conversation away from that crucial slip he'd made, telling her the one almost infallible method of saving her business, and Sam's. Don't let him guess that you're on to him; keep him talking and steer the conversation gently away. "Well," she said. "I'm just a small fish, with a few timid investments in this and that." That was true enough on one level; the only things she held title to in her own name were smallish ones. Frisco's, as a business, was in her name, although the corporation—her's and Sam's, with her own participation still secret—held title to the land it stood on. "I wouldn't know about those matters."

"You could, though," he said, smiling down at her, responding to her changed tone. "You're bright and alert enough. You have the guts to make a living on the land market. You might even have a bit of the necessary killer instinct, which is all your father lacked."

You're damned right I do, she thought. *But keep talking, Beau. You're cutting your own throat with every word.* "I admit it is interesting," she said. "It's just an extension of cards and dice, with bigger stakes and slightly different rules."

"Exactly," Tolliver said. "And if you can win with the rules of one game you can win at another. It's a matter of getting adjusted to the new circumstances." He grinned at her as the pony slowed in the flat and settled into a gentle walk. "I have to say, my dear, it's a pleasure talking to you. Most women profess to be bored to tears by the whole business. You, on the other hand, have a healthy curiosity about the world of affairs. It's a good sign. Myself, I like winners, male or female. I picked you for a winner first time I met you. I'm gratified to see I was right. You *are* a winner. You've already proven that many times over, my sweet. And I'm sure you'll prove it again."

You bet I will, she was thinking. *Just wait. Just you wait.*

Chapter 47

It was too good an opportunity to let pass for so much as another day. She sent runners out for Sam and to Oscar Talbot's. And in an upstairs room, as the patrons downstairs tried their luck at faro and poker, the three of them held a council of war.

"The question is, Sam," Frisco said, "if the matter of the legitimacy of the title is dropped, do we have any property we can turn over quickly for funds? Is there anything we have that fast a market on?"

"I think so. Matter of fact, I'm pretty much sure so. And if the bank won't loan the money there's a businessman or two in town still unconnected with this unholy consortium of theirs. Most of 'em would like to hang my head up on the trophy-room wall, to be sure, but they'll put up money secured by the right property, if only on the hope that I'll default."

"All right. But can we raise the money by the time the note payments and the loan come due?"

"Maybe I can help there," Talbot said. Unruffled, bland, unhurried, the lawyer opened the file folder on Wes's holdings which he had brought along. "Wes Falligant left you not only land holdings and shares in the corporation, but some cash as well."

"I know about that," Frisco said. "But it's nowhere near enough."

"Don't be too sure. There was a safe deposit box at the bank. There was more cash in that. It's only just turned up and been certified: Wes, for some reason of his own, had taken the box under a pseudonym: 'Tshatshimo Romano.' He—"

"Oh, for God's sake," Frisco said. "It's a Gypsy

334

phrase: it means 'the truth is best told in Romany.' Go on."

"Well, one of the things in there, besides some cash, which will come in handy as the very devil right now, is a stack of stock in the bank itself. This will automatically revert to you as his established and only heir." Talbot almost smiled, he was so pleased with himself. "It makes you a fairly large minority stockholder, and I really doubt the bank will call your loan. Outside interests or no, the bank's board is seriously divided on a lot of questions, and many of them have been settled in recent months by the very group of proxies the Falligant stock represents."

"Then we've licked them!" Frisco said, grinning. "Sam, we've stopped them!"

"Not so fast," Sam said. "The main thing, right now, is the up-country problem. We have installment payments on all that all-but-worthless property up there, and we have to secure that somehow. Do we have the cash for it?"

"I think so," Talbot said. "Barely. But you'd better get up to Yuba City and do what you can to reverse the exodus from there. And in the meantime any ruse you can use, bribery included, to get the steamer captains to stop at Yuba City instead of Marysville, well, I'd use it, and fast. It's no use saving your investment up there if making the payments is just going to be a matter of throwing good money after bad." He started folding up his papers. "I'd see to it as soon as I could. Meanwhile, there'll be a board meeting at the bank tomorrow. Frisco, I'd make plans to attend. I'll be there with you, with the relevant information in hand. I'm sorry this will mean you'll have to give up your anonymity as a member of the corporation, but it couldn't last forever, particularly under stresses of this kind."

"You're right," she said. "Maybe the time for that sort of thing is over, anyhow." Then it hit her again, and she smiled broadly. "Sam! I think we've licked 'em!"

"I hope so," Brannan said. "Incidentally, Oscar, did I hear something about one of the big cheeses from Wheeler's syndicate coming in today on the clipper from the East?"

"That seems to be the case," Oscar said. "Somebody

335

in court mentioned it today. They're represented by a friend of mine, and he said his partner was complaining about the fuss the man was putting him to. First day in town, mind you. Well, that's the East for you. Always making things difficult that ought to be easy. Of course non-lawyers always make the law difficult and complicated. It isn't. Now Wes, he knew that. Of course, he had an uncommon knowledge of the law. I wouldn't be surprised if he'd passed the bar somewhere back East once himself. He could argue a case as well as I could. I once asked him why he continued to pay me to do work that was within his own capabilities. He said it was just to have somebody to talk to in court." He rose, briefcase in hand. "Frisco? I'll see you at the bank tomorrow morning. Ten sharp? Thank you." He left, with no more than a polite nod to Sam.

Frisco looked at Brannan. "Sam, you're moping. Cheer up! Look, I'm feeling so confident I think I'll throw a party tonight, up at the casino. Come on up and I'll buy you a drink."

"I wish I could join you, both in the drink and in the festive mood. But something in me keeps telling me the trouble isn't over yet, not by a long shot. It's just a sort of a foreboding." He frowned, looking at her. "You know Brigham Young's put a curse on me," he said.

"Oh, Sam," she said. "You haven't believed in Mormon blessings for a long time. Why should a Mormon curse mean anything to you? The first day I met you you broke with Brigham and the Utah church forever."

"Well, maybe it's just force of habit. Brigham's an uncommonly powerful personality, after all. Folks who've been around him much have a tendency to jump when he hollers. But you know I was pretty deep into the L.D.S. Church at one time. There's a sort of Mormon turn of mind in me to this day. I have a bad conscience about liquor, coffee, pork chops in the summertime. Somehow, though, I don't think it's just habit, or anything like that. I have a feeling that they still have something to throw at us."

"Well, I'm sure they will. I'm sure we're not dealing with a bunch of school children. But Sam, whatever they throw at us, we can handle. It's as simple as that."

"I hope you're right," he said. But his drawn face, haggard from loss of sleep, showed his lingering doubts in the matter.

The party that night was the biggest, most elegant, most wasteful San Francisco had seen so far. Frisco flushed out the cellars for the best liquor she had, and gave it away. Nobody who could get in the door—and, as usual, the Ducks shooed away anyone who wasn't dressed for the place—went dry. When Frisco got the C.O.D. bill for the catered free lunch she whistled—it was three thousand dollars—but she paid it with good grace. She'd saved them! And she'd done it all on her own hook, without any help from a man!

Best of all, she'd outflanked Beau High-and-Mighty Tolliver, with his patronizing attitude toward what a woman could and couldn't do. She'd singlehanded managed to turn around his damned little plan to put Sam and her out of business! That'd show him! She couldn't wait to see the look on his face tomorrow.

But Beau didn't show up at the party, and he wasn't at the bank when she came down to meet Oscar in the morning. She was a little disappointed at this, although, on reflection, it now occurred to her that there wasn't any real reason why he *should* show up. The firm he was dealing with was represented by Wheeler and Wheeler's lawyer, a fairly well-known Montgomery Street figure named Frank Petty.

There was a trifling amount of surprise at her appearance at what was supposed to be a closed meeting of the bank board, but Oscar Talbot talked for a few minutes with the board chairman, Harry Waterman, and Wheeler's lawyer, and Frisco was seated over the obvious reluctance of Wheeler and his faction.

Waterman introduced her as the meeting opened, as the new heir to a bloc of stock amounting to twenty-two percent of the total. Her welcome was tepid on one side of the long table, warm and friendly on the other. Then Waterman introduced Wheeler as the San Francisco representative of Continental Investments, Ltd., holders of forty-five percent of the firm's stock. *Ah*, Frisco

337

thought. *They've been voting Wes's proxies. They can't anymore. I'm the swing vote, and without me they don't have a majority anymore. We've got them!*

When the meeting broke up the board had voted to extend the deadline on the loan payment for one month. Frisco was elated: that would allow Sam plenty of time to scotch the government challenge to their land titles. Thanking Talbot, she set out for Sam's office. But he was out, and remained out when she sent a runner, one of the Ducks, down to his office with a note later that afternoon.

And, oddly enough, no Beau Tolliver, either. Not that night or the next or the next. This was more than a bit of a disappointment; she'd been looking forward to seeing his face, and showing him how she'd outsmarted him. There was something else, something else besides mere pique, or the budding rivalry between the two of them which his heedless disclosures had set off the other day.

Damn it, she *missed* him.

She was looking forward to—well, to just seeing him again. And hearing his voice. And touching him. And— at further thoughts, she felt a hot flash run through her. God, he was a handsome devil and a marvelous lover.

Now, sitting alone with a cup of hot tea in her room above the casino, she found herself suddenly hoping against hope that he wouldn't take her little coup against him too badly, after all. The other day, on the hill, before he'd let slip his little revelations about the nature of his business in the city, things had gone so nicely. She hadn't felt like that with a man since . . . since Shandor.

Damn it! One could fall in love with a man like that! Hopelessly, helplessly, painfully in love! She'd have to guard against *that*!

There was a knock on the door. She looked up. It was Lyuba. She had become the second-shift dealer on Table Three. "Oh, hello, Lyuba. What can I do for you?"

"Here," Lyuba said. She handed over a folded letter, sealed in red and bearing the mark of Beau Tolliver's signet. "Mr. Tolliver left this."

"Thank you," Frisco said. "Lyuba, don't go. . . . Mr. Tolliver, what was he like? Was he mad? Cold? Distant?"

338

"No, he was like he usually is. Jokes. That sort of thing." She smiled. "He never forgets a compliment for the dealer. It's a nice touch."

"Lyuba, could I be happy with a man like Tolliver? Could . . . could you be happy with a man like Tolliver? I mean, you know what he's like."

"I—he's very handsome. And gallant, and he makes a girl feel good about herself. Me, I'd be frightened about whether I could hold him. But you, ..." Lyuba's eyes opened wide. "Oh," she said. "You're not considering. . . ."

"Well, I don't know," Frisco said. "He hasn't asked me, after all. Maybe he won't. I think I've angered him by something I did a day or two ago. He'll just be finding out about it now, and well, if I were Beau I'd be mad as hell about it, and mean as a wolverine right now. But Lyuba, if he weren't mad, if he were to ask, should I say yes? Should I consider it? *Could* I hold him?"

Lyuba said she would study their horoscopes and compare them. She went downstairs.

Frisco poured another cup of tea and opened the letter. It was brief and pointed:

Frisco,
Touché! You had me completely flummoxed. Wes taught you even better than I knew. No hard feelings; I'd have done the same myself. I'm sure you'll look at whatever counterstroke I devise with the same critically objective eye. With admiration and affection, I am, of course,

Your devoted servant
Beau

Well, he wasn't mad. Perhaps. But why hadn't he dropped by to see her? And why the brief, almost curt note? And what was this "counterstroke" he was referring to? Did he mean he had another plan up his sleeve to outflank her and Sam Brannan? Or would it be something more personal, more specifically tailored to her own individual perfidy?

She bit her lip and fretted over the matter. She had to know. She had to see him. There was something wrong, something much worse than just the relatively minor business coup she'd pulled off. Not that there was anything in his letter to suggest this, specifically, but there was the feeling, the nagging feeling. . . .

In the middle of the night she woke up suddenly, cold as ice, full of fear. She knew, almost immediately, what it was.

Time is running out for you.

You have built a house of cards, which will fall. You have everything. You will have nothing.

You will know when the day of your ruin is upon you. You will know by the blood of the Rom inside you. The blood of the Rom will tell you.

"*Señora!* Come quick! Help! *Socorro!*"

The cry came from the baby's room, where Juana usually slept on a cot of her own. Frisco rushed out in her nightgown, barefoot, her hair down. Juana, the child in her arms, stood whimpering in the doorway. She freed one hand to cross herself again and again: "*Ave Maria, llena de gracia . . .*"

There was a strange acrid smell from inside Alex's room. Frisco pushed open the door, but before she opened it she already knew what she would see.

There it was: a burning sliver of white-hot metal, scorching the oak table it had been driven into, glowing with a malevolent light.

"Oh, my God," she said. "*The Nail!*"

Chapter 48

It wasn't a night for sleep. Alex cried and wouldn't be solaced; Juana and Frisco took turns trying to calm the boy, with indifferent results at best. Frisco had at least this distraction to keep her from brooding over the terrible foreboding feeling that haunted her.

Nevertheless, as the sleepless night progressed, she found her ability to avoid the obvious steadily diminishing. It was, after all, something she *had* to think about. The one and only time Lyuba had predicted for her in a vision like that had been on the night of Shandor's death, a night in which the Nail had appeared. And now several days had passed, and nothing had happened. Yet.

The Nail—oddly, it had suddenly grown cold on its own. There was nothing left to convince them they had not been the victims of a mass hallucination except the scorched wood around it. What had caused it to flame up like that? And, just as suddenly, to cool off again? Then she somehow knew that it meant the Nail would never bother anyone again. The prophecy had been fulfilled.

Frisco remained puzzled, disquieted. Part of her, by now, was a City girl, sophisticated, unsentimental, unsuperstitious. Part of her wanted to stay that way.

What would her life have been like, she wondered, if she had never learned she was a Rom? If she'd stayed the half-Irish, half—but what was she before that? Spanish, as she'd thought she'd been? Or black, as the city of New Orleans and the state of Louisiana thought she was?

Well, there was no sense in going on in this unprofitable direction. What-might-have-been was the most worthless game in the world, bar none, and all it did was to confuse you and depress you and, incidentally, keep you from appreciating the good in what-had-come-to-be.

There was much that was bad, even tragic, about the things that had happened to her since that terrible day when the convent had turned her out and she had been given to one of her father's creditors in settlement of a debt. But on the other hand, out of that single fearful event had come much that was good, and much that was perhaps even better than she'd ever have come to know if she'd led the secure, predictable life her father had intended her to have.

She'd learned some things about herself that she would not now willingly part with for anything. She'd learned that she was, at bottom, smart and strong-minded and independent, fully capable of competing in the world of affairs like any man. She'd learned about her Romany heritage. She'd learned to fend for herself and she'd learned useful skills both practical (the games of skill Wes had taught her) and occult (the irreplaceable lore she'd learned from Pesha and Lyuba). She'd learned about love and sex. She was having a rich and exciting life, when you came right down to it. When she was a happy wrinkled old granny lady she'd have a wonderful time entertaining her grandchildren and scandalizing their parents with tales of her own wildly adventurous youth. Nobody would quite believe her, but that'd be all right: she'd have her own memories, and she'd smile to herself, remembering.

And yes. She'd known love.

It'd been a long time since she'd thought of Shandor that way, really. They'd had such a short time together, but it had been so intense, so much a nightly trip from one peak to another, that the liaisons she'd had since all had faded, to paling beside the single shattering memory of the man she'd had and lost.

All except one.

A sudden feeling of panic swept through her, thinking of the cool courtesy of Beau Tolliver's note to her and his complete absence since her betrayal of him. Why hadn't she spoken up, somewhere along the line? Why hadn't she let him in on who she was in business terms and what she was up to? Why had it been so necessary to her to set him up that way, to embarrass him before his business associates and friends? No, there was no letting herself off the hook on this one. She'd done it because she wanted to, because she wanted to hurt him, deflate him, get back at him.

Why? He hadn't meant her any harm. He hadn't known she was Sam's partner. Why had she suddenly acted so vindictively toward him? Was it resentment at his apparent abandonment of her, back in Louisiana? But of course that hadn't been his fault either. She and Josh had simply had to run before Beau could come back for them, and they'd had to keep running. Good God, he'd laid his life and liberty and reputation on the line for her, stupid and ungrateful girl that she'd been. How many men would have done as much for a friend of many years' standing as Beau Tolliver'd done for her, a stranger with no particular claim on him at all?

Suddenly a new picture of Beau Tolliver came to her: one which belied his lighthearted attitude toward life, his half-mocking, semi-satirical view of existence, his deliberate portrayal of himself as a happy-go-lucky good-for-nothing.

He wasn't any of these. These were the few defenses he customarily put up against a world that was all too prone to deride the wonderful things he actually was, under the skin-deep pretense at amorality.

He was honest and brave and true, gallant and warm and loving, ardent and passionate and thoughtful all at the same time. He was a man of principle but one who could, without compromising his principles, not only survive but prosper. More discriminating in women but how like Wes he was, in some ways. That thought gave her further pause. Imagine a young Wes Falligant, tall, handsome, in the prime of life, vigorous and formidably intelligent, a man of breeding, a man who followed his own star, always. A man generous, sensitive, protective, who hid his sensitivity under a lightweight exterior that fooled no one but the foolish.

Imagine such a man and you had the catch of a lifetime. The sort of man most women prayed for for years before they settled for less. The kind of man who'd come by no more than once.

Oh God, she thought in a sudden panic, *have I lost him? Me and my stupid pride?*

Oh, there was only one thing to do. That was to seek him out and apologize to him, and if that didn't work, to woo him with every ounce of charm, intelligence, guile that she could muster. She'd make it up to him. She'd win him back, she'd *be* that wonderful woman he'd thought she was, that afternoon up on the hill when he had made love to her so tenderly and lustily on the green grass, under the golden sun in the bright blue sky, before that gorgeous backdrop he'd picked out for their first afternoon of love.

The average man pawed at you, groping aimlessly. It was like cow and bull mating in the stockyard, in the dust: a lot of grunting and sweating and heavy breathing. But he'd seen this would not do for her. He had picked out the loveliest time and place he could find, and had worked to make it the bewitching, utterly memorable day it was—or could have been if she hadn't spoiled it.

Well, she told herself. *Let's hope I haven't spoiled it for good. If he can be regained, I'll get him back. So help me almighty God, I will.*

She wasn't quite sure when she'd slipped off to sleep. The candle-powered lantern beside her had guttered out, and the three of them had fallen asleep where they lay, Alex in Juana's tired arms. She herself had dozed off in a big armchair.

There was a noise, loud, insistent.

She sat up. Someone was pounding on the door, again and again. She shook her head, and stood up on the cold floor. "Who is it?" she called in a voice thick with sleep.

"It's Sam! Frisco, please. . . ."

She shook her tousled locks. "I'll be there, Sam. Just a moment."

Why, it was morning! And late—ten a.m. by the big grandfather clock in the sitting room. How could she have overslept like that?

344

"Please, Frisco. There's no time to lose!"

She opened the door. "Sam!" she said. "Do come in—but what's the matter?"

"I got an advance copy of the *Alta*. Damn Kemble! When he first bought the paper he'd have called on me to clear this sort of thing, just to make sure he didn't print anything that wasn't true, or that wasn't responsible. But now. . . ."

He held the paper out. Frisco, blinking, looked down at it. "Sam, I can't see. What do you want me to look at?"

"Here," he said. "Halfway down the page." He pointed to an unsigned column of chatter, gossip and various tidbits the *Alta California*, a reborn version of Sam's old *Star*, had added recently. The item he indicated was run in with the other items in the column:

. . . What "lady" proprietor of what fashionable San Francisco gambling establishment—herself a major stockholder in a City bank and a heavy investor in local real estate—is in fact an escaped runaway slave? Doesn't she know that there are laws against runaways and that women of color, whatever their charms, cannot under law vote, homestead, give testimony in court, or hold real property in the City of San Francisco? . . .

"My God," she said. "There's certainly no mistaking who he's talking about, is there?"

"I sent a messenger down for Oscar Talbot," Sam said, his eyes blazing. "We're going to hit them with the damndest lawsuit they ever heard of. I'm going to sue Kemble, and whoever wrote that scurrilous piece of—"

Then he caught her eye and saw the expression on her face. "Why . . . we are going to sue, aren't we? I mean. . . ." His words trailed off. "Frisco," he said weakly. "It isn't true, is it? Is it?"

"Sam, it's a long story," she said wearily. "It takes some explaining. I don't know how they. . . ." But then her face changed, and shock took over where simple hurt had reigned alone. "Well, yes, maybe I do know. But, well, there's two sides to every—"

"Frisco! You've got to answer me straight. For God's

sake, it's your status at the bank—if you have any—that keeps them from foreclosing on most of my properties. It's your money—if indeed it's legally yours, and you can touch it—that'll be bailing out my properties up north in Yuba City. And the whole question of my salvation or ruin hangs totally on whether or not you legally own the two-thirds of the property we hold in common. If you don't, then I can't put up anything at all for sale to meet my obligations."

"Sam, I assure you it'll all be straightened out. I'll talk to Oscar."

"We may not have time to 'straighten out' anything. You can bet Wheeler and Frank Petty have read this and are already sitting on the court's doorstep, ready to file something. Frisco, for God's sake tell me it isn't really so. It's all a big mistake. It's libel."

"Sit down, Sam," she said, feeling as old and weary as the world itself. "You're going to have to know it all sooner or later. I might just as well give it to you now. But first, is your man Ellis anywhere around right now?"

"He's right downstairs with the cart. I rushed up as fast as I could, as soon as I saw this. Why?"

"I want to send him somewhere with a message. Bring him up. In the meantime. . . ." She opened a drawer and pulled out pen, inkwell, and letterhead.

Brannan stood and watched over her shoulder as she wrote:

Mr. Tolliver:
Business is business, as you say, but I like to think that there are certain kinds of "counterstrokes" so low I would not stoop to pick them up, much less use them against a friend. I had thought you similarly scrupulous; you cannot imagine how sorry I am to have learned better.

Frisco McGee

"Tolliver?" Brannan said. "What does he have to do with this?"

"I'll tell you in a moment. Go give this to Ellis while I dress. I'll be as quick as I can. I'll tell you all about it when you get back."

"Frisco, what can we do about this?"

"I don't know, Sam. Delay things. Stall while I try to figure out how to fight them. Perhaps a libel suit *would* be best. Make them prove the allegation." She stopped dead, her eyes blazing. "Yes! Make them prove it! This'd all rest on Beau's testimony anyhow. He doesn't have any papers to prove anything. Yes! Throw it back in their teeth! Make them prove it!" Her eyes were bright and fierce, her face flushed with anger. "Yes, Sam. We're going to fight it. We're going to sue them for every cent they've got—them and Kemble and anyone else they choose to throw at us."

Chapter 49

Some time around noon a rock smashed through Kemble's window. He boarded it up, but as he worked at this another passer-by heaved a brickbat at his head. He called back the messenger he'd sent to the glazier. There'd be time enough for that. Meanwhile, the entire edition of the *Alta* had sold out within the first hour. This was unprecedented. He'd have to go back to press, even if it meant locking the front door to give himself time to reprint. He bellowed at his apprentices to get downstairs and lay in more paper.

Sentiment was sharply divided around town. Sam's former flock, for the most part having stayed the pious God-fearing Mormons Sam disdained to be these days, tended to disapprove, and to applaud Kemble for exposing Frisco's supposed shady past to public view. *There!* the stiff-necked Mormon wives said. *That'll show her.* Privately their husbands disagreed, but they kept quiet about the matter.

Businessmen meeting one another on streetcorners tended to be divided on the question along the lines of their own political affinities. There was, for all practical purposes, a Sam Brannan party and a hate-Sam-Brannan party, and the latter had a tendency to gloat. But things were not quite so simple. Even Sam's enemies, with the most to gain, thought in passing about the end of Frisco McGee's meteoric career—if that was indeed what it was—and shook their heads in regret. They liked Frisco; she had style and charm, and there wasn't anywhere near enough of either quality in 1850 San Francisco to go around. Frisco's place was a place to see and be seen; a place to talk business in a corner; to make deals; to strut an accomplishment or drown a failure.

At the El Dorado one might have expected unalloyed jubilation; after all, a prosperous rival was getting her comeuppance. But proprietor and patron alike remembered how Frisco had been the first person in town to speak up for contributions for rebuilding the El Dorado when it had burned to the ground, and they remembered her own check had been the largest in the hat when they came to count up the proceeds. Yes, the lady had a way with her. So who gave a goddamn if she had a touch of the tarbrush? She had what it took. She had heart. She was a real Frisco lady, one of the right kind.

Sometime in mid-afternoon some loudmouth made a crack about "that nigger gal that runs the big faro house up the hill" within earshot of Pat Clancy, barkeep of the El Dorado. Clancy snapped his fingers and pointed wordlessly down from his six-foot, eight-inch height, and two stout guardians of the El Dorado's internal peace materialized from the shadows. The patron found a huge hand on each arm, holding him fast, and then, somehow, he was on his belly in the gutter outside, with the breath knocked out of him. There were things you simply didn't say in front of Pat Clancy.

The packet from Sacramento landed at four p.m. Beau Tolliver, carpetbag in hand, jauntily stepped down the gangplank to meet Wheeler on the dock. "Evening, Wheeler," he said. "I've got the deal. The lots are ours. All we have to do—"

"Forget that," Wheeler said, his usually bland face showing signs of strain. "Tolliver, what the devil are you trying to do to us?"

"Excuse me," Tolliver said. "That's Sam Brannan's man Ellis over there, and he seems to be waving something at me."

"Don't take it, you damned fool! It's probably a subpoena!"

"Nonsense! Does that look like legal foolscap? It's tinted paper, and if it isn't from a lady I'll eat it. Here, Ellis, here's for your trouble." He took the paper but Wheeler grabbed his arm. Tolliver yanked the arm away, his eyes blazing. "Wheeler," he said in a low voice, "I'll tell you but once. Don't ever touch me again unless you're invited to. You lay another hand on me, for any reason, and I'll break every finger in three places. Do you get me?"

"Tolliver," Wheeler said, his face flushed, "that note you seem to have put in Kemble's paper. . . ."

"Yes?" Tolliver said, reading the note. His face, already long, grew longer. He frowned. "Why, what the devil . . . ?" He looked up. "I'll be goddamned. Ellis? Confound it, the man's gone. What were you saying, Wheeler?"

"That piece of backyard gossip you took such pains to insert in Kemble's paper, you damned fool. They're suing us for half a million!"

"Whoa, there! Look here, I haven't the smallest idea what you're talking about."

"This! This, you goddamned idiot!"

Wheeler thrust a piece of newspaper forward, awkwardly conscious that he had overstepped himself. Tolliver was widely regarded as a dangerous man, and took target practice daily, when he was in town, at a local quarry—very publicly, where everyone could see him. His accuracy was said to be phenomenal.

"Here, what the devil?" Tolliver said. "For God's sake—of course she would have thought I was the one who . . . what the devil is this all about, Wheeler?"

"Brannan's lawyer specifically implicated you in the libel. You mean to stand there and tell me you had nothing to do with this?"

"Worse. I had no knowledge of it at all until you handed me that paper. When did this come out? Today? Why—look, Wheeler, have you spoken to Kemble?"

"No. He's been boarded up. Someone broke his window. He's back to press with another batch of the same. Look, I thought you—"

"Broke his window! By Christ, I'll break his neck!" He started away down the street; then stopped, turned, and approached Weeler again, fire in his eye. "Wheeler," he said, that deep voice low and penetrating. "You give me your oath before God that you knew nothing of this? Because if you tell me you didn't, and I later find out you were behind this, so help me almighty God, Wheeler, I'll nail you to the cross myself, with

350

these two hands. You'll wish to hell you had never been whelped."

"Tolliver. I could have licked them without this." There was a certain dignity in Wheeler that Tolliver hadn't seen before. "I have my own limits, as you do. Past a certain line I will not go, not in the service of this or any other employer or aim. And I tell you I had no knowledge of this at all."

"All right," Tolliver said. "But who? Well, time enough for that. You say Kemble's reprinting? But hasn't he been enjoined against it?"

"There seems to be a sort of *tertium quid* active in the matter. A lawyer here named Edgar Lynch seems to have got to the presiding judge and stopped the injunction for twenty-four hours. I haven't been able to find out who Lynch is representing. Some anonymous fly-by-night firm."

"Fly-by-night firm? It wasn't Warwick Enterprises, was it?"

"Why, yes, I think it was. Why?"

"I've run across their damned footprints all over Sacramento—yes, and Marysville too. They've outflanked me on three separate deals so far. Yet up to now I'd thought them a small-potatoes outfit. Look, Wheeler, we've got to get to Kemble's place before—"

"Too late!" Wheeler pointed at a barefoot ragamuffin running past them with a stack of freshly printed newspapers under one arm. "There they go."

"Well, the deed's done anyhow. The cat's out of the bag. You get down to Brannan and tell him we had nothing to do with this. Tell him right now. And send someone up to Frisco's. Yes, and tell Oscar Talbot and Frank Petty to get their heads together. Tell them we'll be acting with them, not against them, on this one. Tell Sam the moratorium on calling the loan still stands, and we'll guarantee his installment payments. Pull out all the stops."

"You've got the authority to order this? But I thought. . . ."

"You thought what I wanted you to think. Look, Wheeler, for all that I don't like you much personally you're a good man within your limits as long as you feel nobody's looking over your shoulder. If you'd known I

351

was a sixty-percent stockholder in the corporation in the first place, rather than just its agent for Sacramento and the north country, you'd have felt I was cramping your style." He looked Wheeler in the eye. "You want proof? It's on file at the bank. I'll show you this evening, if we've time. Meanwhile, get moving. There's no time to lose."

Wheeler put up one hand. "But Tolliver, if we had nothing to do with this, and if the woman's being libeled, then why the emergency measures? It seems to me that if the allegation's untrue. . . ." Then he stopped, and it registered on his no longer bland face. "Oh," he said.

"It's true, all right," Tolliver said, his eyes hard. "Although if you pass that fact along to a living soul, you'll answer for it with your life." He handed over the carpetbag, keeping his silver-headed stick. "Now get going."

"But what are we going to do?"

"We're going to prove it a lie. And there's only one way to do that. *Hey! You!*" A passing face had caught his eye: the big Sydney Duck who guarded Frisco's stairs at night. "Here," he said. "Your name's Bill, isn't it?"

"Yeah, that's right. Oh! Mr. Tolliver! Good to see you, sir."

Tolliver took the man's arm conspiratorially. Then he turned back. "Wheeler! Get moving! There's no time to lose!" He led the big man away. "Bill, I've got some work for you—that is, if you're a man who knows his way around Sydney Town."

"You've come to the right man, sir. What I can't find I can find me a man to find."

"Good. First thing I want, my friend, is Alf Beamish. In a word, I want the best bad-paper man in Sydney Town, Little Chile, and parts west."

"Within the hour, sir, if I'm lucky, and two hours if I'm not. And you're right on the mark about Alf. He has a fist like a Dago painter."

"Good. He'd better have. And Bill: how far can you be trusted? I mean, if we're talking about a retainer of five hundred dollars in gold? Payable on the quiet? If . . . ah . . . if a man takes the king's shilling, you get my meaning, would you say he was the king's man? No questions asked, no peaching, and loyalty on both sides all the way to the dock?"

"It would, sir, depend on who the king was. Now if it was you, sir, and I were to see the color of your . . . ah . . . you said 'retainer'? It's a new word to me, sir."

"Weigh this in your hand, Bill." He handed over a small poke of dust. "It's high-grade dust. I won it off a miner up Marysville way two nights ago. It hasn't been to the assayer's office yet, but if it tests out at under five hundred I'll make up the difference or eat the dust in a griddle cake. It's yours for a handshake."

"Done," the big man said, baring broken teeth in a big grin.

Tolliver banged with the silver head of his stick on Kemble's door. "Open up, Kemble!" he bellowed. "Open up early or late, but you'll open up if I have to burn you out."

A voice called out from inside. "Who's there? Look, the process server's already come and gone."

"Open up, Kemble, or I'll open you up. If I have to shoot the door open, so help me God almighty, you'll never set type again. I'll break your fingers like straws. *Kemble?*"

The door opened. The printer, still in his ink-stained apron, motioned Tolliver inside. "Look," he said, "I've had enough trouble already. If you've got business with me, state it and go away. I never saw such a can of worms in all my life."

"You haven't seen the worst of it, Kemble. I'm hitting you with a lawsuit tomorrow that'll make the one Oscar Talbot just hit you with look like child's play. Unless— look, how did you get that item? The one about the supposed runaway slave?"

"I'll tell you what I told Oscar Talbot. I've got an affidavit, sworn and notarized. I've got—"

"Never mind. Any damn fool can swear to anything. I can swear the moon's made of Liederkranz cheese— yes, and have it notarized. What I want to know is who gave it to you?"

"Why, Edgar Lynch."

"Sure, and I'll bet he slipped you a fat bundle to print it. No, don't deny it. So help me God, Kemble, you've

353

got my Irish up, and if you deny the plain gospel truth I'll take the skin off you right now. Who did Mr. Lynch claim to be representing? Warwick Enterprises?"

"Yes, that's correct. But—"

"All right. Kemble, let me see the affidavit."

"But it's on file in—"

"The hell it is. It's right here on the premises. I know damned good and well you wouldn't let a paper that important twenty feet out of your sight. Hand it over, Kemble."

"But. . . ."

Tolliver twisted the head of his stick and slid it back slowly to show three or four inches of razor-sharp steel inside the hallow handle. "Kemble, I'm not going to rob you of anything. I just want to see the signature on the affidavit. And if I don't see it within thirty seconds, so help me, I'll cut your tripes out."

"I—all right," Kemble said. He pulled a strong box out from under a rack full of California cases, unlocked it, handed up a paper. "I wish I'd never seen the thing. Why, I've had three threats today already: people tell me they're going to wreck my presses, pi the type. . . ."

Tolliver read the affidavit, handed it back. "All right," he said. "I've got what I came after. The statement was taken before the Parker House notary? Then I can assume he's staying there?"

"I assume so. If he's still in town."

"Oh, he'll be here all right. He wouldn't miss a moment of it. Thank you, Kemble." He slid the steel back inside the cane. "Don't worry about your presses. I'll put a guard on them. Otherwise, well, I'll see you in court."

"But I've been thinking. A retraction—"

"A retraction's not good enough, although it might mitigate some of the anger you've unleashed here. No, the lady's reputation has to be cleared, and there's only one way to do that."

"Tolliver, this man—you're not going to. . . ."

"Goodbye, Kemble. I'll have you a nice headline for your next number. I'd get out the seventy-two-point type if I were you. If you have a larger font, you might want to use that."

"But this man—you're not going to—"

"That's up to the Almighty, as it always is," Tolliver said. "But I know this man, and the world's not big enough to hold the two of us. If he can be killed, I'll kill him." And, with a tight controlled smile, Tolliver swept out the door, slamming it hard behind him.

Kemble's hands were trembling. *God*, he thought, *how did I get into this?* He reached into a cabinet, pulled out a brown bottle and drank deeply, shuddering as the raw stuff went down. One thing he was sure of: he wouldn't want to be Louis Thiebaud, of Warwick Enterprises, right now.

Chapter 50

Frisco, dressed warmly, sat on the edge of a couch in the middle of the casino. The staff had been called, bade farewell to, and dismissed. Only Lyuba remained, and Juana, who held a sleeping Alex on her knee. "All right, Juana," she said. "You can take Alex to the coach. Tell Wong I'll be right out. Wrap Alex up securely; there's a cold fog out."

"Frisco," Lyuba said. "You . . . you have to go?" The woman's eyes filled with tears.

"I'm afraid so," Frisco said. "I don't know what else to do right now. I mean, if it were just the businesses, the property I held in common with Sam, well, I could earn that back. But technically the allegation's right. They have me, unless I can get out here before I can be—what's the word? Impounded as stolen property?"

"But, dear. . . ."

"You're in charge now," Frisco said. "Frankly, I don't know who you're working for, precisely. Sam? The government? The federal receiver? It's an interesting question. If an escaped slave becomes the illegal owner of property and then is found out, who owns the property? The slaveowner? Well, a motion for admission to the Union, with full statehood, is before the Congress right now. Whether or not we'll be admitted slave or free is an open question. If we're admitted free, though, I still won't have property rights, or voting rights or much of anything else. And if we're admitted slave, well, I'm some man's property. And Lyuba: I'll never be another man's property again. I'll die first. I'll kill before that."

"Frisco," the woman said, her voice husky. "We love you."

"Lyuba, I. . . ." But no! Damn it, she wouldn't cry! She wouldn't let them make her cry! She stood up, her mouth firm, her eyes hard, but so close to tears that the smallest thing could have forced her over the edge. "Look," she said. "Say goodbye to Bill and the rest. I—"

The door opened just then, and Sam Brannan rushed in. "Frisco!" he said. "That's Wong outside in the landau with Juana and Alex!"

"Yes," she said. She smiled bitterly. "Goodbye, Sam. I'd have liked to stay and help you fight it out. But you stand to lose money and property, and I—I stand to lose my liberty, and for good. I'm leaving at eight on the *Penobscot*. The moon's full and the tide high." She sighed, a deep shuddering sigh that spoke eloquently of how close she was to exhaustion. "Tell Tolliver he's won."

"But Frisco! Tolliver's on our side! I talked to Wheeler's lawyer. Tolliver's the majority stockholder in the firm; Wheeler's just an employee. He's told Petty to file suit against Kemble, and he's guaranteed your loan, and out installment payments, and—my God, he's saved us! And you're leaving? Leaving all this?"

She sighed again and looked him squarely in the eye. "That's all very nice, Sam. I'm glad you're not ruined. But the rest of this . . . I suppose Tolliver feels he has to make amends."

"He swears he has nothing to do with it! And Frisco, he's telling the truth. That is, if Kemble is to be believed. Kemble says he got the item from a man representing Warwick Enterprises, a man named Thiebaud. . . ."

Suddenly the earth fell out from under her. If Sam hadn't caught her and eased her back onto the couch she'd have passed out cold.

Sam knelt before her. "Frisco! Are you all right?"

"Sam," she said weakly. "Thiebaud—he's the one who. . . ."

"Oh," he said, rocking back on his heels. "Oh. Then—oh, my God."

"Lyuba," Frisco said. "I think I left my bag upstairs. Could you ask Bill to bring it down for me?"

"Bill's gone. I'll get Stanley."

Frisco turned to Sam again. He stood up wearily. "You see?" she said. "They've got me boxed, any way you look at it. No, not 'they,' I suppose. Oh, God, tell Beau I apologize. It's just that I thought—well, it doesn't matter. Not now. The main thing is making it down to the *Penobscot* before it weighs anchor. Sam, I've left a power-of-attorney paper in the safe deposit box for you. I had it made up some time ago. You have my full confidence. I know you'll act in my best interests. I'll write from—oh, God, wherever I land. I've got a little money. London, perhaps."

"Write to me immediately," he said. "I'll arrange for immediate transfer of credit wherever you put down. No, I'll come down to the boat with you, and I'll write you a letter to my London representatives authorizing you to draw on funds I have on deposit there."

"That's good of you," she said, smiling sadly. "Sam, I'll miss you. I'll miss all of this."

"Frisco," he said. He started to say something, stopped, sighed, and smiled ruefully. "I'm no Beau Tolliver. I'm just a good small-town businessman. Even knowing who I am and what my laughably small chances were, I—well, I'd have left Liza and the children a long time ago for you if you'd have had me. And," he grinned, "if I hadn't been scared half to death of you."

"Sam," she said, and leaned over to kiss his cheek. "That was just what I needed. A touch of flattery was just what the doctor ordered right now. Well, I've forfeited my right to that sort of thing on every other front. It's nice to know I've one dear friend left who has a touch of it left for me. Give my best to everyone." She took the bag from the big, scarfaced Sydney Duck who'd come down the stairs with Lyuba. "Goodbye, Stanley. Thank you. Here's five dollars to bet on the ponies Saturday, and a tip to boot. Campeador on the nose. The race's fixed." The big man grinned and muttered his thanks. "Lyuba," she said, her hand on the woman's arm. "Talk to Sam here Monday. I've settled five percent of the casino's net on you. You've done a splendid job. You're in charge now. You report to Sam.

358

Goodbye." The two women embraced. Sam, his heart heavy, led Frisco to the door.

They met Bill at the door. His battered face bore a puzzled and excited expression. "Miz Frisco! The coach—you're not leavin', ma'am?"

"Bill, I'd better! Why?"

"Mr. Tolliver, he sent me up to tell you, he thought you'd do something like this. He said don't let you. He said for God's sake, Bill, don't let her do anything foolish."

"Bill, I haven't any choice."

"But, ma'am, look," he said, his face calmer, his voice lower. "Please, ma'am. Trust him. He's workin' on this thing. If you can hang in there another day or so. . . ."

"But Bill! There's a man in town who—"

"Yes, ma'am. He knows about that. But, well, that might not be a problem much longer."

"Not a problem? But for God's sake, Bill—"

"It's Thiebaud, isn't it, ma'am? I mean, him bein' here in town and all."

"Yes, but how did you know?"

"No matter, ma'am. But Mr. Tolliver, he sent me and the Ducks out to find Thiebaud. We found him at the Silver Slipper. Mr. Tolliver, he's gone down there to call Thiebaud out and kill him."

"Oh, my God," she said. "Beau. . . ."

Beau Tolliver halted for a moment outside the Silver Slipper. He looked around. The moon was large and full; there was a chill fog out, but it wasn't thick enough to keep out the bright light from above. Outside, then? It was a good enough place. No matter. Wherever Thiebaud chose, and with whatever weapons.

He took a deep breath and walked in the open door. He stood outlined in the doorway, looking around.

Traffic had largely cleared out by now. There were a few people playing faro in the rear, and one man slept at a table to one side. The barman stood frozen, transfixed, towel and clean glass in his hands, looking at him.

Thiebaud stood at the bar, a glass in one hand. He turned slowly to look at Beau Tolliver.

"Well," he said. "I've been waiting for you. For more

years than I care to remember, I've been waiting for you."

"Thiebaud," Tolliver said. "Let's not waste time or words. I'm going to kill you. How do you want it?"

"Don't be in such a hurry. You'll be up for charges soon enough as it is. I have a warrant for the girl's arrest issued in the morning. I'll have a warrant for yours by afternoon. Conspiracy to commit grand theft, for openers. You know what a slave's worth nowadays?"

"Thiebaud, you're a coward. You talk because you won't fight me."

"Why should I fight you when I can destroy you in court? By the time you've fought your way out of the legal thicket I've prepared for you, I'll have you boxed in here so badly you won't be able to see daylight." He tipped up the drink, signaled to the barkeep for another. "You were right about one thing. You certainly picked the right arena. San Francisco and the gold country, they're up for grabs. But you picked the wrong adversary. Tolliver, I've had men here watching your activities ever since you landed. The only thing they didn't know was the business about the nigger. When I came here the other day, I saw her in the street and recognized her. Then I knew I had you—you and Brannan too." He chuckled. "I never forget a face. I also never forget a slight, or an ill turn. I've owed you one of each for quite a while."

Tolliver took one step closer, and his gloved hand reached out to jog the drink in Thiebaud's fist. The liquor went in Thiebaud's face.

Thiebaud smiled. "Arthur," he said. The barman handed him a dishrag; he wiped his dripping face. "Thank you. Tolliver, I take it I'm challenged."

"You are."

"Splendid. Let's not fool around. We don't need seconds and calling cards and all the rest of the drivel the New Orleans bloods surround this business of killing with. Clausewitz said war was the logical extension of diplomacy; well, a good gutter fight is no more than the logical extension of business. You've crossed me in business twice. Let's not fiddle around like a couple of cadets."

360

"At your service. I agree: the sooner the better. What'll it be, Thiebaud? Pistols? The sword?"

"Ah," Thiebaud said. He picked up his empty glass and looked at it, twirling it in his hand. "Much too hoity-toity for my blood. I'm one of those vulgar Frenchmen you used to be so fond of denigrating. I have simpler tastes.

"Besides," he said, giving Tolliver an insolent up-and-down glance and dismissing him, "you're a known quantity with the pistol: a dead shot, everyone in town says. I've a touch of presbyopia which makes this an inopportune choice for me. And with the foil you'd have eight inches' reach on me. No, that's a bad idea, too."

"You're just playing rhetorical games with me," Tolliver said in an icy voice. "Choose, you cowardly bastard."

"All right," Thiebaud said. "We'll see who's a coward. I've a short arm and a bad eye. I naturally choose the medium and place which nullifies those disadvantages." He smiled a small deadly smile. "San Francisco rules, then," he said.

"San Francisco rules?" Tolliver said. "You'll have to explain. I haven't had occasion to kill anyone here—yet."

"Very well," Thiebaud said. "Arthur here has an empty barn out back. He'll join the two of us in the barn but he'll sit in the loft. The two of us will be armed with bowie knives, and there'll be a lantern on the floor between us."

"Yes? And then?"

"At the count of ten Arthur will shoot out the light."

Tolliver's eye hardened. Then he smiled a cold and terrible smile. "Done," he said.

Chapter 51

Hoofs clopping on the dry streets, the horses gathered speed, drawing the rattling landau steadily onward through the waterfront. Up on the high driver's seat, Wong, the driver, heard Sam Brannan's anxious knocks on the walls of the passenger cabin and touched the animals' backs lightly with his long-handled quirt.

Inside, Juana calmed the baby again. Beside her on the big seat Bill watched apprehensively out the window. And on the opposite seat Sam Brannan fidgeted beside Frisco. "You're sure you're doing the right thing?" he said.

"I'm not sure of anything, Sam." Frisco's voice was full of tension. "I haven't been sure of anything since the day Thiebaud raped me. Anything, that is, other than the fact that I'd die before I'd let him touch me again. And now? Now it's a choice between—well, just look, Sam. If Thiebaud kills Beau, why, my God, I'm lost! Unless I can get out of town." She sighed. "That's one side of the scale. On the other side is the fact that Beau's risking his life for me, as he's done before. God knows what I've done to deserve it."

"Beggin' your par'n, ma'am," Bill began. But he stopped, biting his cracked lip. "I'm sorry. I almost spoke out o' turn."

"No, Bill, you had something to say."

"No, ma'am. I got orders to keep my mouth shut."

"Orders?" she said. But Sam Brannan, looking out the window, stood up suddenly and leaned out the open window to yell at Wong: "Wong! Right! Turn right here!"

Sam settled himself again in the seat. As he did the

landau lurched crazily from side to side as Wong, punishing the ponies bitterly, turned them at near full speed. The wagon careened, righted itself as the passengers desperately leaned the opposite way to overcome the coach's tendency to top-heaviness. "Well, he's not sparing the animals any, at least," Sam said.

"I gave him a talking to," Bill said. "He knows time's important."

Up ahead, their destination loomed. The coach slowed, shuddered, came to a stop. Bill jumped down first and dashed to the open door before them; Sam came second and lingered to help Frisco down. "Here," Sam called up to Wong. "Take Juana and the baby home. See they're settled. Here's something for your trouble."

The Silver Slipper was crowded. Sam and Frisco walked in, and Sam pushed a way through the crowd to make way for her. Bill joined them halfway down the bar.

"They're out in the barn," he said in his husky voice, "with bowie knives. I don't know if they've—"

A single pistol shot interrupted him as he broke a path for them through the crowd. "That means they've started!" he said over the tavern's din.

"Oh, my God," Frisco said. "We're too late!"

"You couldn't have stopped 'em nohow," Bill said. "Mr. Tolliver—I never seen anybody madder. Nothin' short of killin' somebody could ever satisfy a man that mad. There's bad blood between those two."

Someone tried to stop them at the back door; the yard was already full of people. But the big bouncer took one look at Bill's even more imposing bulk and menacing look and waved them through; it wasn't worth the challenge.

Frisco looked at the ominously closed barn door. There was a round of scuffling inside. "That shot, Bill, that wasn't . . . ?"

"Naw," Bill said. "They're fightin' with bowies. The shot just started things. It'll be pitch dark in there, and they'll be fightin' on dirt, not straw. Dirt don't make much noise. A man can come up on you real sud—" Then he realized what he was saying and stopped, biting his lip again. "Sorry, ma'am. But Mr. Tolliver, he can take care of himself if anyone can."

God, bring him through it, she was praying. *Please, just bring him back to me. Please, dear God, save him.* She hadn't prayed for a long time, and even then she'd seldom meant it, seldom felt she was really praying. Now it all seemed so real. God seemed real. Her prayers soared above, with her heart hanging on every word. *Bring him through this.*

Why was it that you never knew how wonderful the thing you stood to lose was until you lost it? And why couldn't she make a little covenant with herself, from now on, to try to appreciate the things she had while she had them and not wait until it was too late? To let the people she loved know how much she loved them now, not later?

There was a grunt of pain from inside the big building. She caught her breath and listened. Any further noises were drowned by the crowd.

"My God," she said to herself, "and to think I almost left him."

"Oh, you wouldn't have left, ma'am," Bill said beside her, his husky voice rasping in her ear. "I'd orders from Mr. Tolliver to stop you. 'If Wong tries to drive you away, shoot the horses,' he said. 'If Wong complains, shoot Wong.'"

"And you'd have done it?"

"You would've too, ma'am, if you knew what I—"

There was a gasp from the crowd. Frisco wheeled.

The barn door opened a foot, two feet. A bloody figure stepped into view. Its shirt was in ragged red shreds. One hand held its stomach. Its face was all gore and dirt; out of this two mad eyes stared, full of hatred, resentment, insatiable blood-lust.

Frisco's heart froze. She clutched Bill's arm. "Oh God," she said. "*Thiebaud. . . .*"

And then the figure seemed to come apart slowly, like a puppet whose strings have been cut. The hand fell away from the cut stomach, and blood gushed forth, blood, and other things. Frisco turned away and felt, rather than saw, the body fall forward on its face.

There was a pause. Then she looked back at the door. Beau Tolliver, his forearms a mass of cuts, his shirt in hanging ribbons, stepped arrogantly through the door, his red hair askew, his green eyes darting back and forth, daring anyone to stop him. He had a knife in one hand—a knife tipped with red. "Well, that's all," he said. "You can all go on home now. Are there any constables here? Militiamen? All right. I'll be at the sheriff's office bright and shiny in the morning."

He turned and threw the knife at the barn door with a powerful overhand motion. It stuck an inch and a half deep in the soft wood. "Arthur," he said. "Keep it for evidence. It's what I killed him with. The more evidence, the more witnesses the better. When you hear what I killed him for you'll wish to God I'd left enough of him alive for you to hang." His voice took on a certain finality. "That's all, friends and neighbors. Go home now. Arthur?" he said jauntily, the touch of arrogance still in his strong voice. "Thanks for the use of the hall."

Then he was plowing through the crowd, his eyes on nobody but her, the smile on his face changing, softening. And his arms around her, bleeding and covered with dirt, gave her the finest, most warmly comforting feeling she'd ever felt. It was a moment she never wanted to end.

Frisco insisted on doctoring him herself, using ancient Romany folk remedies she'd learned from Pesha. As she bent over his lacerated arms she could feel his eyes all over her, peeling the clothing away, searching for the warm, naked flesh underneath the cloth.

"Well," he said. "All's well that ends well. Only it doesn't feel like an ending. It feels like a beginning."

She looked up to see his suddenly gentle and protective smile. "Well, it is. The beginning of our new life together."

"Yes," he said, touching her cheek with a battered, infinitely gentle hand. "And stop worrying about tomorrow. It's as I told the crowd: when I'm done pleading they'll give me the keys to the city."

"I don't understand."

"Why, what man would allow even his *estranged* wife to be slandered that way?"

"Wife? I—I don't understand."

Beau reached inside his coat for a paper, handed it

over. She read it and couldn't believe her eyes. "Married? Mrs. James Beaudry Tolliver . . . Cairo, Illinois, September 12, 1847?" She almost let the paper fall. "I—what is this?"

"Something I paid Alf Beamish a pretty penny for. Alf's one of the finest engravers I've ever run across. You should see his fifty-dollar bills, for the love of God. They're masterpieces. They make this look like something an urchin would scrawl upon a wall. But this will do, unless a former magistrate from Cairo shows up here and ask for a look at it. Short of that we're in the gravy, my dear. Alex has a father who loves him, I have a wife I love, Sam has a viable business, we all get rich. Unless you have some objections to advance?"

"Oh, *Beau*," she said, hugging him tight, her eyes full of tears. "Oh, Beau, this is the happiest day of my life!" But then the happiness dissolved in tears. He held her and suddenly it was all right to cry, after all this time: all right to be a vulnerable human being who at times liked being taken care of, just like anyone else.

"Frisco!" Sam said. "My God! Look out the window! The whole top of the hill—your casino, my building next door—they're on fire!"

"Oh, my God," she said. "Oh, no." She rushed from Beau's arms to the window. It was true: the flames were leaping high, lighting the whole top of the hill. "Oh, Beau, I hope all the girls are out! Oh, God!" She turned to watch him sitting there looking at her, a complacent smile on his face. "Beau, aren't you concerned at all?"

"No," he said, leaning back and putting his big boots up on her coffee table. "And don't worry about the girls, or the Ducks either, or about that strong box you've been keeping under a panel upstairs. The strong box is at my place, the girls are safe at home, and the Ducks are downtown having a drink on ole Beau Tolliver, that generous and open-hearted friend of all mankind. And a couple of specialist friends of Bill's are splitting a thousand-dollar payment they've earned tonight for putting a torch to Frisco's and getting my wife out of the card-sharping business." He reached for the cognac bottle they'd been cleansing his wounds with and poured some in a teacup full, sloshing it around in the cup before drinking.

"Beau, *you* did this?" She stared at him openmouthed.

"Not exactly. Thiebaud had ordered it done in the event he was killed in our fight. The men told me and I just figured that it would solve a lot of things to let them go ahead. You've mentioned you were tired of running a casino, and as my wife and partner we can manage our San Francisco real estate, and other investments, along with Sam, here."

"Beau, you actually knew they were going to set the casino on fire? And my warehouse next door?"

"And why not? You're both insured to the hilt. And guess who bought out your insurance company a month ago, and is going to be paying you both handsomely for your losses? Why, Warwick Enterprises, that's who."

They both stared at him, wordlessly. "Here," he said, "come out on the balcony. Frisco—no, I'm going to go back to calling you Graciela, it's a better name—get your wrap; it's chilly. But come along." He took the cup and the bottle. "Sam, bring a glass. No, make it two."

Outside on the balcony, the evening fog was chilly and visible, particularly down below in the flat where it hung low on the bottom. Up on the hill, Frisco's blazed away merrily, the flames soaring, the black clouds billowing. "There!" he said appreciatively. "Your glasses? Here. . . ." Then, having poured, he held his cup high. "Every six months or so part of the damned city burns down anyhow, you know. It's the City's way of renewing itself. Frisco's wasn't bringing you an adequate return, for all its popularity. We're going to build up there: hotels, apartment houses, anything you want that'll maximize the profits per square inch. This is going to be one of the great cities of the world." He held his cup high. "To that cheerful phoenix among cities, San Francisco." He laughed. "No, goddamn it, call it Frisco! That's a handle to grab a city you love by! To Frisco!"

Graciela—now Graciela again, and happy to be so—snuggled into the crook of his free arm and held her glass high. Somehow, down inside her, she felt as though it was still her name as well as the city's, that it was she as well that they'd toasted. And there was a thrill in the thought. "Frisco" she'd been, and would be no more. But the woman she'd been when she was Frisco? Well, for all her faults, she *was* a woman worth toasting, worth drinking to. Now, though, it was time to say goodbye to Frisco, and to her casino, and to all the things she'd had to do for herself on the way up.

Well, good riddance! Let it burn, all of it, the pain and the fear and the loss and the bad memories. All gone! In their place a new, fresh slate, a new life in which she'd at last found her place in the sun. Now that Beau and she were together, they would fulfill themselves *with,* rather than *through,* one another. Together they would create a new life for themselves. But right now they had a city to rebuild.

And as she watched the city burning, she thought to herself, *Yes! Lyuba was right! All was well.*

Dear Reader:

The Pinnacle Books editors strive to select and produce books that are exciting, entertaining and readable . . . no matter what the category. From time to time we will attempt to discover what you, the reader, think about a particular book.

Now that you've finished reading *Frisco Lady*, we'd like to find out what you liked, or didn't like, about this story. We'll share your opinions with the author and discuss them as we plan future books. This will result in books that you will find more to your liking. As in fine art and good cooking a matter of taste is involved; and for you, of course, it is *your* taste that is most important to you. For Jeraldine Saunders, and the Pinnacle editors, it is not the critics' reviews and awards that have been most rewarding, it is the unending stream of readers' mail. Here is where we discover what readers like, what they *feel* about a story, and what they find memorable. So, do help us in becoming a little better in providing you with the kind of stories you like. Here's how . . .

WIN BOOKS . . . AND $200!

Please fill out the following pages and mail them as indicated. Every week, for twelve weeks following publication, the editors will choose, at random, a reader's name from all the questionnaires received. The twelve lucky readers will receive $25 worth of paperbacks *and* become an official entry in our 1979 Pinnacle

Books Reader Sweepstakes. The winner of this sweep-stakes drawing will receive a Grand Prize of $200, the inclusion of their name in a forthcoming Pinnacle Book (as a special acknowledgment, possibly even as a character!), and several other local prizes to be an-nounced to each initial winner. As a further induce-ment to send in your questionnaire *now*, we will also send the first 25 replies received a free book by return mail! Here's a chance to talk to the author and editor, voice your opinions, and win some great prizes, too!

—The Editors

READER SURVEY

NOTE: Please feel free to expand on any of these questions on a separate page, or to express yourself on any aspect of your thoughts on reading . . . but do be sure to include this entire questionnaire with any such letters.

---

1. Are you glad you bought this book, and did it live up to your expectations?

   ---

2. What was it about this book that induced you to buy it?

   (A. The title_____) (B. The author's name_____)

   (C. A friend's recommendation_____)

   (D. The cover art_____)

   (E. The cover description_____)

   (F. Subject matter_____) (G. Advertisement_____)

   (H. Heard author on TV or radio_____)

   (I. Read a previous book by author_____ . . . which one? _____)

   (J. Bookstore display_____)

   (K. Other? _____)

3. What is the book you read just before this one?

   And how would you rate it with *Frisco Lady?*

   ---

4. What is the very next book you plan to read?

   How did you decide on that? _____

371

5.   Where did you buy *Frisco Lady?* _____

     (Name and address of store, please):

     _____

     _____

6.   Where do you buy the majority of your paperbacks? _____

7.   What seems to be the major factor that persuades you to buy a certain book?

     _____

8.   How many books do you buy each month?

     _____

9.   Do you ever write letters to the author or publisher . . . and why? _____

     _____

10.   About how many hours a week do you spend reading books? _____ How many hours a week watching television? _____

11.   What other spare-time activity do you enjoy most? _____ For how many hours a week? _____

12.   Which magazines do you read regularly? . . . in order of your preference _____,

     _____, _____,

     _____

13.   Of your favorite magazine, what is it that you like best about it? _____

     _____

14.   What is your favorite television show of the past year or so? _____

15. What is your favorite motion picture of the past year or so? _____

16. What is the most disappointing television show you've seen lately? _____

17. What is the most disappointing motion picture you've seen lately? _____

18. What is the most disappointing book you've read lately? _____

19. Are there authors that you like so well that you read *all* their books? _____
    Who are they? _____

20. And can you explain *why* you like their books so much? _____
    _____
    _____

21. Which particular books by these authors do you like best? _____
    _____

22. Did you read Taylor Caldwell's *Captains and the Kings*?_____ Did you watch it on television?_____
    Which did you do first? _____

23. Did you read John Jakes' *The Bastard*? _____
    Did you watch it on TV?_____ Which first?_____
    Have you read any of the other books in John Jakes' Bicentennial Series? _____
    What do you think of them? _____

24. Did you read James Michener's *Centennial*?_____
    Did you watch it on TV?_____ Which first?_____

373

25. Did you read Irwin Shaw's *Rich Man, Poor Man*? _____ Did you watch it on TV? _____ Which first? _____

26. Of all the recent books you've read, or films you've seen, are there any that you would compare in any way to *Frisco Lady*? _____

27. Have you read any books by Patricia Matthews? _____ Which ones? _____

28. Have you read any books by Marie de Jourlet? _____ Which ones? _____

29. Have you read any books by Rosemary Rogers? _____ Which ones? _____

30. In *Frisco Lady*, which character did you find most fascinating? _____ Most likeable? _____ Most exciting? _____ Least interesting? _____ Which one did you identify with most? _____

31. Rank the following descriptions of *Frisco Lady* as you feel they are best defined:

	Excellent	Okay	Poor
A. A sense of reality	_____	_____	_____
B. Suspense	_____	_____	_____
C. Intrigue	_____	_____	_____
D. Sexuality	_____	_____	_____
E. Violence	_____	_____	_____
F. Romance	_____	_____	_____
G. History	_____	_____	_____
H. Characterization	_____	_____	_____
I. Scenes, events	_____	_____	_____

374

J. Pace, readability   ___   ___   ___

K. Dialogue   ___   ___   ___

L. Style   ___   ___   ___

32. Do you have any thoughts regarding the length of this book?____ Would you have liked it to be longer? ____ Shorter? ____

33. Would you be interested in a sequel to *Frisco Lady?* _____

34. Would you be interested in reading a similar story, but in a different locale? ____ Where, for example? _____
_____

35. Which historical era do you find most appealing?
_____

Least appealing? _____
_____

36. What, in your opinion, is the best or most vivid scene in *Frisco Lady?* _____
_____

37. Did you find any errors or other upsetting things in this book? _____
_____

38. What do you do with your paperbacks after you've read them? _____
_____

39. Do you buy paperbacks in any of the following categories, and approximately how many do you buy in a year?

A. Contemporary fiction (like *this* book) ____
B. Historical romance ____
C. Family saga ____
D. Romance (like Harlequin) ____
E. Romantic suspense ____
F. Gothic romance ____
G. Occult novels ____
H. War novels ____
I. Action/adventure novels ____
J. "Bestsellers" ____
K. Science fiction ____
L. Mystery ____
M. Westerns ____
N. Nonfiction ____
O. Biography ____
P. How-To books ____
Q. Other _____

40. And, lastly, some profile data on *you* the reader . . .

A. Age: 12–16____ 17–20____ 21–30____
31–40____ 41–50____ 51–60____
61 or over____

B. Occupation: _____

C. Education level; check last grade completed:
10____ 11____ 12____ Freshman____
Sophomore____ Junior____ Senior____
Graduate School____, plus any specialized
schooling _____

376

D. Your average annual gross income: Under
$10,000_____ $10,000–$15,000_____
$15,000–$20,000_____ $20,000–
$30,000_____ $30,000–$50,000_____
Above $50,000_____

E. Did you read a lot as a child?_____ Do you
recall your favorite childhood novel? _____
_____

F. Do you find yourself reading more or less
than you did five years ago?_____

G. Do you read hardcover books?_____ How
often?_____ If so, are they books that you
buy?_____ borrow?_____ or trade?_____ Or
other?_____

H. Does the imprint (Pinnacle, Avon, Bantam,
etc.) make any difference to you when considering a paperback purchase? _____

I. Have you ever bought paperbacks by mail
directly from the publisher?_____ And do you
like to buy books that way? _____

J. Would you be interested in buying paperbacks via a book club or subscription pro-
gram?_____ And, in your opinion, what would
be the best reasons for doing so? _____
_____ . . . the problems in
doing so? _____

K. Is there something that you'd like to see
writers or publishers do for you as a reader
of paperbacks? _____
_____

THANK YOU FOR TAKING THE TIME TO REPLY TO THIS, THE FIRST PUBLIC READER SURVEY IN PAPERBACK HISTORY!

NAME _____ PHONE_____
ADDRESS _____
CITY _____ STATE _____ ZIP _____

Please return this questionnaire to:

The Editors; Survey Dept. FL
Pinnacle Books, Inc.
2029 Century Park East
Los Angeles, CA 90067